# TALES OF THE
# SHADOWMEN
## Volume 11: Force Majeure

# TALES OF THE
# SHADOWMEN

## Volume 11: Force Majeure

edited by
Jean-Marc & Randy Lofficier

stories by
**Matthew Baugh, Nathan Cabaniss, Matthew Dennion,
Brian Gallagher, Martin Gately, Emmanuel Gorlier,
Micah S. Harris & Loston Wallace, Travis Hiltz, Paul Hugli,
Rick Lai, Nigel Malcolm, Christofer Nigro, John Peel,
Pete Rawlik, Frank Schildiner, Sam Shook, David L. Vineyard**
and **Jared Welch**

translations by
**J.-M. & Randy Lofficier**

cover by
**Mariusz Gandzel**

A Black Coat Press Book

ISBN 978-1-61227-344-0. First Printing. December 2014. Published by Black Coat Press, an imprint of Hollywood Comics.com, LLC, P.O. Box 17270, Encino, CA 91416. All rights reserved. Except for review purposes, no part of this book may be reproduced or transmitted in any form or by any means, electronic or mechanical, including photocopying, recording or by any information storage and retrieval system, without permission in writing from the publisher. The stories and characters depicted in this anthology are entirely fictional. Printed in the United States of America.

# Table of Contents

*Most of the time,* Tales of the Shadowmen *doesn't dabble in "parallel univers-es" or "alternate histories," but we have been known to make the occasional exception, such as with Xavier Maumejean's brilliant reinterpretation of Bat-man as a soviet spy in our last volume. This retelling of the myth of Gilgamesh, recast with modern archetypes, by Matthew Baugh, is another strikingly original story that deserved to be published in these pages...*

## Matthew Baugh: *Gilgamesh Revisited*

*I*

Gilgamesh stood at the peak of the ziggurat and gazed out across the city he ruled. Of all the metropolises of the world, none was as grand as New Uruk, the City of the Towers. Her greatness came from the richness of the surrounding lands, the industry of her people, but mainly from the greatness of her king, who was two parts god and one part mortal, so it was said.

He looked upon the slender, white-stone ziggurats that he had designed, and the mighty airships and nimble autogyros—also his inventions—that flitted and flew from place to place.

A frown creased the king's perfect, bronzed features as he lowered his gaze to the streets of the city. Workers from every corner of the world crowded the streets of the great city. They had come to revel in the lights of New Uruk and to work in the factories manufacturing the many inventions of the king's matchless genius.

Nor was it his mind alone that set the king apart. When Gilgamesh walked among his subjects, he towered a full head above other men and his powerful muscles seemed sculpted out of bronze rather than formed from flesh. Never had Gilgamesh lost a contest of strength or agility, though he had competed against champions from places as far as Ys, Hy-Brasil, and Shangri La, but none were his equal.

Gilgamesh sighed and turned his eyes to Heaven again, for in the entire world, there was no one like him, and he was alone.

In the city below, many passed by the great ziggurat, surmounted with a mooring mast for the king's personal dirigible, and would turn their eyes up in awe and adoration, for Gilgamesh was beloved of the people of New Uruk. They loved him; not only for his accomplishments, but for the many times he had saved the city from the criminals and mad scientists and monsters who roamed the Earth.

Yet some looked up with hatred, for Gilgamesh was such a virtuous king that he allowed no vices of any kind. He shut down the gambling houses, the brothels and the speakeasies with righteous zeal. As for the criminals who profited in vice, he had invented a brain treatment that made them into mindless zombies, who labored at building the wonders of the city.

Those who loved Gilgamesh built shrines to him and worshipped his glory, but those who hated him met in secret temples beneath the city. There they prayed that the gods would sent them a savior; a champion greater than Gilgamesh who could throw him down and free them from his rule.

The gods must have been pleased with the people's prayers for, that year, his nemesis was born.

It happened in this way: a noble merchant-prince from the far city of Ys was forced to flee into the jungle after a tragic brawl. Injured, he was rescued by a native princess. Unfortunately, her father wanted his daughter to marry another man, so they had no choice but to elope. Eventually, a baby son was born.

However, the jealous suitor managed to find the two lovers and killed them both. He would have murdered the baby too, if a lioness whose cub he had previously killed had not leapt to his defense. The baby was then raised by the great lions of the forest and grew to be mightier than any among them, or indeed than leopard or rhino, crocodile or hippo and even the lions acknowledged his supremacy. And so the boy was called Enkidu, the Lord of Lions.

Now, the greatest of Gilgamesh's enemies was the immortal Ut-Napishtim, who dwelled in the City of Gold and Lepers. He was the leader of the sinister cult of the Scorpion-men and a great genius himself. Ut-Napishtim had come to the Dark Continent and sent his Scorpion-men to procure animals for his insidious experiments.

Soon the Scorpion-men returned empty handed. They told Ut-Napishtim that they were unable to capture any of the jungle creatures for a wild man called Enkidu broke their traps, destroyed their snares, and bent the bars of their cages, releasing the animals. They had tried to oppose him, but their skills were no match for his savage strength.

Ut-Napishtim realized this must be the one whom the enemies of Gilgamesh had prayed for.

"Forget the animals," he told them. "Go and capture this Lord of the Lions, for I would pit him against the Man of Bronze. The beast-man shall throw down the god-man and then I shall be free to seize the city of New Uruk."

The Scorpion-men returned to seize Enkidu. They were the deadliest warriors in the world, skilled in the arts of Kung-fu and ninjitsu, pentjak-silat and kalari-payat, and many other devilish fighting styles. Yet, they returned, broken and few in number, for Enkidu was more than their match.

"We tried, O Master," the leader of the Scorpion-men said. "Alas, no mortal man can defeat Enkidu. He is strong as the elephant, swift as the leopard, agile as the monkey and cunning as the snake. The animals of the jungle obey him and the lion, the wildcat, and even the kangaroo are his companions."

This made Ut-Napishtim even keener to capture Enkidu, and so he sent messengers to his daughter Shamhat, the beautiful Priestess of lost Atlantis. In seductive beauty, Shamhat was as far above all other women as Enkidu was above men in might.

"You have sent for me, my father," Shamhat said, bowing before the insidious Ut-Napishtim in his camp on the Dark Continent.

"I have a task for you," Ut-Napishtim said. "There is a man whose services I require. I need him to seduce him for me."

"Is that all?" Shamhat asked, stifling a yawn. "As you know, there is no man who can resist my beauty. Surely, you remember my collection of former lovers, whom I have dipped in orichalcum when I grew weary of them."

"I have admired your unique statues many times," Ut-Napishtim said. "But this man is like none you have ever met, for he is wild, and said to be half man and half beast."

"How intriguing," Shamhat said. "What would you have me do?"

"Show him your beauty," the fiendish one said. "Lure him to your bed, for when he lies with you, he will lose his wildness and will do as you say. Once he is yours, take him to New Uruk and show him Gilgamesh. Persuade him to fight the god-king and throw him down. Then, when Gilgamesh is no more, and New Uruk is mine, I shall reward you richly."

And so, Shamhat donned her finest gown and traveled to the spring where Enkidu and the animals went to drink every day. She pitched her tent on the shore. When the animals came to drink, they were afraid at first, but Shamhat was soft of voice and gentle of manner, and soon they ceased to fear her. But while the animals did not fear her, Enkidu remained in the trees and watched, for he had never seen a woman before, and did not know what to make of her.

Then Shamhat removed her gown and went to the spring to bathe. The Lord of Lions was enchanted by her beauty and left his trees to meet her on the shore. Shamhat took him by the hand and led him into the tent where they remained for twelve days and twelve nights. When they left the tent, he was no longer interested in living with the animals or in being Lord of the Lions.

## II

Shamhat dressed Enkidu in clothes and took him to the city of New Uruk where he was dazzled by the bright lights, the zeppelins, and the towers that reached almost to the realm of the gods. But when he saw the zombie workers who built the wonders, Enkidu was disturbed, for there is nothing more sacred to a wild man than freedom.

"Why do these men behave thus?" he asked. "They seem to me like the dog that has been tamed, or the wild ox that has been gelded, and have no will of their own."

9

"It is worse," said the fair Shamhat, "for it is their minds that have been gelded."

"Who has done this thing?" asked Enkidu.

"This is the work of Gilgamesh the Strong," Shamhat said to him. "Gilgamesh is proud and claims that none can equal him in a test of strength. Gilgamesh is the one who takes his enemies and turns them into docile beasts."

"Then take me to this man," said Enkidu, "and I will contend with him and he will learn that there is indeed one who can equal him in strength."

"I dare not," said Shamhat, "for I fear that he would geld your mind. Then, without strong Enkidu to prevent him, he would take me, for he desires me greatly."

"Take me to him," repeated Enkidu. "I will throw him down three times: once for his pride, and once for gelding the minds of free men, and a third time for thinking he could possess you."

So Shamhat brought Enkidu to the great ziggurat of Gilgamesh, where he stood in the square outside and shouted his challenges up to the pinnacle. When Gilgamesh looked down to see what the shouting was, he saw Enkidu and Shamhat in the square below.

"Who is this beast-man that challenges me?" he said. "I will go down and overthrow him and take his fair companion, for I recognize her as the daughter of Ut-Napishtim. If I have her in my hand, I can lure her father hither and put an end to his insidious plans."

So Gilgamesh descended the ziggurat in a special elevator of great speed and he came forth from the tower and said, "Where is the man who would challenge Gilgamesh?"

"Here am I!" the beast man bellowed. "Enkidu am I, Lord of the Lions!" He tore away his clothes until he stood as naked as he had been in the wild, then he roared the challenge of the lion and lunged at his foe.

Gilgamesh met Enkidu, hand to hand and chest to chest. The towers trembled as they came together and the pavement under their feet crumbled as they strove mightily, each to cast the other down. As they struggled, the people of New Uruk came and watched and were amazed at the spectacle. The police of the city cheered for Gilgamesh, for they knew that they would never be able to stand against the stranger without him. The mobsters and racketeers—all but a few—cheered for Enkidu, for they longed to see the city's hero overthrown. Those racketeers who did not cheer were busy taking bets from all the people of New Uruk, and the odds that they offered were five to three in favor of the king.

But Shamhat watched as the two contended with one another. She marveled at the physique of Enkidu, which was as graceful as that of the sun god, Shamash. She gazed upon Gilgamesh as his exertions tore his shirt to shreds of fabric, exposing mighty muscles and bronze skin.

"Mighty is Enkidu," she said, "and mighty indeed is Gilgamesh." And in that moment, she forgot about her father, Ut-Napishtim, and her loyalty to his Scorpion-men.

From dawn until dusk, Gilgamesh and Enkidu struggled, yet neither could cast the other down. Finally, they broke from each other and each stepped back a pace.

"Mightiest of men is Gilgamesh," said Enkidu. "Mightiest of men and destined to be king over them, just as Enkidu has been king over the beasts of the wild."

"Mighty is Enkidu," Gilgamesh said. "From this day forth, he shall be my brother and dwell with me in my ziggurat, looking out over all of New Uruk."

Then the two embraced and, taking Shamhat, they went into the ziggurat. The people of the city dispersed to tell the story of the wonders they had seen and to reclaim their bets from the racketeers.

### III

Gilgamesh and Enkidu stood at the peak of the ziggurat and watched over the city. Enkidu was filled with wonder, but Gilgamesh's heart was troubled, for there was no challenge left for him in the entire world.

"All that I have set my hand to, I have accomplished," he said. "In the whole world there is nothing that I have not prevailed over; only Enkidu who is my beloved brother."

"There is another," Enkidu said, "for on the island of Mu there dwell many dinosaurs, and other strange monsters."

"Alas," cried Gilgamesh, "I have already striven against dinosaurs, for three times criminals and mad scientists have brought them to the gates of New Uruk, hoping to breach the city and topple her towers. No... I fear that dinosaurs are no more a challenge to me than death rays, or invisibility potions, or mechanical men."

"Ah, but I do not speak only of dinosaurs," said Enkidu, "for on this island lives the mighty Humbaba. He is an ape of greater size and ferocity than any other. The gods themselves have set Humbaba as guardian over the island, and none may prevail against him."

Then Gilgamesh clasped the hands of his sworn brother, Enkidu, and they agreed to sail to the island and fight against Humbaba.

### IV

Gilgamesh went to the elders of the city and told them of his plans but the elders were upset.

11

"Great king," the chief elder said. "We have heard tales of the great ape, Humbaba and fear for your safety. What would become of our city should Humbaba slaw Gilgamesh?"

But Gilgamesh laughed.

"Surely, you do not doubt my strength," he said. "And, even if you do, remember that my sworn brother Enkidu goes with me, and nothing on Earth or the Heavens could stand against both of us."

"But what of the gods?" the chief elder asked. "They placed Humbaba over his island. Will not they be offended if any overthrows their mighty guardian?"

Gilgamesh laughed again.

"Let them be offended," he said. "Even the gods must give way to progress, which conquers all things. Is not your king the very avatar of progress?"

"But what of the city?" the chief priest said. "Will we not New Uruk be vulnerable to the menace of Ut-Napishtim while Gilgamesh and Enkidu were away?"

"But proud Gilgamesh laughed a third time.

"I do not fear Ut-Napishtim and his Scorpion-men," he said. "Even if they were to conquer the city, they would flee in terror when Gilgamesh and Enkidu returned, having conquered great Humbaba. Now, bother me no more you're your timid concerns for we have a mighty quest to prepare for."

And so, proud Gilgamesh made his dirigible ready for the flight to the Island of Mu. He took Enkidu with him, traveling first to his Fortress of Solitude in the frozen north to supply himself with potent weapons. Afterward, he and Enkidu travelled to Mu.

## V

As the two brothers rode together in the dirigible, Gilgamesh lay down to sleep and there came to him strange dreams. In the first, he was walking through the forest when a mighty mountain fell on him.

In the second dream, he was walking on the savannah and a wild bull of the wilderness came and charged at him, bearing him to the ground.

In the third, he was walking through the mountains when lightning struck at his feet, and fire rained all around him.

Finally, he was walking through an ancient ruin when a mighty gate opened and a great ape, who stood fully eighteen cubits and a span tall, strode out.

Gilgamesh woke and was terrified. He wakened Enkidu and told him of the dream, but Enkidu told him not to be afraid.

"The mountain in your dream is Humbaba," he said, "and we shall cast him down. The bull is me, for I am your strong ally and protector. The lightning and fire are the terrible weapons with which you have armed yourself. Finally, the great ape is a true image of the mighty Humbaba, but do not be afraid, for we are destined to overcome him."

Hearing Enkidu's words, Gilgamesh was comforted, and returned to sleep.

## VI

Gilgamesh and Enkidu arrived at the Island of Mu, where they tethered their dirigible and went into the forest to find Humbaba. At length they discovered an ancient ruin with a massive gate and knew that the giant ape must be on the other side.

Enkidu called out their challenge in the language of the great apes and mighty Humbaba bellowed back his answer. His voice was like the roar of the wind and it made the earth tremble.

"What says Humbaba?" Gilgamesh asked.

"He calls me traitor," Enkidu said, "for I was raised by animals, yet I have come with a man to stand against a beast. He says that he is my kinsman and not you, and that he shall crush me for my treason."

"And what says Humbaba of Gilgamesh the Strong"

"He says that your strength is nothing to him and that he shall crush you until your bowels burst forth from your body. He says that he will slay you and feed your flesh to the birds of the air."

Gilgamesh trembled at this and would have fled back to the dirigible, but Enkidu spoke again. "Do not be afraid, Gilgamesh," he said. "Humbaba the mighty cannot stand before the Man of Bronze, for you have your weapons and you have your sworn brother, and you are destined to prevail."

Gilgamesh took heart at these words and stood fast.

Then the great Humbaba pounded his fists against the gate until it shivered into splinters and he strode through. In form, Humbaba was a mighty ape but his size was greater than a bull of the wilderness, or of an elephant, or even of a great tyrannosaur. The ground quaked with his footsteps and the trees shuddered at his roar. He raised his mighty arms and smote at Gilgamesh and Enkidu, but they were fast and dodged away.

Then the sworn brothers moved close to the giant Humbaba and smote him with the many terrible weapons with which Gilgamesh had armed himself. The beast howled in pain but did not succumb. He seized Gilgamesh in one hand and raised him high, as if to dash him to the ground. Then Enkidu struck with his spear and hunting knife, wounding Humbaba hip and thigh. The giant roared in pain. Dropping Gilgamesh, he seized up Enkidu and made as if to devour him. But Gilgamesh did hurl one of his weapons into the great ape's mouth; a bomb that let forth a powerful gas, bringing sleep to all who breathed it. Humbaba breathed the gas and soon was fast asleep.

Then Gilgamesh and Enkidu made Humbaba fast with ropes. When the giant awoke, he pleaded for his life.

"Have mercy, great king," the ape said. "You have proven your strength by defeating me. Now let me go free and I promise to be your friend."

"I shall never release you," Gilgamesh said.

"If you do not release him, you should kill him," Enkidu said.

"We shall return to New Uruk with Humbaba as out prisoner," Gilgamesh said. "There we shall exhibit so that the people can see the strength of Gilgamesh, their king."

"He will escape," Enkidu warned. "And he will bring great destruction to your city."

"No," said Gilgamesh. "Once I have displayed him I will operate on his brain to make a zombie of him and he will labor at the building of the city."

This did not please Enkidu either, for he hated to see the mind of the great beast gelded, but he bowed to his sworn brother's wisdom and said nothing.

## VII

When Gilgamesh returned to New Uruk, all of the city was amazed at his mighty feat and came to see Humbaba, who was displayed in chains in the city square.

"Mighty is Gilgamesh," the people said, and, "great is Gilgamesh the wise, who bends even the great Humbaba to his will." All the people loved Gilgamesh, but Enkidu was troubled in his heart and retired to the park in the center of the city to be alone with his thoughts.

Then Shamhat came to Gilgamesh and, letting her dress fall, uncovered her nakedness to him.

"Mighty is Gilgamesh," she said, "and worthy to claim the daughter of Ut-Napishtim as his lover."

But Gilgamesh turned away from her beauty and would not lie with her.

"Are you not the lover of my brother, Enkidu, and thus my sister?" he asked.

"It is true that I have loved Enkidu," she said, "but now I have found one who is even more worthy of my love. Enkidu is strong of body and fair to look upon and he possesses the strength of many men, but Gilgamesh is his match in every way. More, Gilgamesh is wise enough to confound the gods with his learning. His mind is a match even for that of my father."

But for all her words, Gilgamesh would not lie with her.

Then Shamhat, in her anger, remembered her loyalty to her father and to his Scorpion-men. Taking the secret of the brain surgery, she fled from New Uruk and returned to the Dark Continent where she gave him the secret.

"You have done well, my daughter," said he, "for with this secret, I can make all of Gilgamesh's zombies act as my servants. They will rise up and devour the living until the city is mine."

## VIII

So Ut-Napishtim created a device that would control all who had been made into zombies. He travelled with his daughter Shamhat to the city of New Uruk. When they arrived, he activated his device and the zombies rose up to devour the living. The city fell into a panic as zombies stalked the inhabitants and ate their brains. The police were helpless before this threat, as were the mobsters and the racketeers, for the zombies were immune to all but the direst wounds.

Then mighty Gilgamesh descended from his ziggurat and fought the zombies. Alas, he soon discovered that they were immune to his weapons, even the gas bombs which he had used to overcome Humbaba. Then, he fought them with his matchless strength, with his great agility, and with the many forms of unarmed combat he had mastered in his travels. Even so, Gilgamesh found himself hard pressed by the ravening hordes.

But Enkidu had also become aware of the zombies and went to the great zoo of New Uruk where he had bent the bars and broken the locks of all the cages, releasing the wild beasts kept there. He had freed the elephants, and the apes, and the lions, and the bears, and the hyenas, and the crocodiles, and every manner of wild beast imprisoned there. Enkidu spoke to them, each in their own language, and told them to sweep through the city, crushing the zombies underfoot, or rending them apart with biting jaws and slashing claws.

He rode through New Uruk on the back of a great elephant until he found Gilgamesh, hard pressed by a horde of the zombies, and he scattered them and swept his sworn-brother onto the beast's back.

"My thanks, brother," Gilgamesh said.

"We have overcome these zombies, but what caused them to turn against you?" Enkidu asked.

"It can only be my enemy, Ut-Napishtim," Gilgamesh said. "He has sought revenge on me ever since I defeated him in his City of Gold and Lepers."

"Then we must find him and kill him," Enkidu said.

"There is only one place he can be," Gilgamesh said. "He will have gone to the great ziggurat."

Indeed, Ut-Napishtim had arrived at the great square below the ziggurat, along with Shamhat and his Scorpion-men. Ut-Napishtim gazed with wonder and awe upon Humbaba and ordered his men to undo the great ape's chains.

"Why have you freed me?" the monster asked.

"You and I have the same enemy," Ut-Napishtim said. "Gilgamesh, who chained you up, is also the man I hate most in the world. Now that I have freed you, you can destroy him and be my servant."

"You are a fool!" Humbaba said. "Mighty is Gilgamesh, who overcame me and placed me in chains. He has earned my hatred, it is true, but he has also earned my respect. Because of my hatred for Gilgamesh, I shall crush him but because of my respect for him, I shall crush you first."

"Scorpion-men, protect me," Ut-Napishtim cried.

He fled as the mighty ape fought with the Scorpion-men. Soon Humbaba had crushed all of Ut-Napishtim's minions except for Shamhat. Finding her beautiful, the great ape spared Shamhat's life. Seizing her in one hand, he began to climb the great ziggurat.

Gilgamesh and Enkidu arrived at the square to see the destruction and the bodies of the Scorpion-man. When they saw that Humbaba was climbing the ziggurat, they parted ways. Enkidu held his knife in his teeth and began to climb after the ape, while Gilgamesh hurried to a storage building on the waterfront where he kept his private autogyro.

The machine rose into the air and crossed the city quickly. When Gilgamesh reached the ziggurat, he saw that Humbaba had climbed to the pinnacle and clung there with Shamhat still in his hand.

Gilgamesh dove on him, firing the autogyro's mighty guns. Humbaba roared and lashed out at the wondrous machine, but the Man of Bronze was as skilled in piloting as he was in all other things. He turned the craft and slipped away from every blow.

They dueled thus for many minutes. The weapons of Gilgamesh were not powerful enough to slay the ape, but Humbaba was not quick enough to catch the autogyro. Finally, in desperation, the great ape flung the fair Shamhat into the air. Gilgamesh spun the craft with matchless skill, and leaning far out of the cockpit, caught Shamhat in one powerful arm. But not even the skill of Gilgamesh could pilot an aircraft while performing such a feat and his flight took him close to the building, where Humbaba waited, ready to strike.

As the zombie ape raised his mighty hands, Enkidu reached the top of the Ziggurat. Uttering a lion's roar, the beast-man flung himself onto Humbaba's back and smote him many times with his hunting knife. Humbaba flailed at the Jungle Lord, but Enkidu held tight and continued to strike. Then, unable to keep his balance, Humbaba toppled from the building. Enkidu still clung to the beast and, together, they plummeted to the street.

## IX

At the base of the ziggurat lay the body of Humbaba, crushed and broken by the fall. There too lay the brave Enkidu, still living but shattered in body. Gilgamesh landed his autogyro and went to his sworn brother, but even his medical skills were of no avail. He was able to wake his sworn brother but could not save his life.

"Cursed be Ut-Napishtim," Enkidu cried in his agony, "for he created the monster that has slain me. And cursed be Shamhat, for she lured me out of the forest and brought me to this place where I must die." But as he cursed he did not mention the name of Humbaba, for he felt a great kinship with the giant ape.

Then Shamhat went to him with tears in her eyes. "Enkidu, do not curse me," she said, "for it was I who brought you to civilization with all its pleasures, and it was I who taught you the joy of human company."

"Then blessed be Shamhat," Enkidu said, and having spoken, gave up his spirit to death.

Thus Enkidu died at peace, but Gilgamesh lived in turmoil. Shamhat encased the body of the Lord of Lions in a veneer of orichalcum, as was her habit with former lovers, and they placed his body in a great monument hidden within the park at the center of the city. There Gilgamesh buried the remains of Humbaba, praying that the giant ape would be the guardian of his sworn-brother's resting place.

X

For weeks after the death of his friend, Gilgamesh mourned. He did not eat, nor did he bathe, nor did he shave, but came to look and act like a wild man. He was grieved, not only that his friend should die, but at the thought that all men die, and that even the mighty Gilgamesh must one day follow his friend into the darkness.

XI

Then Shamhat came to Gilgamesh.

"You need not die," she said. "And Enkidu need not remain among the dead. My father possesses an elixir that brings life to the dead and immortality to the living. Come, and I will take you to him that we may restore your brother, my lover, to life."

So Gilgamesh rose and ate and washed and shaved his beard and went with Shamhat to the City of Gold and Lepers, where Ut-Napishtim had gone after fleeing from New Uruk.

XII

Together, Gilgamesh and Shamhat crossed the ocean in the Man of Bronze's dirigible and came at length to the City of Gold and Lepers, which was guarded by the Scorpion-men. When they saw Gilgamesh approaching, the Scorpion-men assumed their kung fu stances and readied their throwing stars, and their butterfly swords, and their hook-sickle sabers, and their flying guillotines, but Shamhat spoke harshly to them and they lowered their weapons and allowed Gilgamesh to pass.

"Why have you come?" Ut-Napishtim asked.

17

"I seek the answer to death," Gilgamesh said. "I do not wish to die, and I wish to restore Enkidu to life. Give me the secret of your elixir."

"There is no elixir," Dr. Ut-Napishtim said. "This is a lie that I have told to Shamhat and many others. It is true that I am ageless, but this is a gift that the gods granted me long ago, before the waters of Heaven flooded the Earth."

Then Gilgamesh's anger blazed fiercely and he struck down the villain with a single blow. The Scorpion-men assumed their kung fu stances again and advanced to slay him, but Shamhat stopped them and went to sit on Ut-Napishtim's throne.

"My father is gone. Now I rule the Scorpion-men," she said. "I owe this to you, O Gilgamesh, and will give you anything that you desire in return."

"Then give me your father's elixir," he said, "for I do not wish to die, and I wish to restore Enkidu to life."

Shamhat sent the Scorpion-men to her father's laboratories, and they soon returned to her with news of what they had discovered.

"Alas, my father spoke the truth," Shamhat said. "There is no elixir and it is the will of the gods that every man should die in his time. But I beg you to stay, Mighty Gilgamesh and the two of us shall share power and pleasure such as no mortal has ever known. Though we may be mortal, we shall live with a passion that shall outshine the gods, if only for a brief span. And when you die, I shall encase your body in the sacred metal, orichalcum to preserve your likeness for all time."

"No," Gilgamesh said, "for your heart is fickle and the monuments you make of your lovers are a sham. If I cannot have true immortality, shall I be satisfied with a counterfeit?"

Then Gilgamesh turned away from the beautiful Shamhat and left the City of Gold and Lepers to return to his home

## XIII

Gilgamesh stood at the peak of the ziggurat and gazed out across the city he ruled, and his heard was grieved. Wisest and mightiest of all was Gilgamesh the king, but in all the world there was no one like him, and he was alone.

*We will not spoil our readers' enjoyment of Nathan Cabaniss' tale by revealing here which modern-day thriller inspired the dark events contained within that take place in the 18th century Louisiana Bayou. The two sleuths being forced to join forces here to unravel a veritable web of evil are certainly as different and yet just as resourceful as their modern-day counterparts...*

## Nathan Cabaniss: *The Darkness in the Woods*

*New Orleans, 1766*

The fog hung over the bayou docks in a swirl as thick as soup, as footsteps echoed softly against the planks and the water beneath. Slowly, it began to dissipate, as if sensing the macabre presence of the dark figure passing through, parting for the man himself. His cloak seemed to suck whatever light was visible right from the air. A figure both towering and formidable, he was known throughout the world by many names, but for the purposes of his current trip, he was Doctor Joseph Balsamo.

He reached the end of the dock, his feet touching dry land for the first time in months. Balsamo had important business to attend to in France, business entrusted to him by the Freemasons, but before he could get on with the particulars of that task, the Order first wanted him to attend to an affair in the Colonies that required his... *specific* talents.

Balsamo stopped and looked around, as he searched for the agent he was to contact. Only one other figure was out this night, a man huddled near a signpost with a dim lamp. Upon being approached by Balsamo, he instantly straightened and cleared his throat. He looked increasingly worried, a nervous type who seemed to carry an invisible weight upon his shoulders at all times.

"*Will no one help the widow's son?*" the man called out, a slight crack in his voice.

The first test passed, Balsamo offered his hand for the second. The man took it, and gave and received the Masonic handshake. Passing inspection on both ends, the two of them relaxed a bit in the other's company.

"You're the one they call Doctor Balsamo?"

"At the moment. And you?"

"Capitaine Charles-Philippe Aubry, acting governor of the colony of Louisiana, at your service."

"*Acting* governor?"

"My predecessor passed on suddenly, leaving me to bear the title. A burden I am eager to be rid of, believe me," Aubrey said.

Balsamo did—the man could hardly keep his hand steady as he produced a handkerchief to wipe his sweating brow.

"And the reason you have requested my services?" Balsamo asked.

Aubry was taken aback. "Doctor Balsamo, you have only just arrived. Surely you wish to catch some rest before embarking upon this endeavor...?"

"There's time enough for sleep in the grave. I have other businesses waiting for me, and wish to be done here as quickly as possible. Now tell me what ails you."

Aubry looked deeply into the dark pool of the man's eyes, which were unwavering. Immediately feeling uncomfortable, he turned his gaze downwards.

"W-well, we're at a very tenuous place right now. Louisiana, that is. France has sold us off, and Spanish rule is imminent. Our population is a tangled mass of various factions: Frenchmen, soldiers unable to return home, displaced Indians of all tribes, freed slaves—it is a kettle under constant threat of boiling over. And the looming acquisition of the Spaniards hangs ever in the air, like a black cloud in the east signaling a coming storm..."

Balsamo was growing impatient.

"Your problem, Captain! The reason for my being here."

"Yes, yes... apologies, Doctor. I'm having a hard enough time keeping order until the Spanish arrive, and this recent ugliness has the port of New Orleans in a stir."

Aubry pulled the collar of his coat tighter about his neck, and looked about nervously.

"Someone's been killing Indians," he said, softly.

Balsamo raised an eyebrow. "Killing Indians? This is why you've invoked *the widow's son*—a simple murderer?"

"There's more to it than that. They've been leaving them in public places—in front of taverns, in the middle of the street, and so on. At first, it was just one at a time, the bodies scalped, with crosses carved in their chests. But the most recent find was a whole group of them, their corpses arranged in strange patterns, their insides..." Aubry let his words trail off, hoping that would be enough to provide a suitable description. "Men, women, children—the killer has no preference, as long as they're Indian. The scattering of tribes we've got are already scared out of their minds. *Everyone's* scared out of their minds. Couple that with the precarious position the colony is in, and you can see that already my hands are quite full. I mean, I can't hand over New Orleans to the Spaniards with the city in a riot!"

Balsamo thought the matter over—sending him all this way to handle a simple outbreak of murders still seemed an extreme measure on the part of his benefactors. But, if this were how the Freemasons thought best to use his talents, he would see the task through.

"What do you know of the murders? Have you any suspects already in mind?"

Aubrey's tone turned harsher, in a fashion more fitting to a man of commanding stature.

"Doctor Balsamo, please do not take my frankness for impudence, but if I knew any more than what I have already told you, I would not have seen fit to call upon your services. There are other pressing matters that call for my attention, and thus I require someone to handle this affair with the utmost expedience and efficiency."

Balsamo sighed. Aubry had revealed his true colors. He was a simple-minded fool, one given far more responsibility than he could ever handle or even want, but still a simple-minded fool. Balsamo decided then and there that the man could be of no further use to him.

"Very well. I shall begin by visiting the taverns and inns within the area. Can you tell me which is closest?"

"Closest? The hour is quite late; I doubt any will be open..."

"Time is of the essence, Captain Aubry."

Aubry hazarded a second glance into the man's otherworldly eyes, found within them an unbreakable steely reserve. There was to be no arguing with him. "The nearest tavern opens three hours hence."

"Then the innkeeper shall find me waiting when he arrives."

By the time the Sun reached its peak in the sky, Balsamo had visited every tavern, inn and eatery in the area. In each, there were hushed murmurs of the spate of Indian killings, but nothing more than the broadest details of what had already occurred. Fool that he was, Aubrey was at least right about one thing: the people were frightened, and the looming threat of Spanish occupation did little to calm their nerves.

As always, it was in the last tavern he visited that Balsamo gleaned the only bit of information that would be useful to him. There was an individual at the bar, already in his spirits, though the day had scarcely begun. Balsamo found his tongue to be especially loose.

"Aye, I know of the Indian killin's," the man said. "Certain savages've taken to call it the work a' the *Jibbenainosay*."

"*Jibbenainosay*? What the Devil is that?" Balsamo asked.

"*Spirit that walks*, in the heathen tongue. Or, at least, in one of 'em. Got near as many languages between 'em all as there are leaves on the trees, if'n you can believe it."

"Do *you* believe it?"

"A spirit that goes aroun' killin' Injuns?" the drunk asked, chortling under his breath. "I believe only what my eyes see, an' they ain't never seen anythin' like that."

"Has anyone seen this *Jibbenainosay*?"

"They say there was a child that survived the band of 'em bein' kilt and splayed about as they was—a girl not even twelve."

"Where is this girl now?" Balsamo asked deliberately.

The drunk hemmed and hawed, shrugging his shoulders this way and that. "Funny thing, my memory. Just like any other tool, it needs the right amount a' greasin', if'n it's to work properly..."

Balsamo sighed, ordered the man another tankard of ale from the barkeep.

"Well?"

"She's bein' kept at the convent on the far side a' town, with the Ursulines," the man said. "Although I don't know how much help she'll be to you. She ain't said a word since they found 'er, way I hear tell..."

Balsamo left without another word to the man, not even a simple gesture of gratitude. Immediately, he set his sights towards the convent the man had mentioned. Before the Sun had the chance to turn upon the face of the dial, he was at the place, speaking with the Ursuline sisters therein. Although at first reluctant to discuss the Indian girl they had in their keep, Balsamo's invoking of Captain Aubry's name gave him the access he needed. He also made sure his gold cross necklace was clearly visible to the sisters, which did not hurt their general opinion of him.

He was taken to a room in the back, where the Indian girl sat unmoving on a small bed in the far corner, dressed in a humble dress provided by the sisters. There was no change in the girl's expression as Balsamo knelt before her. Her gaze remained glassy and far off.

"Tell me what happened," he asked to the sister behind him.

"They found her hiding in a grove not far from where the... the bodies were found. This was the most recent one, where they were found all arranged and..." The sister closed her eyes, crossed herself. "Well, it's too horrible to mention. There were seven in all; most likely her family, exiled by the war from some land or other. No telling how she was able to escape, but we've kept her here secretly, as a precaution. With the killer still at large, there's no telling what could happen."

"Are there any of the sisters who can speak the native languages?" Balsamo asked.

"I can, a little. But it's no use—the girl hasn't spoken since she was found. She barely does anything but stare at the wall."

"I can get her to speak," Balsamo said, reaching deep within his cloak. Producing his hand at last, he held a shiny, polished coin between his fingers. He moved it from one finger to the next with astonishing grace, which to the sister's surprise got the girl's attention. With another movement of his hand, the coin disappeared from Balsamo's grasp.

Smiling wryly, he reached behind the girl's ear, pulled his hand back with the coin between his fingers once more. The girl smiled, finally looked him in the eye, which was all Balsamo needed.

"Look into my eyes, girl, and listen to my voice," he said, in tones surprisingly deep and calming. The girl was transfixed. "What is your name?"

The girl answered in her own tongue, shocking all in the room.

"Can you understand her?" Balsamo asked.

The sister was at first too stunned to respond, but quickly regained her composure. "Y-yes. She says her name is Atala, after a woman her ancestor loved very much."

"Atala," Balsamo said, his voice so soothing even the sister was beginning to fall into a trance. "Can you tell me what happened the night they found you?"

Atala spoke once more, and the sister translated: "She says she was travelling with her family—they were thrown from their lands and decided to head further south. Upon their arrival in town, they met a kindly white man who smiled big and offered to feed them. Tired and hungry, they agreed, and the man led them to a clearing in the woods.

"As they ate, they noticed the white man disappeared. Not long after, he returned, with a different face... Or, I guess the proper word would be, 'mask.' He apparently approached the group calmly, proceeded to plant a tomahawk in her brother's scalp. She says she didn't see what happened after that; her mother grabbed her and told her to run off into the woods, where she hid until she was found."

Satisfied, Balsamo broke his stare from the girl, gave her the coin from earlier. He pulled the sister aside to speak with her privately.

"You said they found the girl in a grove—where exactly were the bodies of her family discovered?"

"In town, right in the middle of the street."

*Curious*, Balsamo thought. *He moved them—wanted them to be seen...*

With nothing further to be learned, Balsamo made for the door, but was stopped by the sister.

"How did you do that? Get her to speak like that?" she inquired.

"A new medical procedure," Balsamo said. "Something I picked up in my travels."

He had learned that and a great deal more on his travels; occult practices that would surely turn the sister's hair grey if she were to learn the particulars. He decided it best not to share them, and promptly left the convent.

A murderer on the loose who wanted the public to know what he was up to... Was he seeking attention, or did he secretly wish to be caught? Armed with this new information, Balsamo once more hit the streets in pursuit.

The next few days proved fortuitous for Balsamo's investigation. Liberal deposits of coin and drink with several of the town's more agreeable constituents provided bits and pieces of useful information; bits and pieces that Balsamo slowly shaped into a whole.

The first of the bodies began showing up in early October—Atala's family were found on 5 November. Balsamo made a list of persons who arrived in the port at that point, narrowed it down by who was still in town within that

23

timeframe. Further questionings of those on the list's accountability for that evening in November whittled the list down to two persons: a pirate captain by the name of Clegg, and the Quaker frontiersman known only as Wandering Nathan."

Balsamo found the Quaker first, sitting alone in the back of a particularly questionable tavern. To call the man humble in appearance was something of an understatement. His dress was largely composed of leather—dried animal skins sewn together so haphazardly they barely held their shape. He was still young, perhaps twenty or twenty-five, but his face was already marked by a certain haggardness that came from a life lived in no great comfort.

Balsamo approached him curiously as he sat and stared off into space, with nothing to eat or drink on the table before him.

"You are the one they call Wandering Nathan?" he inquired.

The man looked up from his daze, imparted upon Balsamo a simple, good-natured smile.

"Aye, I am he, friend. What, may I ask, troubles thee?"

Balsamo sat down in the seat across from him, studied him closely with his piercing stare. His first read of the man suggested him a simpleton, but there was something indistinguishable about the Quaker's eyes, dull as they were.

"Would you mind if I asked you a few questions?" he asked.

"Whatever thee asks, this humble servant shall answer."

"You've only been in the port of New Orleans for a few months, correct?"

"Aye, that is the truth."

"And what has your business been here?"

"I am but a simple wanderer from Pennsylvania, with no home to return to, nor family of mine own. I travel from town to town, to trade animal skins and furs, least 'til I am run oft."

"'Run oft'?"

"Aye. It is to mine great displeasure that most find me deplorable company, and 'tis never long 'til I am chased back to the woods from whence I came." Nathan's mood became melancholy for the briefest of moments, before returning at once to its good-natured state. "But mayhap that's the better fate—the woods provide far better company."

Balsamo decided to move in for the kill: "You've heard of the recent Indian murders, yes?"

"Aye, a terrible thing," Nathan said, removing his patchwork of a leather cap. His reaction proved hard to gauge.

"The night when the family was found arranged in the street—would you mind telling me where you were at that time?"

"Friend, is thee making accusations of poor Nathan, just because he was in the woods at the time? Does thee think Nathan responsible for the killing of the savages in the very same woods?"

Balsamo shrugged. "I'm merely asking a question, is all."

"I tell thee true, sir, that I am a man of peace. I detest violence in all its forms. But I shall answer thee's question, if it eases thee's conscience. I was out late trapping for small game, and thus decided to spend the night in the woods. I returned only three days after the family was found, and was sad to hear of it, tell thee true."

Balsamo studied the Quaker's dull eyes carefully for any hint of a lie, but he found nothing there. The man was a simpleton—there was little doubt that not much of note transpired in the region connecting his ears. Balsamo could always turn to the trick of hypnosis, and although he had little scruples when it came to the morals of the modern world, performing such an action on a man of Wandering Nathan's wits did not sit well with him. Still unsure of the man, Balsamo gleaned that this would be all the information he could infer.

With nothing left to discuss, Balsamo stood from the table.

"I thank you for your time, sir, and apologize for any inconvenience. I do ask of you one thing: you spend much time on the fringes of town, do you not?"

"Aye, that I do."

"Then I must humbly ask you to keep a weather eye at all times. I have been tasked with locating this Indian killer, and a man familiar with the outskirts and those who travel there would be most useful to me. Will you agree to be my eyes and ears?"

Nathan thought it over, as much was possible for the mind behind those dull eyes, before finally answering:

"Thee has my word. I shall keep an eye out for all things suspicious or queer."

Balsamo tipped his cap, left Nathan to continue his staring at the wall, or whatever it was he found the Quaker doing earlier. He was still unsure of the man's innocence, but at the very least he now knew his true purpose for being in town, and by keeping an eye out on his behalf, Balsamo in turn could keep an eye on Nathan, as well.

Tracking down the pirate captain Clegg proved to be a trickier proposition. Smugglers and the like were pulling into harbor all the time in New Orleans, and often leaving just as quickly. Balsamo wasted an entire day inquiring from the sea-merchants and dock owners about Clegg, but came up with little. They all seemed reluctant to discuss the rogue, who apparently was a man of quick temper and great violence. When asked of Clegg, one ship-hand only shook his head and walked away, muttering, "I'd rather keep me tongue, than risk loose talk a' that devil."

By chance Balsamo finally discovered Clegg's ship, the *Imogene*, still anchored at a small dock. He was loath to approach it in good manner—the general mood towards Clegg from all around made him leery of questioning the man as he did Wandering Nathan. Balsamo decided the better course of action was to sneak aboard and gather what information he could from the captain's quarters.

The ship was largely abandoned, with only two of its crew left behind to stand guard. Sneaking past them was easy enough—a minor distraction or two, and Balsamo was on the ship, in the captain's quarters, without even the slightest hint of alarm.

The room was fairly modest for one belonging to a captain of a ship, the decorum befitting of a man who favored simplicity and functionality. Balsamo first rifled through the desk, finding nothing truly of note, although several captain's documents had been signed with a name other than "Clegg;" names such as "Christopher Syn" and, curiously, "Black Satan."

Balsamo continued his search to a large chest kept in the corner of the room, which held items of greater concern. Inside there was an arrangement of various swords, cutlasses, stone daggers and other jeweled artifacts of the ancient New World. What raised Balsamo's alarm were the ephemera of the Indian: there was a tomahawk with a polished, black blade, and a breastplate and several necklaces hewn from animal bone and skins.

One item in particular was especially curious, and Balsamo lifted it from the chest for further inspection. It was a burlap sack, nothing remarkable to it at a glance, but holding it up to the light of the Moon revealed two holes cut in the center—giving the sack the ghastly appearance of the face of a scarecrow. Balsamo remembered the girl Atala's words from before, of the white man who disappeared while they were eating, only to return later with a different face. A mask...

"What in God's name do you think you're doing here?" a voice called out from behind, followed quickly by the cocking of a firearm.

Balsamo turned his head over his shoulder to see a large man in the doorway to the cabin, holding a pistol steady and aimed right at him.

"Why don't you be a good chap and turn around, so I may get a better look at the intruder on my ship? Slowly, if you please," the man said.

Balsamo discreetly lifted a hand to his own belt as he began to turn around. Before revealing the fullness of his face, Balsamo's arm shot out from the darkness of his cloak, let loose a dagger that went spinning across the cabin and knocked the pistol right out of the man's hand.

In an instant, Balsamo cut the distance between himself and his assailant, drawing his sword and slicing the air straight at the man's neck. But before Balsamo's sword struck home, his movements were halted by a pressure at his ribs—a glance down revealed that the man had pulled a cutlass of his own. The two of them stood there in the cabin's darkness, Balsamo with his sword at the man's throat, and the man with the point of a cutlass at Balsamo's heart.

"Captain Clegg, I presume? Or is it Christopher Syn, or Black Satan?"

"I killed Black Satan, mean old bastard of the seas that he was."

"And you fancy killing, don't you?" Balsamo asked with insincerity. "Men, women, children… doesn't matter as long as they're Indian, eh?"

"The Indian killings? You think me responsible?"

"The game is over, Clegg. I saw the Indian trinkets in your collection. I saw your mask."

"Mask?" Clegg asked, then saw the burlap sack with the holes lying on the floor. "You mean that? I assure you that bullet holes attained during a galleon siege are not uncommon… Curious that you saw it as a mask. Besides, I'm a feared pirate captain… what need have I to hide my face?"

"Enough. You will come with me to the barracks on shore, alive or dead. My benefactor did not specify a condition."

"Listen to me very carefully, sir," Clegg said, slowly pulling his cutlass away and returning it to its scabbard. "I am not your enemy. I am a killer, 'tis true—and not always of deserving parties. But I swear to you on all that is holy that I have never taken lives so senselessly as the killer you pursue."

His eyes were unwavering and his breathing was steady. He wasn't lying.

"And the Indian items in your trunk?"

"Sir, I have traveled the world, traded with men from cultures you would scarcely believe. I have items from many places."

"I don't believe you. You're keeping secrets…"

"Oh, I have my secrets, as all men do. My given name is Christopher Syn, and I am not a true pirate. Or at least, once I was not. I took the pose of a pirate long ago for just reasons, although now I have fallen into the life of a scoundrel so far, I fear I may never recover. But the longing for justice still beats within my breast, and I might even be inclined to offer my services to you and your cause… *if* you can trust me long enough to take your blade from my throat."

Balsamo ran the thoughts over in his head—Clegg seemed a reasonable man, despite his dubious profession. He gave off no sign of madness or insanity. That meant the killer had to be the Quaker Nathan… didn't it? Balsamo cursed himself, cursed his rush to complete the task at hand. He was so blinded by the need to return to France that he was willing to cut down innocent men at the flimsiest of reasons.

He lowered his blade from Clegg's neck, bowed his head in apology.

"Forgive me, Captain. I am afraid I have not used my best judgment as of late," he said, then offered his hand to Clegg. "My name is Doctor Joseph Balsamo, and I would be glad of your assistance, if you are so inclined."

Clegg looked at his hand for a moment, finally shook it. "You seek the Indian killer—that means you're working for Aubry, correct?"

"Hardly. Aubry called upon the assistance of my true benefactors, the identity of whom I am not at liberty to discuss."

"Secret societies hold no interest for me, anyway," Clegg shrugged. "Well, besides myself, what else have you found?"

"The only other man I've come across is a strange Quaker everyone refers to as 'Wandering Nathan,' but he claimed to be trapping in the woods at the..."

Balsamo halted himself in mid-sentence. He suddenly remembered what Nathan had said earlier: *"Does thee think Nathan responsible for the killing of the savages in the very same woods?"*

He had not told Nathan of the family being murdered in the woods—no one knew that except for Atala, the sister who translated and himself—and yet Nathan knew. Balsamo cursed himself again for this oversight, but allowed no time for further discouragements. He headed for the door...

"Doctor? What is it?"

He had told the Quaker nothing of Atala or the convent, but by now Nathan had surely inquired after the mysterious stranger who had questioned him, and all the places he had visited prior. It was only a matter of time until that led him straight to the girl...

"Come, quickly. I fear I have made a grave error..."

Balsamo and Clegg arrived at the convent just in time to hear the scream. They rushed inside, only to find the sister Balsamo spoke with before huddled in a corner, the others gathered around her worriedly.

Balsamo broke through the crowd and bent low, putting a hand to the sister's shoulder. She turned to him, face streaked with tears.

"The girl—Atala—it took her. Oh, it was horrible. So horrible..."

"Where, sister? Which way did they go?"

"Out the back, towards the swamp. It was covered in fur... It wasn't a man—I promise it wasn't a man!"

Balsamo exchanged a look with Clegg. The two nodded, both proceeded to run out the back and into the dark of the wood. Clegg pointed at the ground—the barest hint of footsteps traced a path, one pair smaller than the other. The two of them lit off after the prints in hot pursuit, travelling further and further into the woods with nothing but the light of the Moon to guide their way.

Finally they came close enough to catch a glimpse of the thing they chased—it was large, covered in whitish-grey fur which shone in the moonlight briefly before disappearing into the thick brush.

Balsamo and Clegg quickened their pace, eventually found the girl curled up in a ball on the ground. Fearing the worst, Balsamo went to inspect her. Atala's hands and feet were bound, but she was still alive.

Just as Balsamo realized he had taken the bait, an inhuman yell echoed out from the inky black spaces of the woods. From out of nowhere, the Quaker Nathan leapt at Balsamo, sending him sprawling to the floor with a kick. He was dressed from head to toe in wolf furs, with the head fashioned into a gruesome mask from which Nathan's eyes burned through holes carved in the face with far more rage than anything Balsamo had seen in any natural animal.

Clegg drew his blade first, charged at Nathan with a yell. The Quaker produced a tomahawk and sent it spinning straight at the pirate, whereupon it pegged the shoulder of his sleeve to a nearby tree.

As Clegg struggled to free himself of his shirt, Balsamo came to his feet once more. He charged at Nathan, his cloak expanding out from him in an infinite darkness as he drew his sword in an arc of gleaming silver. Nathan unslung the musket from his back, and a plume of smoke and fire discharged from the barrel, as the swamp was filled with the sound of sand striking a hollow, wooden basin. The round passed through Balsamo's cloak, narrowly missing his side by inches, and he thrust his sword forward at the wolf-skinned Quaker...

Nathan deflected the blow with a swing of his musket, leapt over to Clegg to retrieve his tomahawk from the tree. Now free, Clegg swiped the air with his cutlass aimed at Nathan's throat, but the Quaker hooked his tomahawk behind Clegg's knee, swiping him right off of his feet.

Balsamo was at him again, and Nathan caught the blade of Balsamo's sword with his tomahawk. He pulled a knife from his boot and slashed at his shins, causing Balsamo to drop to his knees. Now towering over the crouched Balsamo, Nathan raised his tomahawk against the face of the Moon. His eyes were wild with a violent lust, in anticipation of the bloody strike home to Balsamo's skull...

Suddenly Nathan cried out—with his back still in the dirt, Clegg had driven a knife into the Quaker's thigh. Balsamo rose once more, brought the hilt of his sword straight into Nathan's face. He fell over to the ground with a bloodied nose, and at last the conflict was over.

Clegg went over to Atala and cut her bonds, as Balsamo reached down and pulled the wolf's head from Nathan's face. The kindly expression of the simpleton of earlier was entirely gone, replaced instead by the twisted snarl of a madman.

"The Indian has no right to live," the Quaker spat, "He is barely above the station of a dog, with only a dirty shirt to separate him from that of the beasts..."

"That will be quite enough of that," Balsamo said, lifting Nathan's discarded musket and striking him in the head, knocking the Quaker out.

Now holding Atala in his arms, Clegg approached from behind.

"I'll take the girl into town, bring Aubry and his soldiers back to take him into custody."

Balsamo said nothing, only nodded. He heard the brush give way as Clegg and the girl made their way through the swamp, but Balsamo's eyes remained transfixed on the unconscious Nathan.

His task in the New World, it would appear, was finally at an end.


"What do you mean, 'he got away'?"

Clegg paced Aubry's office in a fury, as the acting governor sat behind his desk shuffling through a mound of paperwork.

"I mean just that. He was under watch by my men the entire night, but still the Quaker found some way to slip away unnoticed. My men have searched the area thoroughly, but found no trace of the man. As far as I am concerned, the one called Nathan Slaughter is no longer the problem of Louisiana." Aubry stopped, considered his words. "Slaughter... should have been obvious, really, with a name like that."

Clegg pounded his fist on the table.

"And you're just going to allow that to transpire? Allow this killer to roam free?"

Aubry looked up from his desk at Clegg, his patience wearing thin.

"The watch commander on duty last night was a man named Childress. You have any more questions, Captain, then I suggest asking him. Otherwise, I have a great deal on my mind at the present time. Slaughter has fled the colony, and is unlikely to return. The matter is settled."

"Settled?" Clegg shouted. He turned to Balsamo, who had been quietly sitting in the corner the whole time. His thoughts, as always, were elsewhere. "What about you, Balsamo? You're all right with this?"

"He knows when a task is finished," Aubry said, standing up from behind his desk. "Louisiana thanks you both, gentlemen, for your service and aid. Please be gracious enough to accept it."

With that, Aubrey left the room. Clegg threw his hands out in exasperation.

"Coward... spineless, sniveling coward! A dog caught between two masters, he cares for nothing more than saving his own skin." Noticing that Balsamo had not moved for some time, Clegg turned to the man. "And what is it with you? You've been sitting there all morning, without uttering a single word. What's the matter?"

Balsamo turned his head, finally meeting Clegg's gaze, and abruptly stood.

"Come with me."

Balsamo led Clegg back into the woods, deeper than they had gone the previous night while chasing after the Quaker Nathan. Balsamo was quiet the entire time, so Clegg decided it best to wait and see whatever it was the man had to show him before making inquiries.

Eventually they arrived at a cave dug deep into the Earth, where they paused a moment to gather their breath.

Staring into the mouth of the cave, Clegg finally deemed it appropriate to speak.

"What is the meaning of this, Balsamo?"

"Last night, after you took the girl back into town, I saw in the corner of my eye another with us out in the woods. He fled the scene, and I followed after him, which led me here. The figure entered the cave, but before it disappeared completely from sight, I caught a glimpse: it was a tall man in a robe, with a mask made of sticks adorned to his face."

"Another in a mask?" Clegg asked.

"Yes," Balsamo said, before stepping forward boldly and entering the cave.

Clegg hesitated in following after, as a chill went over his spine. The wind whistled out of the cave, in a sound not dissimilar from that of a human whisper. Something was severely wrong with the place before him—something that Clegg could not put a finger to. Feeling uneasy on his own, he followed after Balsamo into the cave.

The interior was damp and eerily silent, and before long it became so dark that Clegg could not see his own hand held up to his face.

"This way, Captain," he heard Balsamo call out. "Follow the sound of my voice."

Eventually light began to peek through the darkness, and before long Clegg arrived to an opening in the cave, where the light of day shone through a wide crevice above. Balsamo stood in the center, admiring a sight which immediately ran the blood in Clegg's veins cold.

It was a makeshift man, put together from twigs and branches and draped in a pale, yellow cloak, with a human skull placed at the top and affixed with the antlers of a stag. The walls had been painted with strange, spiral designs, and all around the opening were other skulls and bones of all shapes and sizes, the details of which Clegg did not wish to focus on too closely.

"What is this, Balsamo?"

"We caught the wrong man last night."

"What? But that's impossible—we caught Slaughter in the act itself, ready to kill Atala…"

"Oh, we caught a killer last night. Perhaps even the one responsible for *some* of the deaths… but not all. Whether he was acting in the service of others, or those very same others used the circumstances of his bloodlust towards the Indians for their own advantage, who's to say. But he was not the only one…"

Clegg approached the center of the opening cautiously, feeling his normally rational mind start to quite suddenly and irrationally think that the yellow-cloaked figure followed his every move with its eyeless sockets.

"What does this all mean?" Clegg asked, motioning to their current surroundings and keeping his voice low.

"I had a mentor once, who was obsessed with finding the secret to immortality. He told me of practices certain occult bodies performed in the hopes of attaining such a thing, and I tell you now, Captain, not a day goes by that I don't wish I could have those images stricken from my memory. Ritual killings, and worse…"

"You think these people were doing all this in the hopes of being granted immortality?"

"I think that there is no depth to the evils mankind is capable of in the service of irrational belief—an evil I sense hanging over this land, and one that will continue to cast its shadow for some time," Balsamo said solemnly. "Or, if you'd rather my true opinion: I do not know."

Suddenly, Clegg heard a soft whispering echo out of the caverns from behind. He turned with a start, but there was nothing there.

Only darkness.

*It is customary for each volume of* Tales of the Shadowmen *to feature shorter, often more light-hearted, stories poking fun at our favorite heroes and villains. Matthew Dennion's take on Sam Raimi's* Evil Dead *is certainly one of these...*

## Matthew Dennion: *Don't Judge a Book by its Title*

*French Country Side, 1993*

Ash Williams cursed as he passed the turn that he was looking for. The map was no help. All of the words were in French. He rolled his eyes and thought: *"Didn't the French realize that Americans came to their country as well? Wouldn't the occasional map written in English be something useful?"*

He shook his head and mused that ever since he had become The Chosen One, the one destined to fight the forces of darkness, it seemed that only bad luck had come his way—and this was no exception.

The bad luck started when all of his friends turned into monsters and tried to kill him, forcing him to slice them to ribbons. Just when he thought he was done battling corpses, he got sucked back in time to fight an evil version of himself and an army of skeletons. Finally, he got back home where all he wanted to do was live out the rest of his life working at a department store. Then, on his first day back at the job, he was attacked by a possessed dead woman. So what did he do but unleash a little Deadite Fu on her boney butt and sent her back to hell in a hand basket.

Ash sped further down the dark county road as he continued to reminisce. You would think that saving a store full of people from Frankenstein's ugly little sister would qualify you as a hero, but not at S-Mart. There, you get reprimanded for firing a shotgun in the store.

The next day it happened again, and once more The Chosen One fought off the bad guy. This time his supervisor called him into the office and said that they couldn't keep having him attacked in the store like that. The boss gave him two weeks of vacation time to solve the problem, and if he couldn't solve it, he was to stay on permanent vacation. When Ash asked if it would be paid permanent vacation, he was told to get the hell out of the store.

Ash left the store and sighed; he knew what he had to do in order to stop all of these crazy corpses from attacking him. He needed to find the *Necronomicon* and destroy it once and for all. With that book gone, it would be nothing but the S-Mart, cold beer, and hot babes for old Ash. The problem was, where to find the darned thing. It was not like you could just check the book out of the local library. He had already searched the cabin where all this craziness started when he went *Back to the Future*.

33

Further down the road, he could see another small cabin. If his information was right, this was the place he was looking for. He continued to replay the events that had brought him there in his mind. He reached out to people in the paranormal community for leads on the *Necronomicon*. He tried everyone from psychics to some screwball Ghostbusters in New York. He finally got a lead when he talked to a French guy by the name of Sâr Dubnotal. The old man told him that he knew where the *Necronomicon* was, and how he could destroy it if Ash were to bring it to him.

It turned out that the damned book was in France and had fallen into the hands of someone who, of course, was using it for evil purposes!

Ash stopped the car outside of the cabin. When he got out of the car, he could hear the sounds of a struggle coming from inside. He ran to the trunk, opened it, and said to no one in particular, "Go time, baby."

He removed his prosthetic hand and put a chainsaw in its place. With his good hand, he grabbed his shotgun. He screamed, ran at the door, and kicked it in. What he saw stopped him dead in his tracks.

Inside the cabin was the most beautiful woman that he had ever seen, lying naked on a bed. Normally, this would have been a welcomed sight, were she not surrounded by massive tentacles crawling out of a swirling vortex in the middle of the room. In the corner of the room stood a giant with a book in his hand that could only be the *Necronomicon*. While tentacles were not the typical Deadite manifestation Ash was used to fighting, he figured they came in all shapes and sizes—and he knew a virgin sacrifice when he saw one.

Ash let loose a battle cry, jumped into the room, and began using his chainsaw to slice the tentacles off the monster from the portal. As chunks of calamari fell to the floor, the tentacles began to recede into the quickly closing portal. Ash pointed his gun at the giant in the corner.

"Don't move, chuckles. Boom Stick beats brawn any day of the week."

He turned to the girl and saw the stunned look on her face.

"It's okay, miss..."

Before he could finish his thought, the naked girl flew across the room, disarmed him, grabbed him by the throat, and pinned him to the wall. The vampire bared her fangs and hissed at the hero. The giant in the corner spoke:

"Countess Irina is angry with you. She and Baal had a mutually beneficial agreement that suited both of their unique needs..."

"Look," yelled Ash. "I see a girl being attacked by a reject from a Ray Harryhausen film and I save the day. How was I supposed to know Vampirella here actually wanted to be attacked by that thing?"

"She was not under attack," replied the giant, smiling. "Now, who are you and how did you find us?"

Ash swallowed hard as Irina continued to look at him as if he was a steak dinner.

"My name is Ash. I came here looking for the *Necronomicon*."

The giant looked down at the book in his hands.

"Why do you seek the dreaded book?" he asked.

Ash kept his eyes on the vampire.

"Because the Deadites it attracts have it in for me. I can't even show up to work without being attacked."

A puzzled look ran across the giant's face.

"Deadites? This book does not call forth the Deadites. My sad friend, you are chasing the wrong book."

Ash tried to free himself from the vampire.

"Look here, Hagar the Horny, I dealt with the *Necronomicon* before; and, as sure as you guys think Jerry Lewis is funny, that book does bring forth Deadites."

Irina shook her head and the giant spoke for her.

"You seek the lesser *Necronomicon Ex Mortis*. This is the *First Necronomicon* written by the mad Arab Abdul Alhazred."

Ash squirmed in the grip of Irina.

"There are two *Necronomicons*, and one of them is supposed to be written by a wrestler? I supposed next you're going to tell me that your book summons Paul Bearer and the Undertaker?"

The giant and Irina look at each other as they clearly did not understand the reference.

"Whatever you believe, it is nevertheless true," said the giant. "There are two books by that name and this is not the one you seek. Now how did you locate us?"

"Some Sâr-something said you would be here," said Ash, rolling his eyes.

The vampire scowled as the giant spoke:

"Sâr Dubnotal! Yes. He has long sought to destroy this book. Tell me, why such a powerful mage would send a pitiful fool like you to retrieve the book instead of coming here himself?"

Ash could feel his anger building up inside of him.

"Look, buddy, you are not just talking to the S-Mart employee of the week. I also happen to be The Chosen One! So tell Morticia here to let me go before I kick her butt all the way back to Mockingbird Lane."

Irina's eyes opened wide and the giant stepped forward.

"Wait... Deadites, Chosen One... Are you the one destined to fight the forces of darkness?"

"The one and only," said Ash, smiling, "although I did hear something about a girl named Buffy who hangs out with the band *Slayer*, I think."

The giant looked at the vampire woman.

"Mistress, if he is the Chosen One, you no longer need Baal. This man can fulfill all your needs, and, as the Chosen One, he will be unharmed in the process."

"If you think that I am just going to let her drain me dry of my blood," protested Ash, "you got another thing coming."

Irina smiled as the giant spoke.

"It is not your blood she desires."

Ash gazed into Irina's eyes and uttered his best pick up line:

"Give me some sugar, baby!"

*In last year's collection, Brian Gallagher used Marie Nizet's Captain Liatoukine, from her ground-breaking 1879 novel* Captain Vampire *(available from Black Coat Press), to introduce us to the complex and murky world of vampire politics, and their intersection with the very real and equally dangerous realm of human politics. This new story jumps forward in time and brings us to the eve of World War I...*

## Brian Gallagher: *The Trial of Van Helsing*

*St. Petersburg, 1913*

Rasputin considered his visitor, tall, upright and thin. There was something about the eyes—like those of a cat. In some circles, he was known as "Captain Vampire." However, he was now a General of the Russian Imperial Army. Yes, thought Rasputin, up close he could tell that the General was not quite human. But many did not listen to the rumors. Liatoukine was a man of influence. And it seemed he wanted the help of none other than himself; also influential in certain circles, although perhaps a lot less liked.

For his part, Boris Liatoukine was also considering Rasputin, but he thought him to be nothing but a degenerate. They were both at a particular lady of the court's home. Rasputin was sitting on a divan. He was leant back, his shirt undone, with a semi-clad noblewoman on either side of him. Liatoukine was not above such behavior himself, but he disapproved of it in others. Especially peasants—and he considered the monk Rasputin to be little more than that. But his influence was unquestionable. Liatoukine had, in fact, expected to find a supernatural being, but he had found someone who was only human and nothing more. Given the peasant's power, he found that unsettling. One day, something would have to be done.

They had already exchanged pleasantries when Liatoukine finally got to business.

"I understand you can help me find a certain individual, a renowned professor named Van Helsing—a Dutchman. You are aware, of course, that the Tsar relies on me to look into areas of... er, *special interest*, shall we say? I firmly believe the Professor could assist in these matters. We have approached the Dutch government, but they say he is studying and does not wish to give private consultations. I am sure I could persuade him to help, if only I could speak to him myself."

"My dear General Liatoukine," cackled Rasputin. "No need to be so coy. You advise the Tsar on supernatural matters. I, too, advise him—and the Tsarina—on many matters. We both do God's work." Rasputin looked heavenwards, rolling his eyes upwards. Liatoukine, too, felt like rolling his eyes, but restrained himself.

"Of course, I can help you," the monk continued. "In recent years, Van Helsing has become known in many religious circles for his esoteric knowledge. I have already obtained the information for you. Of course, I had to incur certain expenses..."

Liatoukine tossed a small pouch at Rasputin. The monk took a quick glance inside. He was not greedy, but money helped him be the center of attention. Satisfied, he placed the pouch on a table in front of him, then took a small envelope which he gave to Liatoukine.

"I think you will find the information necessary to assist you in finding Van Helsing," he said. "Now, if our business is concluded, I have many spiritual matters to discuss with my guests."

Liatoukine was displeased with the monk's attitude. Had it not been for his closeness to the Tsar, he would have drained him of his energy, giving the peasant an excellent opportunity to have a real spiritual discussion with his maker. Instead, he simply bade him a good day and left.

Liatoukine entered his carriage and looked at the document he had just been handed. Van Helsing's location was a surprise to him. It was a place he had visited in the past, whose master was now dead, but somehow, it seemed appropriate. Of course, Liatoukine had no real intention to merely have a conversation with van Helsing. He was to capture the Dutchman and take him to the Vampire City—The Sepulchre, sometimes known as Selene amongst the humans. There, Van Helsing would stand trial for his role in killing the greatest vampire of all— Count Dracula.

*Castle Dracula, Transylvania, the Austro-Hungarian Empire.*

On a mountain high above a village, a most foreboding castle stood. Within its corridors, soldiers of the Austro-Hungarian Empire patrolled, and certain officials worked. The soldiers would patrol and look into anything odd; a mysterious sound perhaps, or an odd drop in temperature... Nothing was ever found. Such things were unsettling, but only temporarily. These men knew their business and were confident. The one who had once been the master of this castle had been destroyed some twenty years before. They were the masters now, and used the castle for their own purposes.

In one of the many rooms, now converted into a study, two men were having a conversation. Baron Vordenberg, whose office it was, was talking to a distinguished guest. Vordenberg, a man in his late thirties, was experienced in supernatural matters and had gained a high official position within the group tasked by the Emperor to deal with such things.

"Well, we know the vampires of Selene have been looking for you for a while," he said. "They seem to have become a little braver of late, we believe, of which trying to get to you is a large part, but you already know this."

His guest, a noted expert on many supernatural matters, including vampirism, was Professor Van Helsing. It had been a few years since his encounter with Count Dracula, but he remained active.

"I am most grateful not only for informing me of the threat," he replied, nodding his head, "but also for the access you have afforded me to study the many documents and artifacts left behind by Dracula"

"My friend, it is we who should be grateful," said the Baron, laughing. "Your efforts disposed not only of a grave vampire threat, but also provided the Empire with a most useful base of operations. Cost free, too!" he added, slapping his hand on his desk in amusement.

"What about the locals? Do they have any inkling of what you're doing here?" asked Van Helsing.

"Possibly—but only as rumor. Our public face is merely that of minor functionaries with a small troop of soldiers, operating in a part of the Empire that is so remote that no one would think anything of it. The legends of the previous, er, owner, persist of course. However, we do feel some of the natives are slowly becoming impressed by the fact we have taken the castle for ourselves. Such stories serve our purpose. The peasantry is consequently less fearful of the supernatural—and the supernatural is more fearful of us!"

"Hence perhaps the vampires' recent interest in me," mused Van Helsing. "No doubt an attempt to tilt the balance back. Especially now that we know where their city is located."

"And that is something else we are very grateful to you," nodded the Baron. "For your work on establishing where it is was of great importance. The city would be better off destroyed. It is unfortunate indeed that it is situated, as was rumored, in Serbia."

"I understand the political situation remains tense," said Van Helsing.

"Yes. Serbia is promoting an assassination campaign in Bosnia-Herzegovina, which is part of the Empire. They seem to be insisting on a war—one which we would swiftly win, of course, even if their Russian friends support them, which frankly I doubt. In such circumstances, we could then attend to Selene. However, we are beholden to a policy over which we have no influence. Vienna will not institute a war over a supernatural city that can only be seen for an hour a day. Serbian agitators, yes—they are real enough for the world to see, but vampires, no—despite rumors and even some official reports. We can only act covertly, and in such a way to not provoke Serbia or Russia. We still don't quite know what the understanding between Belgrade and Selene is..."

Van Helsing pondered the issue.

"Perhaps some form of non-aggression pact? I wonder what they make of the new ruler of Selene—Mircalla Karnstein. From what I learned, and your own organization have gathered, she is being most assertive. Certainly, it seems she is making a real effort to deal with me. I can only assume my research has eager readers in her domain."

"Indeed," chuckled the Baron. "Especially as they are clearly aware of your dispatching the former owner of this castle! However, we are ready for them. As you know, we have given your location to the Russian General Boris Liatoukine."

Liatoukine was a familiar name to Van Helsing; he had long been rumored to be of supernatural origin and had been known as "Captain Vampire" for decades, although the present holder of the title claimed he was just the latest in family line. But it was not an unfamiliar tactic among some vampires... Liatoukine had a brutal reputation. His influence at the Court in St. Petersburg was well known, even feared. Although there was no solid evidence, Van Helsing was assumed that Liatoukine was some kind of vampire, but one who drained life-force instead of blood.

"What you perhaps do not know," Vordenberg went on, "is that the General has assumed some kind of role as supernatural adviser to the Tsar. In matters pertaining to vampires he has effectively total control. You could say he is my opposite number. Of late, due to the political situation, our cooperation with Russia on these matters has declined. With Liatoukine assuming this role, it has fallen even further. We even believe there has been some disinformation. We have only just found out about his position..."

Van Helsing wondered if they had just found out, or if the Baron had only just decided to tell him. Perhaps he was just getting older, and more suspicious due to his experiences. The Baron and his people had been very helpful in his research, despite his not being a citizen of their empire.

"Perhaps it is he who will come to kill or capture me?" said Van Helsing.

"I do hope so," said the Baron. "If we can capture him, we may be able to interrogate him, and if kill him, that's one less enemy to deal with. To all, he will have simply disappeared. He is unlikely to have told the Tsar where he is going. But whoever comes, our trap will send the right signal to Karnstein." He paused. "It is brave of you to act as bait."

"Not so. I have no intention of looking over my shoulder for the rest of my life, however long that may be. The vampires have been afraid of me since they realized my involvement in destroying Dracula. Now, it seems Karnstein has emboldened them. Destroying their agent would throw them back into a state of fear."

There was a knock on the door. A guard came in with a note for the Baron. He read it and said:

"It seems we will soon find out. We have word that strangers are approaching the village. We should prepare. Our trap may be sprung tonight!"

"One moment," said Van Helsing. "I am troubled by Mircalla Karnstein. We know she was destroyed many years ago How is it that she has come back to life? Her resurrection is the key to her rise to power—no vampire has ever come back from such destruction before. Indeed, there was an official report on the matter and her last victim even wrote something on it..." Van Helsing paused. "If she can come back, then perhaps others can too..." He paused again. "...Others such as Dracula..."

"Yes, that had crossed my mind too," said the Baron. "Of course, my own family has its own connection to Mircalla Karnstein. Dealing with such creatures is a family tradition. My grandfather was present at her destruction. He related it to me himself. There is no doubt in my mind that he told me the truth. The official reports from Styria confirmed the matter. Even the famous report by Doctor Hesselius leaves no room for doubt. And the account by Karnstein's last victim, Laura—her own descendent!—also confirmed it, although she was not present at the destruction..."

"All of that is only some of the evidence that the public knows about, and it is often attributed to hallucinations, visions, or what have you, in relation to what some believe was the work of a poisoner rather than a vampire."

Baron Vordenberg looked thoughtful for a moment.

"We know Karnstein was not a poisoner. I have been pondering this and I do have a theory—nothing more than that—that would explain it..."

Later, Van Helsing made his way down to the village, accompanied by a couple of soldiers. Other troops were ensconced there. The Dutchman was staying at a rented farmhouse rather than at the castle. That had been the location provided via intermediaries to Liatoukine. In these remote parts of the world, matters could be dealt with quietly and away from the eyes of the public. Van Helsing had approved of this as there were fewer chances of innocents being harmed. The villagers had been told that tonight they may be better off staying indoors.

Van Helsing entered his house and sat at a desk. He hoped the strangers were indeed vampires. It would be best to deal with them as soon as possible.

The horse-drawn carriage with the two strangers stopped before approaching the village. Liatoukine was the main rider. He was dressed as a trader. He considered this ruse somewhat unbecoming for a man of his stature, but such deceptions were unfortunately often needed—especially as not only his vampire senses, but his soldier's experience, told him something was not quite right in the village ahead.

He turned to his fellow rider, also disguised as a trader. Like Liatoukine, she, too, was a vampire. Originally known as Polly Bird, she had been converted into vampirism by one Otto Goetzi—long since deceased. However, he had used his power to change her into a copy of himself. She stayed in that form for many years, even becoming a member of the Vampire Council of the Sepulchre.

However, Liatoukine was well aware of her original form. She had been lower born than him, certainly, but it was said she was rather beautiful previous to her encounter with Goetzi, and he certainly admired the female form. He made an offer: using certain knowledge he had acquired, he would revert her to her previous female form—still belonging to the Undead of course—and, in return, she would support him on the Vampire Council of the Sepulchre.

Things had not gone entirely to plan, however. Mircalla had objected to Polly's continued presence on the Council due to the change of form, arguing she was no longer quite the same person. Liatoukine found this odd. It was thought that Mircalla had certain tastes and that, like himself, was not averse to the female form. No doubt her attitude was to do with eliminating someone loyal to her from the Council. This was when their rivalry had begun in earnest.

Still, Polly Bird had remained his ally within the Sepulchre, despite no longer being on the Council. Liatoukine could count on her, but knew that she also had a degree of ambition of her own. She desired to reclaim her position on the Council, but not for his exclusive benefit. Observing her long, raven-colored tresses and shapely body, Liatoukine felt pleased with his work.

"I sense something amiss," he said, breaking out of his reverie. "I will visit the local inn, see what the atmosphere is like and gain information if I can."

Van Helsing was still at his desk. He was not alone. There was a soldier masquerading as his assistant in the room. Upstairs, there were more soldiers waiting. And there were more still, hiding behind a false wall of his study.

The Dutchman suddenly some green light on his window—the sign that a vampire was coming. He rapped on the wall twice. Signals would be passed. All would be warned.

Liatoukine entered the Inn and proceeded to the bar. The establishment only had only a few young men there. At first glance, there was nothing unusual—but the Vampire General noticed the absence of older men and barmaids. He ordered a tankard of ale.

"What brings you here, stranger?" the landlord asked.

The landlord was in actual fact a local, albeit a Sergeant in the Emperor's army. All the men were soldiers dressed as villagers.

"I am just a trader, selling my wares," replied Liatoukine. "What I sell is not cheap: jewels, rare books and so on. I aim for those with enough money to appreciate the better things in life. I understand that to be Castle Dracula outside?"

Nobody reacted at that—the other patrons simply carried on talking. The landlord replied, handing over the drink:

"Yes. The Count died a while back and it's all in the hands of the state now."

Liatoukine had been here before, years ago. The locals were terrified of the very name of Dracula. They may have recovered some of their courage, but surely not to this casual extent?

"However," the landlord continued, "we do have a man of learning in the village, studying books from the Count's collection. He may well be interested in what you are selling."

"My prices are high, but I would like to meet with him. Perhaps I have something of interest to him," replied the Russian Vampire.

The landlord gave him the address of Van Helsing's farmhouse.

The lack of fear, the quick providing of information of Van Helsing's address, the make-up of the pub clientele... All a bit obvious, Liatoukine thought. Still, best not to underestimate these men. He went over to a table and drank his ale—not too quickly—and then left.

He walked back to his carriage and took a case out from the back. Polly was seated there, hidden from view. He quietly and briefly apprised her of the situation.

He then walked over to the farmhouse and knocked on the door. The Dutchman's "assistant" opened it. Liatoukine briefly introduced himself as a trader of books and jewels from St. Petersburg and was let in.

Van Helsing got up from his desk to greet his visitor—crucifix casually in hand. Liatoukine saw no reason to delay matters. It was indeed his quarry. They had met before, just a handshake, at a diplomatic function.

The Vampire General spun around and killed the young "assistant" with a blow to the neck. Another blow to Van Helsing's arm and the crucifix was on the floor. Without a word, he grabbed the Dutchman by the throat and pulled him out of the house. Why delay things with dramatic utterances? That can come later at a more congenial time.

The soldiers behind the fake wall—nothing more than paper—burst through and gave chase. There were two of them; their pistols had bullets which contained the ashes of vampire's hearts—a rare commodity that could destroy vampires.

"Halt!" they cried.

Liatoukine held Van Helsing aloft with one arm. With the other, he shot the soldiers with his own pistol. A bullet to their hearts. Had these humans not yet accounted for the speed and superior reflexes of a vampire? Clearly not.

He landlord and his men came running from the Inn. From the first floor of the farmhouse and other directions came more soldiers—in military dress. They were armed in a number of ways: pistols, swords, stakes, holy water and other weapons known to defeat various forms of vampires.

Liatoukine assessed the threat in but a moment. As indeed had Polly Bird, who burst out of the carriage.

She carried a machine gun in her hand that might have been too heavy for a normal human to carry as lightly as she did. She leapt onto the carriage roof and started mowing the soldiers down. Then she jumped off and ran around, firing at everyone—whilst not hitting Liatoukine or Van Helsing.

For his part, the Vampire General was also moving swiftly, using a knife, cutting and slashing any soldier who got near him. The bloody scene looked like a grotesque speeded up ballet with Liatoukine and Polly leaping and jumping and spinning and killing.

Within a minute, they had won. All the soldiers lay dead or dying.

In the distance, the two vampires could see more soldiers coming down from the castle at high speed, but for a few precious moments, they would savor their victory. This they did by feeding on the dying. Polly went for their throats, taking their blood whilst they were still breathing. She did this to three of them, taking enough to convert them. She did this knowing that their comrades would destroy them as soon as they reached them. It was an act of deliberate psychological cruelty—these Austrian upstarts must be taught as disturbing a lesson as possible.

For Liatoukine's part, he swiftly drained the life force of two soldiers, including the landlord. The man was saying the Lord's Prayer as he died, causing Liatoukine some pain. For that, he left nothing but a skeleton behind, even if it did take a few moments more.

A horrified Van Helsing had already started running towards the coming soldiers, led by Baron Vordenberg. But Polly caught up with him, grabbed him by the neck, and pulled him back to the carriage. There, she threw him into the back and attached him to a chain hanging off the compartment wall.

Swiftly, she jumped next to Liatoukine in the rider's seat. With a crack of the whip, the carriage was away at enormous speed. Both Liatoukine and Polly, intoxicated on their success and their feeding, laughed almost uncontrollably.

At the village, the soldiers lay dead, their blood seeping into the ground. They had come from all over the Empire: Austria, Dalmatia, Slovakia, Ruthenia and Slovenia. They were Austrians, Croats, Czechs and more. They had served their Emperor and indeed their God under one banner. Their loyalty and service had been rewarded with death. Such were the thoughts of Baron Vordenberg as he surveyed the scene. Despite his experience, he found himself shaking in shock at what had happened. They had not been prepared for such tactics. How dare these creatures use such barbaric technology as a machine gun in the heart of civilized Europe?

Meanwhile, after a frenzied ride of no more than an hour, Liatoukine's carriage had come to a halt in a deserted field. There, guarded by a couple of peasants—they had their uses after all—was an aircraft. It was a Russky Vityaz, of which only one was built. However, Liatoukine had had a secret version especially made for him. Furthermore, using certain knowledge gleaned from the Sepulchre's library, he was able to make certain modifications to the machine.

Liatoukine considered himself a modern vampire. He had visited an air show in Brescia, Italy, in 1909, and was fascinated with what he'd seen. Technology was here to be used and, indeed, enjoyed in the furtherance of power. He cared not if it came from the humans. Many other vampires preferred more traditional methods of doing things. Fortunately, Polly was advanced in her thinking and was most enthusiastic about using the machine gun—his idea, of course. Such tactics had given them the edge.

Now, with this other piece of human technology, he would foil the Austrians again. They bundled a protesting Van Helsing into a compartment, not bothering to respond to whatever he was saying, and took their places in the flying machine.

They took off into the dark Transylvanian sky. Liatoukine was still intoxicated by his draining of the soldier's life force. He wanted to demonstrate his superiority over the Empire he had just defeated and test his aircraft modifications.

One of his fellow countrymen had just performed the first loop the loop. This was a matter of great pride for Liatoukine. He was a proud Russian. Many of his kin suspected his loyalty to Russia outweighed that to the Sepulchre. They were right.

Liatoukine pulled back the control stick and the aircraft started the loop. Liatoukine roared with delight. Polly screamed her joy. On the ground, the plane was barely seen, but their unearthly cries could be heard by many, causing deep fear. Liatoukine was exhilarated. What a joy it was to be Undead in this new era! In his tiny compartment, Van Helsing's reaction was somewhat less enthusiastic.

The aircraft landed in Serbia, where the Sepulchre was based. There, they transferred to a horse and carriage supplied personally by Mircalla. It had no driver—a supernatural trick intended to cause fear amongst the locals. Liatoukine was all in favor of causing fear, but wondered if this might bring too much attention to the Vampire City. The Serbian authorities and the Sepulchre had some kind of informal agreement. He would have to find out what that was; Marcella's behavior may endanger it.

Liatoukine discussed the current situation with Polly.

"I daresay Mircalla will be most pleased with our results," he said, with more than a hint of sarcasm.

"You mean, your plan was to kill Van Helsing in revenge for his destruction of Dracula?" she replied.

"Yes, his impertinence could not be allowed to stand. Humans have destroyed prominent vampires before—including Mircalla herself before her resurrection—but he was the lord of the vampires. A direct insult against all of us."

"And of course, your personal standing and influence amongst our kind would have been most enhanced."

"Naturally such a thought never crossed my mind," he replied with a sly smile. "Of course, that would be a pleasant outcome, but my motives are entirely altruistic."

Dracula may well have been "Lord of the Vampires" or whatever, but Liatoukine's respect for him had, in fact, diminished. His actions in Britain appeared almost naive. He seemed not to care if he drew attention to himself, and inevitably was destroyed. So much for that education at the Scholomance, the school of the evil one himself.

"Of course, Mircalla heard of my plans," he continued. "I fear I may have been indiscreet. She commanded that I take him prisoner instead, giving me an arrest warrant for him would you believe. She intends to reap glory as the one who puts him on trial. She even intends to notify the great powers of the inevitable execution. A simple killing without boasting to the Empires would have been better. Her Austrian arrogance will simply increase the danger to us all. Dracula and Orlok were vampires of power; they pushed things too far, and where are they today?"

"Mircalla was once destroyed," said Polly, thoughtful. "Yet she came back. No other vampire has ever achieved that. It is that resurrection that enabled her to awe others into eventually letting her take over Selene. We should not underestimate her."

"Indeed, we should not. Given her position, I am not able to stand against her openly. As for her resurrection, I am not convinced of it. Why has not Dracula returned? Or Orlok? We often know when one of our kind dies and, in this case, the Austrians were obliging enough to produce a public record of the affair. They have been more circumspect since, of course."

"Are you saying she is an imposter?" asked Polly. "Or that she did not die? I must say, there is much speculation about her taste in lovers, and yet she has taken little interest in me." She gave a deliberate fake look of hurt.

Liatoukine laughed. "That could be because she knows you are my ally as much as anything else. It was sensed in the city when Mircalla died years ago. And as for being an imposter... she certainly has great vampire skills, just as the original Mircalla did. She operated alone, aside from her immediate servants, and few knew her. None are Un-dead today."

"In itself, that is most curious," said Polly. "They have all been destroyed, apparently by humans discovering them. A possible coincidence, of course, but most convenient for her, if she is not whom she claims to be. Although these few who knew her were not necessarily her friends—another reason to dispose of them?"

"Whatever the case," responded Liatoukine, "we should assume that Mircalla intends for us to be also 'accidentally' discovered by humans. I have never been impressed by her, and she knows it. Had we failed in capturing Van Helsing, or been destroyed in the process, that would have served her too. No doubt someone would then have been sent to destroy Van Helsing as per my original plan."

The carriage came to halt outside Selene. The gates of the Vampire City materialized. It was both invisible and intangible during the day, except for one hour when it could be seen by all. For Liatoukine, this was a dangerous tactical disadvantage in a world where humans were becoming ever more scientifically advanced. One day, soon, the whole world would know of the city's existence. Unless the Sepulchre could be made intangible for the whole day, some kind of arrangement will have to be made with the empires. The one with Belgrade would no longer suffice.

The carriage entered, pulling the cage containing Van Helsing. Two vampire guards took him from his cage and walked him through the city. The expert in Van Helsing came to the fore, helping to balance his terror. The city seemed constructed from some form of black marble. There were many bizarre-looking shapes and statues. And although it seemed empty, he could feel that he was being observed by many, those who wished to see the man who had killed Dracula. Some psychic effect, probably? This was all most informative.

They came to a rectangular building with many different sized triangles on the roof. Van Helsing was placed in a cell and given some food. He felt he had to learn more about this place. He was also determined to escape, but how?

The next day, the Dutchman was taken to the courtroom. He was placed by his guards in the dock. There, he took in his surroundings. To his right was a high bench for the judge. Past that, also next to him, were empty tables, presumably for prosecution and the defense. Would he have a defense? By a vampire? No! He would defend himself. He was avoiding the sight in front of him, the public gallery. There seemed to be at least a hundred vampires, hissing at him. A particularly hideous crone in the front row was clawing in the air. He could see his captors there too. Liatoukine was, as he had suspected, a vampire, too.

For his part, the Russian was irritated at having to sit next to the peasant crone. He suspected this may have been a local only just converted in order to provide some theatrics.

From a doorway behind the high bench, Mircalla entered. The hissing ceased. All rose, including, somewhat grudgingly, the Russian general.

Van Helsing did not rise. His vampire guard simply grabbed him by the back of the neck, held him aloft, and dropped him back in his seat when she sat down.

She wore elaborate robes, based on those of the judges in Vienna, albeit configured to her comely form. Her Styrian background had not been affected by her time in the Sepulchre. What else might she look to Vienna for? Liatoukine doubted that she intended to create a non- aggression pact with the human empires. If such things were to be achieved, it would be under the influence of St. Petersburg, not Vienna.

He turned his attention back to Mircalla. She had been followed by her lieutenant, Countess Marcian Gregoryi, also known as the legendary vampire Countess Addhema. Rather than immediately sit down, Mircalla hovered above the courtroom.

"We have before us the Dutchman Van Helsing, who is accused of the murder of Count Dracula!" she finally proclaimed.

"Murderer!" shouted the crone, attracting everyone's attention.

Given that she sat next to him, Liatoukine felt rather awkward. He hoped that people would not think she was with him. At least, Polly was on the other side. Lowly born as she was—a failing, of course—her beauty and her fighting prowess made her much respected.

"In two days' time," Mircalla continued, "we shall hear opening statements on the charge of the murder of Count Dracula. In a matter as grave as this, only I am fit to be charged with the duties of a judge."

The crowd roared its approval.

Predictable, thought the Russian general. Mircalla wishes to dominate the masses in such a manner, appearing to control everything. Even the Vampire Council seemed to have disappeared altogether.

"The prosecutor shall be Countess Marcian Gregoryi!"

Another roar. No surprise there: her Austro-Hungarian compatriot, albeit from the Magyar side.

"And the defense shall be..."

"If I may interject," said Van Helsing, causing much hissing, "I will represent myself in this ludicrous farce. I will tell you all about what happened, so that you will have an inkling about what will happen to you all and this foul city soon enough."

Again, this was predictable. Mircalla would no doubt make the most of the opportunity. He had to admire the Dutchman's nerve though.

There was again much hissing. Mircalla smiled, revealing her splendid fangs. How unfortunate she was an enemy, thought Liatoukine.

"Oh no," she said. "You are unfamiliar with our laws, and that would put you at a disadvantage. We are a fair people. You will be assigned counsel—one of our greatest denizens in fact." She pointed at the Russian General. "General Boris Liatoukine shall be your defense counsel!"

That development had not been so predictable.

In the office provided for him, Liatoukine was incandescent with rage. Mircalla had placed him in a position he could hardly have refused. Not if he wanted to get out of the city. He was hardly likely to win the case. More importantly, he knew this would damage his reputation. Defending the killer of Count Dracula, even though he had had no choice in the matter, would not be forgotten. He suspected that Mircalla had plans for some unfortunate incident to happen to him soon after the trial.

His best stratagem would be to go along with this trial lunacy and then get back to St. Petersburg as quickly as he could. Let her try and eliminate him there! He would plot against her from his beloved homeland. Let the Serbs provoke their war with the Habsburgs. Russia would come to Belgrade's aid and crush Vienna within weeks. Then, Russian influence would reach new heights. And, under his control, St. Petersburg would make a new arrangement for the safety of the city of the vampires, taking over from the Serbs. The cost would not be too high: merely his appointment as military governor and the staking of Mircalla in the heart of the Sepulchre! He would even get Countess Gregoryi to do it, perhaps.

Liatoukine turned his mind to the current situation. He had had a brief meeting with Van Helsing. He hoped to persuade him to plead guilty. He was going to die anyway, probably by Mircalla draining every drop of his blood. Why prolong the wait? He might even be granted some form of last request. Getting him to plead guilty could have served Liatoukine well. However, Van Helsing refused to see reason.

Now, the trial was about to begin. He had a strategy—it was a strong one, but it might fail. If it did, he would not go down attempting to curry favor. There was also a slim chance of getting the mob to respect his effort.

Liatoukine left his office and proceeded to the courtroom. He was clothed in full dress uniform, complete with ceremonial sword. He considered the silver-edged sword a useful precaution.

Mircalla opened the trial by addressing Van Helsing.

"Professor Abraham Van Helsing, you are charged with the murder of Count Dracula. How do you plead?"

Van Helsing decided to go for theatrics. He got up and, directly addressing the court, responded:

"Certainly, I am not guilty of murder. I plead guilty only to the destruction of a foul creature, nothing more than a bit of vermin extermination."

The crowd went wild with hissing. Liatoukine grabbed the Dutchman and pulled him back into his seat.

Mircalla put up her hand and all went silent.

"Let the record show a plea of not guilty. The manner of his plea, however, will be taken into my consideration. Let the prosecution open its case."

She knew she could have enforced a plea of not guilty, but she wanted a full trial to glory in—and to force Liatoukine to defend the murderer of the Lord of Vampires.

Countess Marcian Gregoryi, resplendent in her rich Hungarian garb, began:

"Over the next few days, I intend to show how the accused and his compatriots, whom sadly we cannot yet locate..."

Or because Mircalla is not reckless enough to draw the attention of the British Empire just yet, thought Liatoukine.

"...plotted and carried out the destruction of the man known justly as the Lord of the Vampires. Even more foul, they murdered the newly-created vampire Lucy Westenra and those three known as his 'Brides.' I request that he be also charged with those murders."

"I object!" exclaimed the Russian vampire. "My client has only been charged with one murder. We have not prepared for others. Van Helsing must be treated fairly, so that we can all have confidence in our justice."

Mircalla considered this. She intended at some point to widen the system to deal with vampires who opposed her in any way. For the time being, it would serve her just as well to give the illusion of fairness.

"Your point is well taken, General Liatoukine. The original charges will not be expanded..."

The Countess looked startled for a moment. Clearly, this was not part of the plan, thought Liatoukine. Mircalla quickly continued:

"...However, the killings will be considered as part of the overall main charge. Please continue, Countess Gregoryi."

The Countess had fully recovered her composure.

"Thank you, my lady. I intend to show how Count Dracula had meant to start a new existence in London. Quite reasonably, he had already taken an interest in English women as his servants. Or brides, if you will. It is the undisputed right of vampires to use humans as they see fit, after all will. I will show how the Count traveled to London, passing through the town of Whitby, all the while harassed by Van Helsing and his criminal associates. The Count was eventually forced to retreat from England, but even this was not enough for Van Helsing. He pursued him across Europe..."

The Countess was interrupted by a wail from the peasant woman, accompanied by much hissing from the vampire mob in the public gallery. But she continued, coming to the end of her presentation, her voice getting more strident:

"And then, in the final act of this symphony of horror, Van Helsing presided over the driving of a wooden stake through his very heart!"

The Countess dramatically clutched at her chest. The peasant vampire screamed and collapsed to the ground. The mob hissed again, this time seeming to move forward. Mircalla stood up and raised her hand. The hissing subsided at once.

"Actually," Van Helsing said, standing up, "we destroyed him with a knife slashing his throat and another straight into his heart."

He sat back down. Liatoukine almost burst out laughing, but contained himself. Still, he had to grab the Dutchman and exit the courtroom before the enraged mob could get to them.

The court reconvened the next day. This time there were more guards and fewer vampires in the public gallery. Liatoukine was pleased to see that the peasant woman was no longer there.

Mircalla began by addressing the court:

"There must be no repetition of yesterday's disturbances, whatever the provocation. The consequences of any further disruption will be severe." She did not care if the mob destroyed Van Helsing and Liatoukine. It was the challenge to her authority that concerned her. "General Liatoukine, please deliver the opening statement for the defense."

The Russian General rose to speak.

"It is clear that the human Van Helsing did indeed—either by his own hand or by leading others—murder Count Dracula. It is also correct that we vampires can do as we see fit with humans. Yet, there is a natural balance. Sometimes the humans have a right to defend themselves—but only until the balance is restored. The Count had effectively begun an unspoken war against the most powerful force in this world, the British Empire.

"Such behavior is unheard of amongst vampires. We always strive to remain in the background. We have had sometimes had to restrain our own kind. Some here may remember having to deal with Graf Von Orlok, who was himself connected with Dracula, a few years ago.[1] Orlok was going too far with his plans involving our city. They may also recall my own part in the successful conclusion of that affair..."

Here, he gave a meaningful look at Mircalla. This was clearly an unspoken challenge, one that those in the public gallery would understand. It would do no harm to put some doubt about Mircalla into the minds of the other vampires, and remind them about his own considerable abilities.

"What an interesting defense you present," responded Mircalla. "Van Helsing isn't even British. Nonetheless, you will have your chance to present your evidence soon enough. The prosecution will present her evidence tomorrow; the day after the defense will do the same. Two days after that, I will deliver my verdict. Let no one say our justice is not swift and effective."

Van Helsing had been watching this with some interest, as he might, given that his life was at stake. But what really interested him was the rivalry between Mircalla and Liatoukine. He did not quite understand what was going on, but he saw an opportunity. He quickly wrote a note and passed it to Liatoukine: *Get a recess of a few days*, it read.

The Russian vampire wondered what the human was up to. He knew that Van Helsing was no fool. This was not likely to be a simple way of postponing his demise. Further, this was the first time he had communicated with him in any meaningful way.

He decided to see where this led.

"My lady," he said to Mircalla, "I would be like a three-day recess. We need to consider the evidence of the prosecution further, in particular how they have come by some of their information."

Mircalla looked at him. He must be desperate, she thought. He might also be up to something. She decided to give him only one day, in order to be seen to be fair.

"General Liatoukine," she said, "you have already had time to examine the evidence. Nevertheless, I will grant you an extra day."

With that, she left the courtroom.

Liatoukine went to see Van Helsing in his cell.

---

[1] See "City of the Nosferatu" in *Tales of the Shadowmen* No. 10.

"You have something in mind?" he asked.

"Quite so," replied the Dutchman. "I think there may be a way out of this for both of us. I have certain information that may—if it is accurate, and I cannot vouch for that yet—let us both come out ahead. It is only a slight opportunity, but at the moment we appear to have none. It is clear to me that you have some problem with Mircalla. I sense she wishes you out of the way as much as me, is that not so?"

Liatoukine ignored the question.

"What is this opportunity?" he asked.

Van Helsing responded with a list of demands:

"I will need assurances regarding my safe passage out of Selene and my return to areas safely under human control. Further, I will require a solemn guarantee as to my own, permanent safety and that of my colleagues involved in the demise of Count Dracula in the future. In return, the information I shall give you will see an end to Marcella's reign. I assume this trade may be of great benefit to you?"

The General wondered what it could be that Van Helsing had that could result in such an outcome. He could, of course, torture him. However, the Dutchman was hardly young anymore and may not survive the ordeal. It was perhaps surprising that he had already survived his trial without any apparent ill effects.

"If this information of yours gets Mircalla out of my way," he replied, "how do you know that I won't just kill you?"

"I don't," the Dutchman replied. "That is why I need some kind of witness to our agreement. No doubt you will choose your associate, this bizarrely named 'Polly Bird' However, she may not always be your ally, and should you betray me, she will be in a position to reveal your deal with me, and how you broke it. But by keeping to our agreement, you will send a signal to the powers of Europe that you can be trusted. From what you said in the courtroom, I gather that you do not seek a war with Mankind, not least due to your own life of privilege. I suspect those of us who deal with your kind already suspect your true nature. Assassinating you would prove too difficult and diplomatically risky, given your position of power in Russia. So it makes sense to strike a bargain now. That said, my information requires verification—I am not even sure we have enough time..."

Van Helsing was indeed no fool, Liatoukine thought. He was clearly outlining some very good reasons to let him go. The removal of Mircalla would be a prize well worth the Dutchman's freedom. And he was also correct in his assessment of Liatoukine's situation—it was important that the powers of Europe realize that, when it came to vampire matters, he could be a man with whom they could do business. He had certain plans.

"I can agree to a witness," he responded, "and I can certainly get you over the border to Slavonia, in the Austrian empire. I cannot give the assurances you seek regarding permanent safety—you are hardly popular amongst my kind. But you are in no position to guarantee my own safety form various human agencies. However, I think that both of us coming out of this situation victorious should be enough, don't you agree?"

Van Helsing did. Polly was called in to witness everything that was to be discussed and agreed. The Professor began by relating what Baron Vordenberg had told him a few days earlier at Castle Dracula.

"We must indeed move fast," Liatoukine said. "Polly will have to get the evidence we require. Using my aircraft, and her own natural speed, it can be achieved in the next couple of days. She will leave at once. Tomorrow is our one-day of recess and the next day will be taken with the prosecution case. No doubt Mircalla will have her spies follow her, but I am sure she is more than capable of dealing with them."

Polly smiled, and was gone. The vampire and the human then started to prepare for the first day of the prosecution.

The first day of the prosecution proceeded with a vigorous case presented by Countess Gregoryi—matched by an equally vigorous cross-examination by the Vampire General. He knew the ridiculously brief trial could not be won and Mircalla continually intervened, usually in favor of the Countess. However, he remained confident throughout. As well he might, given that word had reached him from Polly. She would shortly arrive back at the Sepulchre, already in possession of the evidence required to deal with Mircalla.

The next day, the trial reconvened for the beginning of the defense.

"General Liatoukine, you may begin your defense," Mircalla said.

He stood and said, "I wish a mistrial to be declared."

"On what grounds?" a clearly amused Mircalla asked. She could not wait to hear whatever desperate reason this Russian barbarian had found.

This was Liatoukine's moment. He addressed the whole court, rather than just Mircalla.

"On the grounds that the judge is not who she claims to be. You are not the real Mircalla Karnstein. You are an imposter!"

Countess Gregoryi and Mircalla threw a swift glance at each other.

"Prove what you say. Immediately," demanded Mircalla.

She knew the shared glance had been a mistake. All had noticed it, and undoubtedly did not interpret it as a glance of incomprehension.

"Mircalla Karnstein is famous in the human world, as most of us are not," Liatoukine began. "Indeed, for those humans who believe in us, this manuscript is of great importance." He waved a book in the air. "This is a study on the case written by one Doctor Hesselius. It contains the official report on the matter. It also contains the manuscript of Laura, Mircalla's last victim, relating her experiences. It makes it clear that Mircalla was destroyed by human hands. That form of destruction is one that our kind never survive.

"Then, some years ago, this person claiming to be Mircalla Karnstein appeared, claiming that she had returned from the dead. I don't quite know how she convinced so many, but surely her close associate the Countess here," he pointed at Marcian Gregoryi, "had much to do with it. The Countess has a formidable reputation and her vouching for the woman claiming to be Mircalla would indeed help convince many of us..."

"You talk nonsense, Russian," the Countess said. "You can prove nothing—you seem to forget it is your client who is on trial here."

"Oh, but I can prove what I say," Liatoukine simply continued. "The imposter we see here today was helped by a very real link to Mircalla. Her last victim, Laura, also happened to be her descendent. And that is who we have before us—Laura."

Mircalla looked impassive.

"What is your evidence?" she asked. "And may I remind you that Laura was not one of us."

Liatoukine again addressed the court.

"It is true that Laura was not a vampire—not at first. She was only a descendent. She had been bitten by Mircalla. Then after Mircalla's destruction, I believe Laura gradually became one of us. The bite and familial link must have been the cause. Perhaps when she died, she became one of us, or perhaps she did so beforehand and only faked her human death? Certainly, it must happened some years after she wrote her manuscript that appeared in Doctor Hesselius' work. At some point, Laura's vampiric legacy took over. She wanted power and thus took the persona of Mircalla. The details need not concern us, whatever they may be, but the evidence I have should. First, we have a copy a Laura's manuscript and Mircalla's signature—in reality, Laura's—on her arrest warrant for Van Helsing..." He held both items aloft. "Look! The handwriting is the same!"

Many vampires had superior eyesight; those in the public gallery could see that what he said was the truth.

"However, my ultimate evidence was obtained recently by Polly, whom many of you know," Liatoukine continued.

"Your associate!" hissed the Countess.

"Yes, my associate," countered he Russian, "but one who is well known by many of you. And the evidence she procured is incontrovertible..."

Polly entered the courtroom—in a pre-planned manner—with two large portraits, held easily aloft in each hand. She explained their meaning.

"In my right hand is a portrait of Mircalla Karnstein, taken by myself from Karnstein Castle. In my left, taken from her former Styrian home, is one of Laura."

The women in the portraits were similar. However, it was clear who the woman seated in the judge's chair was—Laura.

Many vampires were old. They had a sense of age. Their eyesight could see the details of the art. Those in the public gallery could see within seconds that the portraits were from two different time periods. Laura's would have been painted long after Marcella's death—that was clear to them, as Van Helsing and Liatoukine knew it would be.

He briefly wondered how it was that Laura had not destroyed such evidence years back. Styrian arrogance, no doubt.

There was great unrest in the public gallery. The vampires moved forward, as a mob. The guards did not try to stop them—they joined with them. This imposter had made fools of them. They did not take that lightly.

"I am Mircalla," Laura bellowed.

She looked for support from the Countess—but she had somehow disappeared. It was over. She glared at Liatoukine. She still had one chance—destroy him and perhaps she could restore her authority.

She levitated. The mob stopped, some residual fear remaining.

She swooped down towards Liatoukine, arms outstretched. She would remove his head from his shoulders and crush it. If that did not work, she at least would have had her revenge. But the Russian vampire was ready for her. Aside from his powers, he was a true soldier. Laura could not match his combat experience. The Vampire General drew his sword and, as she came down, sliced her outstretched arms off.

Laura screamed in agony, blood splattering everywhere. Her arms slowly moved back in the air to re-attach themselves, but even before they reached her, Liatoukine had grabbed her by her throat, dropping his sword. He glared into her eyes and started to absorb her life force.

Laura thought of her childhood, her innocence. When Mircalla had come to her, when she was so young, so pure in spirit. It was only years after Marcella's death that she felt the changes, a corruption taking root within her. She tried to resist it at first, but eventually gave in. How she wished now that she had resisted it more. How she wished now to have remained in that state of innocence, to somehow return to it. Then she thought no more.

Liatoukine had taken her life essence. She became old and wizened, her floating arms became bones and fell to the ground, disintegrating. Even the blood that had gushed from her severed limbs dried away. Held aloft in Liatoukine's arm, Laura rotted into a skeleton; even her clothing disintegrated. Then she was just dust floating down between the Russian vampire's fingers.

Van Helsing watched, transfixed and terrified. He had been silent throughout the trial, as agreed, in order not to antagonize the vampires any further. Somehow he remembered what he had to do—and that was to get out whilst all eyes were on this grim spectacle.

He moved towards the door and was out of the courtroom. He missed the sight of the Russian Vampire casually brushing off bits of dust from his uniform.

Van Helsing left the city and was taken to the border of the Austrian Empire in the same carriage that had brought him to the Sepulchre—albeit this time he was not in a cage. He crossed the border on foot and soon made contact with Croatian officials. He was taken to Baron Vordenberg without delay. Van Helsing considered that a victory had occurred. He was still alive for a start. More importantly for the wider world, the information he had gathered would soon be in the hands of the Austrians, and those they cooperated with on such matters. Their understanding of Selene and its politics—something not really considered before—would now be vastly enhanced. A dangerous vampire, Mircalla, had been removed. It was possible that Liatoukine may be even more formidable, but the information gathered about the Vampire City would outweigh that.

On the journey to Vienna, where he was expected to brief some of the Habsburg Empire's top officials, Van Helsing considered the political situation. He did not believe there would be war. Humanity was moving beyond that, at least in Europe. The incidents in Bosnia-Herzegovina were just that—not sparks but perhaps cinders of all previous wars. The great powers instead would cooperate to prevent war. Were not all the royal houses related to one another? Was there not new, forward-thinking policies in the empires? Indeed, he expected them to cooperate on matters related to vampirism. There would perhaps be a war—but one of a united Europe against Selene. Despite an experience that may have driven many to madness, he felt content.

For his part Liatoukine was satisfied. He was still intoxicated with the life force of Laura. Now it was time to return to St. Petersburg. As her reward, Polly had been reinstated on the reconstituted Vampire Council, ensuring his influence. He had his position in St. Petersburg to return to and thus could not be on the Council himself. However, his reputation had soared. Perhaps now he was considered almost as great as Dracula?

Laura's lackey, Countess Gregoryi, had fled. Perhaps she may turn up somewhere else. He might even offer her forgiveness, if she agreed to be in his service. Apart from anything else, he admired her countenance.

He took a horse to get to his aircraft. He knew it would be one of the last times he would do so, as he intended cars to replace horses. Modernization was one of many of his plans for the Sepulchre.

He was pleased that Van Helsing had gotten away safely. This would help open lines of communication when needed. His reading of the political situation was that there would be a short war against Vienna. Russia would soon crush the Austro-Hungarians. He would take control of whatever deal Belgrade had made with the Sepulchre. From Russia's position of strength, he could secure their safety in a world ever moving faster with scientific progress. A non-aggression pact was the best option. Vampires would be grateful for the security and look to him for protection. He would use his position to find out all the supernatural secrets the Sepulchre had. These would be put at the service of Imperial Russia, which would become the most powerful force in the world—beyond that even of the British.

In such a position, the political rabble in his country would also be dealt with. The weak who preached democracy and worse would be swept away in days. He foresaw a glorious Russian Imperial future, under his quiet but firm guidance. Whatever could stop it?

*Over the years, Martin Gately has assembled a series of clever mystery tales starring Gaston Leroux's sleuth, Joseph Rouletabille, whose* The Mystery of the Yellow Room *and* Rouletabille at Krupp's *have been released by Black Coat Press. Following "Leviathan Creek," published in our Volume 8, and "Rouletabille vs. The Cat," published in our last volume, here is the third chapter in the saga of the indomitable French detective...*

## Martin Gately: *Rouletabille and the New World Order*

*Philadelphia, May 1926*

### 1. Slow Train Missing

It was less than ten minutes since Rouletabille had left the P.R.T Trolley Station and he had already spotted the man to whom he needed to speak. The crowds at the Sesqui-Centennial Exposition celebrating 150 years since the signing of the Declaration of Independence were thinner than he had anticipated. The sudden, sharp torrents of rain were scaring people away, and that was a terrible pity since there was so much to see in the exposition grounds.

He needed a picture of the giant illuminated reproduction of the Liberty Bell for his newspaper, but right now he didn't want to lose sight of James Worth. The man he had come to see was dressed as Robin Hood—Lincoln Green outfit, pheasant-feather cap, tights, quiver and longbow. He was with a gaggle of individuals who were masquerading as Robin's *'Merrie Men'* and to a man. they were soaked to the skin following the last downpour. They huddled together under the canopy of the Exposition Administration Building and grinned widely at the press photographers who were snapping them.

The next group to parade into view was an orderly line of Plymouth Pilgrims; at least their wide-brimmed hats had given them some protection from the rain. Seeing then that James Worth was no longer required by the press cameramen, the Frenchman moved forward to introduce himself.

"Mr. Worth? I am Joseph Rouletabille," he said, extending his hand.

"I am most pleased to meet you, sir," said Worth. "Come let's head up towards my office. I really need to get out of these wet things anyway. All I can say is, I volunteered to play Robin Hood in the history pageant a good while before the long range weather forecast came in."

Worth ushered Rouletabille into the entrance hall of the administration building, where he was immediately struck by a beautifully executed mural showing the history of the United States. Every significant event from Penn's treaty with the Indians, through Washington crossing the Delaware to the Wright

Brothers at Kitty Hawk was lovingly depicted. Above the mural the following words were written in gold: *"For I dipt in to the future, far as human eye could see; Saw the vision of the world, and all the wonder that would be."*

"I don't recognize that quotation," admitted Rouletabille.

"Ah, then you don't know your Tennyson," said Worth. "It is a line from that poet's greatest work—Locksley Hall. And this administration building borrows its name from the title of the poem; you are now in Locksley Hall."

They took the elevator up to the fifth floor and passed the desks of dozens of clerks and press aides before finally reaching Worth's overly palatial office. The American invited Rouletabille to help himself from the cylindrical walnut cocktail cabinet while he disappeared into a private washroom to disrobe, towel himself dry and change into his suit. Obviously, prohibition was little enforced amongst the higher echelons of society. Rouletabille swiftly rustled up a matching pair of Rickety Scotch cocktails, using a generous amount of warming Talisker and probably a few too many drops of grapefruit bitters. After a gap of a few minutes, Worth emerged and gratefully sipped at the drink.

"That's one hell of a concoction, young man," said Worth, smacking his lips. "But let's get down to business. I am one of the organizers of this exposition; it's been many years in the planning and, because of the weather, we're losing money hand-over-fist."

"You need an Indian witch Doctor to improve the weather, not a detective," said Rouletabille.

"Don't think I haven't considered it," said Worth," but that is not why you are here. In an effort to promote the exposition, I laid on a series of special free trains to transport people who might not otherwise have been able to afford to come. Last Thursday, one of these trains disappeared with everyone on it. There is simply no sign of the train at all—it's like it vanished off the face of the Earth."

"Hardly, a unique problem, Mr. Worth. It puts me in mind of the case of the 'Lost Special' in which the great detective Sherlock Holmes was peripherally involved. If memory serves, the train was concealed on the disused railroad leading to a mine. I assume that this train too was lost in a mining area?"

"Yes, in fact, in the heart of anthracite mining territory, up in Luzerne County. But this train won't be concealed down a disused mineshaft or some such, since every single mine in that vicinity is open for business and busy as a bee hive. No, someone wants to stop people from coming to the exposition by generating bad publicity. Doubtless they expected the story to break by now, but I can tell you that every newspaper publisher on the eastern seaboard is a personal friend of mine. The lid is on this story tight, just not forever. I want you to go to Luzerne and find that train. Your reputation as a solver of impossible crimes precedes you. Surely this is right up your alley?" said Worth.

"I don't know, Mr. Worth. The lack of uniqueness in this case is not attractive. Holmes and at least one of his successors have been involved in very similar puzzles. While I have every sympathy with the families of those who have disappeared in such circumstances, this is likely to be a case where manpower will be key to solving the crime and finding the locomotive. It is a matter for the official police, not a lone detective, even one with skills such as mine," said Rouletabille.

"Well, that certainly disappoints me. I won't insult you by offering you vast amounts of money. But I believe I do have something that could entice you to commit yourself. I know that you are greatly interested in the events that took place on the so-called 'Mysterious Island' some decades ago and that Cyrus West and General Herbert Brown were personally known to you..."

"They were, indeed. God rest their souls," said Rouletabille.

Worth moved to the area behind his desk and slid to one side a wooden panel revealing the portrait of a belligerent looking man with heavy side whiskers.

"This is my father, Adam Worth. He was an associate of Cyrus West, and like him he was a Civil War *bounty jumper*—a man who enlisted in the army under false names in order to claim a bounty and then deserted, only to re-enlist under another false name. I'm not proud of my father. In fact, he was something of a villain. But he never painted himself to be a hero in later life, like West and Brown. The Mysterious Island castaways were not what they pretended to be. And the tales of their adventures on Lincoln Island were a pack self-serving lies. I know this because my father was on Lincoln Island with them—although his name was expunged from all the stories," said Worth.

Worth then tugged open his desk drawer and pulled out a worn and water damaged leather bound journal.

"This book is my father's record of what really happened on Lincoln Island and if you find the missing train for me, I'll happily let you read it," said Worth.

Rouletabille considered carefully, while reining in the surge of anger inside him. He could not believe for one moment that Cyrus West had been a dishonest man. In the case of his old friend Herbert Brown, it seemed even more unlikely. He was consumed with the desire to grab the book from Worth's hand and commence to read it now. He suppressed the urge and lit his pipe instead.

"Very well. I shall take on this case, in order to have access to that journal. You have succeeded in piquing my curiosity in a most extreme fashion," said Rouletabille.

"I am very pleased to hear that," said Worth. "Now I realize that this information has probably come as a shock to you. But there is really no need for you and me to fall out. Instead, why don't you show me how to make that cocktail? It really is delicious."

And so, after a few more drinks, Rouletabille came to find himself liking James Worth irrespective of the man's rather manipulative nature. He was, admittedly, a little superficial, but there was a high gloss of charm and a personal magnetism about him that was difficult to ignore. He had diverse business interests in pharmaceuticals, agriculture, armaments and tool manufacture. His knowledge of the history of the United States had the pedantic completeness of the self-educated man, and he made no reference to having attended university. Plainly, he was one of the richest and most influential men in Philadelphia.

"Tell me, Mr. Worth, why did you play the part of Robin Hood in the History Pageant; and more importantly, why was Robin Hood including in a pageant of American history at all?" asked Rouletabille.

"Robin Hood is more than merely my favorite character, he is an early embodiment of the spirit of rebellion, just like Ned Ludd or the Scarecrow of Romney Marsh. In that rebelliousness lies the genesis of the United States, just as much or perhaps even more than in the desire of the Pilgrim Fathers for religious freedom," said Worth.

"Ned Ludd?" queried the detective.

"Perhaps you're not familiar with him. His followers, the Luddites, destroyed machinery in an attempt to halt the creeping mechanization that has ultimately soiled this world and profaned the glorious rural idyll of the past," said Worth.

"You are a most unusual man, Mr. Worth. I don't think I've ever heard an American complain that there is too much mechanization."

"To be honest, my friend, I don't even like guns, let alone machines. I prefer a good longbow in my hand for hunting, especially when I'm stalking deer. Let's go down to the shooting gallery in the basement and I'll show you how good a shot I am."

They took the elevator down into the sub-basement area, which opened up into an expansive area about the size of a football field. There was a trestle table sagging under the weight of various weapons, including crossbows and a full-sized six-foot longbow. Fifty yards away various targets had been set up and one of them was a metal suit of armor. Worth deftly picked up the bow and nocked an arrow to the string, pulled back effortlessly, aimed just for a moment, and let fly the arrow. There was a muffled clang, as if a bullet had struck an old galvanized bucket at extreme range and the suit of armor was impaled by the arrow. Now, as if prove that this was no fluke, Worth shot three more, and the plate mail started to resemble Saint Sebastian at his martyrdom.

"You give it a shot," said Worth.

And so, with some hesitation the Frenchman picked up the bow and clumsily got the arrow into place. The draw weight of the bow seemed immense to Rouletabille's unaccustomed muscles. He drew back and drew back until his shoulder burned. It felt like at least 150 lbs of pull was required. His arm started to shake, so he released the string. The arrow flashed past the target: a miss, but perhaps not so wide as Rouletabille had been expecting.

"Not bad for a beginner," said Worth. "Now, I don't want to keep you here too late since you need to be at Vermissa Junction in Luzerne tomorrow. But if we just practice for a couple of hours, I think you'll be surprised how much your aim improves."

It seemed that Rouletabille had again encountered a man that one simply could not say no to. He sighed inwardly and reached for another arrow, rather desperately wishing that he had brought the makings of another Rickety Scotch cocktail down here with him.

The following morning, Rouletabille was in the restaurant car of the all-stopping slow train to Scranton. He'd finished up his late breakfast of bacon and eggs and was now savoring some strong black coffee. He'd already laid out a large scale map of the county on his table and weighted down the corners with the salt and pepper shakers and a bottle of Hunt's tomato ketchup. Perhaps some inspiration would strike him soon. He could not imagine that anything would be possible other than simply narrowing down the territory to be searched as much as possible, disembarking to gather a posse with the local sheriff's office and roving endlessly, perhaps fruitlessly, over the terrain.

The detective took to staring out of the window, desperate for some sort of inspiration. The steady rhythm and movement of the train had the opposite effect on him to what he was accustomed. It did not lull or relax him; instead it set his nerves on edge and generated a feeling as if a ball of ice were slowly forming in his stomach. Lunchtime came and went, and he chewed without real appetite on sandwiches filled with blue-veined Chester County cheese.

The arrival of one particular man in the restaurant car burned off the mist of his despondency. The man was very tall, at least six and a half feet tall and built more powerfully than a circus strongman. He wore a tailored blue woolen suit with a white shirt and red tie, as well as sporting large wire framed spectacles which served to give him a scholarly, almost owlish appearance. Rouletabille wondered if he might be a fellow reporter. Yet, perhaps the most striking thing about this giant was the streak of white hair that ran through his otherwise jet black tonsure from the center of his forehead hairline all the way to the nape of his neck. Rouletabille could not account for the sudden rush of goosebumps that originated somewhere near his shoulders and descended quickly to his forearms. He had seen this man before. He recognized not so much his face as his unique physiognomy and lithe, pantherish movement. Could he be mistaken? No, the more he looked, the more certain he was.

Rouletabille got up from his table and approached the bar, where the newcomer was ordering a glass of lemonade.

"Pardon me, sir," said Rouletabille. "I believe you are a veteran of the French Army. I too served under Captain Crouan during the Great War. I remember all too well the day that you carried an immense canvas bundle of rations and ammunition through no-man's land to relieve our position. You leapt in great bounds across the wire and the mud. It was almost as it you had the power of flight. Afterwards, they tried to tell us that it was all an illusion; some form of mass hysteria. But my eyes do not play tricks, not then or now. I remember you. You are Private Danner."

At first, Rouletabille thought that the man might deny it. But instead his weathered face cracked into a sardonic smile.

"Speak softly, my old comrade-in-arms and call me Mark Rainham—that's the name I'm currently travelling under," said Danner. "You will have to refresh my memory on your monicker. I'm afraid I cannot recall the names of all the soldiers I served with," said the Adonis-like warrior.

"You never knew my name. I was just one of many you helped that day. I am Joseph Rouletabille."

"Perhaps I did not know you then, but I know you now. The detective who solved the *Mystery of the Yellow Room* needs no introduction. Yet, you are far younger than I would have supposed," said Danner.

"I am here to investigate another mystery—the disappearance of Exposition Loco 481 bound for Philadelphia. Though I have little confidence that this is a puzzle that I can solve."

"Good Lord!" said Danner. "This surely cannot be a coincidence. I have been hired to travel on trains during the Exposition to guard against any nefarious attack such as may have befallen the missing train."

"And who has given you this commission?" asked the detective.

"Why, the organizer of the Philadelphia Exposition, James Worth," said Danner.

"It is curious that he did not inform me of your involvement. He did not seem the sort of man to allow something to slip his mind," said Rouletabille.

The two men sat together for half an hour or so, trying to imagine in what circumstances a locomotive could disappear from its prescribed route. The discussion went swiftly in circles. With no long tunnel on this track, the only thing that might account for the disappearance was the train being diverted onto a mining company track—the exact same thing that had happened to the 'Lost Special;' in effect, it was a non-mystery. Sherlock Holmes, according to the article in *The Times* which Rouletabille half-recalled, had not even bothered to leave his Baker Street rooms in order to solve the conundrum. The problem with a train was that it left traces of its passing, but to deduce how it was done would not necessarily result in the discovery of the missing train. In country such as this, with mines, slag heaps, industrial waste lagoons and foundries, a thousand men might look for a locomotive for weeks and never find it. And what if the locomotive was now hidden in plain sight? Repainted, disguised... The problem was maddening in its complexity. Where were the passengers? Had none of them escaped? What dreadful fate had befallen them?

As if in answer, a sudden whine emanated from the axles and couplings and the slow train to Scranton heaved to the left. Crockery and silverware slid to the floor, women squealed, then regained their composure with a giggle.

Rouletabille looked around. There were certainly plenty of beautiful young women in the carriage.

"We took those points far too quickly," judged Rouletabille.

"Then it's begun," said Danner.

Rouletabille consulted his map for the last time and pondered the situation. Worth had been wrong to think that only trains heading for the Exposition would be targeted. The slow train for Scranton was quite plainly no longer bound for its original destination.

Danner downed the dregs of his third lemonade.

"No reason to alarm the other passengers," he said.

"No. But we need to get to the engine cab," said Rouletabille.

The two men got up without a further word and worked their way through the two first-class cars towards the luggage cars, where they could most likely converse without being overheard.

"So, we've been diverted off the main railroad onto a private track that runs North East of Wyoming Valley. This is very isolated anthracite mining country. We need to find out if the engineer and fireman are in on this, and if not, get them to stop the train or reverse it," said Danner.

"They didn't slow down for the points change. And they haven't stopped. We better go look and see," said the Frenchman.

Rouletabille opened the door onto the coupling platform. Smuts and cinders from the smoke stack swirled around him, but his view of the engine was blocked by the tender car. The detective ascended the ladder at the back of the car and readied himself to crawl over the coal down and into the cab. His suit was going to get ruined. As Rouletabille reached the top of the ladder, he saw that there was a man in a strange military uniform in the cab aiming a rifle at him. His brain barely had time to compute that the weapon strongly resembled the pneumatic carbines used by the crew of the legendary submarine, *The Nautilus*, when with a spitting hiss a projectile was launched at him. The bullet, or dart, clipped the fabric of the suit at the shoulder. Then Rouletabille was aware of a powerful pair of hands pulling him back to safety.

"I knew I shouldn't have let you go first," said Danner, with a smile. "Stay here, pal, I'll deal with this."

Danner leapt on top of the tender car and stood on the heap of coal, seemingly oblivious to the danger in which he was putting himself. He was a sitting duck target for the marksman in the cab. He was struck several times by bullets, which did little more than blast away the fabric of his suit and leave angry dark welts on his skin.

In fact, there were two oddly uniformed soldiers in the cab; aside from the one blazing away at Danner, there was one keeping the driver and fireman covered. Danner strode confidently across the coal, knowing that his steel-hard skin meant that he was virtually invulnerable to bullets. During battles in the Great War, there were times when he had been constantly raked by heavy machine gun fire, but had suffered little more than bruising. Then his hawk-like eyes noticed that the marksman was swapping the steel grey ammo magazine of his rifle for a light powder blue one which he had removed from a satchel at his shoulder. Shooting from the hip, the man fired at Danner again, just a split second before the veteran planned to jump down into the cab and smash open the skulls of the two soldiers.

Danner reeled back in the most agonizing pain that he had ever experienced in his entire life. The impact knocked him backwards and he found himself lying on the coupling platform, having fallen from the top of the tender. Danner could barely keep himself from screaming; the agony did not diminish one iota. Rouletabille rushed to his assistance and, immediately, saw the source of the problem. Sticking into Danner's skin was something like a tightly wound glowing glass corkscrew. He placed his fingers around it and tried to wrench it from his old comrade's flesh. Now it was Rouletabille's turn to suppress a scream. The glass corkscrew was white-hot and the Frenchman could smell his skin burning like meat on a griddle. He let go and blew on his scorched fingers.

"Lay still, my friend," soothed Rouletabille, although he suspected that the almost super-human warrior could no longer hear him. His eyes had rolled far back in his head and he was jerking like an epileptic.

A few moments later, Danner was quite still, unconscious and breathing shallowly. The detective theorized that he would need something like a pair of pliers to get the dreadful projectile out of his comrade's skin. There might be such an implement in the toolbox in the cab, but how on earth was he supposed to reach it?

As usual, the powerful engine that was Rouletabille's deductive powers worked away unbidden. The presence of the soldiers with a weapon that could immobilize a man as apparently unkillable as Danner suggested that his presence had been expected, and catered for.

Now the train began to slow, and Rouletabille looked up at the stark, blasted countryside of this anthracite mining area. It seemed as bleak and lonely as another planet. Incongruously, a painted sign with a cheerful motif and bold black letters seemed to welcome them to their final destination. The sign said simply *CATHARUS MINE*, and depicted on it was a rather deft and delicately drawn picture of a bird with a mottled breast.

## 2. Into the Mine

The locomotive slowed to little more than walking pace as it traversed the mine's railyard and neared the great man-made cave which served as the entrance to the mine. More soldiers in black and white uniforms, armed with *Nautilus*-style pneumatic carbines emerged from out of the workings. Some of them had shouldered their weapons and carried portable wooden steps to allow easy egress from the train carriages.

65

While Rouletabille did not jump down from the coupling platform to the black and dusty ground, he did take the opportunity to crane his neck and see what the other passengers were doing. Well, he might've been forgiven for thinking that the train had pulled in to Scranton Station. The other passengers were disembarking as if nothing were wrong. Taking their luggage with them, they cheerfully strode to the gaping stone mouth of the mine. He noted that about seventy percent of the people on the train seemed to be women. And from their appearance and mode of dress, he guessed they were young women, mostly under twenty-five. A sudden inexplicable fear took hold of him which manifested as more iciness in his stomach and the feeling that these were virgins about to be sacrificed to some Dark God.

When the passengers, guards and restaurant staff were gone, one of the soldiers called out: "M'sieu Rouletabille, please come down and do not be afraid. Medical attention has been arranged for Mr. Rainham."

For a second Rouletabille's mind was blank; then he recalled that Danner had said he was travelling under the name Mark Rainham. Two men in white uniforms, carrying a stretcher between them, were almost at the train. Rouletabille jumped down and the soldiers made no hostile move towards him. Then, without warning, the carbines cracked twice and the driver and fireman fell from the cab dead. Quite obviously, these men were neither needed, nor welcome within Catharus Mine. The Frenchman resolved that if he ever got out of this situation, he would go about heavily armed. The world had changed since the war, and it seemed that firepower was more important than brains. A regrettable state of affairs, but one that he could do very little about. He had not expected to have to go up against a foreign or private army here in the United States.

Rouletabille was escorted to the mine; he walked just ahead of the stretcher carrying Danner. Inside, he saw that the shaft elevator was huge, large enough to hold perhaps fifty or sixty men comfortably. They had to wait for three more lots of passengers to be taken down. While they waited, Rouletabille looked around. This was quite plainly no ordinary mine. He also couldn't help but notice that the lift smelt strongly of horses. Yes, of course, some mines still used 'pit ponies' in the same way that they still used canaries to check for gas, but here, it did not seem right. The sheer obviousness of it all was causing speculation to gel into assumptions—and much too quickly for his liking. All the circumstantial evidence pointed to the fact that this mine was not being used as a mine. It was being utilized as some sort of citadel or sanctuary. There was a whole population down there. He could feel it in his gut.

The elevator went down and down and down; into velvet darkness that was illuminated only by meager flickering light bulbs. He felt like Orpheus descending into Hades. The winding gears complained as the brakes engaged and the elevator car came to a shuddering halt. More soldiers appeared and dragged open the folding metal gates. They emerged into a well-lit tunnel, where they were met by a man in flowing black and gold robes. The robes had a hood, not dissimilar to that of a monk's habit, which obscured his features. The figure lifted both hands to the material of the hood and gently pushed it back.

"Welcome, M'sieu Rouletabille," said James Worth. "I hope that you are not too surprised. Welcome to the main enclave of the Catharus Society. This is where you'll be living for probably the next two years."

There had been very few times when Rouletabille was so thunderstruck that he couldn't speak, but this was one of them.

Just along the tunnel, a man in a white doctor's coat stood by a small metal trolley. As they processed by it, with James Worth in the lead, the doctor picked a syringe from the trolley.

"Stop and take off your jacket and roll up your sleeve, please," said the doctor.

"No harm will come to you, my friend," said Worth. "Quite the opposite, in fact. You are receiving an inoculation. Hugo Danner will need to be inoculated too, at some stage. We'll need to figure out a less traumatic way to get something through his tough hide than using our new carbines."

Rouletabille winced a little as the needle went in.

"Inoculated against what?" he said.

"A particularly nasty strain of Viral Hemorrhagic Fever which we developed right here in our underground laboratories," said Worth.

The stretcher bearers and the doctor passed into a side-room that was some form of medical facility. Rouletabille was reassured by Worth that they would simply remove the white-hot corkscrew projectile, called a 'plasma dart' from Danner, following which he would be sedated and restrained. After receiving some medical aid for his finger burns, Rouletabille continued with Worth. It was getting harder and harder to remember that he was down an anthracite mine. The internal architecture was starting to resemble the dungeons of some medieval castle. They passed into a room which could only be called a throne room, and naturally Worth (or was he 'King Worth' now?) took his place on the ornate golden chair.

"You probably have many questions," smiled Worth.

"You plan is to release a deadly fever at the exposition. The attendees will leave with it, incubating inside them and return to their home towns—or home countries. Perhaps within a few weeks, all but the most inaccessible parts of the world will be struck down by the epidemic. The only question is, why? What could you possibly gain? And you seemed like a rational man. Have you issued a ransom demand? What could a man as wealthy as you possibly want?"

"There will be no ransom demand," said Worth. "I want nothing except a great winnowing of humanity. I have taken the time to consider precisely where the ship of history is taking us. There will be nothing but bigger and bigger wars with bigger and bigger weapons. Ultimately, there will be armaments that could threaten and destroy entire cities. If these proliferate, then the entire world might be rendered uninhabitable. Imagine the entire planet shrouded by phosgene gas. Someone has to take control now and steer us away from the rocks. Even if I'm wrong about the destructive nature of war, the alternative is worse—overpopulation. A hundred years from now, there might be ten or twelve billion people. There won't be enough food or resources. We need an alternative to the chaotic nature of so-called progress. We've already seen what works best. An agrarian society with a low technology base, governed by feudal overlords, just like England in the middle ages. It will be a return to the rural idyll. With over ninety per cent of the global population dead within two years, virtually all knowledge and skills relating to high level technology will be lost. Only Catharus Society enclaves like this one will have access to the old ways, the old medicines. And only our ruling elite will benefit from them."

"Then why bring Danner and myself here? We are nothing to do with your New World Order, and I, for one, would rather take my chances with hemorrhagic fever than hide in this hole while civilization goes to hell," said Rouletabille.

"My friend, your incredible problem-solving mind could not be allowed to be destroyed in such circumstances. You squander your potential by acting as a journalist, detective, spy or soldier. In my New World Order, as you call it, you will be one of my feudal overlords. Don't rule it out now while anger governs your mind. I will win you around eventually. I have preserved other extraordinary individuals in much the same way. Danner presents more of a problem—he could never be allowed to become part of the lordly caste. Yet, had I left him on the surface, with his super-powerful constitution. he might have survived the fever, and gathered around him an army of survivors. That could have been a threat. I needed to find an effective way to enslave him; so far nothing has presented itself," said Worth.

"You said that if I took on the case of the missing locomotive, you would show me your father's journal—an alternative version of the events on Lincoln Island—too perfect an inducement, surely. I am not easily tricked, but I believed you completely," said Rouletabille.

"You were right to do so. It was no trick, unlike the story of the missing train. The missing loco merely brought Catharus Society members to the mine, men whose skills I will need in the years to come. The second train brought a stock of willing, fertile women for them to breed with. But I'm sure you guessed that," said Worth.

"And your father's journal?" said Rouletabille.

"Adam Worth was a genius. A man whose inventions and scientific knowledge were at least 50 years ahead of their time. You already know almost everything about him, for you know him under a different name. Adam Worth is the true identity of Captain Nemo. Prince Dakkar was a ludicrous fiction invented by Cyrus West. The journal reveals everything—well, almost everything. We can only infer my father's ultimate fate. Cyrus West murdered him for his inventions, and registered patents on most of them upon his return to the United States. Many of the patent blueprints in West's name are noticeably signed with my father's initials. West was a brazen thief indeed. Other drawings that were too obviously recognizable as being components of the *Nautilus* were kept by Herbert Brown; until, for reasons that are not entirely clear, you allowed them to fall into the hands of the German Air-Pirate, Kapitan Mors.[2] I will bring you the journal after my final trip to Philadelphia tomorrow."

The door to the throne room opened and a man in a wheelchair entered, he was accompanied by a couple of the black and white uniformed Catharus Society guards. The man would have been tall and spare had he not been confined to the chair, and although perhaps no older than his late twenties he was already balding. Nevertheless, there was an obvious intellectual intensity and, rather oddly, a certain friendliness to his demeanor.

"Rouletabille, this is Ward Baldwin, one of the senior officers within my organization, and, like you, a veteran of the Great War. The advanced surgery techniques here in the enclave will hopefully restore some function to the leg he nearly lost in the Macedonia campaign," said Worth.

"I am very pleased that you could join us," said Baldwin. "Your mind will be a great asset to the Catharus Society."

"I have not, by any definition, joined you. I am your prisoner. I will do my best to escape and frustrate your machinations, but keeping in mind your vastly superior numbers, I imagine I will die trying. I am quite happy to accept that," said Rouletabille, flatly.

"It is not possible to escape from this place. I understand how you must feel right now. But within a few days there will be nowhere worth escaping to, and then, a man of your unusually high intelligence will be forced to accept the reality of the situation," said Baldwin.

"Until then, take him away," Worth instructed the guards.

Rouletabille was marched through the mine past living areas, great kitchens, storage facilities and (as he has suspected) stables towards a secure holding area which oddly resembled a collection of zoo cages. Just before he arrived at the cages, the procession passed a combat practice arena in which two men in chainmail and surcoats fought with maces. It seemed the final proof that Worth and his band of madmen were deadly serious. The world was to be reduced to a state resembling the 13th century and held there in stagnant perpetuity. In a couple of years, the inhabitants of the mine would emerge to find an almost uninhabited United States. An empty landscape, to be restructured to their will. There would be fields to be ploughed and castles to be built. The handful of survivors would most likely be reduced to serfdom.

The cage door clanged shut and Rouletabille was left alone. He marshaled every cell of his brain, every scintilla of mental energy to a single resolute pur-

---

[2] See "Leviathan Creek" in *Tales of the Shadowmen 8*.

pose: escape. Rouletabille thought back almost sixteen years to his adventure in London, reported in a certain popular metropolitan magazine of the day as *The Adventure of the Snaresbrook Assizes.* At that time, he had been captured by the fiendish German Agent, Dr. Grierson. Grierson was a psychiatrist and briefly had the Frenchman committed to an insane asylum. After receiving torture by means of electric shocks and intra-muscular injections of camphor, Rouletabille managed to escape even though he had been placed in a straitjacket. The intervening years dulled the recollection the agony involved, and he felt slightly cheered that he had successfully executed a Houdini-like exit once before in his career.

Within fifteen minutes, the detective had succeeded in breaking apart his belt buckle and was using the pieces to try to pick the cage lock. He was having almost no luck with the tumblers, but even if he had been the exercise struck him as a particularly futile one. It was going to be far more difficult to get out of here than a London insane asylum. When the baton struck his hand, Rouletabille realized that he had been far too wrapped in his task to hear the approach of a guard.

"Gimme what you were usin' to pick at that lock or, so help me, I'll brain ya," said the guard.

Using his uninjured hand, Rouletabille picked up the fragments of buckle from the floor of the cage and tossed them towards the surly, smirking guard.

"Try that again and I'll break your feet!" the baton wielder threatened.

The lower ranks of the Catharus Society had obviously not been made privy to Rouletabille's importance.

A newcomer strode into the dim light of the holding area. He was a tall man, with a handsome and trustworthy countenance; yet unfortunately, he too wore the black and white uniform of the Catharus Society militia, with what Rouletabille took to be officer rank insignia on the epaulettes and sleeves.

"What's going on here, Maddocks? Are you antagonizing a prisoner again? I'll have you on a charge!" said the officer.

"Why no, Captain Rogers," said Maddocks. This prisoner was picking his cell lock. I caught 'im at it."

"What was he using on the lock?" asked Rogers.

"Little bits of metal—looks like part of a buckle," said Maddocks as he stooped to recover the pieces.

Without warning, Rogers kicked Maddocks in the head, just as if he was kicking a football off the tee. The guard rose up with the transferred momentum, then crashed down onto his back: out cold. Rouletabille looked at the Catharus Society officer in disbelief.

"Sir, I know that you've little reason to trust me, but I can assure you that I am not on the side of the people running this mine. I threw in with them under duress. I am Anthony Rogers of the American Radioactive Gas Corporation and I want to get out of here just as much as you do," said Captain Rogers.

Rogers knelt down and removed a ring of keys from the guard's belt, then after a moment selecting the right key, he inserted it into the lock of Rouletabille's cage and released him.

"If this is an attempt to break my spirit by allowing me to escape and then re-confining me it would seem extraordinarily premature," said Rouletabille, somewhat mockingly.

"I'll be proving my good intentions with forceful action against our captors—let that alone convince you. Talk is always cheap," said the Captain, and with that, he removed from his holster a pistol of highly unusual design. Rouletabille was reminded of the pistol that he had seen in the hands of Kapitan Mors a decade ago; perhaps that weapon too had been derived from the designs of Adam Worth.

"The best way out of here might be the ruse that you are a captive being transferred to a different level. I have some handcuffs here somewhere," said Rogers.

"Forget it. I am not being cuffed. I'll need my hands free to fight when the opportunity presents itself," said the detective. "Let's just walk out of here very casually and see if we can make it to the elevator," said Rouletabille. "There are a lot of newcomers here; it may be that they'll assume that I am just another neophyte of the Catharus Society."

"Uh-uh, they are very fussy about who they let back up to the surface. Only James Worth and Ward Baldwin seem to be able to come and go at will," said Rogers.

"Well, I don't intend to stay down here for two years... there has to be a way," said Rouletabille.

"Nobody is going to be down here for two years. I told them, but they didn't believe me. There's a rich vein of carnotite in the lower levels of the mine. It's a hydrovanadate of uranium. It means all the air down here is radioactive. Anyone down here for more than a few months will become seriously ill," explained Rogers.

"Are you sure?"

"Mister, this is my business. I'm a mining engineer with a specialty in this field. The abandoned Vermissa Mine next door is even more badly contaminated, and Worth plans to extend into that. He'll flood the Catharus workings with even deadlier gas," said Rogers.

"How were they planning to break through into that other mine?" asked the Frenchman.

"Well, they should drill through gradually and prop as they go, but these guys are pretty crazy. They've been using dynamite to create additional tunnels. Maybe you can get away with that in a lead mine or something, but in a coal mine, sooner or later you'll hit a pocket of concentrated methane and that'll be all she wrote! Next stop, the Pearly Gates or..."

"The gateway that says 'Abandon hope, all ye who enter here,'" completed Rouletabille. "How thick is the wall between this mine and the Vermissa?"

"Maybe just two or three yards in some places… I see where you're going. We could make our way to the surface from the abandoned mine. You're not loco enough to want to blast through, are you?" asked Rogers.

"We won't need to blast through. We just need Danner," smiled Rouletabille.

Rogers walked into the medical bay very confidently, as if performing an inspection on behalf of James Worth himself. He then pistol-whipped the doctor who was standing over Hugo Danner rather mercilessly, sending him into a temporary dreamless oblivion. The attendant nurse sought to flee but had her exit blocked by Rouletabille. The two would-be escapers were both far too gentlemanly too engage in violence against women, but that did not stop them from threatening, restraining and binding her. Once the woman was taken care of, they both examined Danner's situation. The plasma dart had been removed from his chest and a dressing placed over the wound. Over his face a rubber mask was fastened in place, and from the mask a thick rubber tube led away to a black gas cylinder on which where stenciled the words DIETHYL ETHER. There was a small brass control wheel at the top of the cylinder which Rouletabille immediately started to turn counter-clockwise to the shut position.

"They're keeping him heavily anaesthetized," said Rouletabille.

"And how exactly is this man going to help us?" asked Rogers.

"Well, I know nothing of his origins, but I can tell you that he is a modern day Samson or Hercules. He has the strength of a hundred men. "

Rogers raised an eyebrow.

"You asked me to accept your word. Now return the favor," said Rouletabille.

"I wonder how long he'll take to come round," said Rogers.

"His constitution is extraordinary: see, he is already starting to stir," observed Rouletabille.

Danner's hands moved slowly to the rubber mask at his face and pulled it off. Then his eyes snapped wide open and Rouletabille instantly realized the terrible danger that Rogers was in. The mining engineer stood before Danner in the uniform of his enemy—possibly Danner might even think that this was the same man who shot him with the plasma dart within his ether-clouded brain. Swift as lightning, Danner grabbed Rogers by the throat and commenced to throttle him.

"Danner! No, he is an ally," shouted Rouletabille.

Mercifully, Rogers felt the fantastic crushing pressure on his trachea suddenly cease. He dropped to his knees clutching a throat that would be black and blue in the morning—assuming they lived that long.

As Danner recovered, Rouletabille regaled him with the full details of his experiences within the Catharus Mine, summarizing each cogent fact with the skill of a highly trained journalist, until finally Danner was fully apprised of the plan to break through into the nearby mine—but this was not what concerned him.

"It is extremely strange that Worth tempted you with this journal telling the true version of events regarding his father, who just happens to be the legendary Captain Nemo, when he also offered me access to an extraordinary and far more incredible journal. He claimed he had access to a secret diary which my father, Professor Abednego Danner lodged in the archives of Indian Creek College, Colorado—officially not to be opened until one hundred years after his death; when the world might be ready for the information therein. Worth suggested to me that my father was, in fact, an alien from another world sent to this planet from a dying world about to suffer an imminent catastrophe when he was only a baby. His crashed miniature space-vehicle was discovered by my grandparents who raised him as their own," said Danner.

"That's very telling. A man might have access to one revelatory tome, but to have two so conveniently related to men he wants to influence smacks of cynical and manipulative fraud," said Rouletabille.

"Fellows, we don't have time for this," judged Rogers. "Anyway, aliens? Who believes in such fairytales? Let's just get out of here…"

The trio went out into the corridor and almost immediately encountered a pair of guards. Before the men could unshoulder their carbines, Danner had set upon them. A blind rage descended on him as he fought and the two guards fell to the dusty floor of the tunnel as sacks of splintered bone.

Rouletabille recovered one of the dropped pneumatic carbines and armed himself. They moved forward like an army patrol with Danner taking point, Rouletabille in the center and Rogers bringing up the rear. They made their way past a set of women's dormitories where the girls from the train to Scranton were still unpacking their luggage, chatting and giggling, as if they were on the most adventurous sleepover of all time. Finally, Rogers directed them to a spur tunnel which took them closest to the Vermissa mine.

They stopped in front of the blank, black rock face at the tunnel's end and Danner placed his huge hands on the wall in front of him as if considering how much of his tremendous strength to utilize. Rouletabille and Rogers turned to defend their position against a phalanx of approaching guards. Rouletabille switched the carbine to rapid-fire mode and opened up. He wished he'd picked up a spare magazine now. Rogers blazed away with his pistol and proved himself to be an excellent shot. Rouletabille aimed carefully, just as he had back in the Great War, and soon found himself able to compensate for the carbine's propensity to pull to the right. The black and white garbed guards fell back, found cover and sniped into the tunnel from their positions of semi-concealment.

Suddenly, pulverized dust filled their nostrils as Danner's fists whacked again and again into the wall of black-blue anthracite coal in front of him. Danner extended the spur tunnel like some superhuman mole, and the detritus from his efforts built up around the two other men's legs like a rising tide.

Less than a minute later there was a sudden blast of stale, warmish air: Danner had broken through into the Vermissa workings. Rouletabille and Rogers retreated through the newly-opened tunnel, keeping up a suppressing fire at their adversaries. Once through, Danner dragged them to one side, jumped up and punched the roof of the spur tunnel suddenly collapsing it. Away from the electric lanterns that were strung along the tunnels of the Catharus Mine, the three men found themselves to be plunged into total darkness.

"I wish we'd thought to bring a flashlight with us," said Rouletabille.

"Don't worry, my friend. I can see in total darkness just as easily as in noonday sun," reassured Danner.

"One of the benefits of your otherworldly lineage, no doubt," laughed Rogers. "I find it easier to believe now. If all this is real, and not all in my mind."

Danner took Rouletabille and Rogers by the hands and guided them through the foul blackness. After almost half an hour of wandering, Danner came upon the long out of service shaft elevator. He tore open the gate and then got his two companions to loop their arms around his thickly sinewed neck, then started to ascend the greasy steel cable, which was thankfully still in place. Once at the top, a few of Danner's punches destroyed the wooden boards which blocked the mine entrance, and then they were free.

All three of them paused to cough up the anthracite dust they'd been inhaling, and then Rouletabille took stock of the situation.

"They may come over to this mine to investigate, if they have a brain between them. After all, they know where we've gone," said Rouletabille.

"So what's our next move?" asked Rogers.

"We need to get away from here as quickly as possible and travel to Philadelphia. We must thwart the propagation of the hemorrhagic fever virus, if we can," said the detective.

Without a further word, Danner grabbed both Rogers and Rouletabille around the torso with a vise-like grip and then made a prodigious leap which carried them all many hundreds of feet into the air. This process was repeated many dozens of times. At first, the landings were traumatic, but as they progressed Danner became more accustomed to cushioning the impact. While grateful for the speed with which they would get to Philadelphia, Rouletabille was thoroughly nauseated by the acceleration and sense of falling. Rogers, on the other hand, loved it, and whooped as if he were riding an exciting Coney Island rollercoaster.

"This is the only way to travel," he had to scream above the deafening roar of the wind.

Danner's jumps became longer and lower over time as he perfected his technique. Ultimately, the arcs of the jumps were perhaps only one hundred and fifty feet high, but nearly three miles in length. Finally, Rouletabille could see the grounds of the exposition below them. He could just make out the stadium, and to the west, the Treasure Island Lagoon with neighboring Fine Arts building. For a second, Rouletabille thought that Danner intended to land them in one of the various bodies of water in that part of the Exposition. In fact, Danner had judged the descent perfectly and they landed with a not too elegant thud on the flat concrete roof of the administration building.

"This is where Worth briefed me on the disappearance of the loco," said Danner.

"Me too. His office must be directly beneath us," said Rouletabille.

Without a further word, Danner's fists smacked a ragged hole in the roof large enough from them to drop through onto the plush royal blue carpet.

"We have to assume that the virus has not been released yet—search everywhere—wait! A safe behind a portrait is a recurring theme in my life... let's try it here," said the Frenchman. Then he slid the panel behind Worth's desk to one side, to show again the portrait of his father. He wrenched it forward and it swung on concealed hinges revealing an old Brooker 440 safe.

"Take care of it, Danner," said Rouletabille.

The brass and steel of the safe were torn apart by Danner, and the accompanying sound could almost have been the screeching of some gargantuan and monstrous raven. Danner retrieved the papers and handed them to Rouletabille.

"Anything useful?" asked Rogers.

"It's just papers and correspondence about something called *The Maracot Expedition.* Worth seemed to be in negotiations with the Maracot Diving Company to charter their staff and equipment for an exploration in the Pacific, once they had concluded their own excursion to the deep Atlantic. Hmm. I seem to remember that there was due to be a Maracot mission to the Atlantic years ago, but it all fell through when one of their engineers embezzled virtually all of the company's funds—Ian Hassett was the miscreant's name, as I recall," said Rouletabille.

"That doesn't sound like much help," said Danner. "Is there anything more relevant in that sheaf of documents?"

"There are some blueprints of the Exposition attractions: the 1776 Street, the Treasure Island Lagoon, the giant Liberty Bell with all the light bulbs on it..." said the detective.

"Let me see that," demanded Rogers. He took the blueprint of the enormous Liberty Bell from Rouletabille and brought it closer to the lamplight. "Look at this cross-section of the Liberty Bell. Yeah, sure, it is full of electrical cables and wires, but these other things look like air-pumps and plumbing, with reservoirs for holding some kind of liquid. And look at these nozzles near the surface of the bell. You know what it reminds me of? It almost looks like a gigantic, electrically powered perfume atomizer. Probably ideal if they wanted to disperse some kind of airborne infection," concluded Rogers.

"Is viral hemorrhagic fever airborne?" asked Rouletabille.

"Don't forget that this is something the Catharus Society cobbled together in a lab. It could well be spread by the prevailing wind," said Rogers.

"Danner, this is your department," said Rouletabille. "Carry the bell into the sea and destroy it completely. The virus will not survive immersion in salt-water."

"Consider it done, my friend," said Danner.

"You don't suppose that Worth has already activated the mechanism?" asked Rogers.

"I don't think so. I suppose if he has then the Catharus Society has already won. But I think he was waiting for better weather, for capacity crowds.

The two men searched the office for hours hoping to find one or both of the journals that Worth had offered them as an inducement, but there was no trace of them.

Momentarily unnoticed by Rogers or Rouletabille, another panel eased to one side accompanied by the whirring sound of a small servo motor. Behind the panel was a prototype crystal tele-screen, which flared to life with an azure glow.

"Gentlemen," began Ward Baldwin. "I congratulate you on stymieing the plans of the Catharus Society. Mr. Worth underestimated your capabilities and made a terrible mistake by involving you in our affairs. The Catharus Society invited Mr. Worth to atone for his shortcomings by taking the honorable way out. He was allocated the usual period for calm reflection before his suicide by poison capsule; but he has now killed his guards and escaped. We will hunt him down in due course. In the meantime, all traces of his failure will be eliminated. This organization will return in time, most likely with a different name, and hopefully with other more effective schemes. But rest assured that one day, humanity will be subjugated to our will."

Before Rouletabille could marshal within his mind some sort of coherent reply, the image on the screen ceased to be Baldwin's face. Now the screen showed the interior of the Catharus Mine. Technicians and militia were walking along the tunnels, some purposefully, others as if taking an afternoon stroll. Rouletabille noticed that a few of the girls who had arrived on the train with him were now walking along hand in hand with men. Without warning, a powerful explosion rocked the scene. Bodies were blasted apart by high explosives. The roof commenced to fall and the moving picture on the screen flickered and died; then there was nothing but blackness.

"You realize that we can never tell the world of this?" said the detective. "It would be like waking a somnambulist on a cliff edge... the shock could cause the human race to never know peace of mind again."

"I had sometimes thought that a big enough war might bring about some kind of Armageddon, maybe destroy the world. But the development of the sort of weapons that would be necessary seems to be still decades in the future. Now to find that doomsday can creep up on you like a thief in the night, and that people want to bring it about is, well, sickening," said Rogers. "I agree that we need to keep our mouths shut, but I can't help feeling that the world needs a united network command of law enforcers to guard against the return of the Catharus Society as some kind of technological hierarchy for the removal of undesirables and the subjugation of humanity."

The two men left the office and strode through the lobby on the way out. Outside, the Sun was rising and the pink early morning rays were hitting the mural of American History. Rouletabille realized that a pair of wood and canvas freestanding screens were obscuring the very end of this piece of art, which it seemed had been added to very recently. He pushed the screens aside. The mural now foretold history that would never come: of the arrival of a great plague, with people dying in the streets. Of the coming of a new lordly caste of knights. Of the building of great castles and the forging of an empire, with contented serfs toiling in the fields. And above this tableau, words of incredible cynicism and hypocrisy were neatly painted in black.

*"Till the war-drum throbb'd no longer, and the battle-flags were furl'd*
*In the Parliament of man, the Federation of the world."*

There was a sound in the air like the tuneless whistle of an approaching shell; it was Danner returning. Rouletabille resolved to get him to destroy the new part of the mural and gouge out those dreadful words. He too was sickened by how close James Worth had come to erasing the human status quo and replacing it with his absurd and idealized Ivanhoe-type future. Yes, Rouletabille still looked young, but he was starting to feel old in his attitudes, starting to wonder if peace was the just the hiatus between wars that came about when people were too fatigued to fight. Tennyson's words chilled him. What force, what tyranny would it take to truly unite the world? With all the disparate brands of politics and religion on the planet, if they were to be brought under one banner, a lot of people would have to die to achieve that end. The Catharus Society had been right about that.

*Dedicated to David McDaniel—he paved the way for all of us.*

*Emmanuel Gorlier has, over the years, become the semi-official chronicler of the adventures of Leo Saint-Clair, aka The Nyctalope, who teams up here with Briar Rose/Belle, a.k.a. Sleeping Beauty, who first appeared in "The Reluctant Princess" in our Volume 4 to uncover a Nazi plot and ask himself whether the supermen to come will be French or German...*

## Emmanuel Gorlier: *Once More, the Nyctalope*

*Villefranche-sur-Mer, January 1936*

He was making slow progress in the dark, walking against the strong, freezing wind. A storm was coming. At a short distance ahead of him, the mansion appeared in a flash of lightning, just before the first drop of ice-cold rain hit his face. He shivered a little. By the time he reached the estate, he was completely soaked.

The doors were unlocked. He entered.

This nocturnal visitor was invisible. Only the sound he made or the movement of the objects he might be handling could identify his presence. An observer located in the sitting-room into which he had just stepped would have seen only the double-paneled door open, as if by itself, then close a few seconds later. Had our observer been more attentive, he might also have noticed the small pools of water in the approximate shape of footprints that appeared on the carpet where the Invisible man walked.

After having cursorily inspected the sitting-room, the Invisible Man walked quickly towards the grand staircase leading to first floor. The traces stopped briefly in front of a large oil painting representing a man and a woman holding hands. The man sported a piercing gaze that seemed to follow the observer with his two extraordinary, gold-speckled eyes, large like a night bird's. The woman at his side was a beautiful blonde with blue eyes, equally fascinating, drawing attention to her despite her companion's charismatic presence.

"Sylvie Saint-Clair and her husband, Leo—the Nyctalope," whispered the Invisible Man. "How unfortunate that she died so young... I must act quickly if I don't want my own children to suffer the same fate!"

The visitor felt a shap pain in his heart at the thought of his family. He shook his head. *Nothing must distract me from reaching my goal,* he thought.

He resumed walking and climbed the stairs to the first floor. On stepping onto the landing, he heard a series of dull thumping sounds coming from a room just above. It sounded like two or more people... doing what? The Invisible Man had a moment's hesitation. He knew that Leo, a widower, would not be without female companionship... Could he be with a new girl-friend? But the reason that

78

had brought him here was urgent... His need, desperate... *He will forgive me if I interrupt him in his lovemaking,* he thought. *Others may already be after me.*

He started up the stairs towards the room from which the sounds had originated. The door was open. The Invisible Man entered, despite his embarrassment.

The room was, in fact, a dance studio. A bar ran along its four mirrored walls, a few feet above the floor. Reflected into infinity was a handsome couple. The man was his old friend, Leo Saint-Clair, whom he had not seen for several years, but who looked exqactly the same, forever young. He appeared to be barely forty when he was over sixty. He was shirtless and wore black tights as is the custom when practicing the French kick-boxing discipline of *la savate*. His partner was a young blonde woman of outstanding beauty, dressed in the same black tights with a white shirt that hid little of her generous curves. They were facing each other, each focused on their respective opponent. Suddenly, the young woman sent a kick flying at Leo, which demonstrated her mastery. But the Nyctalope moved slightly, almost imperceptibly, and her foot missed his chest by mere inches. He made a movement of the arm, barely grazing the back of the foot of his companion, but she immediately winced in pain. She took a couple of steps back, limping slightly, trying to regain her balance. Leo used that opportunity to grab her forearm and, with a fluid motion of his hips, he hurled her into the air. She managed to land back on her feet, but a little unsteadily because of the lingering pain in her foot.

Leo then approached his opponent... and stole a kiss!

He lowered his guard and helped to steady her back.

"You see how being able to hit certain pressure points on the body can be decisive in a fight. With a simple gesture, it is possible to neutralize an opponent, even if he is much stronger and better trained than you."

The young woman was about to respond when the Invisible Man, who felt pressed for time allowed himself a slight cough.

They both turned around abruptly and moved into a position of defense. They scanned the studio to see who could have interrupted their practice. The Nyctalope used his uncanny vision but it did not detect the presence of the Invisible Man.

"It's me, Leo, Jacques, the Invisible Man, your old companion. Sorry to disturb your peace, but I need your help in a matter of the utmost importance!"

"Jacques! I thought you had stopped adventuring and you were now devoting all your time to your family!"

The Nyctalope walked towards the spot where he thought his friend was. The young woman buttoned the top of her shirt, then joined the two men.

"May I present to you Mademoiselle Briar Rose," said Leo, "whom her friends also call Belle—or the Phantom Angel. You can speak in her presence. She and I fought Belphegor together, and I would trust her with my life!"[3]

"Very well! The reason I have to come to you is, as I said, of the utmost importance. It involves not only the lives of my family but also the vital interests of our country. And we must act quickly because I think the enemy is already after me!"

"After you? But you are the Invisible Man! How could they...? But let's go into my study. We'll be more comfortable there to discuss the matter."

Leo led Belle and the Invisible Man into another room where they all sat in leather armchairs. Leo took a cigarette from one of the boxes that contained the Turkish brand he favored. He lit it with delight. He nodded at his guests, but neither Belle nor the Invisible Man wanted to smoke.

"As you said," began the Invisible Man, "I had decided to retire to spend all my time with my wife and our five children. Finally, I had even decided to destroy my invisibility formula, but before I could I was attacked by a merciless enemy. This is what happened: While I wasout, our house was invaded by armed men who took my children prisoner and left a message for me and my wife, whom I found tied to a chair when I returned. She told me that five persons had broken in. I checked and saw that they had twisted the wrought iron gate to force the lock! My wife told me they were led by a young man and a young blonde woman, both with blue eyes, beautiful, and very fit. They both radiated such charisma and strength of will that she remembered being completely passive in their presence, almoat subdued. Within minutes, they had taken the children and left.

"There was nothing left for me to do but read the message they had left. It was very clear: either I delivered somedocuments I possessed and my children would be returned, or else... The delivery was to take place at an old cross in the country at 10 p.m. the next night... I had no choice..."

"If it is not indiscreet to ask," interrupted Leo, "what was the nature of these documents?"

"When I was briefly President of the Council of Ministers, ten years ago, I had a series of files compiled on several prominent politicians and business figures. I even used a few of these when I fought crime as the Invisible Man. When I stopped my activities as crime fighter, I promised myself, and I have kept that promise, to never use these files for any reason whatsoever. I'm even surprised that someone knew I had them in my possession. As you must realize, the present government is on its last legs. It's likely that the workers' party will prevail in the next election. The leader of the coalition, who will be appointed by the unions to take over as President, will probably be Auguste Cahizac. However, many years ago, he was involved in a corruption scandal—a youthful indiscre-

---

[3] See "Una Voce Poco Fa" in *Night of the Nyctalope*.

tion, nothing more. But whoever holds the file I have on him will have significant leverage on the future head of our government!

"Although the lives of my children were at risk, I had no doubt that I should intervene, especially since there was no real guarantee that they wouldn't be killed even if I surrendered my files. So I decided to once again become the Invisible Man.

"I delivered the documents at the appointed time and place, and walked away as I was supposed to do, but secretly returned five minutes later as the Invisible Man.

"I saw a large car approach the cross. Its occupants watched the neighborhood, then a man dressed in a black coat stepped out of the vehicle and retrieved the documents. I took advantage of this to climb on the running board of the car on the opposite side. Moments later, the car left. The two young blond villains were not present.

"The car drove off and eventually arrived at a country estate located about thirty miles outside the city. It was closed by a metal gate. On a stone pillar on the left, there was a brass plate reading *Professor René Belloq*. A guard appeared and opened the gate to let the car pass. It was then that, for the first time, I had the strange feeling *that I was being watched!*

"I took a good look around but saw nothing suspicious. The car drove through a park—more like a small wood—and arrived at a large, two-storied country house that spoke to the wealth of its owner.

"On the front steps were the two young blond villains I mentioned earlier. Between them stood a man of about forty who appeared to be their leader. I assumed it was Professor Belloq.

"Unlike the Professor, the two blonde characters seemed to follow me with their eyes. I felt they could see me. As I got closer, I realized was right! For some unknown reason, their eyes had the power to pierce my invisibility. I had to jump or risk falling into their hands. As the car slowed down before stopping, I jumped off and ran towards the wood.

"At its edge, I turned around to look at my foes. The car was parked in front of the porch of the house, but the two blond figures were already running towards me.

"I started running through the wood in order to reach the gate as quickly as possible. I was lucky because when I reached it, it was open, and the guard was talking to a biker who sought entrance.

"I ran towards them, making as little noise as possible.

"Then, I knocked the guard on the head and pushed his body towards the rider. This man went down with his motorcycle, his eyes filled with surprise as he didn't understand what was happening. I took advantage of that to take his bike and cross through the gate while it was still open.

"I was just in time because I saw the two blonds running out of the wood towards me. They moved with incredible speed, worthy of Olympic champions.

But they were too late—I had already gone out of the gate and reached the main road. Behind me, my pursuers slowed down, realizing that, they could no longer catch up with me, despite their superhuman endurance.

"While riding down the road, I still felt as if someone was watching me. Obviously my opponents had the amazing power of being able to detect my presence even from afar! If I had given most of the documents in my possession to Professor Belloq's men, I had held onto a piece of the utmost importance in order to keep a bargaining chip in case they wouldn't release my children.

"Once back home, I made sure that my wife left town, then I searched the satchels hanging on the back of the bike. In them, I found letter announcing the imminent arrival of a Dr. Karl Haushofer who was going to be visiting the Professor.

"I did not know from whom to seek help in this delicate matter when I suddenly remembered reading in *Le Matin* that you were staying at the family home of your late wife, not too far from my own village. I thought you could help me save my family and retrieve the documents that I was blackmailed into giving to Belloq.

"We must act quickly, because even now, I feel I am being watched!"

"So the infamous Doctor Haushofer, one of the most important members of the Nazi party that governs Germany, a member of the Thule Society, a confidante of Chancellor Adolf Hitler himself, is about to pay a visit to the renowned Professor Belloq of the French Université! I wonder why... Still, right now, we must cut off the mystical link that seems to connect you to these two blond characters. I think I know how! Follow me!

Leo headed downstairs followed by the others.

"Below this house is a series of secret rooms that were used by Sylvie's stepfather, the wise Mathias Lumen, in his fight against Leonid Zattan. I have since turned them into a laboratory where I've stored some of the devices that I've used in my own struggle against evil."

The Nyctalope pressed a molding in the wall, revealing a hidden flight of stairs. Still leading his friends, he took them into a well equipped, modern laboratory, filled with a variety of unique devices. Among them was a unit not unlike a bell-shaped diving unit with a glass dome on top. The Nyctalope opened a hatch and asked the Invisible Man to step inside.

Once he was in, Leo pressed a button and the bell became filled with a greenish, iridescent gas.

"You are now completely isolated from your external environment, including mental or mystic forces," explained Leo. "This is a device that allowed me to overcome Lucifer in the early 20s. Our opponents shall no longer be able to track your aura and should therefore lose all contact with you. Now we can plan our counter-attack... Let me think... First, we must of course locate your children and set them free. We also need to retrieve the documents in their possession..."

"We must neutralize the power of those two blonds," added the Invisible Man. "Do you have a smaller version of this protective device?"

"I do," replied the Nyctalope, "but they're hardly discreet."

"If they're not too large, I could treat them so to make them invisible, which should greatly facilitate our task."

"It's feasible," confirmed Leo. "I've just thought of a way to infiltrate the enemy's lair... "

"I bet I know what it is," said Belle. "I assume you plan to use the invitation you received from Professor Belloq?"

"What invitation?" asked the Invisible Man.

"As unlikely as it seems, the good Professor has invited me, along with some other archeologists and explorers, to his home for a lecture he plans to give on the theme of the 'Emergence of the Super-Man.' There was nothing about it that led me to suspect that it might be connected to Haushofer and the national-socialist theories. I think many of the guests are in for a surprise. Maybe there is a connection with these two blonds?... It's the best way to infiltrate Belloq's home without drawing undue attention. You can accompany us inside a protective device that you will have turned invisible. Tomorrow night, we spring into action!"

The following night, the Nyctalope, Belle and the Invisible Man, concealed in the back of the car, arrived at the gate of Professor Belloq's estate. They were let in by the same guard whom the Invisible Man had knocked out a few days earlier. The driveway was lit by a row of torches planted in the grass on either sides.

The car parked in front of the house. A butler greeted the Nyctalope and his lady friend. Unbeknownst to him, they were both equipped with psychic protection devices under their hats, but although Belle could keep hers on, Leo had to surrender his in the lobby. Meanwhile, the Invisible Man began to explore the surroundings, looking for the location of his children.

Leo and Belle were ushered into a large room where many guests talked freely, glasses of champagne in hand, before the start of the lecture on the Super-Man. A cocktail party was to follow that would allow them to comment on the speakers.

They immediately noticed that Belloq had invited most of the leading scientists of the times. Some had even come from Paris, like Paul Langevin, the eminent physicist, who was also a notorious anti-fascist and probably surprised to find himself in such company. Also present were the renowned archeologist Aristide Clairembart and Tryphon Tournesol, notoriously hard of hearing, who was demonstrating something with the help of his pendulum. The guests, lured by Belloq's reputation, had not realized that they were going to attend a lecture based in part on Nazi beliefs.

In addition to the scientists, Leo also recognized other personalities such as journalist Jerome Fandor, who had been dealing with a sinister master criminal who did deserve the title of "Super-Man," and famous science fiction writer Marcel Priollet. There was also a grim older, one-eyed man who stood silently in a corner of the salon, and, at the opposite end, Dutil-Parot, who had been President a decade before, a few months before Jacques Roll, the Invisible Man. Leo wondered if he hadn't been the one who had told Belloq about the existence of the secret dossiers.... Before he could ponder the subject further, he saw Belloq approaching him, accompanied by a man who was unknown to him.

"Good evening, Monsieur Saint-Clair," said the Professor, smiling. "I am honored that you decided to come after all. May I introduce you to Doctor Haushofer, our keynote speaker tonight?"

"Good evening, Monsieur Saint-Clair," said the German doctor in a heavily accented voice. "So you, too, are interested in the notion of the Super-Man? It is a subject that fascinates many influential people on the other side of the Rhine."

"Indeed—and I understand that you are an expert on the subject. However, this concept always seemed somewhat abstract to me. Frankly, I do not see what possible practical application there might be..."

"I am surprised that you, of all people, think so, Monsieur Saint-Clair. I have had the opportunity to read the newspapers of your country. They are full of praise when talking about you. A few weeks ago, I even read an article in *Le Matin* called '*The Nyctalope: Is the Super-Man French?*' It seems everyone in France is proud to be the nation of the Super-Man, who was fated to serve the 'Greatness of France.' But I hope to show that the natural home of the Super-Man is, and will remain, Germany."

"Whatever gave you that idea?"

"I will show you! I brought two friends with me. Siegfried! Brunhilde! Come here! I have someone who wants to meet you!"

Haushofer turned to welcome the two young blond figures who approached him. They looked as if they were about twenty-five. Both had blue eyes and appeared to have been created in the image of Norse gods. They were truly resplendent in both beauty and strength.

Haushofer introduced them to Leo and Belle with a sweeping motion of the arm:

"Mademoiselle, Monsieur Saint-Clair, here are the first two Super-Men! Look well, Monsieur Saint-Clair, these are the first two to come out of my research. The seeds of the future Master Race!"

Leo instantly felt the mental power of the two newcomers. Without his helmet, despite his training by Tibetan masters, it was difficult to not surrender to their almost supernatural presence. They truly were Super-Men. He did not understand how Haushofer's theories, which he had always considered as no more than a fanciful exercise, could have produced such specimens.

When Haushofer had turned to introduce his two marvels, Leo had caught a shiny reflection on one of his fingers. Looking at it more closely, it turned out to be from a ring engraved with ancient symbols...

"Siegfried and Brunhilde are the precursors of the New Race that shall soon rule the world," continued Haushofer. "Soon, the Aryan Race shall reclaim the dominant place that they should never have lost!"

He seemed inexhaustible on the subject. Meanwhile, Leo tried to fathom the truth behind his words. Haushofer had mentioned an old race... These names... Siegfried... Brunhilde... An ancient ring... The Ring of the Nibelungen! Of course! That was what had enabled Haushofer to summon these beings from the most ancient past!

All the elements now fell into place in the Nyctalope's head. Somehow, Haushofer had come in possession of the fabled Ring. Maybe it had been discovered by Belloq, who had recently been conducting excavations in Germany, waiting to obtain similar permits from Egypt.

Using such an object of power, it was, in theory, possible to summon legends from the past. Haushofer had obviously used it to bring back to life the demigod Siegfried and his lover, the valkyrie Brunhilde. He had molded them into his own vision of the "Super-Man," which explained their strange new powers, not mentioned in the ancient texts. Perhaps Siegfried's invulnerability was not the result of having been dipped in the blood of the dragon Fafnir, but came from some unknown mental discipline? The legend mentioned a weak point, due to a leaf that had stuck to his back, something to be exploited perhaps... Haushofer was a charlatan, but the powers of the two young gods were awesome and terribly dangerous in the service of someone like Chancellor Hitler...

Haushofer at last took his leave and walked to a lectern in order to begin his speech. Belloq introduced his guest to the audience:

"Ladies and Gentlemen, we are pleased to have with us this evening the notorious Doctor Haushofer of the Thule Society. He will present his work tonight, in particular the results of his research on the use of Vril as a psychic energy source allowing ordinary people to bravely take the steps that will turn them into "Super-Men." Now I yield the floor to Doctor Haushofer...

As the German Doctor began his lecture, Leo and Belle exchanged glances. They had retreated slowly to position themselves at the back of the room and their eyes searched for potential exits.

Suddenly, Leo heard a whisper in his ear:

"Leo, I found where my children are being held captive. They are in an outbuilding near the wall of the estate."

"Let's go then," Leo whispered back. "Their safety must be our priority. We will see to the recovery of the documents later..."

Leo took the Invisible Man's hand and he and Belle left. They entered an empty salon, one window of which was ajar. Leo asked the Invisible Man to fetch him his hat in order to retrieve the psychic protection device. Once he had it back on his head, he pointed to the window and said:

"Let's go!"

They crossed the small wood at their left without incident and eventually arrived at a small one-story house, probably a gamekeeper's residence, built against the stone wall that surrounded the estate. There was a guard at the entrance. He tapped his foot, as if marking the rhythm of a song.

"Wait for me," whispered the Invisible Man, "I'll take care of him!"

He silently approached the house. A few yards away, he heard a German song escaping from an open window. He grabbed a stone and hit the guard on the head. The man collapsed soundlessly.

His two companions moved towards the house, taking precautions so as not to be seen by any of the occupants who might be looking through a window. Once at the door, Leo recognized the song: it was *Horst Wessel Lied*, the anthem of the Nazi party.

He tried the doorknob and found it was not locked. He made a sign to Belle, who nodded. They thought that the two of them could easily surprise and overcome their opponents. Leo counted down to zero on his fingers and they burst into the room.

The Germans were taken completely by surprise. One minute, they were drinking beer, singing; a minute later, they were attacked by three opponents—one of whom was invisible—who rained a shower of blows upon them!

The three Frenchmen gave their foes no chance to fight back. In less than five minutes, the four Germans were out of action.

In a small bedroom to the side, they found the Invisible Man's five children sleeping.

"The first part of our mission is accomplished" said the Nyctalope. "Now, we still have to get the documents back, but I think we should split up. Belle and I will return to Belloq's house to find them. You, Jacques, should take your children out of harm's way."

The Invisible Man marked a hesitation, but Leo insisted:

"Come on! There's no time to waste! They may have already realized that we left the lecture and gone looking for us."

The Invisible Man agreed:

"OK! I'll take care of the children."

As he walked away, looking for a way to cross the wall with his children, Leo and Belle walked back towards the house. They had almost reached it when they saw Siegfried and Brunhilde rushing toward them at the head of a group of four men armed with machine guns.

Leo motioned for Belle to fall back into the woods. Then, he pulled out a strange-looking gun from his holster. The weapon sported an unusually long, thin barrel. Belle had the same gun strapped to her right thigh under her dress. They settled behind some bushes and prepared to shoot their assailants. With his night vision, the Nyctalope had a clear advantage. For their enemies to go after him at night in a dark wood while he was armed was pure madness. He was surprised that Siegfried and Brunhilde had made such a mistake.

Soon, he saw one of his opponents approach, machine gun in hand, ready to spray death. He adjusted his aim and fired. There was a slight hissing sound and the Nazi collapsed, a bullet between the eyes. The weapon Leo used was a silent air pistol that he had developed years earlier and used in his fight against Lucifer. Another man appeared and suffered the same fate. The silence was briefly interrupted by the noise he made falling in the bushes. Leo had, so far, only seen the "stooges. The "two "Super-Men" had remained invisible. A third man appeared in his sights, trying his best to hide in the vegetation. The Nyctalope put a bullet through his heart. Everything went silent. Leo heard a faint whistling sound coming from Belle's direction. One of the Nazis who had managed to approach without being detected had just been spotted and neutralized by the young woman. Only the two "Super-Men" were left.

Suddenly, Siegfried and Brunhilde simultaneously attacked Leo and Belle. The fact that they could even surprise the Nyctalope was pure magic. They had moved silently through the wood, making a wide detour so as not to be seen by Leo. Only their superhuman senses and ability to move in total silence had made this ruse possible. The two Germans struck the arms of their opponents, forcing them to drop their guns.

Leo now faced Siegfried and Belle Brunhilde. The odds in favor of the Nyctalope and his friend seemed small. How could they defeat two mythological characters with awesome powers?

Siegfried struck first, but the Nyctalope managed to avoid the attack. The German warrior looked surprised as if he should have foreseen his opponent's action. Leo thought this was due to the psychic protection helmet, the effect of which was to confuse the enemy by blocking his uncanny ability to sense his opponent's actions. Now, he would have to employ all the martial arts skills he had learned over the years, first in Tibet and China, then with his friend Gnô Mitang who had initiated him into the Japanese fighting disciplines.

Siegfried moved towards him, leaning forward, his arms slightly away from his body. Leo thought this was an ancient battle technique and he should be very attentive to what was going to happen next. His opponent suddenly charged but, at the last moment, twisted around to try to strike Leo's arm, intending to break it. Fortunately, Leo had anticipated the move and seized the opportunity to grab Siegfried's arm, then, bending his back, threw him above his head. The German warrior flew through the air but, by twisting around, still landed on own two feet. Seeing this, Leo thought that this could well turn into the toughest fight of his life!

For her part, Belle faced the valkyrie. She positioned her body in the purest style of French boxing and delivered a mighty kick, but her opponent didn't even flinch. Belle felt as if she had hit a wall of granite. Worse, she felt she had reinjured the same ankle that was still sore from her training session the day before. Brunhilde then launched a counterattack, unleashing a rain of blows upon the French woman. Their strength and accuracy were such that Belle found it increasingly difficult to parry them. Soon, her guard was broken and the valkyrie delivered a punch to the temple that sent her to the ground and would even have totally put her out of action if she had not partially deflected the blow by turning her head at the last minute. Brunhilde lunged at Belle and tried to strangle her. A black veil fell over her eyes...

Meanwhile, Siegfried charged Leo, but he stumbled, his feet catching on a root that he had not seen in the darkness. The Nyctalope had the advantage in a combat of this kind because of his night vision. He seized that opportunity to deliver a series of blows on his opponent's pressure points. The German warrior fell to his knees, wincing in pain. Hardening his fingers through mental concentration, Leo struck him on that secret spot that his Tibetan Master, who had taught him the blow, had made him swear never to reveal. Siegfried stiffened and collapsed.

"The leaf on his back," whispered the Nyctalope, struck by the coincidence.

As she sank into oblivion, Belle remembered the Nyctalope's teachings on pressure points. She had to chance a final blow, even though she hadn't yet mastered the technique, otherwise all would be lost. She hit a specific spot on the back of Brunhilde's neck. Instantly, the pressure on her throat relaxed. The valkyrie was out of action! She got up and saw that Leo had already triumphed over his adversary.

"The proof is now in," he said, smiling. "The 'Super-Men' are indeed French! Now, we have to return to the house and get the Invisible Man's documents back!"

As they reached the edge of the wood, they saw what seemed to be the glow of a fire. Indeed, when they stepped out of the trees, they saw that Belloq's residence was ablaze. They helplessly watched the roof collapse.

They noticed Doctor Haushofer and Belloq pacing back and forth while all the guests—no one seemed to have been harmed—were being evacuated. Curious about what had happened, they approached the doctor,

"The one-eyed man... It was Votan all along..." he stammered.

"What do you mean?" asked Leo.

"Votan... The All-Father... He came back for the Ring..." continued Haushofer. "Who knows what calamities will now befall us?..."

Haushofer's words were all but incoherent. However, Leo was able to piece together a scenario. While they were fighting in the wood, the one-eyed older guest had revealed himself, or claimed to be, the god Votan, who, according to legend, was the owner of the Ring of the Nibelungen and had come to reclaim his property. In some way or another, the house had caught fire during the encounter.

"I don't think we'll ever know exactly what happened," concluded Leo, "but our mission is over. The documents must have been destroyed in the fire. Let's go home."

He walked to their car, followed by Belle. No one tried to stop them. When they left through the gate, the Nyctalope thought he saw the shape of an old man riding a horse with eight legs on a rainbow bridge amongst the stars. The old man stopped and looked at him with his single, fiery eye. Behind him were the two youthful figures of Siegfried and Brunhilde. Then the clouds obscured the stars and when they blew away, the vision was gone, as it had never existed. Leo could not swear it hadn't just been an illusion...

An hour later, they rejoined the Invisible Man, who thanked them profusely. With the secret dossiers destroyed, he said there was one last thing he had to do to ensure his family's safety.

A few days later, The Nyctalope read in *Le Matin* that Monsieur Cahizac had suddenly resigned from his position as first secretary of the union; no explanation was given. Leon Blum was to replace him and lead the opposition in the upcoming legislative elections.

*Translation: Jean-Marc & Randy Lofficier*

*A volume of* Tales of the Shadowmen *would not be complete without a good old fashioned rip-roaring Eastern yarn, harking back to the days of Rudyard Kipling, Robert E. Howard and John Buchan. Micah Harris and his collaborator, Loston Wallace, team up their own hero, Blaylock, with the indomitable French journalist and occasional secret agent Joseph Rouletabille to take us to the mountains of Samaria where they will face one of the most evil men in History...*

## Micah S. Harris & Loston Wallace: *Meeting with the Mir Beg*

*Jerusalem, Samaria 1917*

### 1.

Their hooves spewing up earth in their wake, the horses propelled the two men astride them toward their destination.

Looming before them in the Samarian night, frosted by moonlight, the mountain Gerizim with its plateau for a peak, littered with remnants of temples and sanctuaries: Samaritan, Greek, and Christian.

Gerizim's summit was where they were headed. Though some still held the mountain itself holy, reverence did not draw them there. The two men intended that a dangerous weapon not come into German hands and add to the atrocities wrecked upon soldiers in this war to end all wars. That was the common goal.

But the American? He wanted something else as well. He wanted revenge.

A third man, dressed in black hooded cloak, and also on horseback, appeared upon the horizon. His black robe and hood and black horse all but rendered him unperceivable. He carried with him his rifle and a small mortar, as well as a gun the world had not yet seen. Through field glasses he watched the two. In addition there were saddle bags that bore nothing else than something that could turn the Great War.

He was perpendicular to the two who rode together. His megaphone was useless to him—he could draw unwanted attention and bring desert bandits down upon himself. Readying his riffle, he jabbed his spurs into the sides of his mount, and shot off to intercept them.

### 2.

"I am here for my government to seek out some element here called 'the Mir Beg,'" the young, blond French man said.

"Find the man called Blaylock," said Emir the leper with a low voice and a perfect British accent. He sat beside a parched-until-it-had-cracked dirt road just outside Jerusalem. "During the heat of the day, he usually takes refuge in a tavern called *The Three Blades*."

"When is it *not* the heat of the day in this place?" Rouletabille, the young Frenchman, asked and wiped the back of his neck with a handkerchief

Emir ignored his remark and Rouletabille suddenly blushed at how trivial his complaint was compared to that which could be made by the man in his shadow. Emir's leprous arms, swathed where they otherwise would be exposed by his garment, and the way he bowed his head to be sure that his hood concealed as much of his disfigured face as possible, made Rouletabille think the poor man's condition must be especially extreme. A terrible fate, he thought, to befall an agent in service of his country.

If Emir had taken offense at Rouletabille's comment, it was not evident in his tone as he continued: "If he proves incorrigible, you only need one word to convince him. You know it already from the intelligence document you read: *Belasco*."

"*Belasco?*"

The beggar mutely nodded. Rouletabille tossed him two coins to maintain the pretense, and then, with a slight tip of his broad brimmed hat, which protected his face from the desert sun, began to make his way along the dusty streets of Ottoman-occupied Jerusalem. He sighed, thinking of the casinos, mansions, and passenger ships to which his former journeys had taken him compared to that of his current situation. He especially thought of ice cubes clinking together in a droplet covered glass. He swatted at the irritating flies intent on buzzing and crawling over his face, or over the hand that he had lifted to brush them away. He wished he had brought a brim with mosquito netting or a bee-keeper's head attire.

The tavern offered respite from the mid-afternoon sun, but little from the heat. Bodies of Ottoman Turks and Arabs pressed close upon him, bodies that had never experienced a daily bath. Although Rouletabille had very much wished otherwise, the stench out doors from the nearby citadel moat, in which bobbed carcasses of donkeys and dogs, was still pungent inside. And now, added to it, was this reeking from the pores of devoured Middle Eastern foods.

He struggled to the bar—though not for alcohol since Islam prohibited it—to inquire of a burly Arab on its other side, first, if he spoke English, and when this was answered in the affirmative, where he could find one "Blaylock"—he had been informed this was a favorite haunt of his.

The Arab's lips peeled open to expose large, yellow teeth. "Are you sure you want to meet him, young sahib? That Blaylock, he can be a devil."

"Quite sure. I could use a devil about now," Rouletabille said. "It would be an answer to prayer."

The Arab nodded toward a table set in a nook of the far wall, one in position so that Blaylock could see anyone who entered the tavern before they had a chance to see him. There, Rouletabille saw a rangy proportioned man of thirty or so. He wore earth colors: a dark green shirt of the current fashion in the West and khaki jodhpurs with calf-high brown leather boots. He had taken off a colorfully stripped robe which was spread over the back of his chair. Rouletabille noted that Blaylock's skin had been burned so brown by a merciless Middle Eastern sun that, in that robe and the accompanying hood slipped over his brown hair, but showing his beard, he would not be easily recognized as anything other than one indigenous to the area.

In contrast, Rouletabille wore a short-sleeved white shirt with Arrow collar unbuttoned against the heat. His pleated trousers were also decidedly Western, as were his street shoes. He was blond with a fair complexion. He and Blaylock could not have been in higher contrast.

As Rouletabille tentatively came closer, he addressed the seated man:

"Monsieur Blaylock?" he said, extending his hand and then withdrawing it when it became obvious that the man he believed to be the one he sought was not going to shake it. "I am Joseph Rouletabille. My business is in regard to the Great War in which we are currently embroiled..."

"Only thing I'm embroiled in is this heat," the man said, wiping across his forehead with a handkerchief that looked like, sometime in the antediluvian past, it once may have been white. He then resumed cutting into pieces the pastry of thin *phyllo* dough he was preparing to eat.

"Oh," Rouletabille said to the man, whose American accent was as strong as that of Rouletabille's French. "You still subscribe to a separatist philosophy, and haven't followed the rest of your country when they changed theirs."

"Sure. Why not?" the man said, as he lifted the pastry on his blade to his mouth and bit it off.

"What is it that you do here?"

"*Here*? Eat. Drink."

"I mean, here in *Jerusalem*, and, I suppose, the general environs of the Holy Land. Samaria perhaps? I'm told you may be able to help me contact the 'Mir Beg' whom I feel are..."

At a table nearby, an Arab overheard and looked worriedly at the Frenchman. He made some sign to ward off evil and exited the tavern as fast as he could.

"What's wrong with him?" Rouletabille said.

The man grinned. "Because, having said the unspeakable name out loud, you risk making him appear."

"The Mir Beg? What exactly is this Mir B..."

With the hard toe of his boot, the man pushed a chair on the other side of the table out from under it. "Quit saying that so loud. And have a seat. I'll explain things to you."

"But are you Blaylock?" Rouletabille asked as he was seated.

"Yes, I am," the man said and leaned over the table, speaking in a notably hushed voice. "The Mir Beg you're so keen on is the vicar of the Peacock King, the Yezidees's god, Melek Taus. The 'Black Pope' is only how most Westerners hear of him and only how they must speak of him. The other way is as 'Melek Taus.' The Black Pope is the right hand of Shaitan, Melek Taus's true name, forbidden to be spoken by Westerners, Arabs, and Jews. This is because others outside their cult easily confuse 'Shaitan' with 'Satan.' The Yezidees argue that the two are in no way related. To my thinking, Melek Taus is the embodiment of an almost Oriental dualism. The Mir Beg, however, definitely comes down on the dark side."

"Well, thanks for clearing that up. We had thought that the Mir Beg was some group that would help me in my mission to secure a natural resource here that the Germans are trying to obtain. Now, it seems, I have only you."

Blaylock threw his head back and laughed. "I don't know what form the Mir Beg takes in our world, and I'm not the least bit eager to learn that first hand. I have to stay alive, you see. I have my own old scores to deal with. So, go on. Go find someone else to help settle your hash.'"

"Please, reconsider, Monsieur. Allow me to tell you more about why I am here. Our intelligence recently intercepted a message from the Krupp's weapon factory. It concerned shells they had prepared. They were waiting for their partner in this intended slaughter to give them the element with which the shells were to be filled. This was some type of gas –a new type of gas—which would be unleashed on our troops.

"Krupp's part was only to house the gas in the shells. Their partner was going to harvest the natural materials that created it. His men are even now headed to take control of their location: the top of Mount Gerizim."

"And you and I are supposed to secure it before they get there and then turn them back? That's the former location of the ancient Samaritan temple," Blaylock said. "There's nothing up there but ruins, pieces of an old church, remains of a fortress. Why has no one noticed this natural resource until now?"

The Frenchman shrugged. "It has become the topic *du jour* of the occult fraternity. Their agents are always out there gathering old scrolls, reading runes on whalebones… Enochian language in pamphlets dating from Elizabeth… before they ever have a chance to become known to the world at large. And if they reveal that there is a treasure to be found, or a power to be gained from what they have to say, then there are those who *will* have it.

"A recent discovery was a codex purported to be the depository of the wisdom of Simon the sorcerer, also known as Simon Magus. He apparently at least appeared to have some kind of power, but the Book of Acts, where we read of the historic Simon, gives no details as to what it was. The spread of the early church into Samaria there put an end to whatever public sway he had.

"This codex he left behind him, apparently revealed the nature and source of that power…"

"This gas out of Mount Gerizim," Blaylock said.

"This codex of Simon's explains how he discovered it, and reveals that he was fully aware that it was natural. But he rightly surmised the simple Samaritan peasants would not understand it as such. While the codex of Simon gave the nature and general location of this gas source, the last page had been ripped away. Probably for the mutilator to possess the information by him alone."

"Interesting story there, Monsieur, but I hope you'll understand why I still have to say *non*. I have my own battle I'm waiting to complete and getting killed in your project would put a serious crimp in my plans."

"Very well, Monsieur. But before I leave, you should know one more thing…"

"Oh? And what would that be?"

"Regardless of what you might think, you *have* a vested interest in seeing Krupp's partner, the one who is to deliver the crimson mist for their shells, fail."

Blaylock leaned forward, his eyes narrowing. "Who is he?"

"Belasco."

### 3.

Blaylock had his own horse and obtained another from a man whom he had come across one night, staked out spread-eagle and naked, about to be flayed by some Syrian bandits. Rouletabille was impressed with how fluent Blaylock was with the language.

"How did you come to speak Aramaic as a second language so well?" the Frenchman asked as they began their ride to Samaria with the sun hanging low in the western sky.

Blaylock shrugged, "I've always heard the best way to learn a language is to live where they speak it. You pitch your tent here for three years and you'd pick it up, too. You handle English very well. Do you speak any more languages—other than English?"

"My work requires some knowledge of different tongues. I know enough Italian and Russian to get by. I do much better with Spanish. And speaking of Spain, just what exactly has this Belasco fellow done to you?"

"What *hasn't* he done? He's had a vendetta against my family that goes back for generations. When we were children and we first heard the adults talking about him, they passed him off as inhabiting the same plane of reality as Santa Claus and the Sandman. It's only later, when you're older, that your father calls you into his study, closes the doors, and tells you that Belasco is very real and gives you the evidence. If you respond to this revelation the right way, you are then acknowledged as having become a man in the family—with all the privileges and responsibilities. Killing Belasco being both."

For a while, no one spoke. Then Blaylock said: "He has a cousin who probably was the one who informed him of this codex by Simon Magus. Emeric Belasco is into the occult deep. Yeah, I'm betting he's the same guy who tore

94

out that page with the instructions on what Simon Magus had cooked up and gave it to Belasco. That would explain how he learned the secret of this power.

"Emeric's group practices sexual degradation as a form of worship. It's also rumored that any babies that are born from these unions are cut open while still alive and their still steaming entrails used in divination. Last I heard, he's getting ready to build a mansion to house his activities."

*4.*

Now night embraced the desert, and the mysterious rider in black was upon Rouletabille and Blaylock before they realized it, the sound of the intruder's horse's galloping hidden under the cacophony of their own. Blaylock was the first to notice him.

"Rouletabille! Trouble!" Blaylock shouted as he reared his steed, his hand already on his rifle. Rouletabille followed suit and by the time he had turned his horse about and withdrawn his pistol the mystery rider had come to a halt almost three yards away.

With one hand, Blaylock cocked his rifle, then trained it on the stranger in black, his face hidden within the folds of his hood. The man's own rifle was at his side, but pointed toward the ground. He made no move.

"Who are you? What do you want? "Blaylock asked in Aramaic.

"As for what I want, Blaylock," the stranger said in perfect English with an American accent, "you already have a general idea of that." There was mirth in his voice.

Blaylock huffed and put the safety back on his gun. "You keep practicing your theatricals outside the theater, and you are going to get killed," he said.

"And have you forgotten me so soon, Monsieur Rouletabille?" the man said, now speaking with a British accent.

"Emir the leper? This is the informant, who told me where to find you," Rouletabille said, and stared at Blaylock. "You know each other?"

"Oh, you know him too, chances are," Blaylock said. "Ever hear of Houdini?"

"The escape artist of international renown?" asked Rouletabille .

Taking the cue that had been handed him, Houdini flipped back his hood. "The same!" he said, and grinned. He scratched the scalp of his black hair with one hand. "I do believe there are lice in this garment. Do either of you have the same problem? No? Well, I had to get some attire quickly, couldn't be picky. Intelligence was shared with me about the German's seeking to harvest Mount Gerizim's crimson gas. And that was something I could not allow.

"So I came to Jerusalem. Knowing that a French Agent employed in our cause was also on the case. I made it a point to find Monsieur Rouletabille immediately."

95

"But why did you not introduce yourself and together we could have gone directly to Blaylock? Time is short..."

"Agreed. Which is why I needed that time to find out just how far things had progressed. Then I would rendezvous with you on this route which is the quickest to Samaria. Blaylock would be sure to take it."

"How are you so familiar with the Holy Land, by the way?" Blaylock asked.

Houdini smiled again. "I know enough. About Jerusalem. And Samaria. And Mount Gerizim—and the location of its secret."

"You *know* the secret source of this gas? Why have you stayed mum about something that could be invaluable to our side in this war?" Rouletabille asked.

"I have my own plans for it," Houdini said. "And a good magician never reveals his tricks. Unfortunately, a not-so-good Samaritan had noticed my repeatedly coming and going. I tried to be as furtive as I could, but even I can't be expected to catch on to everything that is going on around me.

"I caught him on the mountain watching what I was doing, and we struggled. He knocked me out, and by the time I came around, he was gone with my notebook. I knew he'd probably have to find someone who reads English to see if it was worth anything. Then they would seek out somebody who might find the information in my book valuable It passed through several hands until eventually it reached an agent of an illegal dealer in weapons at war time..."

"Belasco...," Blaylock said and the moonlight shone like sparks in his eyes.

"...who made a deal with the Krupp's factory for those shells to house the gas," Rouletabille said, finishing his thought.

"I have brought a modest armory with me to help our fight against Belasco's men," Houdini said. He handed Blaylock a sheathed weapon. What he uncovered was a strange rifle which loaded on the top in a circular holder of ammunition.

"Your family's name does indeed carry some weight," Houdini said to Blaylock. "I wouldn't have been able to get this prototype otherwise. They're calling it the 'Thompson gun.' You can hold on to that." He patted one side of the saddle bags. "As for me, I've brought a mortar which will fire what's in here."

"And what *is* in there?" Rouletabille asked.

"Look, let's quit jawin' and beat the bastard's men to the top of that Mountain so we can pick 'em off, as they ride up," Blaylock said, tugging on his horse's reins.

"I knew you'd enjoy the opportunity to derail one of his operations," Houdini said with a crooked grin. "But gentlemen, there's something more I need to tell you. *Now* it's about to get interesting!"

5.

They resumed the journey to Samaria; Mount Gerizim continued its eternal looming over the city of stone beneath it.

"Belasco has proven most ingenious in obtaining his operatives for the taking of Mount Gerizim," Houdini said. "They are a militant sect of the Yezidees…"

"What? How is that possible?" Blaylock asked. "The *militant* Yezidees? Those guys are something like the Kali worshippers in Bombay, and they have no use for outsiders… Jew, Christian, or Arab. For *anyone* other than themselves it is even forbidden to call the entity they worship by his true name of 'Shaitan' on pain of death."

"This is incredible! How would it be possible for Belasco's agent to even communicate with this cult as a white man and be allowed to speak to them? What if he slipped up and said 'Shaitan'?" Rouletabille asked.

" 'Shaitan' may be designated by the uninitiated as 'Melek Taus'—the blue peacock king," Blaylock said.

Rouletabille nodded. "Believe it or not, I have seen such a peacock represented in a fresco on the wall in the ruins of a church in Plaincourault."

"A *Christian* church?" Blaylock asked. Rouletabille nodded. "That *is* strange."

"Melek Taus can only transpose into his physical form in one of the seven tower dedicated to him," Houdini said. "They are links in a dark chain that stretches as far as Manchuria to Mount Lalesh. Communications between them flash from one to the other in evil relays."

He continued: "But now the major one of those strongholds of Shaitan, the one of nearby Syria, has been destroyed by the British during the war, and there will be no rebuilding it there, not while the British occupy the area for who knows how long.

"So Shaitan must have a new tower. To this end, Shaitan's hand on Earth, called 'the Black Pope' by Westerners, but known to the Yezidees themselves as the Mir Beg, has done what has not been done in ages: he's descending his tower… after the inhabitants of its location in Baadri saw for six, unholy days dark clouds the color of slate churning and flashing with lightening at its pinnacle, accompanied by a rain of blood."

"And Belasco has convinced this 'Mir Beg'—some impersonating puppet of his—to build the new tower on Mount Gerizim," Blaylock said. "Once they dedicate an icon of Melek Taus where the Samaritan temple once stood, the holy place of Yahweh will be defiled."

"And guarded by these feared Yezidee extremists, who's going to come challenging Belasco for that mountain and what it holds," Rouletabille said. "Life for the people of the little village of Nablus will be hard from now on in the terrible shadow of that tower," he mused with pity in his voice.

"Yeah. And how does he plan to stay chums enough with the Yezidees for them to allow him to harvest the gas after it's dedicated to Melek Taus? That would seem like desecration," Blaylock said. "

"Once he has secured occupation of Gerizim, your friend Belasco will turn on his pawns," Houdini said. "I don't need to tell *you* that. You know his modus operandi, Blaylock."

"Yeah," the adventurer said after a moment's silence, "a lot better than I wish. Well, let's quit jawin' and beat the bastard's men to the top of that Mountain, so we can pick 'em off as they ride up."

"I knew you'd enjoy the opportunity to derail one of Belasco's operations," Houdini said and grinned.

"Oh, I want more than that: I want to hit the Mir Beg so hard that Belasco feels it!"

6.

Racing through the dark desert, they at last came to the foot of Mount Gerizim and the ancient city of Nablus that huddled there. The moon was now low. Passing around the town, they began to climb the mountain, forced to move at a slower gait as their horses picked over the terrain in order to find safe purchase. The mountain was a small one, but its ascent was marked by low shrubs and loose stones. Slowly climbing was at odds with their need to be atop the mountain before sunrise in order to minimize the chance of any early risers seeing them, and thus introducing the possibility that they might lose the element of surprise. To avoid this, they semi-circled the mountain so that it was between them and Nablus before they began the climb, their horses' hooves carefully picked their way up the mountain. As they ascended, Rouletabille fancied he could see above them the lost Samaritan temple in the starlight still dazzling the mountain's plateau summit.

Finally, they mounted the wide plateau that was Gerizim's peak. They passed by the columns of the Byzantine church ruins. Shin-high rows of large ancient brick riddled the landscape, looking like abandoned masonry projects.

They were headed for the small square tower with a dome partially atop it: this, too, was a remnant of the Byzantine church, as were the concentric, uneven stone walls that surrounded it. They climbed up the tower. Below them were the jumbled buildings of Nablus. From here they commanded a view which went far beyond the city, one from where they could see the Yezidees coming literally miles away. They held the high ground. But their weapons for far off warfare were few: the Thompson machine gun prototype that Houdini had brought, and the small mortar he was showing the others for the first time.

"Where's your ammunition for that?" Rouletabille asked.

Houdini grinned and stretched his arms wide and turned in a circle. "What surrounds us: nothing less than the secret of Simon the Sorcerer."

Rouletabille and Blaylock looked around the empty landscape and saw nothing but the remains of the Byzantine church and what traces were left of the dead city that once had surrounded the Samaritan temple.

"What in the world are you talking about, Houdini?" Blaylock asked.

"Among the minerals on this plain on which we find ourselves are two types that, if combined, chemically produce a red cloud in reaction."

"If they lie side by side on this plain, why is it not swathed with this red fog even now?" Rouletabille asked.

"A third mineral, a natural inhibiter, separates them. When removed, this mist initially creeps along the ground like that of the dry ice a stage magician would employ and then begins to rise. Those who breathe its fumes hallucinate. There is a general sense of disorientation, and they become subject to suggestion.

"*This* was the secret of Simon Magus, 'Simon the Sorcerer,' though I haven't a clue how he learned it. Perhaps the old priests of the Samaritan temple cult knew it and left a record of it that Simon was able to translate, or have translated for him? At any rate, it gave him a powerful influence over the Samaritans in the first century. But, like all I've encountered in the present day who make claims of supernatural power, he now stands revealed as a sham and bamboozler."

"What are we supposed to dig these minerals up with? I didn't see you bring any shovels. And how exactly do we identify each mineral needed for the mist?" Blaylock asked. "Isn't this cutting it all rather close?"

Houdini nodded at two of the saddle bags on his horse. "Harvested already. I've discovered the secret, remember? These are in shells; that's what the mortar's for. The two combustive minerals are kept in separate chambers of the shell but come together with the explosion. When the Mir Beg and Yezidees begin to try and take the mountain, they will instead find that they no longer know which way is up. And if they believe it a *haunted* mountain, they're not likely to return, even at the prodding of the Mir Beg."

Blaylock smiled. "And Belasco doesn't get his gas for the battlefield."

"Well," Rouletabille said, "we are digging ourselves in deeper in an increasingly bad spot. But if anyone will be able extricate us from a difficult situation, it would be *you*, Monsieur Houdini."


7.


First came the trilling, wild cries tossed ahead into the air that were the harbingers of the warriors who issued them. They turned the heads of the early risers to the horizon, and then they first saw the crowd rushing toward them. The men of Nablus gathered their wives and children inside their stone homes, barred the doors and pulled out their guns, knives and scimitars.

Having fully expected to be vastly outnumbered, Rouletabille, Houdini, and Blaylock knew that their greatest advantage was surprise. It was also the one they would lose rather quickly if they didn't utilize it early in the raid. Whether they lived or died depended how much of a hallucinating miasma Houdini could create before the Yezidees gained the mountain.

Lying flat on their bellies, stretched prone, the three men peered over the mountain at the mass of killers sweeping toward them, threatening to flood mountain and inundate them. Blaylock had past dealings with this fanatic Yezidee sect, and he knew that mob would pass over them, slitting their throats as they rode by, then trampling under hoof whatever life was left in the bodies of he and his comrades.

The Yezidee mob swarmed through Nablus without taking spoil of it, because the mountain rising behind the village would be their spoil. The horses slowed as they approached Gerizim which necessity required their ascent be a slow one.

Rouletabille nodded at the mortar set near the plateau's lip. "How far are you going to allow them to come before you fire the first shell?" he asked Houdini.

"How high would you say this mountain is," Houdini asked Blaylock.

Blaylock shrugged. "I was estimating on the ride up here. I'd say two and a half thousand feet."

"This is a short range mortar. I'm going to have to let them get a lot closer than we'd like. But I have to be careful not to overshoot"

The Yezidees' horses were picking their way up over the rough terrain with its loose stones. They were not quite half up the mountain when Blaylock said, "My advice would be to go ahead and fire while the wind is in our favor instead of continuing to wait."

Houdini nodded and fired the mortar. The echo from the shot reverberated over the mountains. The shell struck just before the front line of Yezidees. With a bright flash and loud crack, a red mist immediately began boiling out of the broken shell. At the explosion, the horses closest to where it landed reared and whinnied frantically, shaking their heads. The horses of the Yezidees were so close to each other that the front line horses' reaction caught and passed through the throng so that even horses in the rear were startled though they had no idea at what.

The leader of this band had recovered enough to lift his rifle and fire. Immediately, a piece of earth leapt at Rouletabille's face. He shouted in response and rose to his knees: he had just missed taking a bullet to his head.

Then Rouletabille felt a powerful shove to the front of his shoulder. At first, he was at a loss to explain where it had come from. And then he saw his shoulder was bleeding. Blaylock noticed it, too, and pushed him back to the ground.

"Let me take a look at your wound," Blaylock, who lay beside Rouletabille, said. More bullets whistled by, pelting the plain as the Yezidees below continued to fire.

"Wound?" Houdini asked.

"The odds of at least one of us taking a bullet were against us with this big a mob," Blaylock said as the air continue to whistle about and beyond, bullets ricocheting off centuries old stone bricks of the Byzantine ruins. "Looks like Rouletabille drew the short straw. Can you unbutton your shirt enough to pull it down over the shoulder?" he said, again addressing the Frenchman.

"Well?" Rouletabille said after Blaylock had been looking at and gingerly touching the area of his wound while looking at it in silence for a minute.

"You lucked up: only a flesh wound," Blaylock said. "Go ahead and pull up your shirt. If we make it through this, I know Auqbar the barber in Jerusalem. He'll fix you up." Then, noticing the bullets had stopped while he tended to Rouletabille, he said, "What's going on down there, Houdini?"

Below, the gaseous scarlet clouds had risen about the Yezidees' heads, irritating their throats, nostrils, and eyes. They had stopped shooting to allow themselves to put their arms over their noses or swat the air in front of their face to make the smoke part and let in clean air.

"It's show time!" Houdini said, peering over the plateau's edge. "Take the megaphone. Blaylock and say to them in Aramaic what I'm going to say in English…"

From the top of the mountain, Blaylock used the megaphone to shout out into the billowing red cloud below him what Houdini had said:

"You have presumed to intrude upon the djinn of the mountain! His vengeance is turned loose upon you! Flee the mountain lest he rend you as paper! He tears the mountain and hurls it down upon you!"

Through the red vapor the Yezidees looked up and saw the mountainside buckle, and earth and dislodged stones rushing down upon them. Smaller rocks skipped quickly above the moving rubble and hurled ahead of it, seeming to launch themselves at the Yezidees, who, atop their horses, ducked their heads and wheeled their mounts about.

"The ground opens up to receive you!" the amplified voice announced.

Now the mountain seemed to part before them. The new crevice yawned and belched flame.

The leader of the Yezidees held fast. He was not long in realizing that, despite what they were seeing, no stones had actually struck them and the land beneath them was still firm.

"Stop you misbegotten sons of a lame dog!" the Yezidee leader shouted to his men. "This is but illusion! Move ahead! Any deserter will be beheaded! Follow me and move ahead! We will take this mountain for Melek Taus, who is greater than this djinn who has shown himself but a deceiver and must thus possess no real power."

The Yezidees turned their horses about and resumed their ascent, moving through the crimson fog and up into clear air. Then they, like their leader, also were disabused of the belief that there was any real threat.

"Great is Melek Taus, Shaitan, of the Yezidees!" they shouted as one.

"Please tell me you're not out of tricks," Rouletabille said, first looking at Houdini and then Blaylock.

Blaylock's eyes narrowed, his lips pressed together. Then he smiled and said, "How about the same idea, different words? They've moved out of the red fog; fire another mortar shell, Houdini. This trick isn't played out yet!"

The Yezidees were brought to a collective halt as another shell plowed into the earth just before them, and then it, too, exploded and immediately seethed more of the crimson mist. Horses again reared, jerking their necks around so that their riders had to pull hard on the reins to keep them from turning and running back down the mountain.

Blaylock smiling, raised the megaphone to his mouth and shouted out in Aramaic:

"Melek Taus rejects your worship! You are not found pure in your devotion. Behold! The peacock king comes among you to render his judgment!"

The Yezidees screamed as a giant, blue peacock with its tail feathers in full fan took shape in their midst in the crimson fog. Its head darted down and seemed to pick up one of their number. It threw back its head and gobbled the Yezidee down in a series of quick jerks of its neck.

They screamed, each of the peacock god's followers, in fear that they would be next. Up from the mob came the cry, "Flee great Shaitan! Turn back, so that we are not struck down!"

Then, another shell fell, this time landing *among* them. Horses and men at that spot were seared by the fire of its explosion. The horses reared, sending some of the riders tumbling to the ground. The animals snorted and whinnied shrilly as, along with another uncoiling red cloud, shrapnel flying up from the ruptured shell lacerated the exposed flesh of man and beast.

And above it, in the crimson haze, the giant blue peacock king loomed, its eyes narrowed austerely down upon the warriors as if trying to decide who would be next.

The Yezidees' horses were reeling again, dark eyes bulging, and this time their riders let the animals have their way. In their haste they forgot the loose terrain over which they had carefully picked on the way up. Some of the horses fell over on their sides, dislodging their riders who slid with the loose mountain terrain down the mountainside. Of those who were still mounted and followed in retreat, *their* horses stumbled over the now-riderless animals before them, dislodging their riders from their saddles and to the earth. They all tumbled and slid together like a human avalanche down the side of the mountain.

When they reached the bottom, and those who had fallen had recovered and mounted their horses, their leader shouted something in Aramaic and the mob followed him in retreat.

"We've won the day!" Rouletabille said, as along with Houdini and Blaylock, he watched the Yezidees' exit. "Do you have any idea what they saw?"

"Their god," Blaylock said. "Other than that, whatever fears they have concerning him would be what they would see."

"Wait!" Houdini said, looking into the distance. He put his hand above his eyes to shade them. "They've stopped... and now... it looks like..."

"...they're coming back," Rouletabille said, as he and Blaylock joined Houdini in scoping out the returning band of Yezidees.

The group was crossing the land below just as fast as they had fled across it minutes ago. When they came to the mountain's foot, they stopped, and then began to part to allow one of their crowd to ride out ahead from them on his black horse.

"What's that he's wearing on his head?" Blaylock said. Using the field glasses, he looked for any clue as to how this man might have turned their enemies back with intent, no doubt, of reattempting to take the mountain. He also suspected that he was the source of their new confidence.

Blaylock's jaw dropped at what he saw. He all but shoved the field glasses into Rouletabille's hands.

"What is it?" Rouletabille asked, raising the field glasses.

"The Mir Beg," Blaylock said.

## 8.

His headdress of blue peacock feathers rose high above his bare scalp. The face was only half exposed, the area from the bridge of the nose down was covered with part of his cloak which was ebony. The exposed nose, cheeks and forehead were painted white. And over all his pale face were rendered, in black, Arabic characters and strange symbols.

He looked up directly at Rouletabille and pulled away the cloak over the bottom of his face, revealing all there was white as well and also etched were the mystic Arabic characters. His lips were black and turned into a smile. When he opened that mouth to shout something to the Yezidees, the revealed tongue was also black. When he spoke, it was as though the words came from a small pit of darkness that had opened in his face.

The Mir Beg's body was solid, sturdy, and tall as he sat erect in his saddle. Then with a cry the Mir Beg began to climb the mountain. His black horse was sure-footed, and its rider who drove him on relentlessly and seemingly immune to the loose terra that had so discomfited the Yezidees.

"The way he's moving, he'll make it through any of the crimson mist before it's risen enough for him to breathe it in," Blaylock said.

"Still, a projectile might disconcert his horse," Rouletabille said. "He could be thrown…"

"Or the horse might simply rear and be brought back under control," Houdini said. "Did I mention I have only one more shell of the stuff? No? Well, then, you'll understand why this shot has to count… or our heads will be dangling off his saddle horn as he trots back to his dark tower in Baadri."

Blaylock said, "Then we're going to have to let him get up here and fire it at him at close range."

"Wait, look at that, look at that," Rouletabille said, tugging at Blaylock's sleeve.

He and Houdini looked with Rouletabille down to the bottom of the mountain. As their leader ascended it, his followers were moving around its base.

"They're going to come at us front and back," Houdini said. "But I've got the Mir Beg to concentrate on. Take care of the Yezidees, boys. I'll need to be in position with the mortar to let loose on the Mir Beg. Hand me the megaphone, Blaylock. I'll be needing your services again."

"How's that shoulder, Rouletabille?" Blaylock asked as he picked up the prototype of the Thompson gun. "Are you still able to rest a rifle there?"

"I can do it," Rouletabille said as he checked his own pistol, then, satisfied, took up Houdini's rifle, "It's just a little tender."

"Let's go then!" Blaylock said and he and Rouletabille began running toward another side of the plateau, hoping the Yezidees had not yet begun to climb.

They found them not yet at the halfway point where they would begin their ascent.

Rouletabille aimed his rifle, grunting as he pushed its butt against his sore shoulder. He chose to focus his attention on the gang beneath him and pushed the pain back into a deep recess of his mind.

He fired.

The Yezidees who were not struck watched the first of their own lurch and fall to the ground. Only then, like an afterthought, did the sound of the gun's firing register, and as that sound reverberated between the mountains, they looked up and immediately raised their rifles.

Then they immediately sprinted for the shelter of some near-by huge boulders.

Rouletabille was already firing again. Another Yezidee took a bullet, this one to the head, and he spun before going to the ground.

Then Blaylock let loose with the Thompson gun on the running Yezidees before they could gain the boulders. Bullet instantaneously followed bullet, gnawing the limbs and bodies of those struck. Denuded bone shown through their rent garments. For others, the Thompson gun's chattered played like a malignant music to which its victims danced.

Yezidee bullets were now pelting about Rouletabille, some of them pinging and ricocheting off ancient masonry that riddled the plain. He and Blaylock fell flat to their bellies, rising at the waist to take a shot and then flatten back out.

Rouletabille and Blaylock had killed the first men while they held the element of surprise, picking them off quickly enough to take out the majority. By the time the Yezidees had regained composure and were returning fire, the number of the contingent the Mir Beg sent to take the mountain from another avenue was severely depleted.

Blaylock was firing off the last of the Thompson Gun's bullets, when a bullet from the enemy chipped free a small piece of an ancient stone left from the Samaritan temple. This bit of stone flew back, striking Blaylock in the back of his head. He dropped, stunned, face down to the ground.

"Blaylock!" Rouletabille shouted and ceased firing. Houdini looked their way at Rouletabille's cry; he had planned for Blaylock to be at his side by now, ready to speak hypnotic suggestions in Aramaic by megaphone, just as they had successfully done before. But Houdini saw Blaylock now on the ground...

Rouletabille looked down the mountainside. The Yezidee band had begun its climb up. Deciding the more advantageous success would be to kill or neutralize in some manner this Mir Beg, he let his rifle drop and abandoned it along with the Thompson. Although it was agony to his wounded shoulder, he partially lifted Blaylock by his arms and drug him on his stomach as far away as he could from the edge of the mountain to where he hoped might be out of the path of their enemies. Otherwise they would trample him as they crested the mountain and rode onto the plain.

He reluctantly left his comrade and, with pistol ready, sprinted to where Houdini waited...

...when the large, tenebrous shape that was the Mir Beg on his horse swooped in between them.

Wide-eyed at the Mir Beg's sudden appearance, Rouletabille staggered back, looking up at the embodied darkness. The Mir Beg had crested the mountain and come onto the plateau while Rouletabille's and Blaylock's attention had been distracted by their chore. He rode tall in the saddle, unsheathing his huge scimitar from his side, the metal ringing.

But Rouletabille had drawn his pistol.

He fired and the Mir Beg deflected his bullet with his sword, which then came back and sheared off the gun barrel to a stub.

Again the curved sword sliced through the air, this time at Rouletabille's neck. He ducked, the sword's edge only nicking his ear in the passing. He then leapt back, and, as the Mir Beg brought his steed around, Rouletabille saw something that surprised him...

But then the Mir Beg's horse reared and was pummeling Rouletabille about the shoulders and head with its front hooves. He lost what was left of his pistol as he dropped and rolled, always just one roll ahead of a trampling as the Mir Beg followed.

As Rouletabille had sprinted for Houdini and been cut off by the Mir Beg, Yezidees were beginning to come over the plateau's edge from both sides. Houdini turned his mortar on first one group of the Yezidees and then the other, hoping to continue bluffing them back long enough until Blaylock and Rouletabille could offer more resistance.

One Yezidee, however, had made it as far as where Blaylock lay, his lips parted in a smile at the man who laid face down on the ground, and drawing his sword he knelt beside him.

The sword was raised back over the Yezidee's head, poised for the fatal descent, when Blaylock rolled over. He caught the descending arms by their wrists, bringing the blade to a sudden stop. Now Blaylock began to push up against the leverage of his enemy, not only pushing back the hands that gripped the sword hilt, but raising himself.

Seeing that he had almost made it up to the kneeling position, the Yezidee, sweating with the effort, bore down with extra effort and bent Blaylock back toward the ground.

But the Yezidee had lost strength in the effort to counter his victim's unexpected resistance. Blaylock soon regained the inches he had lost and gained more. Now he was in a rising crouch, pressing the Yezidee down. His hair was dripping sweat that trickled into and stung his eyes. He did not blink. Not once.

Blaylock's face was flushing and a blue vein bulged on his forehead. The Yezidee knew if he made it, Blaylock would show him no mercy. He strained to push Blaylock back to his knees, but he made the mistake of looking Blaylock in the face.

He saw resolution emanating from his eyes like heat waves off the desert sand. This expressed a will to win against all odds, something that had been forged and tempered not only in the deserts of Palestine, but before that, Manchuria, and the Himalayas and the Atlantic Ocean. This man was unstoppable. This frightened the Yezidee—he had, after all, expected to have decapitated him and moved on long ago.

He released his hold and the coiled muscles of Blaylock's legs propelled him upward, his fist, with the push from his thighs and lower back behind it, smashed into the Yezidee's head.

While the man was still knocked out, Blaylock, knowing his Thompson gun was unclaimable now, took his attacker's sword. The other Yezidees began to move in on him, though tentatively after what they had just witnessed Blaylock do to one of their number. Rifles were raised, but they seemed uneager to fire. Blaylock did not know how to take their hesitance. Then he saw they were looking behind him. He risked turning to see...

...and Blaylock laid eyes up close upon the legendary Mir Beg. He indeed appeared a demon mounted atop its black horse. He also saw that the Mir Beg was trying to trample Rouletabille, who was rolling away, but every time he started to rise, he received a kick or dodged an attempted one by the horse.

Blaylock sprinted for the Mir Beg, who was still intent on torturing Rouletabille.

In seconds he had crossed the space, and by the time the Mir Beg realized he was under attack, Blaylock's boot was atop the Mir Beg's in the latter's stirrup, Blaylock lifting himself so that, eye-to-eye with the Mir Beg, he thrust his fist into his adversary's temple. The Mir Beg immediately struck back at Blaylock's face. Blaylock's head recoiled, but he did not lose his hold on the saddle horn with one hand, while the other came back in a series of quick hits to the Mir Beg's head in something resembling a one-fisted boxer's drill. He punched so quickly that the Mir Beg could not get in another hit of his own.

So the Mir Beg drew a knife from where he had sheathed it on his thigh...

By now Rouletabille had rejoined Houdini. The Yezidees were starting to surge forward to help their leader. They feared not to.

"Fire the shell on the Mir Beg! At his horse's feet." Rouletabille took up the megaphone. "I can handle Blaylock's part. Hurry! Those savages will be on us in less than a minute!"

Houdini fired.

The incendiary shell struck beside the Mir Beg's horse. The crimson miasma was swathing the Mir Beg, his horse, and Blaylock who had his hand clasped about the Mir Beg's wrist to push back a dagger. At the sight of the red fog rising from the shell brought the Yezidees came to a halt. They had no desire step into that mist and what it held again.

The Mir Beg would have urged his horse forward, except his struggle with Blaylock would leave him out of control. Better to finish this man off and be done before moving on. He had been told what kind of phantasms this gas could create, but his will was iron, while this unrelenting fellow would be confused and that would give the Mir Beg the opening to kill him.

Blaylock, however, grinned. A chance to whisper defeat in the very ear of his opponent would be rare. Now, still struggling for master of that knife, he shouted at the Mir Beg in Aramaic: "Your sins rise up before you! Look at the people you thought you destroyed or left alive maim! They have come for you, all of them..."

Then Blaylock realized his words were not perturbing his enemy. Was this because the Mir Beg was *not* a Yezidee in a costume but, in fact, a being from somewhere *else*?

Then Rouletabille shouted through the megaphone—in Spanish. "Come face to face with your crimes, monster; your victims rise up to accuse you!"

The Mir Beg saw taking shape in the scarlet fog soldiers with only half faces, some whom were waddling up to him on the stumps of their legs. Other skeletal soldiers marched toward him, their bare bones loose and shuffling in their uniforms, and their skulls rattling in their helmets

In the air about him seemed to hang suspended from head to foot wet men and women, little children, skins pale with the chill of ice water, their eyes staring accusingly in their blankness at him. More than one woman clutched a drowned enfant to her icy bosom…a life preserver futilely embraced one such mother and child. On the preserver was written: *Lusitania.*

And then the Mir Beg for the first time focused on Blaylock's face.

"You!" the Mir Beg shouted, his eyes wide. He no longer tried to stab him, for Blaylock's grip had grown as icy on his wrist as the chill of the Northern Atlantic. He looked again at the dead soldiers who would soon be upon them.

"Hyahhh!" the Mir Beg shouted, rearing his horse and shaking Blaylock from his mount and to the ground.

He did not attempt to trample his assailant. The only thing that was on his mind was escape, from the red gas, and the top of the Mountain of Gerizim with its fragments of temples and ancient churches, the handiwork of the long dead, who seemed ready to pierce through the crust of the earth like an insect.

"Follow me, you fools!" the Mir Beg shouted to his Yezidees as he made for the side of the mountain. His men scrambled upon their horses and followed him, all now acting regardless of the real risks of the uncertain terrain on the mountain's sides.

With the Mir Beg's retreat, Rouletabille and Houdini had run to Blaylock, who, back on his feet, was dusting himself off. "He spoke to me in English, but you were speaking Spanish, weren't you, Rouletabille?" Blaylock asked. "When you conjured up whatever demons sent him fleeing. I wonder what he saw that gave him such a shock."

Blaylock watched the remaining wisps of scarlet dissolving in the air. "Look, I don't know about you, but I need some time to process this before we discuss it. What say we go to the Inn of the Seventh Paradise back in Jerusalem? We can get a half-decent bath there and a good meal with some drinks afterward. Then we can chat it up all we want."

He expelled his breath. "I don't know your thoughts on the matter gentlemen, but I'd say we've had a hell of a day!"

9.

Twilight brought breezes across the lunar painted desert sands, and they whispered through the streets of Jerusalem. They whispered at Houdini's ear as though imparting a secret. At least it made him smile to think of it that way.

The three men had cleaned up and were on private, open terrace, seated at a table and downing some alcohol as they waited for their meal to arrive. After their hot exertions that day, they were enjoying a cool night by eating out in the open at one of the Inn of the Seventh Paradise's suites.

"How's the arm?" Blaylock asked Rouletabille, who wore a large bandage beneath his shirt.

"Not as bad as a toothache," he said.

"You'll be feeling tops soon as we get that bullet out tomorrow."

"I will not be here tomorrow," Houdini said and smiled. So, before time gets away, Monsieur Rouletabille, would you enlighten us as to how you knew the Mir Beg spoke Spanish? That he wasn't an Arab or even another Yezidee under that get up?"

"My eye is trained to search for details, gentlemen," Rouletabille said, "just as any good journalist, which is how I make a living between wars." He grinned. "I noticed the brand on his horse wasn't the same as these middle-easterners use on their horses. I had seen it before, during one of my reporting assignments at Arc day at Longchamps. We reporters were allowed to go back-stage, as it were, and see the horses before the race. There I took note of the brand marks: most were of the same design. Only one had an alternative one, a Spanish brand I was told, for that was the horse's country of origin. The mark could have been a sketch of a chess piece, or the tower of a Medieval castle with an upside down U at the bottom to represent some sort of entrance.

"Gentlemen, that was the same brand on this Mir Beg's steed. From this I reasoned he himself was of Spain and not the Middle East. It would explain why Blaylock's Aramaic had no effect on him—he didn't understand you. But when I spoke through the megaphone in Spanish, he understood very well, to judge by his reaction. Blaylock, what did he say to you?"

"He said 'you.'"

"Then he recognized you, but you have no previous connections with the Mir Beg, I'm sure? But there *is* someone, someone who conceivably enough would know your face, who deals in selling weapons at war time, who for just such a purpose, was interested in obtaining this gas to which he fell victim; someone of *Spanish* descent who has been your family's nemesis for generations…"

Blaylock looked at Houdini, Houdini looked at Blaylock, then both looked at Rouletabille who, using his good arm, was calmly downing some wine.

"Belasco!" they said.

*Our story so far: Doctor Omega and his friends were flung from his ship, the* Cosmos, *and into the time-stream. Scattered across history, they have discovered that the strange rifts that caused their situation have also released the Red Lectroids from their other-dimensional prison. Brought back together, Doctor Omega and his friends have now joined forces with the Time Brigade and the peaceful Black Lectroids to deal with the increasingly unstable rifts in space and time and discover what is behind them...*

## Travis Hiltz: *All Roads Lead to Mars*

*Russia, 1812*

It had snowed the day before. By dusk what had once been a field had been trampled and churned into a vast expanse of mud. The occasional broken wagon or discarded corpse littered the ground. There was a feeling of uneasiness amongst the platoon of soldiers gathered on the hill, overlooking the field.

Napoleon's forces were retreating through Russia; the Russian army close behind, to ensure that the French did not change their mind about returning home. Occasionally they would catch up with the French soldiers and provide a brutal reminder of how Russia treated uninvited guests.

Doctor Omega stood on the hill, overlooking the muddy field and its grumbling occupants. He was huddled within his traveling cloak and leaning heavily upon his cane. Gathered around him was a half-dozen mismatched individuals, including his bearded handyman Fred, looking even more like a bear in a borrowed Russian hat and fur coat. On the other side stood two shivering versions of his companion Denis, one middle aged and bearded, the other younger and dressed in the fashion of the mid-1700s, complete with knee breeches and a tricorner hat.

Gathered behind the quartet were members of the Time Brigade, guardians of all human history—or perhaps they were from the Time Patrol? Doctor Omega could never remember which was which) and some Black Lectroids, an interdimensional race of alien beings. They had been gathered in a hurry and so their uniforms and weapons were a mix of several different eras. The Lectroids merely had an eclectic and otherworldly dress-sense.

"Are you sure this is the right place?" Young Denis asked, shifting anxiously, while trying not to fumble the pink hatbox he had been charged with carrying.

"Or even the correct time?" his older counterpart added. "It wouldn't be the first time you were off by an hour... or a decade..."

"Hush, the both of you," the elderly scientist grumbled, reaching into his coat pocket.

He came out with a sheaf of papers, including a bit of medieval parchment and a napkin from Disneyworld's Crystal Palace restaurant. All were covered in intricate mathematical formula, scribbles and computations.

"You are more than welcome to review my calculations…!"

Both men stepped back, making placating gestures. As they did, two other figures, a blond-haired man in a futuristic red bodysuit, and a tall African-American with dreadlocks, clad in the style of a tourist to the tropics approached Doctor Omega. Neither man seemed bothered by the cold.

"You were correct," the man with the dreadlocks said, in a thick, yet difficult to place accent. "There was a rift incident in Grover Mills."

"We were able to get a tech team there and repair the damage," the man in red added. "Between our team and the Lectroids, we were able to capture most of the Red Lectroids."

"My people have made arrangements in case any of the escapees should attempt to recreate the rift," the African-American man said.

"Thank you, Mr. Spell, John Fibhead," Doctor Omega nodded. "I'm sure that John's people will find allies in New Jersey, and we can focus our energies upon this rift."

He took an ornate, but much abused-looking pocket watch and a pair of opera glasses out of his pocket and spent the next few minutes alternating from studying one to peering through the other.

"Just as I'd calculated," he muttered. "Traces of quantum foam and ionic pulses… Mr. Spell, ready your men!"

He tucked the items back into his coat and pulled his traveling cloak tighter around his ancient body.

"Where?" Jason Spell, the commander of the Time Brigade forces, asked.

"Right to the left of the horse carcass."

The man from the future nodded grimly, and moved off to prepare his troops. John Fibhead gestured to his own people to ready themselves.

Soon, both groups had joined the human troops the Time Brigade had 'recruited' to assist them, upon the field. The two groups formed a pair of crescents, facing the predicted arrival point of the space-time rift.

The first crescent was the Black Lectroids. To human eyes, the aliens appeared as a dozen African-American men dressed for either a tropical vacation or a night at the disco. Each brandished a short tube-shaped device, decorated with lights, wires and what looked to be barnacles. As one, the line of Black Lectroids went down on one knee, allowing the human troops to aim weapons over their heads.

A minute passed and then two; the troops began to fidget and the younger Denis finally lost the fight to not ask any more questions, and had just begun to open his mouth, when he started, wide-eyed and mouth still agape.

A strange sound drifted across the field, a hum that seemed to come on the chill winter wind. It rose and fell as it swirled around the assembled soldiers, aliens and time travelers.

A light joined the sound, no bigger than an apple. It hovered ten feet off the ground. It flickered and pulsed, shrinking and expanding in rhythm to the hum. It flared and the rift tore open, unleashing two-dozen hate-crazed Red Lectroids out onto the Russian soil.

The soldiers from the Time Brigade fired, their weapons, a mix of projectile and energy beam based. The Black Lectroids activated their devices, focusing the tubes' energies on the rift itself.

Up on the hill, both versions of Denis stepped forward, only to be halted by the raised arm and cane of Doctor Omega.

"Steady, my boy, both of you," he said, his gaze not leaving the battle on the field. "We all have a part to play and yours does not involve your questionable fighting prowess."

The battle below was savage, but brief. The Red Lectroids were inhumanly strong and driven by a raw animal need to escape their other-dimensional prison, but even that was no match for the advanced weaponry and strategy of Doctor Omega and his allies.

As the smoke and noise cleared, the quartet on the hill spotted Captain Spencer, an English World War I Tommy, jogging up the hill towards them.

"Excuse me, sir," the soldier said, snapping off a hasty salute at the elderly scientist. "Commander Spell says we've got the lobsters under control and you can go ahead with...whatever you've got planned..."

Doctor Omega nodded curtly and then trudged down the hill, his companions following close behind.

The Time Brigade troops were rounding up the subdued Red Lectroids. Off to the side, they had erected a makeshift field hospital to deal with the few wounded from both sides.

The quartet joined the leader of the Time Brigade forces. They watched as a pair of Black Lectroids embedded two of the tube devices into the ground, on either side of the shrunken rift, connecting the tubes with what looked like strings of Christmas lights and plastic clothespins.

"All set, are we?" Doctor Omega asked, peering intently at the odd set up and then at the swirling hole in the fabric of space. He nodded at the Lectroids work and then gestured for the two Denises to move over to the rift.

"What...us...?" They both asked, skeptically.

"You wanted to help," the white-haired time traveler replied, peevishly. "Now is your opportunity. Each of you stand by one of the tubes...young Denis, hand me the box... Now, John Panther, help them with the contact wires..."

"I'm...uh..." Young Denis stammered. "What is this all about...?"

"Oh dear," Older Denis muttered. "I never listened."

"Gentlemen," Jason Spell said, stepping forward to help set things up. "Your presence here, at the same time, creates a paradox. Any form of time travel causes an energy build up, paradoxes even more so. The two of you, in such close contact, will hopefully generate enough chronal energy to keep the rift stable, while we deal with tracing its source."

"Get all that, did you?" Doctor Omega grumbled. "Or were you too preoccupied with your new hat?"

"What...? No, of course not...! We generate...chronic...um...energy." Young Denis stammered.

"So, how did it happen...?" Older Denis started then raised his eyebrows in surprise. "Doctor...you sent that letter that drew me into...all this...!"

"Or will in the future," Doctor Omega nodded, patting at his coat pockets. "Must make a note... Don't want to cause a paradox while causing a paradox..."

"Are you all right, Doctor?" Fred asked. His attempt to lean in and whisper discreetly instead coming across as looming over the time traveler and growling.

"Fine, fine," Doctor Omega muttered, waving away the handyman's concerns. "Just a bit tired. Come now, you two, raise them a bit higher and activate the large stub towards the top."

Both men followed the instructions and both tubes suddenly flared to life. The energy swirled and grew thin, like kite strings made of light.

"Hold them up," Doctor Omega commanded, sounding like an exasperated schoolmaster. "Face each other. The streams need to cross..."

"I thought you weren't supposed to do that?" Fred rumbled, nervously.

"Our options are limited," Spell said, quietly. "And despite our occupations, we are running out of time."

The two versions of Denis anxiously reached out with their devices until the swirling streamers of energy entwined above the rift. Then the streams traced around the ragged edge of the rift until they encircled it.

Everyone held his breath as the circle of light pulsed and sparked for several moments, before settling down into what looked like a solid band of light.

"There," Doctor Omega nodded, as though he'd never doubted it for a moment and couldn't understand why all the others had gotten themselves worked up.

He stepped up to the rift and peered thoughtfully at it, tucking his cane under his arm in order to reach out and run a fingertip across the surface of the distortion. The others all flinched back, while the Doctor merely pulled his finger back and studied it, as though he'd merely been checking for dust.

"Just about there," he said, nodding thoughtfully to himself.

"I don't agree that this is the best course of action," Spell said, his tone a mixture of stern and anxious.

"And as you've also said," Doctor Omega grumbled over his shoulder. "We are running out of options and time."

With that, he adjusted his traveling cloak, tightened his grip on his cane and stepped through the rift.

"What did he mean?" Fred grumbled.

"He'll be all right?" Young Denis asked.

"Won't he?" his older self added.

"I hope so," Spell replied. "I was hoping he'd allow someone else to take the risk…"

"What risk?" Fred growled, one of his large, mittened hands clamping onto the Time Brigade leader's shoulder. "What did you two concoct?"

"My people and the Black Lectroids have been tracking down all the rifts," Spell explained, grimly. "We have sealed off all but two, this one and one in 1980s New Jersey. We arranged with the Doctor that, after a certain interval, our operatives at both rift sites would implode the rifts…"

"That would trap the Doctor… wherever the rifts lead to…?!" Young Denis exclaimed.

"If he survives…!" Fred muttered, anxiously.

An uncomfortable silence fell over the group. Each man glanced about; waiting and hoping for someone else to say something reassuring that would brush away the worry over Doctor Omega's possible return.

Somewhere just to the left of reality, Doctor Omega spent a timeless second, every fiber of his being thrumming like one of Denis' violin strings. The white void made his eyes burn with snow blindness and his limbs felt as unsubstantial as smoke.

Wincing with a vertigo that threatened his senses and sanity, Doctor Omega suddenly found himself standing upon a sandy plain, a vast desert that stretched to the horizon.

Kneeling down, he set the hatbox on the ground and took a pinch of reddish sand between his fingers.

"Hmmm, bit heavy in iron oxidants… I wonder…?"

Picking up the hatbox, Doctor Omega trudged up a red sand dune. Once at the top, he saw a black pyramid in the distance.

"Mars…?" he muttered. "Though, it seems a bit different from my last visit…"

There was a rumble and he could feel a vibration through the soles of his shoes. Off in the distance, he watched as a mountain range blew apart and a dozen craggy, black ships arced off into the upper atmosphere.

"Curious," he muttered. "Very curious indeed."

"Who… Who isss there?" a faint voice demanded.

Stumbling in the loose sand, Doctor Omega made his way down the other side of the dune. Lying at the bottom, was sprawled an alien creature, one massive leg twisted at an odd angle and one arm smeared with what appeared to be its own blood.

The alien was large, close to seven feet tall. Its body was encased in a rough green armor or perhaps an organic outer shell. This armor was textured and green, giving it the appearance of some strange blending of man and crocodile. Its head was encased in a helmet like structure with large red eyes that looked more like lenses. Instead of hands, it had over-sized clamps.

Despite his dire condition, this alien had the bearing of a warrior.

Doctor Omega kneeled down next to the alien unsure what was armor and what skin and so unsure what, if anything, he could do to help.

"You look to be in a bad way," Doctor Omega muttered.

"I... am... dying," the alien told him, his voice coming out as a wet hiss. "But, my life will ensssure...my people will live... we have sssacrificed many lives and our home, but the Setissi... will ssssurvive...!"

"The Setissi...?" Doctor Omega muttered, glancing around at their desert surroundings. "I've met your kind before, long ago, in the depths of the Polar Sea... So, your people eventually came to rule Mars? How curious...?"

He was distracted from his own thoughts, by a soft groan from the Setissi.

"I am sorry I can't do anything to relieve your suffering," the time traveler continued, "but I too am on a mission to save... Well, I guess you could call them my people, and hopefully, my home. You may be able to help... I am unsure how I arrived on Mars, but it seems important that I am here."

"I fear... I... hnn... can be no... help to you, traveler..." the alien gasped faintly before growing silent and still.

Doctor Omega nodded sadly and patted the cold shoulder of the alien warrior.

"A noble fellow. I hope when I next encounter your people it will be as friends."

He stood up, dusting the sand off his hands and pant leg.

"No answers," he muttered. "Only more questions."

With a sigh, he picked up the hatbox and began walking.

He couldn't feel even the slightest breeze, and yet with each step, there was a struggle to move forward, as though he was walking into a strong wind. He closed his eyes, fighting off a wave of dizziness and again felt that thrumming sensation through his entire body and the sensation, as if he was being dragged along, of riding some enormous wave, while something had a hold on the back of his coat.

He blinked and with a feeling like he'd just sneezed, opened his eyes to find that the landscape had changed.

There were still the reddish tones and thin atmosphere of Mars, but the texture of the ground beneath his feet had changed. Also gone was the black pyramid, to be replaced by the ruins of an ancient city.

Doctor Omega shook his head in a mix of confusion and annoyance as he rummaged around in his coat pocket, taking out a handkerchief and dabbing at his forehead.

"Hmmf!" he muttered, tucking his handkerchief away.

Seeing nothing else about, began trudging towards the ruins.

He was within feet of the ancient structure, when he halted, straining his ears to make sense of a distant noise. He soon recognized it as the sound of combat and was pondering if he wished to continue walking or avoid the whole thing, when the noise stopped as abruptly as if a switch had been thrown.

After several minutes, a man came limping out of the ruins. He was tall, with midnight black hair and a muscular form tanned bronze by the desert sun.

He wore a loincloth-like garment, a sword belt, harness and sandals. In his right hand he held a blood-streaked sword, in his left the over-sized head of a gorilla with snow-white skin and fur.

The swordsman took a few more halting steps then sat down wearily on a block of stone. He stuck his sword, point first, into the sand and casually tossed the severed head aside. He took a water skin off his belt and was drinking deep, when he glanced around and spotted the old man with the cane and the hatbox.

The swordsman got to his feet, dropping the water skin and snatching his weapon out of the sand. He leapt the distance between himself and the time traveler in a single surprising bound.

"Omega...?" The swordsman exclaimed. "Doctor Omega? What are you doing on Barsoom?"

"Barsoom?" Omega muttered. "Curious, I thought I was on Mars...?"

"Barsoom *is* Mars," The swordsman said. "What are you doing here? How...?"

"What are you chattering on about?" Doctor Omega snapped. "How could you know who I am? I have never been to Bassoon..."

"Barsoom."

"...Before in my...Carter...?"

"Yes."

"Colonel Carter!"

"Captain, actually," the Swordsman said, lowering his sword. "But, since leaving Earth, I don't use the title much."

"Captain John Carter," Doctor Omega muttered. "Haven't seen you since that incident, during the war, with the..."

"Yes, yes, I was there," Carter interrupted. "How did you get here? What are you doing here?!"

The two men walked back to the block of stone. Doctor Omega sat down and explained about his and his companions' previous encounters with the rifts and the risky gambit to follow them to their source.

"These Polar Warriors... Setissi.. you mention sound like none of the people of Barsoom," Carter mused, wiping his sword clean, while they talked. "But, these rifts... there may be something...?"

"How so?"

"Well, it means something for those of us that have traveled to Barsoom from other worlds," Carter explained. "I thought it was a form of, I guess you'd call it, astral projection, but I've been told that I may have traveled in time or even across dimensions to a Mars very different from the one described by Earth scientists."

He shrugged and re-sheathed his sword.

"Personally, I never cared enough about it to study it further," Carter said, getting to his feet. "This is my home. It's where I belong."

"Yes, yes," Doctor Omega muttered, absently. "I wonder..."

"We can't stay here," Carter interrupted.

"Why not?"

"That," replied the swordsman, gesturing toward the severed head, "will have friends nearby. This may have been his territory, but the noise and smell of blood will make the other apes... curious. I have a flyer in the courtyard. You are welcome to accompany me to Helium. I have a bit of influence there and could put you in touch with the Council of Science."

"That might be best. This whole ordeal has gotten a bit much. I seem to be running hither and yon without much idea of where my destination might be. Feel like I've been blindfolded and given a jigsaw puzzle... Pieces fit, but I can't see the picture... I'm babbling... getting old... I would be grateful for any help you can offer."

John Carter offered a hand to help the savant to his feet. Instead of clasping hands, they passed through each other.

"Oh, bother," Doctor Omega muttered, as the void scooped him up once more.

He was no longer drifting, but rather being tossed about by another-dimensional tempest and the feeling that unseen hands were grabbing and pulling him was even stronger. It was hard to tell if they were trying to pull him out of the swirling, tumbling void or to deeper into the depths.

Reality snapped back into place so abruptly that Doctor Omega stumbled, landing in the red sand on his hands and knees, losing his grip on both his cane and the pink hatbox. While struggling to catch his breath, he also realized that, along the way, he'd also lost his hat.

Shaking his head in weary frustration, the time traveler grabbed hold of his cane and struggled to his feet.

"This is growing tiresome," he muttered, brushing himself off, yet again. "Never going to get this coat clean..."

Still frowning, he glanced up to take in his new surroundings and his eyebrows shot quickly up to the top of his forehead.

The plain was an expanse of rust-colored dirt and gravel. Situated in the center was a clunky six-wheeled vehicle. It resembled a children's toy that had been rendered full-sized. It was an odd collection of devices, thick wires and folded robotic limbs. It had a stout pipe standing mast-like from the front corner, with a white plastic box on the top. It sported a singular red lens. A faint humming coming from it was almost drowned out by a low grinding noise from one of the middle wheels.

"Ah," Doctor Omega mused, a slight smile creeping across his tired features. "A Mars rover... how quaint."

He gathered up his cloak and hatbox and strolled over to the Rover, peering over the various pieces of equipment, appearing more like a perspective buyer than a lost inter-dimensional traveler. He would nod approvingly at a component or frown at a wiring junction.

After pacing a complete circle around the Rover, Doctor Omega stretched up onto the tips of his toes, reaching up to pat the device with its single red eye. His expression was that of someone encountering a particularly talented and lovable dog.

"Now, why are you loitering around here, hmmm?" he asked, kneeling down to look at the Rover's wheels. On the right side one, he found a fist-sized stone wedged in the inner tread.

He then moved to a boxy device on the Rover's side. A couple moments study and, after setting his cloak, cane and hatbox on the Rover, flipped open an access panel and delicately poked a finger at the inner workings with a slightly disapproving expression on his face. He took down the hatbox and undid the twine around it. Reaching in, Doctor Omega brought out a robot head. It was made of dull grey metal. Its vaguely female features were scuffed, scratched and smeared with soot and dirt. One earpiece huge on by a strand of wire and one eye flickered with a faint light. Wires trailed from its metal neck.

Doctor Omega took two of these wires and connected them to points in the Rover's panel.

"Poor child," he murmured patting the metal head affectionately. "If we survive sorting out this whole mess, I will see to it that Fred and I patch you up. You have more than earned your place aboard the *Cosmos*, Thea."

Both the Rover and the robot head hummed and her one eye flickered rapidly. Doctor Omega took out his prince-nez and studied a tiny screen nestled amongst the circuits and wiring of the section of the Rover.

"Ah, here we are!" he muttered. "Time stamp gives us the date.... and... ah, yes, planetary coordinates... helpful... yes, quite helpful...."

He rummaged around in his coat pockets, taking out the tiny stub of a pencil and a crumpled grocery list. He scribbled the coordinates down, straightened up, putting away his various knickknacks and retrieved his cloak, cane and hatbox.

"Now, Thea, I think we may be putting pieces together," he said, as he disconnected her head from the Rover. "Still a bit of a jumble, but we are no longer stumbling in the dark... We have found ourselves a tiny candle."

He smiled at the robot head, and then getting no reply shrugged and returned her to the box. He walked back to the middle wheel and reaching down and pried loose the chunk of Martian stone. With a wheezing-groan, the Rover began to roll off across the plain.

"There's my good deed for the day," Doctor Omega said, walking in the opposite direction. He studied the scribbled numbers and glanced up at the sky. After several minutes he reached a bare spot and scratched an 'X' in the dirt with the tip of his cane. He stood on the marked spot, eyes closed, breathing growing rhythmic and deep.

And the void swallowed him up once more.

Doctor Omega kept his eyes closed, and just felt the flow and rhythm of the other-dimensional energy. He felt the surreal touch of invisible hands and this time willed himself to reach out to them... and found himself standing in a rocky valley.

It was early evening and the stars shown dimly overhead. Three figures stood around him.

They were humanoid, but inhumanly tall and inhumanly thin. Their pale skin had a feathery quality to it. Each one held, in their seven fingered hands, an equally tall and thin metal staff with what looked like a silver lantern on top.

They nodded at him, their features vague and serene and he, respectfully returned the greeting.

"Welcome to Malacandra," the lead alien intoned. "We regret the crude and chaotic manner of your summoning."

"I understand. My own efforts have been a bit on the impromptu side," Doctor Omega replied. "If I had known the Seroni were involved, it would have made matters a bit clearer..."

"We come to you, speaking for the Oyarsa," the Sorn continued, "since it is their bent brethren, the exiled Oyarsa of Thulcandra, who has set these events in motion."

"Celestial beings," Doctor Omega grumbled. "Nothing but trouble. How is it that the black sheep of the host of planetary angels is able to wreck this kind of havoc...?"

"In his exile, the bent Oyarsa was drawn to the cosmic maelstrom that lingers about Malacandra," the Sorn said, grimly.

A chrono-synclastic infundibulum!" Doctor Omega breathed. "Of course! A being like an Eldil channeling the infudibulum's energy... I shudder to imagine... Not that I need to, I've been twirled across time and space like a top because of it... That begs the question: why am I the target of this 'fallen angel'? Why have my companions and I been scattered and hunted...?"

"We were sent by the Oyarsa," the Sorn continued, ignoring the question, "to convey you to the site of the Bent One's containment."

"Why isn't the Oyarsa speaking to me directly?" Doctor Omega asked, a trace of testiness creeping into his voice.

"The Oyarsa of Malacandra is locked in struggle, containing not just the Bent Eldil, but the chrono-synclastic infundibulum from causing further damage to the fabric of the Heavens," the Sorn explained.

"Fair enough," Doctor Omega shrugged. "Let's be on our way then."

The Sorn formed a triangle around him and raised their staffs until the lantern-like pieces touched. Light flared in each one and the light passed over Doctor Omega like a dry wind.

"Getting quite irritated with this mode of travel," he muttered rubbing his eyes.

When he opened them, he was standing in his ship, the *Cosmos*.

He gazed in surprise and wonder at his surroundings, like he was seeing them for the first time, as though an absence of several days had wiped all trace of his beloved ship from his memory. During his quest to return to the *Cosmos*, he had come to accept the possibility that he would never see his beloved space-time ship again.

As he looked about at the cluttered mix of Victorian décor and high-tech equipment, a sudden realization swirled about in his brain and a thin, immensely satisfied smile crossed his face.

"Of course," he breathed, hanging his cloak over the back of a wing-backed chair and leaning his cane against the mantelpiece. "It was you all along! You sensed the turbulence caused by traveling too close to the chrono-synclastic infundibulum and jettisoned us into the void! You frustrated the Eldil's plans by plunging into the infundibulum... Truly you are the finest craft to ply the vast sea of stars and time!"

He patted the wall tenderly. "So, let us see if we can pull off one last miracle."

The hatbox tucked under his arm, Doctor Omega made his way down the corridor to bridge of the *Cosmos*. He strode up to the ship's mushroom-shaped console, pausing a moment to nod happily at its vast array of switches, buttons and levers, before placing the hatbox on the floor by his feet.

His ancient fingers were a flurry of movement across the brass and ivory keyboard then pounded a large red button and the lights around the console room flickered and grew dim.

"Come now," Doctor Omega said, glancing upwards. "No point being coy. You know we are going to have this out. The *Cosmos* isn't big enough for the both of us."

In the far corner of the room, a light appeared, a pillar of rainbow light. It pulsed and glimmered.

"Yes, yes, very dramatic," Doctor Omega muttered, "but, we aren't going to accomplish much if all you do is float and sulk."

He opened a small wooden panel on the console and then drew up a glass rod with a metal prong on the end. He kneeled down, took Thea's head out of the hatbox and set it upon the glass rod, fitting the metal prong into her neck hole.

Her eyes lit up, beams of light pouring from them and her mouth sparked. A thin wisp of smoke trickled from her damaged earpiece.

"What would you have me say, man of time?" the Eldil known as the Bent One said, speaking through the robot head. "Would you have me bargain or barter for my freedom? I hold your ship and even as it fights me, I still have the might to slash through the walls of the universe and send the Lectroid hordes into history!"

"Yes, quite fierce, I can see why your brethren would rather wrestle with the infundibulum than deal with you," Doctor Omega said, reaching across the console, and flicking several switches, then adjusting a large dial. "Any other time, I might even sympathize with your plight: exiled by your people and cast out into the void, but I am tired and apparently getting cantankerous in my old age, because being deprived of sleeping in my own bed has left me with little interest in debate or reconciliation."

Doctor Omega straightened up one hand holding his coat's lapel, the other hand resting upon a brass lever.

"Your disruption of the fabric of the universe was so severe that the *Cosmos* felt she should have to sacrifice herself to keep my companions and I safe. You have intruded upon my ship... my home... and then pursued my friends... perhaps due to arrogance, perhaps due to fear. I believe you were right to feel a sliver of fear about this old man and his eccentric little craft. Separated across the gulf of infinity, we have thwarted your schemes... Now, reunited, you do not stand a chance. So you can release your hold over the infundibulum and the *Cosmos*, return to the void and whatever mercy your brethren feel inclined to bestow upon you, or..."

His fingers merely tapped the lever and his smile was fiercely enigmatic.

The pillar of light flickered and pulsed. It seemed caught up in some invisible struggle.

"What are you... doing?" the robot head growled angrily. "You... do... not have... the power...to..."

"Really?" Doctor Omega mused, absently. "I'm in a ship that can transverse the whole of space and time, which is lodged at the center of one of the most expansive and powerful rifts in the fabric of the universe... I think I have the power to do anything I wish, and you should consider yourself lucky I'm not prone to megalomania or thoughts of violent revenge... Perhaps we'll talk again at a later, or even earlier, date, and I hope you'll have gained some wisdom in that time... Good-bye!"

Doctor Omega pushed the lever forward and the celestial creature began to pulse and flicker violently, the sounds coming from Thea's head becoming evermore incoherent and frantic, till, with a finale tinny screech, the light flared.

When the console room's lighting returned to normal the Doctor and Thea were the sole occupants.

"It would be refreshing," he muttered, adjusting controls with one hand, while scratching his beak of a nose with the other, "if just once, I could encounter a celestial being that didn't act like a spoiled six-year old. Very undignified."

"Whu-what... where..zzzt... di-di-di-didddddd...?" Thea slurred.

Calm down," Doctor Omega said, gently patting the robot head. "Don't over-tax yourself. You have been through more than any of us in the course of this little escapade. Rest, let the *Cosmos'* computer interface work its magic on your internal circuits."

He pulled out a handkerchief and began walking around the console, dusting as he went.

"It was really very simple," he explained as he shuffled about. "I merely used the Infundibulum to anchor the *Cosmos* in place and was then able to sling-shot our unwelcome guest to the far reaches of time. Gave him what he wanted, if you think about it. He should end up back on Earth... just several quintillion centuries in the future. I'm sure subjugating the giant crabs, mutated vampires or whatever he finds there, to his benevolent rule will keep him busy for a good long time. Not a bad bit of work if I do say so myself... hmmm, don't you agree?"

He'd gone full circle around the console and was facing Thea again. Her eyes were dark and a faint hum came from deep within her metallic skull.

Doctor Omega gave her a brief onceover with the dusting cloth, blew his nose and then tucked it back into his pocket.

"Yes, I think a nap would do us both a world of good," he muttered. "But, I suppose I should let Mr. Spell and the others know that the time stream is as stable as its likely to get and gather up Denis, Fred and... Hmm, I just realized, we never encountered Tiziraou...I wonder what he got up to...?"

Loompaland, in the heart of darkest Africa.

Tiziraou drew his sword and hacked away at the underbrush. The child-size Martian wore a loincloth, a sword belt made from vines and a broad leaf tied to his pumpkin-sized head as a makeshift hat.

A cluster of Oompa-Loompa warriors huddled behind him as he scouted the jungle ahead. Despite his own diminutive size, none of the Oompa-Loompas stood taller than his shoulder. They gripped their crude wooden spears anxiously.

The hunting party had barely escaped from a snozzwangler pack and just discovered the tracks of a poison-tusked hornswoggler.

Tiziraou paused, his eyes darting back and forth, his tiny ears straining to catch any sound that indicated where predators might be lurking. He turned back to the hunting party, held a thin, pale finger to his lips and then pointed in the direction he thought they should go. Holding his breath, the Martian pushed through the undergrowth and stepped into the clearing.

Across the way, a blunt, bullet-shaped craft was parked at an odd angle, wedged between two boulders. Standing by the round metal door, Doctor Omega was stirring a cup of tea, while peering at the *Cosmos'* landing site with disapproval.

Tiziraou gestured for the Oompa-Loompas to wait and he jogged across the clearing to the old scientist.

He reached Doctor Omega and tugged at his pant leg.

"Ah! There you are," the Doctor said, looking down with a faint smile. "Denis will appreciate your hat, I'm sure."

The diminutive alien smiled back up at his friend, glanced back the way he'd come with a thoughtful expression. He gestured for Doctor Omega to come closer. The time traveler leaned down. Tiziraou muttered, occasionally pointing back to the hunting party.

He told the story how he'd found himself lost in the jungle and after saving an Oompa-Loompa princess from a wild band of white monkeys was taken in by the tribe and made their warlord and that he wished to do something as a 'thank you' to his adopted tribe.

Doctor Omega nodded, as he straightened up.

"I think we can do that," he said, walking back to the door of the *Cosmos*. "Not too much to ask, for them taking you in, while you were stranded here. "

He leaned into the doorway.

"Fred...? Ah, there you are, could you see if we have some cocoa beans in the pantry?" He then turned back to the diminutive alien. "Though, I will warn you, sometimes people take the gift of cocoa the wrong way."

After bestowing the bag of cocoa beans upon the Oompa-Loompas that had taken him in during his time marooned, Tiziraou returned to the *Cosmos* and his true tribe.

*Paul Hugli has always displayed his love and knowledge of Ancient Egypt in the stories published in our previous volumes of* Tales of the Shadowmen. *The tale that follows is no different. Here, Paul notes that the Pharaoh Akhenaten's brother, Thutmose [Thutmoses], somehow appears to have disappeared from the historical records, after his brother's ascension to power. It's unlikely that he was the same man as the otherwise well-known sculptor of the same name, but it is interesting to speculate what happened behind the curtain of history, and possibly shaped our entire civilization...*

# Paul Hugli: *Dream's End*

*"All religion...evolves out of fraud, fear, guilt, imagination and poetry."*
Edgar A. Poe

*Middle Egypt, 1336 BCE*

In the Bathmose District of the City, set back off the Royal Road by a few cubits to offer some solitude and exclusiveness, sits the tavern Ka-Re-Sa.

Despite what was happening in the City—the Nation—the tavern managed to attract a number of soldiers and minor officials, all in good cheer from sweetened beer, roasted lotus seeds, and cat-calling the sinuous Syrian dancing girls outfitted only in diaphanous gowns and pectorals of beads and flowers. The accompanying musicians played sitars, rattles, harps and lutes as the dancers writhed to the atonal, yet somehow harmonic, music.

Elsewhere, others placed bets on the tavern's two mousers, on which would kill the most grain thieves.

These two activities covered what was transpiring in the dimly-lit back room, the so-called Royal Room because much of the workings of the Great House was planned and plotted there.

Tonight was no different.

"It is all coming unraveled," Mahu, Chief-of-the Medjay, said after wiping beer from his lips with the back of his hand. His hair was just turning white from age, worry and patrols on the fringes of the Eastern Desert.

"Is that what you will report to Vizier Nakht?" General Ramose asked, smirking.

"Well..."

"I thought not. He'd have your head."

"Enough," the third member of the trio grunted.

This was Paatenemheb, General-in-Chief of the North, who was trying to keep order—the *ma'at*—in the Empire. "We are all agreed?"

"But this is mutiny... treason....," Mahu began to protest.

"No," Paatenemheb said, "Pharaoh's experiment has failed. The King worships his God and the people worship him. And what has that brought us? Plagues in the farms across the Blue Nile; frogs have overflowed the River; fleas, lice and boils have killed the livestock."

"If something doesn't happen soon, the Nile will run red with the blood of our first-born to sate Pharaoh's god," Mahu added, after taking a deep tug from his beer.

"That is the *one* thing," Paatenemheb said, "that we know he will *never* do. Otherwise, are we agreed?"

For emphasis he slammed the short wand he had recently found outside Memphis, shattering its crystalline knob on the table. The entire tavern went silent. Musicians, dancers, drunken revelers, all became still. The General thought it was in reaction to him scattering the wand's crystal.

At the door to Royal Room, half-hidden in shadows, a woman staggered, confused, disheveled, her distinctive tall flat blue crown askew. Her linen gown was in tatters and the kohl around her eyes smeared. Her right hand grasped the door jamb tightly as she slurred

"Who am I?"

"Nefer...," Mahu mumbled, falling to one knee, stretching out his right hand in salute.

"...Nefruaten...," General Ramose continued, also saluting.

"...Nefertiti," Paatenemheb said, concluding, "The Queen's Royal titulary: *Beautiful Are the Beauties of the Aten...*" Then, barely hiding his sneer, he added: "Life, Health, Prosperity... May you live a million-million years."

Nefertiti stared at them with confused blue eyes. Little did she know she was not Nefertiti, Queen of Egypt, wife of Pharaoh Akhenaten, but from the 40th century C.E. Earth where she was known as—Barbarella.

*One Week Earlier [Relative Time]*

The squat sled, trimmed in brass ebony and ivory, hit a chronometric bubble, a time-dilation flux created by another time vehicle traveling in the opposite direction, thus knocking the Time Traveler out of not only time but also space, preventing his return to 802,701 C.E.

The Time Machine spun and spun, the ages passing by until the machine came to an abrupt halt with a jolt, knocking loose the translucent quartz control lever, tumbling in time before the sled halted in a upheaval of sand, scattering the Time Traveler and his meager cargo, including copies of *The Holy Bible, Das Kapital,* and *A Thousand and One Arabian Nights.*

When he regained consciousness, the Time Traveler wiped the blood from the cut on his forehead. His clothes tattered, he crawled back to his Machine, and panicked when he discovered that the quartz control lever was missing.

In the light of the full Moon, and a silvery sky of countless stars, he stared at the Great Sphinx. It was not like the one he had left back in the future, in the time of Weena and the Eloi.

This Sphinx wasn't erected in a lovely garden setting, green and sublime, a world of glass and metal towers. The only things here were sand and stone.

As the Time Traveler pondered his next move, he fingered the petals Weena had placed there only yesterday in relative time.

*USA: 1950s*

"Jumping Gods," Manse Everard exclaimed as the Scotch burned his gullet. "That's smooth."

Life was good. He was an Unattached Agent of the Time Patrol (life expendable, no specific daily assignments), pulling down a princely $15,000 a year. He was thirty, a stocky man with broad shoulders, crew-cut brown hair, and was relaxing between assignments, having just returned from a refreshing Oligocene Age hunting trip.

All that came to an end when he received a call from the Egyptian Milieu Office of Spatio-Temporal Anomalies needing his expertise: Coded Assignment 2152-1615144.

A thief from the 40th century had traveled back in time, seeking a prized religious object. Though Manse put little store in religious mythos, he understood certain icons could move and inspire people in unpredictable ways.

When people messed with history, the Time Patrol swung into action, policing the time-lines with the assistance of the Danellians, a race of "humans" more than a million years hence, evolutionarily as far above us as we were above the amoeba, or, at least, our ancestral insectivores. The Danellians—neither malignant nor benevolent—didn't want to ban time travel, only police it.

After availing himself of the hypnotic conditioner to instruct him in everything Ancient Egyptian, including their language, Manse began rubbing down his Time Hopper. Equipped with a spatio-temporal drive field and an anti-gravity field, the Hopper resembled a two-seated motorcycle, *sans* wheels.

*Earth Orbit: 40th Century; One Week Ago [Relative]*

Barbarella had just returned from the Planet Lythion of the Tau Ceti System via her temporal accelerator and was relaxing with Nado, a gynoide, when her ship's astro-viewer twinkled and Lord Dianthus, President of the Earth and Rotating President of the Solar System, oscillated into view.

"Love, President, Love," Barbarella said, jumping to her feet, saluting, her naked breasts bouncing.

"Love, Barbarella, Love," Lord Dianthus replied with a salute in kind, trying (and failing) to divert his eyes from the flaxen beauty's body. "We received your report. Well done. Unfortunately, Duran-Duran remains on the loose."

"But..." Barbarella began, confusion in her eyes.

"He managed to survive the devastation of Sogo," the President interrupted. "You need to go after him again."

"I was expecting a short vacation," she said, glancing over her shoulder at Nado, then back to the President, and again saluted. "But the duty of a 5-Star Double-Rated Astronavigatrix comes first."

The President's briefing revealed that Duran-Duran had used the chrono-rays from his positronic generator to escape the destruction into the past, over 5300 years ago, and was now seeking a piece of antiquity with which he hoped to return to the future and rule the Universe.

All the relative data was fed into Barbarella's on-board computer as she dressed in a shiny green and gray plastic one-piece and white knee-boots.

When the computer informed her all was ready, she engaged the positronic generator installed in her ship by Professor Ping when he had repaired it back on Lythion.

The ship time-warped, the on-board chronometer smoothly rolling back until it was approaching the eve of the 20th century. Suddenly, it began to spin out-of-control. Barbarella's fingers flew over the control panel buttons, trying to get the system back on line.

She could have sworn she saw a squat, brass, ebony and ivory contraption fitted in red Victorian velvet out of the window.

*Middle Egypt, 1336 BCE*

The Time Traveler checked his own chronometer, discovering the year was 1336 B.C.E. He knew he was in Egypt: the pyramids and Sphinx gave that fact away. He had to find his quartz control lever, but he couldn't do it dressed as a turn-of-the-20th century Englishman. Fortunately for his return to the future, he had packed some meager supplies: pens, paper, boxes of Lucifers, and various items of clothing, including a linen tunic and belt, similar to those wore by the Eloi.

The last item he retrieved was an electro-magneto-locator, or EML, to help him track the stolen quartz lever; he didn't want a repeat of what had happened with the Morlocks when they had stolen the lever.

The pulse on the EML gauge-screen indicated due South.

Barbarella's ship popped out of warp, twisting and turning, crashing into the Ancient Nile. Shaken, she picked herself up off the floor. A good thing it had been that it was upholstered in thick, shock-absorbing shag. The ship was taking on water so Barbarella quickly dressed in a linen shift before crawling into the ejection tube, which propelled her to the surface in a transparent flexo-plast-bubble. She surfaced on the East shore of the North Distinct of the City of Akhetaten. The bubble's hatch popped open and she stepped out, adjusting the miniature galactic tongue box wrist-translator.

Once in the city, Barbarella began asking about strangers, about an older man named Duran-Duran. Her inquiries eventually reached the ears of the occupant of the North Palace, and she was summoned.

Chief Steward Merye led the Woman of the Future into the bed chamber of the exiled queen—Nefertiti.

Manse Everard popped into airspace over Akhetaten and landed behind the Eastern hills. Stepping off the Time Hopper, he sent it to hover high above. Then, dressed as a palace guard he headed west, toward the City proper.

Blessed with a photographic memory, the Time Traveler could read hieroglyphs and speak several foreign tongues, but no one knew Ancient Egypt's spoken word. While waiting for the ferry to cross the Nile, he eavesdropped on some conversions and discovered that gutter-Egyptian was closely related to Syro-Palestinian, of which he had a passing knowledge. Yet, he decided to play dumb, literally, and communicate via sign-language, augmented which the semi-precious stone he carried in his belt. He had planned to give them to Weena, who liked shiny things, but now, to get back to her, he would have to sacrifice these gifts.

His EML continued to point south, up river, a few hundred kilometers.

Barbarella thought she was looking in a mirror. Except for her own flaxen hair which differed from the reddish-brunette of the Queen, and a slight difference in skin tone and eye color—blue vs. black—they could have been twins.

The exiled queen was seated in a chair layered in gold leaf, turquoise and ebony, attended by two young Nubian servant girls. Nefertiti immediately dismissed the girls, inviting Barbarella to come closer, examining her, comparing the Woman of the Future to her own reflection in a bronze mirror with a handle in the shape of Hathor.

"If I believed in witches..." the Queen said, shaking her head.

"I am nothing of the sort. I'm just a plain woman looking for a lost, er, uncle."

"This 'Duran-Duran' about whom you have been inquiring?"

"Yes."

"It is a strange name. Is he one of the Hyksos?"

Barbarella smiled. The Queen was correct in her own way since the term "Hyksos" collectively referred to the "rulers of foreign lands," who had upset the *ma'at* and ruled Egypt during the Second Intermediate Period, before the founders of the 18th Dynasty, over 200 years before the *ma'at* prevailed and established the New Kingdom. Duran-Duran couldn't be from a more "foreign land" than the future.

"He's... we are from Ceti," Barbarella said.

Nefertiti nodded with a dismissive wave of the hand, obviously never having heard of Ceti before, but too proud to admit it. "Of course. And what does this, ah..."

"He is a merchant. A stranger in this strange land."

"We are *strange*?"

"I mean no offense, Your Majesty. Everyone knows of Egypt's pre-eminence in the world."

Nefertiti shrugged. "What does this *Hyksos* look like?"

"An older man... stocky with white hair."

"That could describe a score of merchants who come into the City. Though, admittedly, fewer have come since the plagues across the Nile, in the farm lands." Barbarella nodded and the Queen continued: "I am in the dark on the present workings of the Court and Palace, having been exiled here two years earlier."

"Exiled?"

Nefertiti looked down. She shook her head slightly, crossing and uncrossing her hands on her lap, wondering why she was confiding in this doppelganger. "Only the Aten knows. I tried to provide my husband with a male heir, but only issued him six daughters. Yes, I tried for fifteen year... it seems like an eternity. Could he ask more from any other woman?"

When Barbarella shifted on her feet but remained silent, the Queen added: "It appears now that the issue of my husband's father and Princess Sitamun, Prince Tutankhaten, will claim the title of heir apparent."

*King Tut*, Barbarella thought, *I've heard of him*.

"And you were exiled for failing to produce a male heir?" she asked.

"Yes. Also, he took up a co-regency with a wanderer calling himself Smenkhkare. Ha! He showed the king some wonders—I know not what—save it was referred to as the *Light of the Aten*. It seemed to have impressed my husband, Pharaoh."

"Magic?"

"Oh, no, we do not believe in magic."

*Ah, still*, Barbarella thought, *perhaps this Smenkhkare is Duran-Duran passing-off some futuristic technology as magic...*

"Is this Smenkhkare an older man with white hair?"

"No, he is not the man you are seeking. The co-regent has seen but twenty-years."

*Damn!*

The Time Traveler's EML led him up the river to the City of Akhetaten. Stepping ashore, he was amazed by what had risen out of the desert in thirteen years. The City was flanked by the Nile to the west and the low hills to the east. When the Sun rose in the morning, the huge red globe hung in the bowl created by the two hills, a perfect match for the hieroglyph representing "Horizon," thus its name: *The Horizon of the Aten.*

Though the City was ablaze with colors—reds, greens, blues, yellows and blacks—in just a few years of existence, they had already begun to fade, to flake, from neglect. Pharaoh Akhenaten's City had, indeed, seen better days.

Still, there were marvels, such as the Great Palace. But the Time Traveler was forced to step aside as a commanding figure, wearing a heavy pectoral around his neck, swept out the door, with two other men close on his heels. From the clothing and scabbard swords swinging at their side, he guessed they were military. Then he noticed something:

*The leader carried in his hand a short metal staff with a quartz crystal cap!*

The Time Traveler's eyes widened. It was his Control Lever! But it was in the hand of General Paatenemheb, General-in-Chief of the North, heading for the North Distinct.

What was he to do now?

Barbarella and the exiled Nefertiti hatched a plan, decided to act on King Akhenaten's behalf against a rumored plot to remove him from the throne. Nefertiti, herself, was incapacitated, due to a minor fall, plus she was nursing an ailing daughter, Princess Ankhesenpaaten.

Nefertiti provided Barbarella with royal accouterments, clothing, and the Queen's trademarked helmet. The servant girls dyed her hair with henna to match the Queen's. Lastly, Nefertiti wrote a note on heavy papyrus to Pharaoh's brother, stating her concerns. After affixing her seal, she handed it to Barbarella and said:

"May the Aten be with you."

Barbarella mounted the chariot behind Steward Merye, who used the reins to coach the team of horses forward along the Royal Road. They were proceeding south at a leisurely pace when a chariot came roaring up behind them, spooking Merye's team, which rose up and tossed its passengers flying.

Just before Barbarella hit the ground, she saw the other chariot speeding away, the driver's head and shoulders barely visible over the top of the basket, his side-lock flowing in the wind.

Paatenemheb stepped towards the person lurking in the shadows of the Ka-Re-Sa's Royal Room, believing her to be the exiled Queen. Meanwhile, General Ramose yelled:

"Is there a physician in the house?"

"I am a physician," a sinewy man with graying temples said, stepping into the Royal Room.

"Sinahu," Paatenemheb said, "what is the Physician to Pharaoh doing here?"

"Looking to quench my thirst with a cold beer."

The General of the North snickered as the physician wrapped an arm around the confused woman. At once, he noticed it was *not* Queen Nefertiti, but held his tongue.

"I will take charge," he said. "No one is to touch the Royal Personage, save Her Physician."

The physician kept his comforting arm around the faux-Queen and led them from the tavern as the patrons made way for them, bowing their heads as a clueless Barbarella allowed herself to be escorted, mumbling: "Who am I? Where am I?"

"Shhh," Sinahu whispered. "We will be alone soon enough."

He walked her into an alley off the Royal Road, and shoved her up against a wall, shaking her.

"You are not the Queen. Who are you?"

"I... don't know."

Her mumblings were translated into Ancient Egyptian via the miniature tongue box on her wrist.

Sinahu had been a physician all his life. He knew of potions, of spells, and of medicines. But there was one sure-fire cure for amnesia. He hauled back and slapped her hard across the face, sending her blue crown flying, revealing her henna-dried hair. He was about to repeat the treatment when she stayed his hand.

"Love, Citizen, Love," she said, rubbing her red cheek.

"Now you're beginning to *sound* like the Royal Couple," said Sinahu, not without a bit of irony. "But why are you dressed as the Queen?"

"I am on a mission for Queen Nefertiti," she said, offering the physician the papyrus roll from inside her linen gown.

Sinahu glanced over it, noting the Royal Seal of the Nefertiti. He handed the papyrus back and she replaced it in her gown.

"You might get lost," Sinahu said, "I will guide you to your destination."

They mounted the physician's chariot and headed south down the Royal Road.

The Time Traveler's EML went dead. Something had interrupted the electrodynamic energy waves, just as he had tracked it to the Ka-Re-Sa tavern. Then he saw a woman wearing an askew crown being escorted by a man in a white tunic; they disappeared around a corner. A few minutes later, the three men he had seen earlier exited the tavern. They appeared to be in a hurry.

The Time Traveler noted that the obvious leader of the trio no longer carried the crystalline lever to his Time Machine and concluded that it was still inside the tavern.

The revelry was back in full swing when the Time Traveler entered. At first, he was unable to find the control lever as he navigated through Syrian dancing girls and drunken revelers. Then, in the back room, he found the lever on the floor. Picking it up, he discovered that the crystal was busted.

He sighed.

Charioting down the Royal Road, the City's main drag, Sinahu entered the South District, approaching a multi-room mansion, sprawled out like a plaza.

They were greeted at the door by a Nubian retainer, who led them through a maze of rooms and into a large studio, cluttered with bits and pieces of statuary. A cloud of masonry dust hovered about their feet, shifting as they moved through it.

The shelves were crammed with busts and body parts in a variety of materials—including a few quartz human skulls—all waiting to be finished. On the floor were various uncompleted *objets d'art,* primarily of the Royal Personages: torsos, reliefs, more busts.

"Thutmose," Sinahu began, with a wave of his hand, "Chief Craftsman, Sculptor and Favorite of the King." He paused, then added: "My brother."

An older man with whitish hair had his back to them. He was slightly stooped, dressed in a filthy tunic; his hands and nails were equally soiled. He was petting his tabby, "Pussy," who purred and arched its back. He turned to face the new arrivals, and Barbarella noted that, despite the man's age, he had a powerfully built of arms, legs and chest.

"Ah, Brother Sinahu," the master sculptor began, then stopped short, rubbing his gray eyes. "It has been a long while, Your Majesty," and again he stopped, stepping forward a few paces. "No, no... you're not the Queen... Brother," he added, turning to Sinahu, "what is the meaning of this?"

Sinahu nudged Barbarella, who produced her document from Nefertiti. Tuthmose squinted as he read it, nodding and mumbling here and there, then rolling up the papyrus, he handed it back to Barbarella.

"It appears I'm at your service. Let us begin."

"Begin?"

"Yes. The Great Lady wants me to make you her double," he said, using his dusty right hand to turn her head this way, then that way, ah-huhing in the process.

While he was checking her out, Barbarella's eyes spotted on the workbench a 19-inch high limestone bust of Nefertiti, wearing the blue crown with red, blue, and green inlays, and a pectoral of colored beads of flowers, fruits, leaves and petals. The eyebrows were painted with kohl, and black pupils were set in transparent crystalline eyes.

"It's beautiful."

"My latest creation for the Great Lady, though it has been a while since she last sat for me. Since you will be taking the Queen's place, perhaps I might incorporate some of your salient features in the bust..."

"Brother," Sinahu interrupted, "I have delivered the woman. Now, I must see to my other brother."

Once Sinahu had left, Thutmose began shading Barbarella's skin with a henna-based dye, to give it the darken-red tan of a native Egyptian.

"Is it common for men to call each other 'Brother'?"

"Indeed, and our ladies are 'Sisters.' It is the Aten's way."

"Aten," Barbarella repeated, looking at her shimmering image in the highly-polished bronze mirror. "I heard Nefertiti speak of this god..."

"Ah, you're truly are new to our Nation. Yes. The Aten... the One... the Foremost..."

"You sound as if..."

"I am but Pharaoh's servant."

"And the Aten?"

"The Aten *is* Pharaoh's *god*... and, until recently, that of the Queen. But the Aten is not the god of the people. The Royal Couple worships the Aten—the Solar disc with its arms radiating down, its hand offering *ankhs* to the Royal Family. But only they are allowed to directly worship the Aten. The people can *only* worship it vicariously through the Royal Couple."

"So he outlawed all the other gods?"

"Oh, no, just Amen, whom he believes is a false god, not a manifestation of the Aten."

"Yet the people do not embrace this Aten?"

"Hardliners and sycophants do. After everything is said and done, this Aten offers nothing for the Common Folks... no afterlife, no Day of Judgment, no Festivals or Jubilees... just the rising and setting of the Aten each day. Nothing more."

"You don't seem to believe in this god yourself."

"I do as I am told. The gods are too far above a mere mortal as myself to be properly contemplated."

Barbarella doubted that, but kept her tongue.

"Back to your earlier question," the sculptor said as he handed Barbarella a white linen gown and indicated a dressing screen, "Sinahu is my half-brother as is Pharaoh."

Barbarella saw no use for a dressing screen, but while in Rome... ah, Egypt... Dressing in fresh and clean linen, she replaced the blue crown on her head, and stepped from behind the screen.

"You see," Thutmose continued, "I was once Crown Prince of Egypt. A Sem -priest at Memphis and High Priest of Ptath. I was a warrior..." he saw the stunned look on Barbarella's face and laughed. "I know, I know, looking at me now... but I was, although under my father, Amenhotep III, the Nation was basically at peace, and I saw little action other than policing. The Pharaoh, my father, discovered I was actually the child of his Queen—Tiye—and *her own* brother, Counselor Ay!"

"Nefertiti's father?"

"Yes. Ironic, yes?"

"And your father disowned you?"

"Yes. I was exiled into the desert, and my half-brother, Amenhotep IV, became Crown Prince, then Pharaoh as Akhenaten—*Glory of the Sun-Disc*. My brother was kind to me, welcoming me into his—this—new City, and allowed me to use the artistic abilities I was born with."

"And what of Sinahu?"

"He was born to Amenhotep III via a Secondary Wife. And Queen Tiye didn't like any heir to the throne not being from her own loins, so she banished him down the Nile in a basket of bushreeds, where he was rescued and cared for by a Thebean couple, the husband a physician."

"Then you and this physician Sinahu are half-brothers of Pharaoh and of each other?"

"Welcome to the court intrigues of Egypt."

Barbarella laughed, then asked: "Now what?"

"Why, we present you to Pharaoh and his Co-Regent."

"Who is this Co-Regent, this Smenkhkara?"

"He showed up one day, a year back, and in some manner enthralled the King. The King married him to his daughter, Meritaten, and banished Nefertiti to her North Palace. Her sin? She had bore him six daughters... yet, not one son and heir."

"Akhenaten hopes for an heir through them?"

"Or through the marriage of his third daughter, Ankhesenpaaten, to the young Tutankhaten, the son of Akhenaten's father and Princess Sitamun."

"Queen Nefertiti tells me this Smenkhkare is but twenty years old."

"Correct."

*Damn*, Barbarella thought again.


As Nefertiti/Barbarella left with Thutmose in the golden chariot Pharaoh had gifted him, the Time Traveler arrived at the estate, having been guided by his EML readings, which had picked up electrodynamic emulations from within.

Climbing the back wall and keeping to the shadows, he followed the readings into Thutmose's workshop. Along a shelf against the back wall was a series of seven crystalline skulls, some three-inches across the width of the cranium. They were a series of studies the artist was developing with crystal imported from Punt.

He ran his EML across the skulls, noting a peak in the far one, an electrodynamic reading almost identical to the crystal destroyed by General Paatenemheb.

Searching the shelves and benches he founds the tools he needed: a mallet, a bronze chisel, a rare nail of iron, and a small pit of graphite.

He applied dabs of epoxy to a sheet of double-ply papyrus, then sprinkled some crushed graphite on it, letting it dry into "sand-paper."

Taking down the selected crystalline skull he turned it this way, then that way. It was completely smooth. It must have taken Thutmose years of smoothing abrasion to create it.

Using a vise, the mallet and iron nail the Time Traveler managed to poke a hole into the bottom of the skull. He used his "sand-paper" to smooth over it. Then the time of truth came.

Retrieving his broken control lever, he eased the distal end into the hole he had just created. It took some effort, but soon they were as one. He held the device up to window and could feel the solar energy energizing it.

He smiled.

"Hey, you!" ordered a voice behind him.

He turned to see a palace guard, a stocky man with broad shoulder, a lance leveled at the Time Traveler's heart. "Why are you here?"

"I..." the Time Traveler began, before suddenly realizing he could understand the Palace Guard!

Disguised as Nefertiti, Barbarella was led by Thutmose past the Great Palace guards along a highly-polished floor brightly painted with trees, birds, other wildlife, and pools of fish and fowl . After a brief announcement, they were taken into the Throne Room of the Great Palace.

The Woman of the Future noted that, on the wall behind the raised double-throne, was the official portrait of the entire Royal Family worshiping Ankhenaten's god, the Aten. Barbarella considered that promising.

Then she studied the man on the raised dais. Though she had seen many portraits of the King throughout the City, they hardly prepared her for the reality. The King's face was elongated and horse-like; his arms and legs were spindly; his stomach and breasts, pendulous. He wore the double crown of the two lands, and held the royal regalia—the Flail and Crook—crossed upon his chest. The soles of his golden sandal rested on a representation of the symbolic "40 Captives and 9 Bows." He appeared to be 33 years or so.

Next to Pharaoh sat his younger Co-Regent, Ankhkheprure Smenkhkare, a rather handsome boy, with darkly brown hair and gray eyes. He was dressed in a simple white linen tunic and broad pectoral. His eyes were everywhere, taking in everything, thinking, calculating.

*What is his game?* Barbarella thought.

"My Wife," the King said, his eyes examining this faux-Queen. "Why have you returned from your retirement?"

"Exile, you mean?" Barbarella replied, having been well-versed in the intrigue of the Court.

Though her eyes were locked on Smenkhkare, she continued to address Pharaoh.

"And how is your little playmate? Are he and my daughter ready to produce an heir to the throne of the Thutmoses and the Amenhoteps? Oh, forgive me, My Pharaoh, I've spoken the false god's name, Amen. Will you banish me? Wait, you have already done that!"

Akhenaten only tilted his head, but the Co-Regent spoke: "Sister..."

"I am not your Sister!" Barbarella coldly exclaimed.

"Very well... wife, paramour... queen," Akhenaten said, his thick lips shaping into a smile. "You have turned your back on the Aten."

"How? Have I not allowed myself to be portrayed with you—and alone!—worshiping the Aten?"

"You have failed the Father Aten... have not produced a *male* heir to the Throne of the Two Lands."

"Neither have you, my Wise Husband. Not even with your *own* daughter or your other paramour."

Now the king's brown eyes narrowed, the humor sapped from them. And Barbarella continued:

"Still, you have your little playmate here, Smenkhkare, and our daughter, Meritaten... in the hope of issuing a male heir."

"Nefertiti... Nefertiti... We have discussed this all before..."

"No! You have *demanded*. I have *obeyed*! But no more!"

Pharaoh sighed and rose, handing the Crook and Flail to Smenkhkare. He stepped down from the dais, approaching her, smiling like a horse.

"And what would you do, *Beautiful One Who Has Come*?" he asked, using the literal translation of her name.

Now Barbarella was lost, confused. This was not going as Nefertiti had briefed her. She crossed her arms across her breasts, fingering her miniature bracelet tongue box. Then a smile came to her face.

"My Husband, must we air own dirty laundry here, in front of the courtiers and gossipers?"

"You suggest...?"

She took his hand and squeezed it. And Akhenaten fell in love all over again as she led him into the royal bed chamber.

The Palace Guard—a disguised Manse Everard—came across Counselor Ay and General Paatenemheb rushing toward the Throne Room. The General spotted Manse and demanded that he follow him, having barely noticed the Time Traveler in tow. They picked up more guards along the way.

They burst into the Throne Room to find only the youth, Smenkhkare, on the Throne, absently crossing and uncrossing the Crook and Flail. The sculptor Thutmose had settled on a settee, hoping that—somehow—this strange woman posing as Queen could convince Pharaoh to abdicate the throne for the good of the people.

"Where is Pharaoh?" Counselor Ay demanded of the Co-Regent.

"With his wife," Smenkhkare replied with a wave of his hand.

"Wife?" Paatenemheb repeated. "Which one?"

"Nefertiti," Thutmose said, brushing an imaginary speck of dust from his tunic.

"What is she doing here?"

"My daughter *is* the Queen," Ay said, trying to maintain his authority, although he cared little for his daughter, or anything else other than his own aims.

"In name only!" Paatenemheb countered, also jousting for a position once this obviously failed administration would end, likely sooner than later.

"The Queen is the only one who has ever *really* understood him," Ay opined. "Understood the Aten. Knew how to please him."

"Or cared to," Paatenemheb two-cented.


"Let me show you what I learned from the Syrian dancing girls," Barbarella said, removing Pharaoh's double crown and her own blue crown.

She handed him some pills from the hidden compartment in her bracelet and a glass of water.

"This will make you as young as the day you were born."

They both ingested the pills and raised their right hands, pressing them together.

After a brief moment smoke was issuing out their ears, their hair standing on ends. And Pharaoh's eyes rolled back in their sockets.


Two hours later, Barbarella-cum-Nefertiti and Pharaoh emerged from the royal bed chamber, refreshed. Present in the Throne Room were Counselor Ay, General Paatenemheb, Sinahu, Thutmose, the Time Traveler and Manse Everard, all waiting.

Pharaoh reclimbed his Throne and Barbarella/ Nefertiti took the throne next to his, forcing Smenkhkare, against his objections, to step down, hand the royal regalia back to Akhenaten, and settle in the seat usually reserved for close advisors, like Ay and Vizier Nakht.

Thutmose rose and approached his half-brother, Pharaoh, bowing royally.

"My Brother, we..." he began.

"We?" interrupted Pharaoh.

"Ay, General Paatenemherb and myself."

"And you also, Physician?" Pharaoh inquired of Sinahu, who bowed his head but did not answer. He sighed, then said: "So be it."

"My Son..." Ay said as he stepped forward.

"Yes, Divine Father?" Pharaoh said, using Ay's title as Father of the Queen, Nefertiti.

"As you are well aware, I have always been faithful of the Aten. My tomb has the most complete *Hymn to the Aten* in all the land. I have served you well..."

"And you have been amply repaid for your loyalty. You and your wife, Tey, have become 'People of Gold.' I have gifted you with broad collars of gold, necklaces, armlets, drinking vessels, in fact, all manners of gold..."

Aye continued, ignoring Pharaoh's statement.

"Now comes the time to end this... er... experiment. To return the gods to the people. To end the plagues killing the people across the Nile, which soon will decimate even this City."

"*Experiment?*" Akhenaten mumbled, then laughed. "Yes, I imagine to you—to everyone else—that is exactly what it is..." He glanced at Barbarella, and squeezed her hand. "Save for my queen, Nefertiti. Not another person has realized, not even you Ay, or your sycophants, that the Aten is One, the Aten is All. For I am *Ankhen-Ma'at... the One Living in Truth...*"

"We all have Truths," Ay countered, "Are mine the same as yours?"

"Truth is Truth!" Pharaoh exclaimed.

"Brother," Thutmose said, stepping forward, "you were kind to me when our father rejected me..."

"You are my brother," Pharaoh sighed.

"Of which I have no regrets. Yet, now is not the time for the Aten. The people *will* see the Light of the Aten sometime in the future. It may take a few years, or scores of them, or even a million years. Yet, at some time in the future, the wonders of the Aten will manifest themselves in the hearts of the people. But for now, you must let our people go."

"*Our People?* They are *my* people. Yet, if this is their wish, to abandon the Aten, then so let it be written... So let it be done!"

The collected audience gasped in disbelief, but none dared speak as Pharaoh continued:

"I have never officially outlawed the worship of the other gods. In fact, Brother Thutmose, your workshop turns a tidy profit making amulets and images of them." Pharaoh's brother bowed his head as the king continued: "Though they are idols for *idle* worshipers, only the false god, Amen, was banned..."

"Yes."

"My Way is the Way. Of that, I have no doubt in my heart. Though I Am Who I Am, perhaps I am not the one to spread the Word of the Aten. If you have not forsaken me, Brother Thutmose, perhaps you are the one to spread the Word."

"Me?"

"Yes. Take the people who will follow you. Provide them with what they can carry. Go North and find your own Paradise, like I once found here. Your name, Thutmose, is most apt: *Son of Thoth...* of Wisdom..."

Pharaoh summoned his Nubian guard, who bowed regally as Akhenaten whispered in his ear. The Nubian nodded, bowed again and left.

"You will need some help," Pharaoh said to his brother.

Four Nubian guards returned, carrying a chest on poles across their broad shoulders. It was six feet long, two wide and two high, carved and inlaid with gold. On the lid, facing each other, where two winged Isis, the tips of their jutting wings almost touching. The Nubians set it on the tiled floor.

"This has been in our family since the time of the Great Ahmose, the founder of our Dynasty," Pharaoh said, stepping down from the dais. "It is the one thing the false-priest of Amen never managed to get their greedy hands on."

He motioned for the four guards to lift the lid, which they did with great effort, setting it to the side.

"To lead your people," Pharaoh continued, "you will need a symbol to rally them with, like an Ankh, or the Living Image of the Aten's Solar Disk. Perhaps, this Ark..."

Calmly, Akhenaten reached into the chest and retrieved a seven-foot living, slithering asp and held it up. Everyone but Palace Guard Everard stepped back in fear. Pharaoh smiled. "What are you frightened of?"

He tossed the snake at Thutmose, who stepped back further. But in mid-air the snake had transformed into a seven-foot long piece of arcadia wood, which clattered to the floor.

"Pick it up, Brother."

Thutmose did as Pharaoh asked, hefting it in his hand, testing its weight, thrusting it in the air over his head. He seemed transfixed in the light shining in through the high windows. Transformed, he shouted: "Behold, the Hand of God!"

"It's mine!" screamed the Co-Regent Smenkhkare as he dashed forward, grabbing the staff, shoving Thutmose aside. He held the staff before him, parallel to the floor, waving it back and forth.

"Stand back! Or you will behold...er, God's Mighty Wrath!"

Everard and Paatenemheb took a step forward, but the Co-Regent leveled the staff at them and pressed a button hidden in a knot of the staff. Fire shot from the Transmutor like a modern-day flame-thrower. Everyone kept back and he let the flames reside.

The faux-Queen Nefertiti took a step toward him.

He smiled and said: "Ah, Barbarella."

"You're Duran Duran!" she exclaimed. "But how? You were an elderly man when you fled the destruction of Sogo."

"I escaped via my positronic generator just as Sogo blew. I was tossed back in time, de-aging approximately a year for each century I passed through."

"And you managed to gain the trust of Pharaoh?" Barbarella said. "In a few weeks?"

"I'd been here for three years before I came to the attention of Pharaoh. He fell in for some slight-of-hand tricks. The guy is an idiot... Aten this, Aten that... I had to bide my time." He raised the staff high. "Then I heard of this amidst the gossip of the City."

"It is just a stick," Barbarella opined.

"Just a stick!" he laughed. "This was once a branch of the *Tree of Life*, brought out of Eden and presented to Enoch, then to his great grandson, Noah, then though the Line of Shem down to Abraham, then to his own great-grandson Joseph, who brought it into Egypt. Joseph rose high in Pharaoh's Court, and the staff became the Treasure of Egyptian Kings. Now it's mine!"

"Great Jupiter," Manse Everard grunted. He was the only one other than Barbarella, the Time Traveler and Duran Duran who knew what was being said. "I've had enough of this."

But before he could act, Duran Duran pointed the Staff at the Time Patroller and issued forth a series of lightning bolts, scorching the walls behind him. Then he yelled for everyone to freeze, or the next time the wall wouldn't be the only thing ablaze.

With that, Duran Duran dashed from the Throne Room, with Everard, Paatenemheb, Sinahu and Thutmose hot on his tracks.

Barbarella was about to follow, but a hand on her shoulder from Akhenaten stayed her.

Duran Duran rushed down the steps and onto the Royal Road. His pursuers stopped in their tracks on the Palace steps and watched in horror.

Galloping at full head were two white steeds, whipped into action by a boy, Tutankhaten, whose side-locked head barely peeked out over the top of the basket.

Duran Duran saw the danger but just stood there, lifting the Staff and yelling: "Behold the Power of..."

The rest of his statement was cut off as the horses and chariot trampled over him, sending the Staff sailing through the air. Everard snatched it out of the air and tossed it back to Thutmose, saying: "Here, Moses, you might need this."

"Moses?" the Time Traveler said.

"Jumpin' Gods, haven't you been paying attention?" Everard said, walking back up the steps, adding, "Now everything is just as it was."

"Amen," said the Time Traveler.

"Aten, you mean," the Patroller corrected with a smile.

Meanwhile, in the Throne Room, Akhenaten said to Barbarella:

"I still do not know who you really are, but I thank you for bringing this." From his robe he produced the papyrus written by Nefertiti. "May I keep it? It will remind me of my Queen... before she forsook the Aten."

"No, she never forsaken the Aten *or* you, but you have rejected her, because she was unable to produce a male heir."

140

"Perhaps, the Queen is correct."

"Love, Akhenaten, Love."

"Life, Health, Prosperity! May you live a million, million years."

Manse Everard gathered together Barbarella and the Time Traveler for their voyage home. She hopped on the rear seat of the Time Hopper, while the Time Traveler positioned himself in *his* Time Machine, plugging the control lever in place.

Since the Time Machine was only a temporal device, moving *only* through time but not space, Everard used an anti-gravity tow-line to take it back to the future Richmond, English area, so that the Time Traveler could continue his journey back to 802,701 C.E. unimpeded.

And since her ship was now sunk at the bottom of the Nile, Everard delivered Barbarella back to the 40th century.

Then, his journey completed, Everard returned to his own mid-1950s apartment. There, he shared a scotch with Dard Kelm, from 9573 C.E., recapping his own recent adventure, and its outcome:

Back in 1336 B.C.E., Akhenaten and Nefertiti were reunited, with Pharaoh stepping down and allowing Nefertiti to rule as *Ankhkhetkheprure Nefernefruaten Smenkhkare*, with her daughter, Meritaten, as "queen." This readied the way for the reintroduction of Amen back into the country's pantheon, with Tutankhaten and Nefertiti's third daughter, Ankhesenpaaten, as King and Queen, under the watchful eyes of Counselor Ay and General Paatenemheb, now calling himself Horemheb, to distance himself from the failed Aten cult.

The King And Queen soon substituted the "aten" in their names for "amen."

Now Nefertiti was free to join her husband on his journey to foreign lands, teaching the Aten, even to uncharted lands aboard a ship of the "Sea People."

Akhenaten's half-brother, Thutmose or Moses, led his people out of Egypt and into a new land, with the help of his transmutor staff.

Both Akhenaten and his half-brother realized Truth was not in Akhetaten but outside. For the only Truth in the City of Akhetaten are starvation, misery and suffering, and no hope.

It was at this point in his re-telling that the reality and irony hit Everard. The Danellians had not sent him back in time *just* to put the Tree of Life staff into Thutmose's hand, but also to send the Time Traveler back to the future, on his predestined course, because from his interaction with the Eloi's gene pool would come the Danellians half-a-million years later.

All this interested Kelm very little. He wanted to know about Barbarella.

"She's off to see Paris," Manse said, after the Scotch had scorched his throat again.

"Paris, France?"

"Oh, no. Paris as in Helen of Troy's lover. Then she's off to see Marc Anthony."

"She must have been a wonder."

"Oh, yes, a real wonder woman!"

*In the original* Shadow *pulp novels, it was frequently mentioned that the slouch-hatted hero was known in the French underworld as* L'Ombre. *One novel,* Zemba, *has a lengthy conversation with a French crook in which The Shadow is only called* L'Ombre, *hence a canonical alias. Rick Lai has seized upon this opportunity to graft his latest epic onto the legends of Judex and the Black Coats (which he has previously explored) and since all the villains in this tale are either French or of French descent, it seems quite appropriate for them to call The Shadow* L'Ombre. *Rick notes that none of the other foreign language aliases mentioned in the opening ever appeared in the pulps, but* El Spectro *popped up in a 1958 Shadow film,* Invisible Avenger...

## Rick Lai: *Shadows Reborn*

*USA, Guatemala, Martinique, 1931-49*

> *I hear the shadows canting aloud,*
> *as ancient whistles beckon the shroud.*
> Humbert Kenneth Allard, *Dark Phantoms.*

The man in the black cloak knew many strange secrets because he walked in the shadows. He inspired nameless terror in the hearts of men and women who lurked in the night. He was a ruthless avenger of which criminals dared not speak.

This singular individual had many names. In the capitals of the world, frightened criminals whispered of *Il Simulacro, El Spectro, Der Schatten, Kage, Yingzi* and *Umbra.* The Black Coats of France knew him as *L'Ombre.* Since World War I, that international crime cartel had been pledged to the destruction of the dweller in the shadows.

In this historical account, the cloaked adventurer shall be referred to by his French *alias.* But no matter what name the mysterious individual used, felons across the globe viewed him with implacable hatred.

There was one criminal in whom *L'Ombre* aroused a different emotion. Her name was Thelda Blanche Bouchard and the only feeling that the vigilante stirred in her was love. Thelda had been the mistress of a master criminal who belonged to the Seven Silent Companions, the New York branch of the Black Coats. *L'Ombre* had fatally ended the career of Thelda's lover due to information given to him by the buxom brunette. After seducing Thelda to gain her trust, the vigilante had allowed her to escape. However, he had banished Thelda from New York and ordered her to go back to her native Louisiana.

143

The subsequent destruction of the other Silent Companions by *L'Ombre* had convinced Thelda that it was now safe to return to New York. She was wrong.

One night, in May1931, *L'Ombre* confronted Thelda in her room at the Ramsey Arms. A slouch hat covered the head of the man in the black cloak. Gloves encased his hands. The upper front of the cape obscured the lower portion of his face. Thelda had never seen her former's lover's true face. He was a master of disguise with multiple identities. He gestured menacingly at Thelda.

"Thelda Blanche Bouchard, I told you never to set foot again in New York again."

"I disobeyed your orders because I was beckoned by the greater power of love."

"We can never be lovers again. The shadow of a murdered man stands between us. Have you so soon forgotten Roger Crowthers? You poisoned him!"

"But all the stolen securities were returned to his rightful heirs!"

"Roger was a young man of great promise. He deserved a far better fate."

"Let me atone for my sins. Let me join your agents."

*L'Ombre* cruelly laughed. "Now I understand your motives. You hope to earn my love by fighting crime at my side. You are a fool! Uprooting crime is no task for a woman!"

"Tell that to the Tocsin! She fought crime in this very city over a decade ago. You must know of her. Your methods are very similar. She directed the activities of a rather dumb vigilante called the Gray Seal. There was also that insanely sadistic woman in Paris, the Revenant."

"How dare you!" shouted *L'Ombre*. His left hand grabbed Thelda's throat. "You're unworthy to mention *her* name!"

Thelda's right hand tried fruitlessly to pry *L'Ombre*'s grip loose. His anger quickly dissipated. He relinquished his hold on her neck. Thelda's right hand pulled off the vigilante's glove. A ring containing a fire opal was exposed on the fourth finger of his left hand. The glove fell to the floor. Quickly retrieving it, *L'Ombre* donned the glove.

"My apologies, Thelda Bouchard. The Gray Seal and the Tocsin are my idols. I am easily angered if they are treated disrespectfully. I should never have assaulted you."

"You can make amends by accepting me as one of your agents."

"My rejection is still in effect. I must punish you for violating your exile."

"What do you intend to do?"

"The police want to question a certain Miss Blanchet about Roger Crowthers's death. Twenty-four hours from now, a police detective will receive evidence exposing Blanchet a.k.a. Thelda Bouchard as his killer. I advise you to leave before that deadline is reached."

After *L'Ombre* had departed, left alone in her hotel room, Thelda smiled. On a bureau rested *The Art of Poison* by Noel J. Hendricks. The middle of the book had been hollowed out to hide a singular object. Opening it, she pulled out a chain necklace and latched it around her neck. Examining herself in a mirror, she admired the gem that dangled at the end of it. It was a fire opal very similar to the one mounted on *L'Ombre's* ring.

The history of the necklace was unknown to her. After she had poisoned Crowthers to steal a fortune in securities for the Seven Silent Companions, she had searched her victim's estate and found the necklace inside a secret compartment near the fireplace. She had selfishly decided to keep it for herself.

Runa Kritchnoff was a jewel thief with only one regular partner, Mimile Justin, who drove the getaway car for her burglaries. Despite their fourteen years difference, Mimile and Runa were passionate lovers. In 1914, when he was twenty, Mimile had been a driver for the Secret Raiders, a European gang of thieves. When they had disbanded after an epic battle with Judex, the French vigilante also known as the "Mysterious Shadow," Mimile had sought refuge in the United States.

One night in California, Runa burglarized the Harrison estate. As she exited the mansion through the window, she had been spied by Mrs. Harrison, who quickly telephoned the police. With a patrol car on his tail, Mimile drove as fast as he could. Taking a narrow turn, he lost control of his car, which went off the road and crashed into a ditch.

In the back seat, Runa was miraculously unscathed, but Mimile wasn't so lucky: his left leg was broken.

"I can't leave you," pleaded Runa.

"Take the swag and run," insisted Mimile. "The cops will be here any minute."

With tears in her eyes, Runa kissed Mimile before disappearing into the night.

Runa conferred with a colleague in a booth of the *Crow's Nest*, a seedy bar in San Francisco. Pierre "the Spotter" Lecoq was reputed to know by sight every crook and detective in America. He earned his income by acting as a paid consultant to other would-be lawbreakers.

Lecoq was descended from two of the greatest criminals in history: Lecoq de la Perrière and his diabolical mistress, Marguerite Sadoulas. They had both been members of the High Council of the Black Coats, led by the supposedly immortal Colonel Bozzo-Corona. Both of those legendary malefactors had died violently in the 19th century. Lecoq de la Perrière's head had been crushed by a safe door; Marguerite had been burned alive.

"I need to raise money, Pierre," said Runa. "District Attorney Bryan is throwing the book at Mimile. Mrs. Harrison suffered a serious heart attack after calling the police. She survived, but the D.A.'s going to charge Mimile for attempted murder. I hired Lee Gentry to defend him."

"A wise choice," replied Lecoq. The beady eyes of the lean man sparkled. "Gentry's the best mouthpiece in the country."

"But he's damned expensive," continued the raven-haired Runa. "I have some cash stashed away, but I'll need to do at least two more robberies in order to afford his services."

"Then do them."

"I'll need a driver to replace Mimile. Can you recommend anyone?"

"Yes. Lefty Vigran's wife, Toni. She's a superb driver."

"Good! There only remains the matter of your fee."

After paying Lecoq, Runa drove her car to the Vigrans' apartment. When she knocked, the door was opened by a different woman than Toni Vigran. She was wearing a necklace.

"I know you," said Runa. "We met at your uncle's Mardi Gras party in New Orleans last year. You're Thelda Bouchard."

"I remember you, too! You're Runa Kritchnoff! The Vigrans and I are old friends. They're letting me stay with them."

"Is Toni home?"

"No. She and Lefty are celebrating their wedding anniversary at the High Hat."

"What rotten luck! I have a business proposition for her."

"Maybe I can help you? Do come in."

After Runa entered, Thelda closed the door.

"Can you drive a getaway car?" asked Runa.

"How do you think Toni and I met? We both drove beer trucks for my uncle."

"I need a driver for two jobs; one is scheduled for late tonight; the other for tomorrow night."

"I'm on the lam for one murder already. I can't afford another one. When we last met, you scrupulously avoided killing. Is that still true?"

"You know my family's history. My mother was brutally slain. I refuse to inflict death on anyone."

"Good. W, there's the matter of my share."

"30 percent of the loot."

"You've been staring at my girasol necklace. If you can positively identify the gem, I'll take 25 percent."

"Agreed. Let's go to my place. My reference books on gems are there."

In her apartment, Runa wore a jeweler's eyeglass as she examined Thelda's necklace. Once she finished, she removed the eyeglass and handed the necklace back to her companion, who placed it back around her neck.

Runa consulted her copy of Bernard Sutton's *Encyclopedia of Fabulous Gems* and said:

"You must have one of the three Szinca Girasols, Thelda. The Szincas are a native tribe in Guatemala. They revere an unnamed stone idol in the Yucatán peninsula. It is said that they possessed three magnificent fire opals. Two became the eyes of their idol. The third was placed in its navel. In 1793, a Spanish adventurer, Juan Gonzalles, stole one of the idol's eyes and the third opal from the navel. Eight years later, he sold the two stones to the Tsar Paul I of Russia, who was assassinated shortly thereafter. While the former idol's eye was openly displayed among the Russian crown jewels, the other opal was inexplicably locked away into a vault. In 1881, Tsar Alexander II asked to see it. Then, a few days later, he was killed by a Nihilist bomb. Convinced that the jewel was cursed, the new Tsar sold it to a wealthy American. The sale was secret, and the name of the purchaser was never publicly revealed."

"My gem has to be that third opal, Runa. It was previously the property of Roger Crowthers, who had inherited it from his wealthy uncle, Jethro Clayton. He must have been the anonymous purchaser. What about the other opal? The idol's eye?"

"According to this book, it was made into a ring."

*That must be my beloved's ring*, thought Thelda. "What happened to that ring?"

"The book doesn't say because it was published in 1910 But when I was a young girl in Russia, I saw a ring whose jewel resembled your necklace's opal. It belonged to Alaric Kentoff, a spy reporting directly to the Tsar. He died in an airplane crash during the Great War."

"Was his ring recovered?"

"It was probably incinerated in the crash."

"How much is the fire opal worth?"

"As much as the Blue Diamond or the Black Pearl. In other words, a small fortune."

"Thanks, Runa. Now, let's pull our first job!"

"As soon as I change, Thelda."

Night had already fallen. The slender Runa retreated to her bedroom. When she returned, her dress had been replaced by a black ensemble consisting of a turtleneck sweater, pants, boots and gloves. She held a gun pointed at Thelda. She placed a glass of water on the table.

"I'm sorry, Thelda, but your opal will save the man I love. This glass contains a Mickey Finn. By the time you wake up, I'll be long gone. Drink it!"

Picking up the glass, Thelda threw its contents into Runa's eyes. She kicked upward and knocked the gun out of the blinded thief's hand. Then she slammed her elbow into Runa's stomach and punched her in the jaw. The thief slammed into the wall, then slid downwards to the floor. Removing her necklace, Thelda looped it over Runa's head and around her neck.

"You wanted my necklace, Runa. Have it as a noose!"

"Mercy," begged the thief. "Remember you wanted to avoid murder."

"May your death be as painful as your mother's."

Thelda tightened the necklace until Runa was choked to death.

Leaving the apartment, Thelda opted not to steal Runa's car. Instead, she walked five blocks before hailing a cab. During her journey, she passed a whistling man in a black trench coat and hat. It was Pierre Lecoq. His eyes narrowed upon viewing Thelda's girasol necklace.

Thelda booked passage on a ship to Guatemala. Then, she traveled across the country to the Yucatán. She hoped to find the other eye of the idol that had not been stolen in 1793. At an inn, she brazenly wore her necklace. She made sure that it was seen by any employee of native descent. While she was having breakfast, a waiter dropped a tray when he saw the necklace. Thelda tracked him down and confronted him.

"I bear one of the sacred fire opals. Take me to the elder of your tribe."

Soon after, Thelda sat with her legs crossed on the ground in a stone temple. Two husky Szincas with machetes stood behind her. Seated on the ground in front of her was an elderly native. Behind the old man was a stone idol with *both* eye sockets vacant.

"Did Kentoff send you?" asked the old man.

Thelda instantly concluded that Kentoff was *L'Ombre*. Runa must have been wrong about the Tsarist agent's death.

"Yes."

"Prove that you are Kentoff's emissary."

"Alaric Kentoff wears one of the sacred opals on the fourth finger of his left hand."

"Who gave Kentoff that ring?"

"The Tsar of all Russia."

"Kentoff has a second ring. How did he come by it?"

Thelda realized that any incorrect answer would result in the two natives slaying her. Since she couldn't refuse to answer, she gave the most logical deduction:

"When Kentoff came among you, he showed you his Russian ring. You removed your idol's other eye and gave it to him; then, a duplicate ring was made to house this opal."

"You are truly the envoy of the Eagle of Darkness. Does Kentoff wish me to make another ring for the opal in your necklace?"

"Yes."

"Does Kentoff still want us only to communicate with him in his false skin of Sanger Rainsford?"

*Sanger Rainsford,* thought Thelda, *is a famous explorer and big game hunter. He's frequently traveling outside the United States. Kentoff must imper-*

*sonate Rainsford while he's journeying in the remote corners of the globe. This is a variation on Arsène Lupin's old ploy of impersonating a man who secretly died abroad.*

"Yes," she replied.

In her hotel room in Guatemala, Thelda wore the girasol ring that the Szincas had forged for her. She was thumbing through a notebook. It belonged to her late lover, a Silent Companion who pretended to be a psychiatrist. He had been one of two bogus psychiatrists trained by *N'a-qu'un-Chasse*, the deceased chief of the Secret Raiders. The other pseudo-psychiatrist was a notorious figure currently confined in a Berlin asylum. Like *N'a-qu'un-Chasse*, his two students had scrupulously written blueprints for future crimes. Thelda read a section from the Silent Companion's testament:

*Dormant Account Swindle*

*William Lane was a secretive English philanthropist. In New York, in 1909, he married Marielle Gibson, the daughter of Benjamin and Angelique Gibson. One year later, she died while giving birth to a daughter. Leaving his daughter in the custody of her American in-laws, Lane returned to England. He set up a trust fund for his offspring to be managed by said in-laws. In 1918, both in-laws perished during the influenza epidemic. Lane then transferred the custody of his daughter to Angelique's cousin, Marie LaSalle. In 1920, Marie married James Dale, a prosperous manufacturer of safes.*

*In the same year, William Lane was convicted of counterfeiting in England. An American court ratified the formal adoption of his daughter by the Dales. Fearful that the press might uncover the connection between the counterfeiter and her foster daughter, Marie LaSalle Dale persuaded her husband to move from New York to the island of Martinique. Marie had inherited an estate there from her mother, Andrée Duprès LaSalle.*

*Just before his arrest in 1920, Lane had transferred a bank account from his name to his daughter's. Containing one million dollar deposited at the Standard Savings Bank in New York, it was to be inherited by her at age of 21. Due to the confusion caused by Lane's arrest, Marie Dale was never notified of the existence of this bank account. After being released from Dartmoor in 1925, Lane completely disappeared. His daughter became eligible to claim the account on February 8, 1931.*

*New York newspapers published a recent advertisement mentioning many dormant accounts at the Standard Savings Bank. The one belonging to Lane's daughter was among them. The bank has been unable to trace her because she is living in Martinique under the last name of Dale.*

*Thelda would be the perfect person to impersonate Lane's daughter. Both women are brunettes. While Thelda was born in 1905, she can easily pass for a woman five years younger. I could dispatch Thelda to Martinique in order to purloin some document to complete the impersonation.*

Since it was impossible for Thelda to return to New York in her real identity, imitating Kentoff's impersonation of Rainsford, she decided to steal the identity of Lane's offspring.

Marie LaSalle Dale and two other women were at a popular tennis court in Fort-de-France, the préfecture of the French colony of La Martinique.

"Too bad we don't have a fourth player," said Marie. "We could play doubles."

"Perhaps I could make up that deficiency," announced a dark-haired newcomer. "May I join you, ladies?" asked Thelda Bouchard.

"Certainly," acknowledged Marie.

"My name is Angelique Blanchet," claimed Thelda.

"I'm Marie Dale." Thelda judged Marie's age to be around 40.

"My name is Maggie Dale," said a younger woman. "I'm Marie's daughter."

"I'm Alice Duprès," said a woman around the same age as Maggie. Alice's accent identified her as an island native. "I'm Maggie's cousin."

Thelda partnered with Maggie in a game of doubles. Once it had concluded, Maggie and Alice played against each other while Thelda and Marie sat watching them.

"From your accent, Angelique, I gather you must be from Louisiana?" deduced Marie.

"Quite right. My family moved from La Martinique to New Orleans in the 18th century. My forebears were worried about a slave revolt after a member of our family was stabbed to death. I'm here to conduct some genealogical research. There's an old story in my family about an earlier Angelique who married a wealthy American. I'm trying to verify her existence."

"Angelique was the name of Maggie's grandmother," volunteered Marie. "She married an auto tycoon."

"Could you tell me more about your family? Maybe Maggie's grandmother and I are related?"

"Maggie is not my natural daughter. She's adopted. I have two other children. Maggie's grandmother was actually my father's first cousin. When my own mother died, Maggie's grandmother helped my father raise me. She was a formidable influence on my life."

Marie then engaged in a lengthy discourse on Maggie's antecedents that provided valuable information for Thelda's planned impersonation.

"Have you or Maggie ever considered returning to the United States?" asked Thelda.

"Crime was always a problem before Prohibition, but now it's spiraled out of control. When I was younger, I might have toughed it out. Now that I'm a mother with children, I have no intention of going back there. My family's only exposure to crime will be my husband's collection of mystery fiction."

"What about Maggie? Does she want to go back to New York?"

"She enjoys herself here. There's no reason for her to ever leave."

Once Alice and Maggie had finished their game, the latter had a question:

"Angelique, did you enjoy chatting with Mother Margot?"

Thelda turned to Mrs. Dale. "Margo? I thought your name was Marie."

"Mother Margot was a nickname of my adventurous youth," explained Marie. "My middle name is Margot. Maggie likes to call me that for a special reason. You probably assumed that my daughter's nickname was short for Margaret. It's actually short for Margot."

"Just like that Broadway actress, Margo Channing."

"No, Angelique." corrected Maggie. "Unlike Miss Channing, I have a 't' at the end of my name."

The conversation ended with Marie inviting Thelda for dinner at the Dale estate.

During her visit there, Thelda stole Maggie's passport. It was child's play to replace Maggie's photo with her own.

Arriving in New York in September, Thelda used the passport to get a copy of Maggie's birth certificate and the adoption decree from the proper government agencies. Armed with these documents, she then proceeded to the Standard Saving Bank. There, she gained immediate acceptance as Maggie Dale. Laying claim to the saving account, Thelda converted it into a checking account.

Upon departing the bank, Thelda was watched by a whistling Pierre Lecoq. The underworld fixer had followed her trail from San Francisco to Guatemala. After losing track of her in the Yucatán, Lecoq had monitored the outgoing ships from Guatemala. Discovering Thelda had booked passage for the Caribbean, he had skillfully shadowed her in both Martinique and New York.

John Sinclair, the extremely successful industrialist, was holding a lavish party to celebrate being granted an honorary lifetime membership by the Boy Scouts of America.

Among the guests were two renowned heroes of the Great War. Both wore their Army uniforms. One was a Major who served in the artillery. He was a broad-faced man with a short-clipped mustache. The other was Captain "Ragging" Rassendyll, one of the greatest aces to fly for the Allied Powers. He was currently assigned to Roosevelt Field in order to evaluate the Curtiss O2C-2 and other Navy aircraft for possible reuse by the Army.

"I've heard a rumor, Major, that you'll be resigning your commission early next year," said Rassendyll.

"Don't tell anyone, Captain," whispered the Major, "but Mayor Walker is considering my appointment as Police Commissioner. "

"Tough job. The Police Department is currently riddled with graft."

"Captain, it's been a long time," interrupted a hawk-faced man wearing a girasol ring.

"Sanger, what a surprise!" said Rassendyll. "Major, this is Sanger Rainsford."

"The world-famous explorer!" exclaimed the Major. "I've read all your books. My favorites are *The Death Tower of Ahriman* and *The Shadows Canting Aloud: Devil Worship in Yian.*"

"Actually Sanger Rainsford is a literary pseudonym," said the newcomer handing the Major a business card. "Printed there is my real name."

The Major read the name aloud. "Lament Granston?"

"What?" uttered a surprised Rainsford. "Let me take a look at that card. The ink is smudged slightly on two letters. Here's a properly printed one."

"Excuse me, gentlemen, may I join you?" asked a young woman carrying a book and wearing gloves.

"Of course," answered the Major. "The presence of a charming young lady is always welcome.''

"My name is Maggie Lane Dale," said Thelda Bouchard. "I'm Benjamin Gibson's granddaughter."

"I remember his life story very well," noted the Major. "He started shining shoes and ended up the founder of a motor car company."

"Grandfather's business was a modest success. When he and grandmother died from influenza, I became the eight-year old heiress to the Gibson Motor Car Company. In 1924, my foster parents sold the company to John Sinclair."

"That company has since become the cornerstone of Sinclair's business empire," observed Captain Rassendyll.

Thelda turned her attention to Sanger Rainsford.

"Mr. Rainsford, I'm your greatest fan. I only came to this party because Mr. Sinclair told me you would be invited. Could you sign my copy of your book, *The Snow Leopard of Tibet*?"

"I'll be glad to," acknowledged Rainsford. He took the book, signed it and handed it back to Thelda.

"I wonder, gentlemen, if you could give a struggling author some advice," stated Thelda. "I've written a novel and need help in finding a publisher."

"What's your book called?" asked Rassendyll.

"*Who Knows What Goodness Lurks in the Hearts of Women*?" revealed Thelda,

"Catchy title," said the Major. "What's the novel about?"

"It's about a woman with a sinful past," explained Thelda. "She is a thief and a murderess, but the love of a highly moralistic man redeems her. I based my hero on two men of your acquaintance, Captain Rassendyll."

"Who are these men?" questioned Rassendyll.

Thelda smiled slyly. "One was a pilot who flew for the last Tsar. He was named Alaric Kentoff."

"Kentoff!" exclaimed Rassendyll. "I remember him well. A man whose fantastic sense of humor always made him good for a laugh. Who's the other man merged with Kentoff?"

"Mr. Rainsford."

"I can find you a publisher, Miss Dale," interjected Rainsford. "We should talk in private. Gentlemen, please excuse us."

Rainsford escorted the fake Maggie Dale to a remote corner of the Sinclair mansion.

"What's your game, Thelda?" asked Rainsford. "How did you discover my identity?"

Thelda removed her left glove. She revealed a ring that matched Rainsford's.

"A Szinca Girasol!" he exclaimed.

"Yes, Alaric. Your Guatemalan friends were very informative. I even learned the basis for your Kentoff alias. Shall I address you by your true name?"

"What do you want?"

"I want you to recruit me as an agent."

"It seems that I have no choice. You'll be receiving your orders either directly from me or from a man known by the initial B."

"When do I meet this B?

"You never shall. Your communications with him will be solely by telephone."

"Can't you tell me B's real name?"

"If you ever fully gain my trust, I'll tell you."

"What are my duties? I could spy on the wealthy elite."

"You will only do that on rare occasions. Your primary duty is to provide transportation."

"Transportation?"

"You're an excellent driver, Thelda. The main deficiency in my organization is the lack of a *de facto* chauffeur."

"Don't you have a genuine chauffeur when you impersonate Rainsford?"

"That nitwit isn't an agent. He was hired by the real Rainsford. I have to engage in needless subterfuge whenever that dunce drives me around New York."

153

On, Monday, October 12, 1931, New York City was packed with tourists. Many had come to see the Columbus Day Parade held that morning.[4]

That night, a horrible murder spree engulfed New York. A monstrous beast had escaped. After massacring several people in a theater, the berserk creature derailed a subway train. The horrible rampage finally climaxed at the Empire State Building the following day. After ascending the floors of the skyscraper, and throwing people out the windows, the monster was cornered by an elite military unit under Captain Rassendyll's command. The soldiers had to be particularly careful because the beast had taken a young woman hostage. Shot in the neck by Rassendyll, the creature fell from the top of the skyscraper. The hostage was luckily unharmed.

A huge crowd gathered around the corpse of Rassendyll's quarry. Among the spectators were *L'Ombre* and Thelda, posing respectively as Sanger Rainsford and Maggie Dale. Thelda was attired in an evening gown and a mink coat.

"Do you think it was the fall that killed him?" asked Thelda.

"It wasn't the fall," replied *L'Ombre*. "It was the bullets that killed the brute."

Suddenly a black limousine with a siren arrived. Standing on the running board of the vehicle was a Herculean figure. He was the most prominent doctor residing in New York.

Elsewhere in the crowd were the Major and Ed Somers, a reporter for the *Daily Register*. Somers carried a camera. He often took photographs that accompanied his stories.

"One of the policemen told me that Doc was here earlier," noted the Major.

"Yes," confirmed Somers. "He drove up in a different car. Entering the skyscraper's lobby, he noticed an injured man receiving medical attention. Doc volunteered to drive the man to the nearest hospital in another of his cars. One of his aides drove the car while he attended to the patient in the back."

The crowd in front of the Empire State Building parted like the Red Sea in order to allow the giant to enter the building.

"Is that your rival?" asked Thelda indicating the tall doctor.

"Yes," answered *L'Ombre*. "I scrupulously monitor his movements."

A thickset man suddenly addressed the couple. "I need your help, Nero and I were travelling on the subway when that fiend attacked it. I survived the crash, but I can't find Nero."

The speaker was the owner of both an extravagant restaurant and a night club. In his guise as Rainsford, *L'Ombre* had frequently dined at each location. At the restaurant, he had been introduced to Nero, the owner's oldest friend.

---

[4] Although Columbus Day didn't become a federal holiday until six years later, it was celebrated locally throughout the United States.

"I saw him hours ago," declared *L'Ombre*. "He was driven by Doc to the hospital. We'll take you there."

"How can you? The police are only allowing emergency vehicles on the road."

"The police aren't as honest as they should be. See that motorcycle cop over there. His name's Don Parker. It's well known that he takes bribes. I'll pay him to give us a police escort."

A 13-year old boy from Illinois then interrupted.

"Hey, Mister! Who's the big bronze guy with the fancy car?"

*L'Ombre* glared threateningly at the young tourist. His gaze shifted back to the restaurateur standing next to Thelda.

"Come on, Marko," he whispered. "I've work to do."

Together with Marko and Thelda, *L'Ombre* melted into the crowd.

"You were very rude to that boy," admonished Thelda. "I wonder how much he overheard."

"It doesn't matter, Miss Dale," said *L'Ombre*. "Excitable lads like him always get details wrong."

On their way towards Parker, the trio passed the Major and Ed Somers. The reporter snapped a picture.

The act of bribery was quickly concluded. Reaching her car, Thelda got behind the wheel. *L'Ombre* and Marko sat in the back seat. As the car sped away to follow Parker's motorcycle, *L'Ombre* spotted a criminal whom he had encountered him in the past. Standing on the sidewalk was Pierre Lecoq whistling in the darkness of the night.

*L'Ombre*, Marko and Thelda reached the hospital. They discovered that the beast had taken Nero hostage at the site of the subway crash. Transporting Nero across New York, the brute had then dropped him on the pavement in front of the Empire State Building.

Despite later recovering fully from his injuries, Marko's friend was extremely traumatized. For the rest of his life, Nero became a recluse. Rarely did he ever venture outside his home.

During March 1932, Thelda found herself suddenly summoned to San Francisco. She knew that her shadowy superior had gone there to smash a narcotics ring. The order to leave for California came through B, the operative whom she only knew as a telephone voice. Her only instructions were to go to the Aldebaran Hotel where *L'Ombre* was staying as Sanger Rainsford.

At the hotel, *L'Ombre* merely told her to accompany him in a taxi cab. To Thelda's surprise, the cab arrived at a cemetery.

"What are we doing here?" asked Thelda.

"Visiting a grave," answered *L'Ombre*.

Alighting from the cab, Thelda followed the vigilante passed several rows of graves. Finally *L'Ombre* halted at a tombstone. Thelda involuntarily gasped when she read the inscription:

RUNA VALDA KRITCHNOFF
BELOVED NIECE
*1908-1931*

"Did you know her?" asked *L'Ombre*.

"Yes," replied Thelda.

"How?"

"My uncle is Emile Bouchard, the New Orleans bootlegger. Runa and I met at his Mardi Gras party in 1930."

"Were you friends?"

"Yes."

"Do you know the story of her parents?"

"Her mother was Sonia Kritchnoff. Her father was the greatest jewel thief in Europe, Arsène Lupin."

"You must never again mention my brother's name. I despise him."

"Your brother? Runa was your niece!"

"Yes, but she never knew it. When her mother died, my brother sent Runa to be raised by Russian Orthodox nuns. He secretly paid for her upbringing."

"You were in Russia during the war as Kentoff. You must have traced her."

"Very perceptive. I tried to be a father to her like my sister had been a mother to me."

*"Your sister?"*

"That's a story for another day. Like my brother, my sister had a somewhat checkered past. Unlike my brother, she atoned for her sins." Tears formed in his eyes. "Runa was such an innocent child. Yet she became a criminal like her father."

"What happened?"

"When Runa was only nine, the Bolshevik Revolution broke out. She was taken away from the orphanage by her father. Under his malign influence, she became a thief. I finally located her in Paris in 1929. By that time, she was already a hardened felon. She didn't even recognize me as the Alaric Kentoff of her youth. I had two choices: kill her or forgive her. I chose to forgive her. I clung stubbornly to the hope that she would somehow find redemption just as my sister had. Runa died last year. I didn't learn of her death until this recent trip. She was lying in a pauper's grave. I had her moved here."

"How did she die?"

"She was strangled by an unknown assailant."

"Do you intend to avenge her?"

"What would be the point? My brother is the person ultimately responsible for her death. Her loss will be enough punishment for him. During the war, I pursued a personal vendetta against a woman named Cagliostro. She taught me that vengeance has unexpected consequences. I have no intention of repeating that experience."

"Why did you bring me all the way to San Francisco?"

"Runa's death hit me hard. I needed to unburden my soul to someone. You're the only one of my agents with any real inkling of my past."

"I thought that I knew all your secrets. I've only scratched the surface."

"Runa's death made me realize one thing." Grasping Thelda's hands, *L'Ombre* looked into her eyes. "I've been alone too long."

Their lips met in a passionate kiss. *L'Ombre* then pushed her gently way.

"My niece's grave is not the proper place for this," he said. "Be patient. I need some time to grieve. You will be returning to New York tomorrow. You will be hearing from the man whose full name lies within this riddle: *The Training of the Human Plant.*"

"A clue to B's identity. I'll figure it out at the New York Public Library."

"I'm sure you will. Your faithful service over the last six months proves you can be trusted."

"When will you come back to New York?"

"Within a few days. I have some loose ends to tidy up here."

As *L'Ombre* and his companion returned to the cab, they didn't noticed a figure hidden behind a mausoleum. As the cab left, Pierre Lecoq whistled strangely. His short physique cast a long shadow.

Back in her room at the Aldebaran Hotel, Thelda was filled with exultation. It was only a matter of time before she would once more share *L'Ombre*'s bed.

A year passed. One day, Thelda was waiting for *L'Ombre* in her car. He was off shooting criminals somewhere in Bergen County, New Jersey. She puffed on a Lucky Strike cigarette as her favorite program, *The Lone Ranger*, began to play on the radio.

Thelda was incredibly frustrated. For a year since their encounter in San Francisco, she had continued to faithfully serve *L'Ombre*. Yet he had consistently refused to make love to her. Nor did he elaborate any further about his secret past. He never indicated any intimacy by calling her Maggie. He usually addressed her as "Miss Dale," but when he was annoyed with her behavior, he sarcastically referred to her as "Margot."

Thelda began to concoct wild fantasies about *L'Ombre*. She imagined that he had taken a vow of celibacy to fight crime. Besides smoking, she also relieved her anxieties with alcohol. She was finding it increasingly difficult to play the role of a refined socialite. Her speech would frequently lapse into profanity.

As Thelda listened to the stirring theme of *The Lone Ranger*, a stranger approached her car...

Two months later, *L'Ombre* knew something was wrong with Thelda. She wasn't answering his calls. Posing as Sanger Rainsford, he knocked on the door at her apartment. When no one answered, he picked the lock and found Thelda sitting in a chair. Her left hand was in front of her face. Staring at the fire opal, she was muttering incoherently:

"The ring talks to me. It promised to place me next to the man I love. It did so, but this man, the man of the shadows, refuses to love me. Now he will never do so. Once he learns the truth, I'll be lost to him forever."

*L'Ombre* drove Thelda upstate to the Hudson Mental Institution in Leeson. Working at that asylum was Dr. Ira Burbank Franklin, the acclaimed author of *Studies in Necrophobia (Exaggerated Fear of Death)*. Following an examination of Thelda, he reported his results to the vigilante:

"My cousin Luther explained everything on the phone, sir. Too bad we couldn't meet under better circumstances. Miss Dale is in the grip of a severe mental trauma. She is in the midst of an identity crisis. In the course of our interview, she contradictorily referred to herself as Angelique Blanchet and Thelda Bouchard."

"Neither of those persons has any basis in reality. They only exist in your patient's imagination, Doctor."

"This personality disorder probably resulted when Miss Dale learned the truth about her physical condition."

"Is something physically wrong with Miss Dale?"

"All potential inmates are given a physical exam in addition to the psychological assessment. Miss Dale is pregnant."

"I'm not the father," asserted *L'Ombre*.

"I do not doubt it. Miss Dale admits she only had sexual relations with you in early 1931. However, her identification of the real father makes no sense."

"Who does she name?"

"Rip Van Winkle."

"Ah! It must have been that lunatic!"

"Please elaborate?"

"Two months ago, Miss Dale and I were in Bergen County. One night, I left her to attend to some private business. When I returned, there was a strange man in the car with her. He was dressed in clothes in the style of the 18th century and claimed to be Rip Van Winkle."

"Miss Dale was frustrated due to your refusal to have sex with her. She obviously must have relieved her anxiety by making love to this stranger."

"I realize that now, Doctor."

"What happened to the stranger?"

"Concluding that he was a madman, I decided to turn him over to the authorities. Sitting in the back of the car, I held my gun on this phony Rip Van Winkle as he sat in the front next to Miss Dale. She drove the car across the George Washington Bridge. Heavy traffic brought our movement to a crawl after we crossed it. Since the weather was warm, the top was down. I must have drunk too much liquor that night. I imagined a blazing flash of purple light. When I regained my composure, my prisoner had vanished."

"Taking advantage of what I suppose to be a momentary hallucination, he must have leapt out of the car and fled."

"I agree, Doctor. The Dale family is rather well known. I would like to avoid a scandal."

"That's easily avoidable. Luther told me that the patient is adopted. She will be listed in our records under the surname of her natural father. Only I and the head nurse, Miss Carroll, know that her real name is Dale."

"There is also the matter of the patient's first name, Doctor. It should be totally different."

"What's the patient's full name?

"Margot Phoebe Lane Dale."

"Perhaps Phoebe Lane might make an adequate alias?"

"An excellent idea, Doctor! I understand that you have a private foundation to fund your research into necrophobia. I would like to make a substantial contribution."

The fake Rainsford made out a check and handed it to Dr. Franklin.

In 1934, *L'Ombre* compensated for Thelda's absence by recruiting a taxi cab driver as an agent to replace her. In the same year, Thelda's son was born. Since she was registered at the asylum under the name of "Phoebe Lane," the child was born under that same surname. At Thelda's insistence, the boy was given the first name of Kenton. With Dr. Franklin's connivance, *L'Ombre*, still acting as Rainsford, took custody of the child. He also imported a husband and wife, both Szinca Indians, to raise him.

Dr. Franklin concluded that his patient's insanity stemmed from her possession of the girasol ring. He hoped to cure her by removing it from her finger. Unfortunately, any effort to force the patient to relinquish the ring resulted in hysterical outbursts. Therefore, he let her keep the ring.

Over the ensuing years, *L'Ombre* made substantial contributions to the Necrophobia Foundation. These contributions cost him nothing. Before committing Thelda to the asylum, the vigilante had the confused woman sign several blank checks as Margot Dale. He then engaged in a money laundering scheme in which Thelda's ill-gotten gains paid for her own confinement. The money from the checks signed with Margot Dale's name was deposited in an account that *L'Ombre* maintained while impersonating Rainsford. Money from that account was then disbursed to both the Hudson Mental Institution and the Necrophobia Foundation.

M. K. Simmons, the rotund manager of the Standard Savings Bank, sweated profusely as he fingered the photographs in his private office.

"Where did you get these?"

"Isn't it obvious?' replied Pierre Lecoq. "The lovely Rhea Gutman was employed by me to seduce you. If you don't want your wife to learn of your love affair, you shall give me what I want."

"How much?"

"You insult me, Mr. Simmons. I desire something far more important than mere money."

"What's that?"

"Information. I've been trying to find a woman. Her name is Margot Dale. She vanished from her apartment two years ago. I know that she has a substantial bank account here. Your payment for my silence is access to her bank records."

Simmons acceded to Lecoq's demands. Perusing the records, the criminal noticed checks written during 1933-1935 to a man who had been with Thelda in both New York and San Francisco.

"You won't be seeing the last of me, Mr. Simmons. Whenever I'm in New York, I shall stop by to scrutinize the transactions against Miss Dale's account."

In early May 1940, Mimile Justin was released from Alcatraz. He had heard of Runa Kritchnoff's death during his imprisonment. Intending to avenge her murder, he sought out the best informed criminal in the underworld. At the *Crow's Nest* in San Francisco, he talked to Pierre Lecoq. Seated at the bar, the underworld expediter was reading a copy of Sanger Rainsford's *The Shadows Canting Aloud : Devil Worship in Yian.*

"Pierre, there's something that I need to know. I can't afford your consultation fee, but maybe we can strike a deal."

"If this concerns Runa, my services are free."

"Do you have any idea who killed her?"

"I saw Thelda Bouchard leaving her apartment the night of her murder. Thelda must have croaked Runa."

"I've never met Thelda. What does she look like?"

"She's a good-looking broad with black hair."

"Any idea where she is now?"

"She's in New York. Calls herself Maggie Dale."

"How can I find this Maggie in New York?"

"Look for her boyfriend. He's a rich swell. His photo is on the back of this book."

Mimile examined the book. "Where does this Rainsford hang out?"

"At a night club owned by a guy named Marko." Pulling out a pen, Lecoq wrote on a napkin. "Here's the address. Rainsford's an alias." Lecoq wrote the author's true name.

Mimile pocketed the napkin.

"Thanks, Pierre. I'll need to pull a few jobs before I can afford the plane fare to New York."

"This will cover the plane fare and more," said Lecoq. Pulling out a huge wad of cash, he placed it in Mimile's hand.

"Is this a loan?"

"No. This is your payment in advance for a murder contract. I want Maggie Dale dead."

"Why?"

"Runa was a classy dame. I liked her a lot."

"Pierre, you're a real pal."

Lecoq whistled to himself as Mimile left the *Crow's Nest*. Some hours later, the enigmatic criminal made a long distance phone call to New Orleans.

"Black Spear Holdings," answered a secretary. *"Will there be daylight?"*

*"It will be daylight from midnight to noon if it's the will of the Father,"* replied Lecoq. "Tell the Colonel that *Toulonnais-l'Amitié* desires an audience."

After a few minutes, an old and yet somehow youthful voice responded to Lecoq's request.

"The prodigal son returns. You left my employment once. Madame Palmyre found you a new home. Your behavior was extremely ungrateful, my boy."

"Forgive me, All-Father. I was frightened by what happened during that witch's séance. I'm now ready to embrace my servitude. Of course, I want a seat on the High Council. There are a lot of vacancies after the Sunlight fiasco in Moscow that nearly ruined the Black Coats."

"You have to earn that position, my lad. You can't demand it."

"I'm more than ready to demonstrate my worthiness to act again as your chief lieutenant, All-Father. You only told me a theory about the parentage of the troublesome *L'Ombre*."

"I believe him to be the Revenant's son. Only Countess Cagliostro ever learned *L'Ombre*'s true identity, but she selfishly took that information to her grave. "

"The Revenant once commissioned your assassination. You survived, but your mistress was killed."

"I curse the Revenant for causing the demise of my precious Desdemona."

"I intend to orchestrate the death of *L'Ombre*'s lover, Thelda Bouchard. It would be a fitting revenge for Desdemona's death to slay the paramour of the Revenant's son. "

"I know of Mademoiselle Bouchard's romantic connection to *L'Ombre*. The Seven Silent Companions sent me a report about her in 1931. Don't lie to me, my apostate apprentice. You targeted Bouchard years ago. You just waited for the opportune time to apprise me of her. My relocation in America due to the current European war is such an opportunity."

"I could never fool my old tutor."

"Does L'Ombre care for this Bouchard woman?"

"I saw them lustfully embrace with my own eyes. L'Ombre cares about Bouchard so much that he's secretly hidden her away somewhere."

"Undoubtedly, my boy, L'Ombre wishes to keep his mistress out of harm's way. Does she perform any role in his organization? We have long known of a communication officer who coordinates all L'Ombre's agents. This operative is known by the letter B. Could it be short for Bouchard?"

"That possibility crossed my mind as well. Bouchard is definitely functioning as a clandestine banker. Impersonating an heiress named Margot Dale, she controls a substantial amount of money. Gaining access to her bank records, I unearthed evidence that she's funding her lover's activities."

"Who have you chosen to *pay the law*?"

"The man who will actually be the assassin, Mimile Justin. He once belonged to your Secret Raiders subsidiary. "

"Proceed with the extermination of the Bouchard bitch. You have my blessing."

"I can also give you a bonus, All-Father. I know L'Ombre's true identity."

"Tell me immediately," commanded the Lord of the Black Coats.

"Sanger Rainsford," disclosed Lecoq.

"You fool! Sanger Rainsford can't be L'Ombre! The two of them have been seen together in New York on multiple occasions! Bouchard's death will only earn you a High Council seat. To fully merit your restoration as my second-in-command, you must discover L'Ombre's real identity."

World War II had broken out in Europe in September 1939. The conflict drastically altered the lives of certain individuals residing in La Martinique. Overwhelmed by patriotism, Alice Duprès left for France in the early months of the conflict. On May 10, 1940, Adolf Hitler finally launched his offensive against France. This caused a major decision in the Dale household. Marie LaSalle Dale explained the situation to the real Maggie.

"If France falls, La Martinique could become a Nazi colony. We all need to return to New York."

"When are we leaving, Mother?"

"As soon as possible, but you'll be leaving ahead of us. There's a single berth available on a cruise ship that will be docking here in two days. It will take you to New York. Do you have your passport?"

"Yes. I regularly check its location ever since my old one got mislaid nine years ago. When are you, Dad and my sisters, leaving?"

"We're booked on a ship that leaves in a week."

On the deck of the *Annette Darrow*, Maggie recognized a famous man. Formerly a Major in the U. S. Army, he had been appointed Police Commissioner of New York in 1932. Maggie had seen his photo in a 1934 newspaper. In that year, he had taken a leave of absence from the NYPD in order to reorganize the Cuban National Police. He also often took vacations in the Caribbean.

Maggie decided to introduce herself.

"Excuse me, Commissioner. I'm Maggie Lane Dale. My grandfather was Benjamin Gibson, the founder of the Gibson Motor Car Company."

"Impossible!" proclaimed the Commissioner. "I met Maggie Dale at John Sinclair's party in 1931."

The conversation was overheard by a muscular man reading a comic-book.

"But I'm Maggie Dale. Here's my passport."

"Passports can be forged, young lady," argued the Commissioner.

"Is there a problem?" asked the ship's captain.

"Captain Driscoll, this woman is an impostor," said the Commissioner.

"That's a serious charge, Commissioner. Is there anyone else on this ship capable of substantiating your accusation?"

"Sanger Rainsford."

"He's not a passenger aboard this ship."

"Rainsford's a pen name. He booked passage under his real name. I'll take you to his cabin."

The Commissioner walked towards Rainsford's quarters. He was followed by Maggie, Captain Driscoll and several other passengers, including the man with the comic-book.

The Commissioner knocked on the door of a cabin. The door was opened by Sanger Rainsford.

"What can I do for you, Commissioner?" he asked.

"Remember that charming Maggie Lane Dale whom we met at John Sinclair's party in 1931?"

"I can't say that I do, Commissioner."

"You must remember her! You were photographed with her in front of the Empire State Building the night all those innocent people were butchered by that monster!"

"Oh, that Maggie! What about her?"

"This woman is impersonating her!"

"No, Commissioner!" protested the genuine Maggie. "Someone must have impersonated me!"

The Sanger Rainsford in the doorway was not *L'Ombre*. This was the genuine Rainsford. He had never heard of Maggie Dale. Years ago, *L'Ombre* had blackmailed Rainsford into acceding to the impersonation. Looking into Maggie's eyes, the true Rainsford saw the anguish that he had suffered upon discovering that his life was no longer his own. He instinctively knew that her identity had been misappropriated by some female accomplice of the false Rainsford. The legitimate Rainsford decided to rescue her from the peril in which his doppelganger had inadvertently placed her.

"The lady is correct. The Maggie of 1931 was an unscrupulous gatecrasher. She pretended to be Maggie in order to get into Sinclair's party. She confessed her imposture to me weeks later. I haven't seen her since."

"But that woman knew all the details about Maggie's family," declared the Commissioner.

"She was Maggie's distant cousin," said Rainsford.

"What was her name?" demanded the Commissioner.

Rainsford chose the first name that popped into his head. "Lois Lane."

"Well, I think that settles everything," said Driscoll. "My apologies, Miss Dale."

The Commissioner also apologized. The crowd began to disperse.

"Thank you, Mr. Rainsford. I felt trapped in a nightmare."

"The best cure for a nightmare is good company. Will you dine with me this evening?"

"Yes."

"I'll see you in the dining room in two hours. Pardon me, Miss Dale, but I need to freshen up." Rainsford slowly closed the door.

As Maggie was about to enter her cabin, she was accosted by the man with the comic-book.

"Excuse me, Miss Dale, here's my business card."

Maggie looked at the card. "*Donald Gale, Confidential Investigations.* I don't need a detective."

"You may decide otherwise once I prove that you're being conned. Take a look at this." The private eye thrust his comic book into Maggie's hands. It was entitled *Action Comics.*

Maggie quickly browsed the comic book. "There's a character named Lois Lane."

"Lois is Superman's main squeeze. She's rather famous."

"It could just be a coincidence. There are odd coincidences in life. Look at our surnames, Mr. Gale. They rhyme."

"You can believe in coincidences if you wish, Miss Dale, but you should have me check it out. I'm worth every penny that I'll charge you. My memory is excellent. I'll prove it. The Commissioner mentioned a photo with the other Maggie in it. The photo's in an October 1931 issue of the *New York Daily Register.*"

"I'll consider your offer, Mr. Gale."

For the next few nights, Sanger and Maggie dined together. She found herself falling hopelessly in love with the world traveler. He thrilled her with an account of how he was once stalked like a wild animal by an insane Russian.

"I'm not sure what to call you," confessed Maggie. "Sanger? La..."

"Call me Sanger. I've never been comfortable with my first name. It's better suited for a prominent banker. My family has a long tradition of changing our names. Some of my relatives are stage actors."

"I read in *Cosmopolitan* that Margo Channing's real name is Margola Cranston."

"Yes. She's my cousin."

Once the *Annette Darrow* docked in New York, Maggie had a question for Rainsford:

"Will I ever see you again?"

"I'll be leaving on a plane for Greenland tonight. I'll be back in New York in a month. With all my travels, there's been no time for a woman in my life."

Rainsford gave Maggie a farewell kiss.

Before embarking on his plane, the real Rainsford made a call from a telephone booth at the airport.

In a room filled with radio equipment, a man was reading the seventh volume of Luther Burbank's *How Plants Are Trained to Work for Man.* Putting down the book, he answered the phone:

"Report."

"B, this is C."

"Why are you calling, C? You should be preparing to leave for Greenland."

"My plane doesn't depart for two hours. If your boss knows what's good for him, he'll get his fancy butt over to a phone and call me."

"My superior gives the orders, not you. If there is any matter to discuss, I'm deputized to speak for our chief."

"He's your chief, not mine. All right, I'll play by your rules. I want to talk about Maggie Dale."

"You were never briefed about her."

"I haven't been briefed about a lot of things."

"I don't know how you found out about Maggie Dale, but she's not your concern. The chief made a decision about her in 1933, and it's irrevocable. Good night, C." The enigmatic B hung up the phone.

"Jackass!" exclaimed Rainsford.

The next afternoon, Maggie went to the offices of the *Register.* There she found the reporter who took the photo cited by the Commissioner. Ed Somers escorted Maggie into the "morgue" where old issues were kept. He quickly located the October 1931 issues. When Maggie saw the photo, she recognized the woman as Angelique Blanchet and realized that the woman must have stolen her passport in 1931. The caption in the photo only identified Rainsford and ignored the people around him.

"Do you know the woman in this photo, Ed?" asked Maggie.

"I don't recall her name, but she used to hang out with Rainsford. I last saw her with him in '33. It's hard to keep track of all the women in Rainsford's life..."

"There are other women?"

"So many that our gossip columnist over there has kept a running tally over the years. Hey, Conroy!"

"I can't talk now, Somers. I just resigned. There's a job waiting for me in California."

"I'll be quick. Any news on Sanger Rainsford?"

"He's dining tonight at the Club Royale with the owner of a Park Avenue beauty salon."

In 1935, James Dale began to attend the annual American conventions of mystery collectors. Since he intended to regularly visit the United States unaccompanied by his family, Dale re-established a residence in New York with servants to maintain it.

Maggie was staying at her foster father's residence in May 1940. Dale's chauffeur, Benson, had gone to Martinique with his employer in 1920. When Dale re-created a New York household, Benson became his butler there while his son assumed the duties of chauffeur.

"Benson, I need Junior to drive me to the Club Royale tonight," said Maggie. She gave Benson a letter. "If anything happens to me, I want you to give this to my mother when she returns from Martinique."

"Miss Dale, you're acting like your foster father did decades ago. He lived a dangerous existence. You seem to be embarking on the same path. If you're walking into danger, I have something you may need. Please come to my quarters."

In his room, Benson unlocked a desk drawer with one of his keys. Inside was a revolver.

"Mr. Dale brought this old weapon from Martinique in 1935. He last used it in 1920."

Maggie put the gun in her purse.

Marko's Montenegrin heritage was not reflected in the establishments that he owned. His restaurant had a German name while his night club, the Club Royale, had a distinct Russian atmosphere. The waiters dressed like Cossacks. Generally Marko spent most of his time at the restaurant, but he decided to party at his night club that evening with the glamorous Margo Channing, the acclaimed actress.

Due to his role in locating Marko's friend on that horrible night in 1931, L'Ombre, as Sanger Rainsford, always had access to a private dining room at the night club.

Mimile Justin quickly learned this upon his arrival in New York. In order to keep an eye on Rainsford, he always took a table next to the entrance of the private dining room. Mimile was packing a '45 automatic in a shoulder holster. If Maggie Dale ever showed up, Mimile was determined to plug her full of holes.

To his chagrin, however, the supposed Rainsford arrived with a statuesque blonde. This woman clearly wasn't Maggie. As the counterfeit Rainsford and the blonde were about to enter the dining room, a brunette ran up to them.

"There you are, you two-timing jerk!" shouted Maggie. "You lied to me on the boat! You said you stopped seeing that other woman in 1931! You actually were with her until 1933!"

"Who is this woman?" asked the blonde.

"This is Miss…Miss…" mumbled *L'Ombre*.

"Don't act like you don't know my name! I'm Maggie Dale! Tell Blondie here to scram!"

"Pat, I think you better leave," said *L'Ombre* as he grabbed Maggie's arm and shoved her into the dining room. Following her inside, *L'Ombre* closed the door. He swiftly deduced the situation. The real Rainsford must have met the real Maggie on some ship. Somehow she had learned about the impostor of 1931-1933. *L'Ombre* had to quickly come up with an explanation to calm the irate Maggie down.

Before he could utter a word, however, the door opened. Mimile Justin rushed inside, holding a gun with his right hand.

"No one move," he barked.

"Who are you?" asked Maggie.

"I'm the lover of the woman you killed. Remember Runa Kritchnoff? You're going to suffer like I did." Mimile's eyes shifted towards *L'Ombre*. "I'm going to kill the man you love, and then I'm going to kill you!"

A shot rang out. Mimile screamed as his gun went flying out of his hand. Maggie had drawn her own gun from her purse and shot Mimile's right hand. *L'Ombre* then punched Mimile in the face rendering him unconscious.

"Good Lord!" exclaimed Maggie. "I shot off his thumb!"

*L'Ombre* grabbed the revolver out of Maggie's hand. He also retrieved Mimile's gun from the floor.

Marko rushed into the private room.

"What happened?" he asked. "I heard a gunshot."

"This man tried to kill me," said *L'Ombre*. "I wounded him in the hand. You'll need to get the police as well as a doctor."

Marko left the dining room. He ordered the staff to prevent anyone else from entering the room before the police arrived.

Maggie and *L'Ombre* were alone with the slumbering Mimile.

"You don't need to protect me," objected Maggie.

"Do you have a license for this gun?" asked L'Ombre.

"I'm not sure."

"You don't want to be prosecuted under the Sullivan Act for illegal handgun possession."

"What about you?"

"I'm the personal friend of the Police Commissioner. That fact alone will cloud the minds of the investigating officers."

"But this crook will say that I shot him."

"He's probably a convicted felon. The circular tattoo on his left hand indicates that he once belonged to a notorious French gang. No one will believe him."

When the police arrived, they proved the accuracy of the phony Rainsford's predictions. Mimile was taken to a hospital.

*L'Ombre* escorted Maggie home. In the privacy of the Dale residence, he gave an explanation for the mysterious conduct of Sanger Rainsford. Not wishing to jeopardize his true identity, *L'Ombre* pretended to be the same Rainsford from the cruise.

"The woman who stole your identity was blackmailing me. Have you ever heard of the Gray Seal?"

"He was a heroic vigilante who crushed crime before Prohibition," replied Maggie.

*L'Ombre* had deduced long ago that James Dale was the Gray Seal. Maggie's prompt reply indicated knowledge of her family's secrets.

"I have sought to emulate the Gray Seal. I am also a secret vigilante. Your impostor was threatening to expose my activities to the authorities."

"What happened to this woman?"

"She's in an insane asylum. Our attacker mentioned Runa Kritchnoff. She was strangled in California nine years ago. Your impersonator must have killed her. Hopefully I've explained everything."

"No, you haven't. You told me that you were going to Greenland. Why aren't you there?"

"I had to cancel my trip at the last minute to resume my war on crime."

"That blonde didn't look like a dangerous criminal to me."

"She's the cousin of a noted adventurer whose activities have the potential to interfere with my own. I merely took her to dinner in order to pump her for information about her cousin."

"It looked to me that you wanted to pump her in a different way. For me to accept your vigilante story, you have to prove it to me firsthand."

"How?"

"Make me your assistant."

"That's impossible. There is no role for you in my group of helpers. You don't know what evil lurks in the hearts of men."

"But I know what brilliance lurks in the minds of women! You mentioned the Gray Seal earlier. It was a woman, the Tocsin, who directed all his campaigns. I demand to battle crooks with you."

"Your request is accepted. You will receive your orders either from me or from a man known by the letter B. He will only contact you by the telephone."

"Baloney. You tell me B's real name right now."

"I'll make a deal with you. Let me give you a clue to B's full name. If you can't guess his name, you'll drop this matter.

"I'm game. Give me the clue."

*"The Training of the Human Plant."*

"That's the title of an essay written by a famous botanist. He died at a ripe old age over a decade ago. Your contact man must have exactly the same name. Since you doubt my intelligence, let me prove my proficiency at riddles. Your agent's first name is the same as the surname belonging to the leader of the Protestant Reformation, and his last is identical to that of a city very close to Los Angeles. When do I meet Luther?"

Ira Burbank Franklin, Luther's cousin, was finally making progress with Thelda.

"Don't you love your son?" asked Franklin.

"Yes," responded Thelda.

"Wouldn't you want your son to have your ring?"

"Yes."

"If you give me your ring, I'll see that he gets it."

Thelda handed the ring to Franklin. The psychiatrist kept his word. He gave the ring to the false Sanger Rainsford with the understanding that it would be bestowed on Thelda's son when he reached adulthood. Franklin promised to keep Rainsford informed about his patient's progress.

Maggie had no secrets from her foster mother, so she told Marie Dale everything when she arrived in New York.

"The celebrated Mr. Rainsford has some rough edges," observed Marie.

"So did Dad before you straightened him out," answered Maggie.

"Hopefully you will do the same with the Gray Seal's apparent successor. You must be careful, Maggie. The gunman at the Club Royale is proof that Angelique Blanchet made enemies while impersonating you. What name did the impostor use? Maggie or Margot?"

"Maggie, except for the bank account which she stole from me."

"Bank account? What bank account?"

"My natural father opened a bank account of one million dollars in my name. The impostor largely depleted it. Sanger has generously agreed to compensate me for the loss."

"Rainsford's not being generous. He's protecting himself. You're going to have to do some things to protect yourself too, Maggie. First, close that account and transfer the money to another bank."

"Sanger has already helped me do that."

"Second, you must change your name in order to never be confused again with that impostor. You must discard your nickname. Alter the spelling of your first name like actress Margo Channing did. Furthermore, you must petition the courts to assume the surname of your natural father."

"I don't want to disown you and Dad!" pleaded the younger woman.

"A change of name doesn't matter. You may cease being our daughter in name, but you will always be our daughter in spirit."

Over the weeks that followed, Thelda regained her sanity. However, she didn't let Dr. Franklin know about the restoration of her faculties. Her love for *L'Ombre* had now turned to hate. She resented him for spurning her. She planned to escape and expose all of his secrets to the underworld. She also loathed Franklin for his role in her confinement.

One day, she overheard the psychiatrist talking to the asylum's director outside her room.

"That New York City psychiatrist is a fool, Dr. Crawford. The patient in Cell 13 is perfectly sane. He pretended madness in order to escape criminal prosecution. You must notify the authorities."

Unlike other patients in the asylum, Thelda wasn't confined in a straitjacket because the staff viewed her as relatively harmless.

Miss Carroll, the head nurse, was taking her blood pressure when Thelda leaped at her. Shoving the nurse on the bed, she grabbed the pillow and pushed it over Miss Carroll's face. It didn't take long for the nurse to die from suffocation. Thelda put on her victim's uniform and walked to Cell 13. Opening the padded cell with the dead nurse's keys, she saw a man lying on the floor in a straitjacket.

"I know you're sane," said Thelda. "I'm an inmate too. We can escape together. What's your name?"

"Mimile Justin."

"How did you get here?"

"A woman shot off my thumb. I pretended to be driven mad by the pain. A shrink bought my act. He had me committed here."

"My name's Phoebe. Let me get you out of that straitjacket."

Dr. Franklin was passing Cell 13 when Mimile Justin reached out and pulled him into the enclosure. The criminal threw Franklin face forward on the ground. Taking the discarded straitjacket, Thelda wrapped one of the sleeves around Franklin's neck and pulled.

"You're a pretty good strangler," noted Mimile once Franklin's life was extinguished.

"I've done this before. Put on his clothes."

Soon, Mimile stood wearing Franklin's clothes. He had found gloves in the doctor's pocket and stuffed a tissue into the thumb socket of the right hand. Thelda was still attired as a nurse.

They managed to leave the asylum without being questioned.

"We need to hitch a ride," said Mimile watching a car approach on the country road. It stopped next to the pair of escapees and the driver came out.

"Pierre Lecoq!" exclaimed Mimile.

"Remember your contract," emphasized Lecoq. "Kill Maggie Dale."

"But Maggie isn't here," said Mimile.

"She's standing right next to you," divulged Lecoq.

"I'm not Maggie Dale!" protested Thelda. "I'm Thelda Bouchard!"

"You killed Runa!" yelled Mimile.

"Wait!" shouted Thelda. "There's something that I have to tell you!"

Mimile's left hand shot out and grasped Thelda's throat. As she was slowly throttled, Thelda mumbled some words

Relaxing his grip, Mimile eventually let the dead body fall on the ground.

"Did you hear what she said?" said Lecoq.

"The title of Rainsford's book," grimly answered Mimile. "*The Shadows Canting Aloud.*"

"That makes no sense."

Mimile shrugged. "What would you expect from a crazy broad who just escaped from an asylum?"

Lecoq immediately realized that his earlier deductions were faulty. He would need to debrief Mimile thoroughly to untangle Bouchard's true relationship to *L'Ombre*.

The two crooks got in the car and drive away, leaving Thelda's corpse behind.

It was later discovered by a motorcycle cop, but by then, Lecoq and Mimile were long gone. Thelda Bouchard would be buried as Phoebe Lane.

Lecoq piloted the vehicle into the night. During their long conversation, Lecoq altered his assessment of Mimile Justin. Rather than utilize the ex-chauffeur to *pay the law*, he saw in Mimile a valuable asset to be hidden away for future use. Capable agents like Runa's lover would be needed in the days to come. For the criminal nicknamed *Toulonnais-l'Amitié* had evolved into far more than a consultant to mere burglars and swindlers during his self-imposed years of American exile. A seat on the High Council was the first step in a fantastic scheme that not even Colonel Bozzo-Corona suspected.

"Mimile, there's a business opportunity awaiting you in Burbank, California. Jerry Mason's organizing an auto theft ring. You're now facing a murder rap. You should change your name and get your tattoo removed."

"Thanks, Pierre. I'll do that. You know it's odd that you suddenly showed up."

"Nothing odd about it. I simply found out where you were confined."

"It's still strange."

"Maybe it's destiny. It was my destiny to drive along this road. It was your destiny to escape. It was Thelda Bouchard's destiny to die by strangulation."

"When you say creepy stuff like that, Pierre, I almost believe those wild rumors about you."

"What rumors are you talking about?"

"Some people say you were a big crook beheaded in Paris a century ago. A sorceress named Palmyre gave your soul a new body."

Lecoq's response was to whistle. Whether Mimile spoke the truth remained the secret of the whistler.

Inside a room lit by blue light, tapering fingers used a long quill pen to write inside a massive journal:

*Thelda died without knowing the truth. I had identified her as my niece's killer eight years ago. When we stood before Runa's grave, I lied about my refusal to seek vengeance. I could have simply shot her like a mad dog, but I chose to punish her more subtly. My scheme of retribution was very simple in its implementation. Fuel Thelda's romantic hopes briefly with a single kiss, and then ignore her subsequently. As I foresaw, her growing sexual torment drove her to madness. My sublime vendetta had its unintended consequences, however. If I had merely executed Thelda that afternoon in San Francisco, the tragic deaths of Dr. Franklin and Nurse Carroll never would have happened. On the other side of the ledger, Thelda's son would never have been born. Kenton's a lovely child. He'll never grow up to be a killer like his mother. While I failed with Runa, I shall succeed with Kenton. I'll be a father to the boy just as my sister was a mother to me. It's fitting that Thelda named him after me. Kenton Lane shall learn to walk in the shadows.*

In 1947, the California State Police broke up the Mason gang of auto thieves. Among the men arrested was an individual with a missing thumb. Fingerprints identified him as Mimile Justin, a man wanted for murder in New York. Extradited to that state, the prisoner was sentenced to the electric chair. The execution was scheduled for the spring of 1949.

While he was waiting on Death Row in Sing Sing, Mimile asked for the copy of *The Shadows Canting Aloud: Devil Worship in Yian.* During the trial, his mind went back to the day of Thelda's death. Why had she mentioned this book? Reading the introduction, Mimile discovered that Rainsford had borrowed his title from a line in "Dark Phantoms," a poem by Humbert Kenneth Allard. The title *The Shadows Canting Aloud* was used by Rainsford with the poet's permission. Rainsford had read "Dark Phantoms" in Allard's poetry collection,

*Laughter of the Shadows*. Rainsford initially purchased Allard's book in the mistaken belief that the poet was an American pilot who had once flown the globetrotter over the Yucatán. Both the pilot and the poet had very similar names.

After reading the book, Mimile still remained confused.

Unlike the other prison guards in Sing Sing, Robert Bianchini Drake was friendly with the inmates on Death Row. He conversed with the convicts on a first name basis. Two hours before his scheduled execution, Mimile handed Rainsford's book through the cell's bars to Drake.

"Please return this to the prison library, Bob."

Drake read aloud the shortened title on the spine. "*The Shadows Chanting Aloud*. What this book about, Mimile? The Mysterious Shadow of France?"

"The Mysterious Shadow! How do you know of him?"

"My mother lived in France just before the First World War. When I was growing up, she told me stories about a weird adventurer wearing a black hat and cloak. The fellow was called the Mysterious Shadow."

"You mean, Judex."

"What?"

"The Shadow's Judex."

"The Shadow's Jewish?"

"No, the Shadow's not Jewish. The Shadow's Judex. It's his name. Judex is the name of the Mysterious Shadow, a cloaked adventurer whose methods resemble those of a later vigilante."

"Is this book about Judex?"

"No, Bob. It's about a remote city in China."

"The title's weird. To cant means to lie. How could a shadow lie? It's a macabre concept."

"The title comes from the works of H. Kenneth Allard."

"I've heard of Allard. He's a horror writer and poet who died in the 30s. Thanks for clearing that up, Mimile. My apologies for mishearing you earlier."

Drake walked away with the book.

At that moment, the truth dawned on the prisoner.


As he was being strapped into the electric chair, the condemned man became incoherent.

"Listen to me! I was wrong! Drake showed me the truth! She didn't say '*The Shadows Canting Aloud!*' She said '*The Shadow's Kenton Al-*'"

Mimile Justin never finished the sentence because the executioner pulled the switch. The prison personnel present dismissed Mimile's dying words as the ramblings of a madman.

As with all executions, Mimile's was opened to public spectators. There was only one witness, reporter Ed Somers of the *Register*. He refused to dismiss Mimile's last words as insane rants. After interviewing Bob Drake, Somers knew that he had the story of the century. His editor agreed. The story was printed on the front page with blazing headlines: *"Judex's Secret Identity Revealed! French Vigilante was American Horror Writer! H. Kenneth Allard exposed as Mysterious Shadow!"*

In a dimly lit room in New York, a shadowy figure read the newspaper. On a sheet of paper, he wrote the names "Kenneth Allard" followed by the name "Kenton." He was tempted to laugh, but he whistled instead.

Elsewhere in a different part of the city, a hand wrote with a quill pen:

*Real identity compromised. It's only a matter of time before the Black Coats or another enemy deduces the truth. K. A. must supposedly die again in an air crash. I shall also cease the L. C. impersonation within the next few months*

*The time of rebirth and reflection has arrived. I must modify my methods. The era of the dark cloak and hat has ended. Bullets are no longer the best solution to crime. I will live elsewhere under the false identity that has long been a closely guarded secret. It's time to return to the land of my ancestors.*

The hand reached for a passport lying on a desk. It was issued in the name of Frédéric-Jean Orth.

*British author Nigel Malcolm wrote this story to pay homage to the long-lived, popular British BBC TV police series* Bergerac, *created by Robert Banks Stewart, which lasted ten years (1981-91) and took place on the Channel Island of Jersey. In the tale that follows, the peaceful (yet, according to* Bergerac, *crime-ridden) isle is suddenly subjected to the return of a classic French vigilante—or is it?*

## Nigel Malcolm: *A Fistful of Judexes*

*Jersey, April 1987.*

Michel Kerjean looked over St Helier Harbor. Mattie Storin scrutinized him as she pretended to make notes. Her dictaphone was recording, anyway.

She was sitting at the café table while he had stood up and walked over by a short way. She wasn't so keen on the designer stubble, but the fashionable mullet showed off his great hair, and the white Armani suit added to his air of authority and control. Powerful men were her Achilles Heel, although normally she would have been attracted to someone older.

"So, Mr. Kerjean, the Judex Society. Why name your security business after Judex? Who was he? Or *it*?"

Kerjean was charmed by this young journalist from the local rag. "He was a masked crime-fighter in Paris, before the War. At first, his motive seemed to be revenge for some wrong done to him. But as the years went by, he carried on until no one knew why he was doing it anymore. Except that his very name means 'justice.'"

He sat down and drank his coffee.

"Justice for whom?" asked Mattie.

"Justice for ordinary, decent, hard-working men and women, far too long ignored by the Law and the Police. That's why I've set up the Judex Society. We're independent from all other authorities. We are unencumbered by police bureaucracy, trade unions and corruption."

"Forgive me, but you sound like you could be, well, vigilantes?" asked Mattie, boldly.

Kerjean seemed slightly taken aback by this accusation.

"Are we vigilantes if we take down the scum who rob and rape and murder our children?" Knowing that he was beginning to sound a bit hysterical, he paused to regain control of his emotions. "Judex is like your very own Robin Hood, and the brave members of the Judex Society itself are—in my opinion—heroes. We've come here to clean up crime and corruption."

"On Jersey?"

"Well, we're going to start on Jersey, and eventually set up offices in Paris, London, and so on."

"I see."

They carried on, sipping their coffees and talking. They didn't notice the brown-haired older man in a blue jacket at a nearby table, drinking a coffee very slowly and listening in on the conversation.

At first, the local residents were amused when a group of about twenty men had arrived from France, wearing black cloaks, slouch hats and masks. One or two of the locals even asked them why they wore these strange garments. Was it part of some sort of pageant or festival? No, they replied, they were inspired by a Parisian crime-fighter from long ago.

Oh, that's interesting, the locals would say, and everything would be fine. But after a while, they noticed that some of these "Judexes" had broken noses, scars, shaved heads or tattoos. And underneath the hats and cloaks, they wore incongruous t-shirts and jeans or Bermuda shorts, trainers or big boots. They could get rowdy together and get into scuffles with others. Especially the more foreign-looking visitors.

Detective Sergeant Jim Bergerac knew about them, partly because he worked in the Bureau des Etrangers, which was a branch of the police that dealt with outsiders visiting Jersey. So when he went into his usual place for lunch and saw four of them together, around a table; being loud and boisterous, he viewed them with suspicion.

He ordered a ham sandwich and a coffee from the proprietor, Diamante Lil.

"You're not getting any trouble from them, are you?" he asked her, nodding at the Judexes.

"No trouble yet, Jim," she said, "but, well, they've spent a long time here already, and I've noticed it's put off one or two of the regulars."

"Well, if they get out of hand, tell me, all right?"

"I don't even know what they've come to Jersey for," said Lil.

"We're not sure yet. Apparently they're part of a private security force from Paris."

"Well, I feel like *I* need private security when they're around," said Lil. "Whatever they're here for, I hope they get on with it and go again, that's all I'll say."

At that point a beer glass smashed onto the floor, and the men cheered.

"Private security's not a highly regulated industry," said Jim. "But usually their officers are a bit better behaved. Often they're ex-army or ex-police."

The men started wolf-whistling and making lewd comments at the teenage waitress. A line had been crossed. Bergerac got up.

"I'll handle this," he said to the grateful Lil, and approached the men.

"Excuse me, lads, could you keep the noise down and treat the staff with a bit of respect?"

The men looked at each other and laughed. One of the Judexes made a comment to the others in French.

"I shan't tell you again. Behave like civilized human beings or get out," Bergerac said.

One of the men, presumably the leader, stopped laughing, but continued to smile. He picked up an iron bar that was lying within his arm's reach on the table, and stood up. He casually walked up to Bergerac, who stood his ground. The man's slouch hat was hanging on the back of his head from a chord around where he should have had a neck. The cape hung down his back as though the man was more used to wearing a green bomber jacket over his tricolor t-shirt. It was difficult to tell if his face was red from drinking or sunburn.

Just outside the café, the brown-haired, blue jacketed man watched the situation through the window.

Bergerac pulled out his police ID badge.

"I hope you're not thinking of assaulting a police officer, sir."

The ruddy Judex carried on smiling: "We are the law now," he said, and he raised the rod to strike.

Bergerac dropped the badge, grabbed the thug's arm and, in a self-defense move, forced him to drop the rod. There was a deafening clang and the scraping of chairs being pushed back as the three other Judexes got up and rushed over.

"GET THE POLICE!" shouted Bergerac, to no one in particular as Lil and the waitress had run out of there. He punched the first thug. The others closed in on him. He used a few street-fighting moves he'd used many times before, but soon two of them were holding his arms and another had grabbed a nearby beer glass, smashed it against the wall to make a jagged weapon, pulled it back and...

"NO!" shouted the brown-haired stranger in the blue jacket. He grabbed the glass-wielding Judex's arm and forced him to drop it. He punched the man unconscious.

Meanwhile, Bergerac freed himself from his captors with a combination of kicks and punches. He and the other man fought on until a second Judex was unconscious; the third had run away and the fourth was restrained on the ground by Bergerac.

He straightened up, out of breath, and looked at his helper properly
"Thanks for that, Mr...?"

"You're welcome," said the older man, in a French accent. He was out of breath too. "I'm getting rusty," he added, before going over to pick up Jim's police badge.

"You weren't bad," replied Bergerac with feeling. "Did you used to be in the marines or something?"

The man handed Jim his badge, pausing to read it first.

"Something like that, Detective Sergeant Bergerac

"I'm sorry, I didn't quite catch your name," Jim said, in a more direct tone of voice, that sounded more "policemanish" than he had intended.

"Teddy Verano," the man replied, not quite managing to hide his reluctance. "Now, if you'll excuse me, I've got to go." He made to leave.

"Well, thanks again, M. Verano."

"A pleasure," the older man said, before adding, "Well, maybe not a pleasure, but you know what I mean." And he left.

Bergerac eventually returned to his headquarters, the Bureau des Etrangers, where he was greeted by the office manager, Peggy.

"Hello, Jim. Have you been taking your work into your lunch break today?"

Jim chuckled. "If that was my lunch break, then I'm glad to get back to work."

"Barney wants to see you; he's in his office."

"Right. Peggy, could you find any details about a M. Teddy Verano? address, occupation, anything? Cheers.".

Peggy wrote the name down.

Jim went into Chief Inspector Crozier's office to find him pacing the room. He asked the detective for his own side of the story, and Bergerac told him. Crozier accepted his explanation.

"But you're all right though?" he asked.

"Yes, I'm alright," Bergerac replied.

"The head of the Judex Society turns out to be a man called Michel Kerjean. He's apparently wined and dined the Jersey Law and Order Committee, and I'm getting soundings that he's planning to make the Judex Society a permanent presence on the island. Has your ex-father-in-law told you anything about this?"

"Charlie hasn't said a word."

Barney Crozier looked grim. "Apparently the original Judex was some kind of French folk hero."

"We learned about him at school," said Jim, who unlike Barney, had grown up on Jersey. "A vigilante out for revenge."

Barney remained grim. "I don't like the idea of vigilantes out for revenge on Jersey. You know the Police's official line on that."

Bergerac agreed, but added: "Doesn't stop them becoming heroes in the papers though, does it? But he's a myth now. There may have been a real Judex once, but that was sixty or seventy years ago."

Crozier pulled some A4 sized photographs out of an envelope lying on top of his desk, and showed them to Jim.

"This is what my counterpart in Paris sent me."

They were stills, evidently taken from CCTV cameras in various streets and shops. All showing a figure in a slouch hat and cape, whose face was completely obscured.

"They've been getting the occasional shot of him ever since CCTV cameras have become more commonplace. I'm even told there were reports of him during the student marches in '68. As myths go, he's very real."

"But presumably, that's not the original. Someone else must have inherited the mantle. So he's set up a business?"

"Maybe it's got too much for just one person? If it was ever just one person."

"Bit of a change in tactics, though. If he's going from a secretive lone crime-fighter to a Private Security company in the public eye."

"Maybe he's just moving with the times?"

The Judex Society had set up a temporary base in an empty house near the coast. It was sparsely furnished and undecorated. Kerjean was standing in what would normally be the living-room, where he had the two surviving Judexes from the café brawl standing in front of him.

"You idiots!" he hissed. "Don't you realize that this has jeopardized my chances of setting up here? What were you thinking?"

The ruddy-faced Judex, reeking of lager and struggling to deal with a situation for which he wasn't in the right state of mind, simply blustered and tried to look like he didn't care.

"Well, no one tells me what I can and cannot do," he managed.

"What a stupid excuse. *I* tell you what you can and cannot do."

The booze-flushed Judex realized he'd made a mistake regarding in front of whom he should look nonchalant. "Er, yeah... obviously, you do, but... but no one else does."

Kerjean turned his attention to the tattooed Judex.

"And what about you? At the first sign of trouble, you run away!"

"Well... er... it seemed to be the best thing to do tactically," the other man said.

Kerjean looked at him in disbelief. "A tactical retreat? That was it? Or perhaps you were going to get reinforcements, weren't you?"

The tattooed Judex struggled to think of a reply.

"Pathetic!"

Kerjean turned his back on his men and looked out of the window at the Jersey's coastline and the sea beyond. He then turned to another, mustachioed Judex, standing guard by the door.

"David, these two are decloaked. Dispose of them."

"Yes, sir." said David.

He pulled out a gun and gestured the door with it. The two other Judexes protested, but Kerjean and David ignored them. They'd be stripped of their slouch hats, cloaks and masks, as well as anything else that distinguished them, and their corpses would be dumped in one of the caves nearby.

Kerjean leaned against the window frame and looked out at the sea. This incident might well be the last straw, damaging their chances of establishing a base here. Yet, oddly enough, he was actually quite unemotional about the Judex Society getting brought into disrepute. He would change the name of the company. Call it the Morales Society perhaps? His backers wouldn't mind the re-branding, surely. But there was at least one more thing to do first...

He went over to the camping table, on which a few different maps of Jersey—one ordinance survey; one tourist; one geological—were spread out. He scoured the details and put his finger on a particular location.

"There," he said. "Right there! Isn't it, *Papa*?"

Peggy had been unable to find any details about Teddy Verano. So presumably he didn't live on the island. He could have been staying with friends, or he'd come over to Jersey for the day.

Instead, Bergerac decided to go and question Michel Kerjean.

Kerjean was at the empty house, in the living-room. The Judexes were all standing around behind him. Various items of equipment needed for potholing, including rope; boiler suits and helmets with flashlights on them, were dumped on the floor between them. Behind Kerjean was one of the maps—a very old, hand-drawn map of caves hung up by blue tack. He had just explained to his men:

"...So, we'll all meet *here* just outside the cave mouth," he pointed on the map, "at nine o'clock sharp. We'll put on *all* our equipment—I don't want to find out that one of you has to go back and get the proper boots, or anything like that. The box will be *there*. So memorize the route in. We'll take the same route back out..."

The doorbell rang. Kerjean frowned. He leaned over and peered across the rest of the room and through the front window. He could just about glimpse part of a maroon-colored vintage car.

"See who that is, will you? Deal with them," he said to one of the Judexes, who had missing teeth. The man sloped out of the room to the front door.

Kerjean continued with the briefing: "David, you will keep a lookout at the cave mouth to make sure no one else comes along. You'll sound the alarm if they do. Any questions?"

"Yeah," said David. "Will we get our share of the gold sovereigns?"

"As I've explained before, you're all getting paid very well for what you're doing. And you'll get a bonus if the job is done well."

"But not a share of the loot?"

Kerjean then realized he would have to frame or kill David after the job.

"No," he said, firmly.

Bergerac walked into the room, having clearly brushed past the toothless Judex.

"I hope I'm not interrupting anything?" he asked.

"Yes, you are, officer," replied Kerjean, irritably. "What do you want?"

Bergerac looked around. "Is this some kind of meeting?"

"Yes, a private one. Let's talk out in the reception area."

Kerjean joined Bergerac in the empty reception area.

"Now, what do you want?"

"What is your organization doing on Jersey, M. Kerjean? We both know some of your men have been involved in a number of public disorder offenses. What are you doing here?"

"But most of us are law-abiding. And what we are doing here is no concern of the police. Now. kindly leave."

"What's all the equipment in there for? A camping trip? Potholing?"

Kerjean finally lost his temper.

"Do you have a search warrant for these premises? Do you?"

"No."

"Then you have no right to come bursting in here asking questions," said Kerjean, as he swung the door open. "Now please go!"

Bergerac just stood there.

"Do I have to get my men to physically carry you out of here?" said Kerjean.

Without saying anything, Bergerac stepped out of the door, which was slammed behind him.

He walked back over to his car, a 1947 Triumph Roadster, and sat in it for a moment, thinking. The blunt approach worked sometimes, but he'd been foolish to go blundering in when there was a whole house-load of those thugs.

He started the car and drove off.


In the early evening, Bergerac drove up to Charlie Hungerford's house. They'd always got on well, apart from before and shortly after Charlie's daughter had divorced Jim. Jim had beaten his drinking problem since then, although he couldn't seem to do anything about his obsessive work ethic.

Hungerford was a successful businessman who lived in a big house. His manservant let Bergerac in, and he found Charlie in the dining room, cigar in mouth, standing over rows of sheets of paper spread out on the dining table— some of which were spreadsheets of figures, others photocopies of newspaper articles from the local library.

"Ah, Jim! I'm thinking of investing in the private security business. What do you think?" he said, in his Yorkshire accent.

"Now let me guess—the Judex Society?"

"That's right. Hey, Jim, maybe you ought to think about working for them yourself," he suggested.

This made Bergerac laugh.

"No, seriously. They'd pay you well, and you're always complaining that the police won't promote you. They could do with someone of your experience."

"Can you imagine me in a hat and a mask and a cape? I'd look like Dick Turpin!"

"Well, you wouldn't have to dress up like that; you could be an Operations Manager. I'd put in a good word for you."

"No, thanks, Charlie, I'll stay in the proper police."

"Oh? Well, the Judex Society are putting the wind up the proper police, I expect."

"They're putting the wind up a lot of people. Did you hear what happened in Lil's place earlier?"

"Yes. It was probably just... a few undesirable elements," said Hungerford, trying to convince himself.

"Those 'undesirable elements' tried to crack open my skull with an iron bar."

"But I had lunch with the head of the Judex Society today, and he assured us—that is, the Law and Order committee—that any over-aggressive elements wouldn't be tolerated. There are always a few rotten apples in the barrel. You know that—the police force isn't exactly perfect!"

Bergerac decided not to argue.

"What's the Committee going to do about the Judex Society?"

"Well, obviously much of the discussion is confidential. They run a successful business in Paris, you know. They want to set up camp on the Channel Islands. They're here for a big job as well, but he didn't go into any details about that."

"Don't you think it's odd that Kerjean wants to set up on the Channel Islands? Why here? Why not London?"

Charlie was obviously stumped. "I'm sorry, Jim, but I can't discuss confidential business matters," he blustered.

Jim knew that Charlie was stalling because he didn't know.

Later on, Bergerac drove back to his home, a converted barn surrounded by trees and fields.

As he approached the door, he could see that a light was on. A desk light, not one of the main ones. He braced himself.

Quickly tip-toeing back to his car, he quietly opened the trunk, opened a toolbox, and picked out a large spanner. Then he returned to the front door. It hadn't been forced open, so he put his key in the lock slowly. Then he threw the door open wide suddenly, and burst into the house, brandishing the spanner and switching on the main lights.

There was just one Judex this time. He was sitting on the sofa, looking elegant and composed. Nothing like the other Judexes.

"Please do not be alarmed," he said.

Still holding up the spanner, Jim shut the door behind him and walked slowly over to the figure.

"Who are you? What are you doing here?"

"Forgive the intrusion, Sergeant, but we have a mutual problem," said the man.

"Go on," said Bergerac cautiously.

"The Judex Society. Effectively a bunch of hooligans hired to bring my name into disrepute."

"Why don't you take it up with them? You're one of them."

"I have nothing to do with them."

"Why are you wearing that getup then?"

Judex slowly stood up. "My 'getup,' as you call it, is made of better quality material. This does not come from a joke shop, Sergeant."

"Oh, I see. So you're a better class of Judex are you?" said Bergerac, drily.

"Yes, indeed. To be more accurate, I am the *real* Judex."

Although this was obvious nonsense, Jim found himself wavering. There was something in the man's sincerity that almost convinced him.

"Look, I'm not in the mood for practical jokes..."

"This is no joke."

"Then, you're mad. And I could have you carted off to a loony bin."

Judex smiled. "I'd like to see you try. But first, we have business to discuss."

"Will you take that hat and mask off first?"

"Forgive me, Sergeant, but no. You've already met my associate, M. Verano..."

"Verano works for you?"

"He occasionally helps me when I need him. And I believe he has helped you too. In a café."

"Yes, that's right. So the Judex Society is split into factions?"

"No. As I have said, I have nothing to do with the private security firm that calls itself the Judex Society. My own society is secret. It executes justice on behalf of the persecuted and oppressed. And believe me, we live in times when persecution is rife."

"So you're part of a vigilante gang?"

Judex thought for a moment. "I suppose we might be labeled that, technically speaking. Although vigilantism is really a destructive cocktail of private anger and public self-righteousness. I execute true justice when the law and the police fail. Anyway, back to business. Michel Kerjean is trying to discredit me. Destroy my reputation and legacy."

"Why?" asked Jim, who was looking closely at the man's face, trying to place how old he was. He couldn't.

"Revenge. His grandfather was a criminal going by the name Morales." said Judex, before seeming to choose his words more carefully. "Morales died. His son, and now his grandson, blame me for it. So he is trying to damage me."

Jim looked out of the front window. It was almost completely dark outside. Out of habit, he closed the drapes.

"But setting up an entire company—a multinational company—just to settle an old score, that's pretty extreme. He'd need a lot of money just to get started up."

"He has some powerful backers. Have you heard of BlackSpear Holdings?"

"It rings a bell..." Bergerac was then struck by an uncomfortable thought. "Charlie Hungerford doesn't have dealings with them, does he?"

"No. They choose their trading partners very carefully."

Jim smiled. "Charlie wouldn't be pleased to hear that."

"He would if he knew what they really were. Kerjean has another motivation—he's after unclaimed gold sovereigns left here during the Second World War. They were originally taken from Austria." Judex produced a thick envelope from his cape. "All the information you need is in here," he said, and tossed it across the room.

Bergerac failed to catch it and it fell onto the floor with a smack. Jim bent down to pick it up.

"How did you find this information?" he asked.

He stood up and Judex was gone.

The front door was open again. Bergerac took a flashlight out of the hall table and went outside. There was no one around. He scanned the bushes and hedges. Nothing.

His car was just as he'd left it, with the trunk and the toolbox open. He closed both and went back inside.

He checked the doors and windows. They were all locked and secured. How had this Judex got in?

Then he sat down and opened the envelope. The contents were sensational. Bergerac could only guess that this "Real Judex" had spies within the private security group.

He immediately rang Crozier and told him about it. They agreed to meet tomorrow at the Bureau at 8 a.m. to take action. Crozier hung up to make further phone calls.

As he showered and went to bed, Jim found himself reflecting that when he was 10, if he'd met Judex, he would have asked him for his autograph, or even to be his sidekick. And here he was in his forties, threatening to have Judex sectioned. Well, that's what growing up does to you, he thought.

On the beach, just outside the cave mouth as arranged, Kerjean was dressed appropriately, and the Judexes had abandoned their hats, masks and capes for practical potholing gear. They were just about to go in when...

"Hush! Listen!" said David.

The sound of a helicopter was becoming more distinct. It was the coast-guard. Armed police officers were beginning to pile onto the beach further along.

Kerjean realized things weren't going to go smoothly.

"This changes nothing—get going!"

Kerjean and the Judexes went swiftly into the cave.

A few minutes later, the police officers approached the cave. They were already prepared for potholing, so they filed in.

Inside, the Judexes followed Kerjean, who had memorized the route from the old map. Finally, they came to a corridor where a box, basically a metallic treasure chest, was sitting, rusting.

Kerjean looked at the padlock on it. It was almost entirely rusted. He grabbed it and yanked it off. He opened the lid, as three or four Judexes crowded round.

Kerjean picked out a handful of gold sovereigns and looked at them under the light from his own helmet flashlight. He smiled.

"This is it!"

They could hear echoes of a scuffle behind them in the caves. The other Judexes were fighting with the police. Kerjean knew that those men were as good as taken down. He just had the handful of men left around him. Fortunately, he had a backup plan. He'd memorized the whole layout of the caves—they weren't especially complicated. He knew that there was another cave mouth slightly further up the coast, that would take them back out to the beach, but further along. The beach there was narrower and there was a steeper climb back up the cliffs, but it wasn't impossible. Two strong men could manage to get the box up to the top there.

"You and you," Kerjean gestured at two of the Judexes, "take the box and take it along *that* way," he pointed at another corridor of caves. "Bare left," he instructed.

The two Judexes dutifully picked up the box and carried it along the route. Giving one last look back, Kerjean followed on. At least, he wouldn't have to pay those other Judexes now.

They moved through the occasionally narrow passages, until they heard the rustle of the sea and saw daylight.

Kerjean was the last to come out and stumble slightly on the pebbles. Squinting, he stared further up the beach to see how many police there were now. The Judex Society was finished, but at least it had fulfilled its purpose.

185

He looked ahead and saw the metal box dumped on the wet pebbles, and four unconscious Judexes scattered around. Standing in the middle of it all was a tall man, clad in the full Judex hat, mask and cape.

"I thought I told you to dress appropriately," said Kerjean, with a faint feeling of dread.

"I apologize if my outfit offends you, but you have been quite happy to let your henchmen adopt it."

Kerjean's dread surged into fear and anger.

"You!" he said darkly. "You murdered my grandparents! You destroyed my father's life!"

"Your grandparents brought it on themselves, M. Kerjean," said Judex, simply, before adding, "although the damage caused to your father's life was—I see it now—regrettable. Be assured that I will send him a substantial check from my Justice fund as fair compensation for his suffering."

Kerjean paused to take this in. A swift and simple solution after all these years of suffering?

"You think you can make things right with money?" he finally managed.

"*You* seem to think so," replied Judex, as he nodded at the box of sovereigns. "I am using the same approach as the legal system, where money is used as legal remedy. Not, as you seem to see it, as something almost magical to take from others."

Kerjean finally lost his temper.

"Give me the money! It is my right!"

Judex remained calm.

"In my experience, it is usually the people who go to such lengths, and destroy other people's lives to get wealth, who are the ones who deserve it the least. That is as true for you as it was once for the banker Favraux."

Kerjean launched himself at Judex in a rage. In one judo move, Judex threw him onto the ground, winding him.

Looking further up the beach, he could see police, including Bergerac, running towards him, and so made go into the cave mouth. But before he left, he stopped and turned to Kerjean:

"I am sorry about the suffering of your father, really I am. True, perfect, absolute justice is sometimes impossible to achieve, even by me. Maybe only God can do that, in the next world."

Cape billowing in the wind, he turned round and ran into the caves, just as the police appeared.

Kerjean and most of the Judex Society were arrested and charged. The recovered gold sovereigns would eventually be returned to Austria. And yet a thorough search of the caves did not lead to "the real Judex." Bergerac didn't think it would, somehow.

That evening, Bergerac went to Diamante Lil's café to relax, and see if he'd bump into any friends. Lil herself was serving behind the bar, so he went up to it. She placed his usual, an orange juice, in front of him.

"On the house, Jim."

"Thanks," said Jim, pleasantly surprised.

"For dealing with those hooligans yesterday."

"Oh, I see." Bergerac looked around the place. "You've certainly put the place back together again quickly."

"Well, most of the mess was broken glass. Don't look too closely at the furniture though."

Bergerac spotted Mattie Storin sitting at a nearby table with an older man who looked like he'd stepped out of the past.

"She's that journalist from the local paper, isn't she? Do we know the man she's interviewing? She *is* interviewing him, isn't she?"

Lil was amused. "You think he might be her boyfriend?" she leaned closer to Bergerac to not be overheard "I have heard she's attracted to older men. Nice to know you're still too young for some things, eh, Jim?"

"I'm with Susan, remember," Jim reminded her.

"Yes, I know. That man's apparently an expert on Judex. Let's hope he doesn't decide to smash the place up," said Lil, jokingly.

Bergerac smiled. "Yeah, he looks like a troublemaker, doesn't he?"

A few feet away, having covered the pleasantries, Mattie Storin started her dictaphone running.

"So, M. de Trémeuse, you've studied the Judex legend for many years now, and are considered to be something of an authority on the subject. Does—or rather did—the Judex Society compare to the original?"

"Apart from superficially—with the hat, mask and cape—the so-called Judex Society bears no resemblance to the original. The proper Judex was not a brawler, a mindless thug. This is why I requested that I be interviewed by you, Mademoiselle. Let me give you just one example of an incident that shows his true character. It took place just after the Great War..."

*Christofer Nigro has already used the character of Felifax, the Tiger Man, a creation of Paul Féval fils, in* Tales of the Shadowmen. *In the following story, Felifax is back in England looking for a potential relative of his in the murky demi-monde of monsters and man-beasts...*

## Christofer Nigro: *The Noble Freak*

*East End of London, October, 1936*

The evening boulevards of Britain's greatest city were currently in a state of upheaval following the recent Battle of Cable Street, which had pit marching fascists against their opposite political number. But Rama Tamerlane had no in-clination to glean a metaphorical relevance between this clash of ideologies and his own purpose in this foreign nation. That indifference was soon destined to change, though not at the moment. This gallant hero from the jungles of India, known to the world as "Felifax the Tiger Man," was on a mission of the utmost personal significance. Little else now entered his thoughts, save for how much he missed his beloved wife Grace and adopted sister Djina, whom he had left behind in Benares when word had reached him of the matter that brought him so far from his native habitat.

Though an urban environment wasn't his usual stomping ground, Felifax nevertheless stalked through the city streets with a proficient stealth. The fact that the London thoroughfares had few pedestrians walking about due to the tu-mult of the recent riots aided his clandestine movements. His finely muscled form moved through the shadows as if he was an actual part of it while he ap-proached his destination: a large building centrally located in the East End. This edifice held records that would confirm the startling news he recently received courtesy of his British government contact, Sir Ralph Napper.

*Sir Napper wouldn't give me false information, not after the debt he owes me,* Felifax mused to himself. *And his permanent return to his native Britain fol-lowing the cessation of his government duties in Benares does not relieve him of that.*

The Tiger Man strode into a back alley of the multi-story building and be-gan climbing upwards towards a window located on the fourth floor. The speed at which he climbed was matched only by the level of efficacy his finely honed musculature displayed in gripping every conceivable handhold to aid his ascen-sion.

Quietly making his way to the correct window, he peered through the glass, his keen eyesight unhindered by the darkness. His vision was further abet-ted by a small electric lamp that partially illuminated the room's interior, which revealed the presence of the three people within. Felifax was fascinated by the advent of electricity, having become only recently acquainted with its widespread use in the developed nations, but this was not the time to indulge his interest in scientific phenomena. What did interest him now was one all-important file from the records, hidden within the top secret government files that were stored there amidst a plethora of manila folders.

Scanning the room further, the primal warrior saw that two of the trio of men were security guards, armed and providing a vigil over the room in general, and the third man in particular. This third individual, who was seated and looking over documents in the scant radiance of the lamp, was dressed in professional attire, which suggested he was a bureaucrat entrusted to keep the files in order. Felifax knew that he would have to move quickly and decisively. Fortunately, this was a feat at which he excelled.

A loud crashing sound suddenly pervaded the room as Felifax pushed himself through the window glass. The two guards immediately jumped to attention, brandishing their pistols.

"What the bloody hell?" the bureaucrat bellowed as he leapt out of his seat.

"Get back, Mr. Stratton!" one of the guards shouted as he fired in the direction of the shattered window.

Unfortunately, the hot lead projectile hit no actual target. The Tiger Man's human sinews were genetically augmented by a fusion with the DNA of a true specimen of the fearsome striped big cat, and this granted him the required speed and agility to roll on the floor out of firing range much faster than the guard could aim.

"Did someone throw something through the window?" Stratton queried to the guards.

"I don't know," the guardian on the right replied. "I think some bloke might have jumped through it."

"That's sodding impossible!" Stratton insisted. "We're on the bloody fourth floor, you know!"

Less than a second later, a muscular arm with bronze-toned skin reached out of the shadows from behind the left guard and grasped the collar of his uniform. The man found himself summarily lifted into the air and hurled into one of the office desks, the impact knocking him cold in tandem with all the papers and utensils on its surface being scattered to the floor.

"Oh hell!" the other guard hollered as he turned his pistol in the direction of his hapless cohort. "Mr. Stratton, get the hell out of here!"

But the sentry's order was cut short as a tall young man leapt out of the shadows faster than the guard could pull the trigger and grasped the man's throat from behind with his steel-muscled arm. The guard gasped for air and managed to let off a single shot in no useful direction before falling unconscious from the brutal constriction of his windpipe.

Stratton was rushing towards the exit and reached for the knob of the door. As he grabbed the chrome handle, he realized to his horror that a powerful human hand with tan skin had grasped his wrist.

"Mr. Stratton, you know any struggle to resist would be futile and counter-productive to your welfare," a youthful masculine voice with a distinct non-English accent told him. "Please do not make me have to restrain you, and let's get the inevitable conversation we're going to have out of the way so you can get back to your ordinary life, hmm?"

"Okay, okay," Stratton agreed with anxiety-ridden anxiousness. "Just don't do anything rash, alright, guv?"

"I won't if you refrain from doing the same, Mr. Stratton. I regret utilizing this means to acquire what I need, but your government refused to so much as acknowledge the existence of a file that is of extreme pertinence to me, let alone grant me courteous access to it. But I know that information exists, as my source—who will remain forever unnamed—is eminently reliable."

Stratton gasped. "Sir, I can't just give you any of the files here. Please understand the position I'm in! It would be my job if I..."

"Mr. Stratton, please consider instead my present mood, due to your government's refusal to grant me access to this very personally relevant file. Consider the long distance I had to travel to get here, and consider the fact that I will not leave here without it. Consider how your refusal to cooperate will increasingly try my patience. Consider what a long night this can become for you if you remain obstinate in your deference to your job responsibilities over my requirement."

"Oh, bloody hell, why me, Lord?" Stratton buried his reddened face in his hands for a moment. "All right, look, I'll give you what you want, just please take it and then let me be, huh? I'm giving you this under duress, so maybe my superiors will be forgiving..."

"Let's get this over with, Mr. Stratton, or are you truly that eager for my continued company? I assure you the reverse certainly isn't the case."

"Okay! What file do you need?"

"I want you to give me the entire dossier of Sir Edmund Sexton, including any and all of his medical and scientific experimentation in regards to genetic splicing."

"Oh, God..."

"Mr. Stratton, make with the file or you will be doing much more pleading to your Christian deity before this night is over."

While traveling outside of London towards the county of Surrey, Felifax carefully studied the documents describing the entirety of Dr. Sexton's work. Even a man with the fortitude of Rama Tamerlane couldn't help but repeatedly wince at the singularly low degree of ethical conduct Sexton engaged in during his pursuit of genetic polymorphism. He couldn't help feeling steep amounts of sympathy, and even sorrow, for the many who suffered for what constituted "scientific progress" in Sexton's demented eyes. His own biological mother was one of those who suffered in this manner, even though she yielded a superior child whom Sexton considered a full success. But it was another, prior genetically manipulated product of Sexton's experiments whom Felifax was immediately concerned with. Though the woman who suffered to bring this child to bear was a different victim than his mother, the DNA was culled from the morphogenically altered and artificially inseminated sperm of the male tiger who was also Rama Tamerlane's biological sire.

In other words, this particular child was Felifax's half-brother, a sibling he never knew. Perhaps of equal importance, this sibling was an earlier attempt by Sexton to create a human child harboring tiger DNA. This prior effort was considered a failure, as the resulting child was much less anatomically human than the Adonis-like Rama Tamerlane. This child resembled a true fusion of human and tiger anatomy, and what Sexton described in his journal as a "freak."

*But he is my brother*, Felifax said to himself. *And no matter what he resembles, I will find out what happened to him and embrace him.*

The dossier made it quite clear that the errant sibling wasn't destroyed, but transferred to a government facility in Surrey for further study. What happened to him after that wasn't listed, as it was clearly of little concern to Sexton. Whatever the child grew into could have been disposed of since then, or used for any number of purposes by the country's many government agencies whose activities are kept partially or fully hidden from the general public. Felifax detested the thought of his sibling being utilized for such nefarious purposes, but he didn't see how such an entity could be compatible with what passed for "polite" society.

Felifax himself had the benefit of not only looking entirely human, but was a handsome sampling of humanity who was readily amenable to mass acceptance. His transformations into his full primal capacity were not only temporary and called forth only when strictly necessary, but they didn't constitute a radical departure from the standard anthro phenotype by any means.

This sibling of his would be rejected by the values of "civilized" society, and considered, as Sexton astutely noted, a freak.

*But he shan't be rejected by me*, Felifax thought to himself. *My values are those of the natural world, and my extended family has long included creatures of every conceivable shape.*

Moreover, Felifax's genetic proclivities included a strong empathic rapport with the natural world, and all the fauna that inhabited it, albeit those of the *felis* family in particular. This potent sense of things told him on a deep level that his sibling was not only still alive, but somehow running wild, alone in the world. This no longer needed to be the case. Felifax simply had to reach his next destination to find out what became of the *other* Tiger Man that he now knew to be kin.

Few individuals anywhere in Britain, let alone the world, had any idea that an unassuming two story cottage home located in the outskirts of rural Surrey was secretly a government research facility. Felifax was among those few, again thanks to the contacts he made in the upper echelons of the British government, one of whom stumbled upon the germane information that he passed along to Rama Tamerlane (he owed him that much, after all). The three government security guards who lay insensate at the Tiger Man's feet weren't happy with his possession of this knowledge, nor were the three still conscious sentinels who now confronted him.

"Her Majesty's government will have your hide over this, Hindu!" one of the guards decreed as he raised his billy club.

"I'll take that risk for family, and because of what your exalted 'Majesty' kept from me," was Felifax's cold reply as he summoned his full genetic heritage to metamorphose into his primal state.

Dark brown stripes appeared across the skin of his torso and back as his eyes took on a yellowish-green, cat-like appearance. He growled and swiped his hand in the direction of the remaining trio of opponents, his now enlarged incisors bared to indicate his readiness for battle.

The closest guard rushed towards him and swung his baton at Felifax's temple. The Tiger Man easily dodged the blow and backhanded the man in the side of his face, sending him careening across the floor. He landed with a fractured jaw that effectively took him out of the mêlée. The other two rushed him simultaneously, their combined weight and inertia pinning the formidable son of Kali up against the wall. But the growling jungle warrior would not be deterred. With a display of his massive strength, he hurled one of his assailants to the ground, while using his left arm to swing the other guard against the wall. The second man's collarbone cracked upon impact, and a subsequent blow to the back of his neck divested him entirely of conscious thought.

The remaining guard on the floor went for broke and reached for his pistol, drawing it from his belt holster. Felifax leapt upon him before he could fire, however, hissing angrily as he tugged the man's gun hand aside and battered him twice in the side of his face. The sentry's cheekbone splintered as the man slipped into unconsciousness. Felifax's subverted human will remained strong enough to compel him not to inflict a fatal blow to a security guard who was simply doing his job. Instead, he sprung off the man and rushed to the other end of the room where a terrified records keeper was hiding.

"Some bloody git that looks like that Tiger Man fellow from India is attacking us," the man whispered into the phone he held under the table with him.

"Can you please speak up, sir?" the voice at the police station replied. "You're whispering, and I can't hear you over that ruckus going on around you."

"Oh bloody hell! Listen, you have to send the bobbies over right now, this place is under attack…"

The next thing the beleaguered gentleman knew was the phone being wrenched out of his hand by Felifax, who had now reverted back to his 'civilized' state.

"My apologies, but your scent led me right to you," the Tiger Man said with a half-smile. "And you also whisper rather loudly."

The bureaucrat put his hands over his head and cowered into the corner. "Oh Jesus, please don't kill me, I'm only a lowly records keeper…"

"It wasn't my intention to kill anyone in this building, but I *will* have what I came for. Give me the information I require and my disposition will improve greatly."

"Do you realize this is a government facility? You can't just barge in here and demand…"

"Can't I? To the contrary, I did both of those things, and I expect my demand to be fulfilled. Otherwise, I will not be so quick to leave, nor have any inclination to improve my mood. Understand?" That last word was punctuated with a fierce tone, along with Felifax's face moving closely to that of the record keeper for further serious emphasis.

"Okay, they don't pay me enough for this anyway. What do you want?"

"I want any and all files dealing with Sexton Experiment #7, which I believe is code named *Felanthus*. I'll accompany you to the appropriate cabinet to make sure you provide me with every available sheet of paper encompassing the file."

The chronically underpaid bureaucrat was by then only too content to comply with his unwanted visitor's request.

Upon reading the full dossier acquired in Surrey, Felifax learned that his sibling—designated Felanthus—was held and cared for in a government facility located within the small Essex county village of Little Abilene. Unbeknownst to the public, this entire village and its columns of modest Victorian-style homes were all rented to government employees. The apparent plans for the housing of Felifax's far more bestial sibling was to train the manimal in following the directives of Her Majesty's government.

The creature proved cunning and intelligent, but was apparently physically incapable of reproducing human speech, and displayed a savage proclivity. His physiology resembled that of a tiger from the waist up, save for his human-shaped hands; and a human from the waist down, save for his long tail. He possessed both teeth in his felinoid maw and retractable claws in his human-like hands that were hard and sharp enough to score steel. His musculature granted him tremendous strength, agility, and speed, and he was able to move in either a bipedal or quadrupedal stance. He was covered with a fine, thin coat of striped orange fur, and his physical senses were as acute as any actual feline.

Upon reaching ten years of age, Felanthus was nearly full grown and appeared to be taking to the training well after a few years of harsh conditioning to break down his initial defiance. Or so it seemed; the creature soon came to comprehend the notion of thespianism in order to appease his captors. After being sent on his first supervised mission into the wooded regions of Surrey to locate an escaped criminal, Felanthus abruptly turned on and mauled his armed chaperones, severely injuring both of them, and then retreated into the wilderness.

His natural cunning proved sufficient to evade exhaustive attempts to locate him, and he had already been taught to survive and adapt to the changing climate and live off the game extant in the British countryside, even though he would have to seek shelter in the colder months and sometimes steal food from the area's scarce number of residents. The creature managed to deftly avoid direct contact with the sparse population, though it's believed that some of periodic reports of mystery big cats in the area may be the result of furtive glimpses of the now feral Felanthus.

*My brother may have avoided capture by both government agents and local hunters, but he will not elude me,* Felifax thought as be began looking for signs of his sibling in the expansive woods. *Not only am I a tracker without peer in any type of wild environment, but I can seek him on an empathic as well as physical sensory level.*

After roughly an hour of careful tracking, the Tiger Man finally came across tracks whose intermittent changes from bipedal to quadrupedal locomotion were obvious to him. The amalgamation of human and feline traits in these tracks clearly distinguished them from any true big cat, who were no longer supposed to be native to Britain despite the sporadic reports which seemed to suggest otherwise. He carefully sniffed the area around the tracks, taking in the spoor. He then sat in a meditative stance and called upon Shiva, using his spiritual belief in this great Hindu god to focus his empathy with nature.

*It's him,* he quickly concluded beyond the slightest doubt. *I can now track him wherever he may be in these foreign wilds. Brother, soon you will no longer have to face this unforgiving world alone.*

Within a few short hours, Felifax had used his various array of senses to track his brother to a large gully. This was after noticing that Felanthus had apparently been circling around, as if concerned about a certain presence. It was then that the trail abruptly ended. There was a large indentation on the ground where a heavy body had clearly fallen. Suddenly displaying great concern of his own, Felifax searched about the grassy grounds for clues as to what may have ensued... and to his horror, he found one. He picked up a small object he saw gleaming in the sunlight, something the average person may likely have overlooked. It was an object he clearly recognized as a tranquilizer dart.

*By Shiva,* he thought to himself in consternation. *I will find who has taken you from the home you found here in the wilderness, brother. And I will unleash the wrath of Black Kali herself upon them, whether they be government or not.*

A few short miles away, hidden within an enclosure of overgrown flora was a small but luxurious and well-equipped laboratory. It was entirely privately owned and constructed, having no connection to Her Majesty's government. Within its walls were surprisingly sophisticated apparatus, along with a quartet of large cages with omni-reinforced steel bars, designed to be able to hold anything. And confined within those cages were diverse beings of an unusual and decidedly lethal nature.

Working within the lab was the owner whose vast wealth had financed its construction, a tall man with a grim and homely countenance, a bald head wrapped in a bandana-like cloth, a long bushy beard, and a distinctive recurring nervous tic. Also present were his recently hired protégé, a shorter young man no older than twenty, with a thin beard and visibly balding crown; and a strikingly handsome third younger man of perfect athletic build who kept to the side of the first man, ever watchful and almost always silent unless first spoken to.

The owner was the most infamous and least scrupulous of the surpassingly brilliant scientists produced by a noted French lineage known as Tornada. The second shorter but also quite brilliant man was graduate student Lance Nolter, a native of Britain. When Prof. Tornada was ousted from his position as a professor of the University of London many months previous for breach of ethical conduct, he was quite pleased that Nolter, his prize student who was an obvious prodigy of grand ambition that was similarly unhindered by scruples, chose to quietly leave the collegiate institute to join the Professor on his private continuation of his renegade experiments. Together they would literally change the composition of the world by way of the fledgling scientific field of genetic engineering, Tornada told an intrigued Nolter.

The third man was a creation of Prof. Tornada, synthesized through an advanced process he called osmotic genesis, a process the scientist culled from the work of several other brilliant men of science who had contributed towards the cultivation of creating synthetic organic life by exposing its base components to a series of electrical and chemical conditions that mimicked and accelerated the primordial environment of the nascent Earth. This allowed for the birth of life via spontaneous generation, a remarkable process that no longer occurs in nature of its own accord. Superior to naturally conceived humans in every way but possessing mental faculties entirely beholden to Tornada's control, this artificially generated young man was christened Adam Danator, after the name given to the scientist's first creation by this process a decade earlier, the false surname being an alias the Professor was also using at the time.

It was Danator who had tracked and captured every entity who filled the cages while directed by Tornada's will. Felanthus was among them, and he looked out of his bars with both curiosity and forcefully suppressed anger at the three men who enjoyed the freedom of movement which he and his fellow captives now lacked.

"The chemical component of this tranquilizer is quite advanced, Monsieur Nolter," Tornada boasted to his student with his deep voice and notable French accent. "Ordinarily, one must calculate the amount of sedative with the weight and body mass of the target for it to be effective and non-lethal. This necessitates tailoring the dosage of each dart for one specific target. But this polymotic cocktail is always introduced in a small dosage, and it will very quickly replicate in accordance with any target's body weight and mass, thus promptly rendering nearly any sized biological entity somnambulant. An adaptable, self-replicable chemical that operates as a single-dosage-fits-all sedative! *C'est fantastique, n'est-ce-pas?*"

"Quite fantastic indeed, Professor," Nolter agreed. "But even more fascinating are these beings whom Mr. Danator acquired for our purposes. You only just revealed each of them to me. What are they?"

"Glad you asked, *mon cher collègue*," Tornada replied. "Most remarkable are these specimens, some of them being members of what appear to be a sizable group that have managed to remain hidden from public detection, whereas others seem to be utterly unique unto themselves. Take this first one for instance..."

Tornada led Nolter to a cage containing a huge humanoid being with chalk-white skin, yellow eyes, and a mane of lustrous black hair. He was dressed in a somewhat tattered dark-colored outfit punctuated with specially tailored boots to fit his enormous feet. He was none other than Gouroull, the Monster of Frankenstein.

"This creature was crafted by a genius of another familial line who, like my own, has tended to produce many prodigies in the bio-medical sciences: the Frankensteins. This particular creature appears to have been grown by some osmotic process crafted long before Stéphane Leduc ever entered a lab. The result was something shaped roughly like a man, yet utterly different and vastly superior to any human being, including an artificially generated person like my Adam. He lives by some bio-chemical process that not even I have been able to discern as yet, and seems resistant to destruction. I'm not even sure what my universal polymotic tranquilizer darts would have done to his queer physiology, for he was discovered insensate beneath a collapsed building in Paris, where he evidently lay for as long as two decades. Yet still he lives! *Incroyable, non?*"

Gouroull merely glared at Tornada with a look of pure contempt, his ever-calculating mind looking for the first opportunity to escape and deliver brutal retribution to his captors.

Strolling to the next cage, Tornada said, "Observe these two specimens..."

The duo within resembled human-shaped but obviously inhuman beings with fish-like features, including scaly greenish-blue hides, bulging eyes, frog-like mouths, and fins protruding from their limbs and head. They were nothing less than the once-human worshipers of the Elder God of the sea known as Dagon, beings from a hidden colony off the coast of Innsmouth, Massachusetts known in shadowy rumor as the Deep Ones.

"These men of Piscean anatomical attributes were recovered from a small New England town in America when rumors of their existence reached my ears. Like the Monster over there, I have just begun my studies of them, but what fascinating creatures they are! They seem to have begun their life with a conventionally human genetic constituency, but were later introduced to some form of polymorphological process that altered their genetic structure so as to adapt them to an aquatic existence. Imagine being able to confer such genetic alterations to any human being of my choosing?"

"My imagination has truly reached unprecedented levels since I entered your tutelage, Professor," was Nolter's response.

"Ha ha, *Cela ne fait aucun doute,*" the Professor said with a self-congratulatory snicker. "Now observe the two confined in these separate cages over here."

Tornada led Nolter to the next two cages. In each of them was a man who had truly disturbing characteristics. The first appeared to be human, but acted extremely deranged, foaming at the mouth and slamming himself repeatedly against the bars of the cage, causing Nolter to jump defensively backwards. In the second cage was a man whose body appeared to be in a state of cellular deterioration, yet he still pushed against the bars and reached out towards the men, his mouth agape and slavering.

"What happened to these men, Professor?" Nolter asked with disgust in his tone.

"Based on my preliminary observations, Monsieur Nolter, it appears these men have 'recovered' from actual death, albeit not as orthodoxly functional specimens of humanity any longer. And apparently courtesy of two very different means.

"The first seems to have been the recipient of a cellular stimulation chemical that I suspect to be derived from a re-agent first formulated by Dr. Herbert West, and later further perfected by Dr. Stuart Hartwell. His cellular composition again lives, but his mind was in no way restored to its previous state. He appears to be spending his second life in a state of perpetual psychotic breakdown, yearning to tear the life out of everyone his eyes lay upon.

"The second appears to have been, and still remain, a corpse which was reanimated by means that appear to indicate some form of bizarre and wondrous pathogen that I have yet to fully identify. Despite his ponderous movements due to the progress of nerve destruction and partial *rigor mortis*, he is every bit as dangerous as the other one, for he seems to have a voracious craving for nothing less than the flesh of living human beings, with no other form of meat able to satisfy his palate. The required sustenance for this appetite apparently forestalls further deterioration and provides a continuously mobile home for whatever mi-

croorganism animates this former man. I also suspect the pathogen may be…
communicable."

"Dear Lord," Nolter said quietly.

"Some might say the Lord would never have created such a thing, Monsieur Nolter," Tornada replied, "but if you look at the world about you, then you will see that nature is often quite predatory, competitive, and avariciously cruel. Is it any wonder that we humans behave no differently in our 'civilized' society?"

"Of course. But…"

"But, Monsieur, if I can isolate and find a means to osmotically synthesize a functional variant of that pathogen, as well as Dr. West's re-agent, just imagine the miracles we could perform upon the world?"

"Or the horrors."

"Considering the encroachment of mankind upon nature, I would say that what constitutes desirability and beauty as opposed to horror and subversion can be quite subjective, *n'est-ce-pas?*"

"Your lesson is far from lost upon me, Professor."

"*Bien!* Now, this last of our freakish specimens also appears to be unique, but my acquisition of various difficult to acquire files suggests this may be the result of some pioneering work in genetic hybridization by the late Dr. Edmund Sexton."

"I've read of his work! It inspired me greatly. Just as yours did, of course, Professor Tornada."

Tornada released his ominous giggle, accompanied by another gesticulatory tic of his face. "Yes, of course, *mon ami.* As you can see, this being appears to be an escaped hybrid of human and big cat, an exquisite marvel if I've ever seen one!"

Felanthus peered out of his cage at the three men with a fierce scowl. But since he was intelligent enough to realize the futility of getting at them for the nonce, the cat-man simply kept visible displays of his ire down to a barely audible hissing sound.

"*Magnifique, non,* Monsieur Nolter?"

"Truly, Professor."

"Though I must commend you, as well, for your application of mine and my predecessors' work towards the use of morphogenically altered botanical matter to utilize the carcasses of mammals as a host to facilitate reanimation. That is nothing less than the creation of a most unusual form of hybrid."

Tornada's proud snicker was directed towards a terrarium containing two dead mice that were nevertheless frolicking about curiously, their small forms completely enveloped by a covering of fetid moss.

"Not so much reanimation, Professor, than the means to creating an entirely new type of plant/animal hybrid by introducing an aggressive mass-replicating form of moss which utilizes the components of a dead animal to form the basis of its own rapid reconstitution into a new fully mobile organism that mimics the movement of its dead animal host."

"*Tout aussi magnifique*, Monsieur! The ladies in your life will be most impressed with your ingenuity, and will doubtless offer you a more natural form of fusion on a regular basis."

"If only my skills were geared towards the propensity for hurling a rubber ball through a hoop as opposed to scientific acumen, that may have been the case, Professor."

Tornada laughed at Nolter's reaction to his innuendo. "How I love your self-deprecating sense of humor, my esteemed student! But by any matter, I am having your new aggressive self-replicating moss put to the test on the field in surreptitious fashion. I have had certain paid agents of mine drop self-dissolving capsules containing small samples of your moss in various secluded areas across the globe where the remains of humans are known to be lying in state. The latest such location was a small wilderness region in America where the remains of my old business rival Roger Kirk are sequestered. Let us see what comes of this."

"Did you say *human* remains, Professor? Most... interesting."

It was late afternoon around Tornada's facility when Felifax discovered it in the midst of his tracking. His empathic and physical senses alike would not lie to him; his brother was within. The exterior of the building was well secured but that never stopped the Tiger Man from entering any other edifice in the past. Stealthily avoiding any obvious security device, Rama Tamerlane climbed to the top of the small building, quickly finding an air vent that would enable him to gain entrance. Slowly removing the bolts of the steel plate by using his sharp ceremonial blade like a screwdriver, he slid down into the upper floor. He discovered the first of the two floors to provide living quarters to those who operated the facility. He could hear the voices of two males speaking to each other within the main room, one with a French accent, the other English; they were obviously on the verge of retiring for the evening.

He then proceeded down to the first floor, peering in cautiously. He saw no person within, simply an array of laboratory equipment and the four cages. The strange beings within glowered at him without uttering any sounds as he approached the cage on the far edge of the room. Gurouill followed the intruder's movements with interest, suspecting an opportunity for escape was about to materialize. Felanthus got up from his position of relaxation and strutted over to observe the finely-muscled young man dressed in nothing more than shorts and a leather belt with his blade holstered to it.

"Brother..." Felifax said with a teary-eyed smile.

Looking at the young man closer, Felanthus first snarled suspiciously, but then felt a powerful empathic rapport with the newcomer. Though he never understood the concept of kin, he now found himself comprehending such a connection on a deep psychic level. His snarls quickly segued into soft noises reminiscent of a purring.

"You understand who I am, don't you?" Felifax whispered back. "I'm going to find a way to get you out of here. Please raise either of your hands if you understand."

Felanthus lifted his right hand into an upraised position.

"Very good. Now, I think I can identify the locking mechanism on this cage that keeps you entrapped, so..."

Suddenly, Felanthus looked past his brother and snarled fiercely, clearly giving a warning. Felifax turned around just in time to avoid being struck from behind by Danator. Rarely had any human being proved able to sneak up on him like that, so he knew immediately that this was no ordinary man. Danator's fist struck a cage bar after Felifax ducked, but he barely seemed to acknowledge any pain from his damaged knuckles. The Tiger Man retaliated with a blow to Danator's sternum, followed by a powerful haymaker to his jaw. The synthoorganic man flew back against the wall with blood dribbling out of his lower mouth. He shrugged off the blows, however, and rushed towards Felifax. The two grappled with each other fiercely, but the Tiger Man could not gain ground against his opponent's remarkable strength and speed.

Danator quickly lifted Felifax into the air and hurled him into one of the tables, smashing all of its contents to the floor. Having been dealt worse in the past, Felifax rose to his feet with impressive promptness and allowed his anger to fully subsume him. Summoning the other side of his genetic heritage with a prayer to Kali, his skin, eyes, and front incisors quickly developed the cosmetic characteristics that marked the release of his feral side.

Snarling in fury, Felifax leapt over the fallen table and slammed into Danator with increased strength and speed. The two tumbled about until the synthetic man pushed himself free of the Tiger Man's grip. Jumping to his feet, Danator drew his firearm and blasted two shots at Felifax. Though his aim was impeccable, the Tiger Man's reflexes were no less so, and he back-somersaulted behind a table, dodging both bullets. As fate would have it, the second projectile struck and damaged the locking mechanism of Felanthus' cage. Realizing what happened, the cat-man pushed against the door, but his considerable might still couldn't fully thrust it open.

In the meantime, Felifax continued to dodge Danator's shots by leaping between tables until the gun clicked empty. The Tiger Man then leapt over one of the tables in a single bound and landed on his adversary, his weight knocking him back against the wall. Danator seized Felifax by the throat and exerted pressure that he realized would soon crush his trachea. Before this could happen, however, Felifax drew his dagger and shoved it into his enemy's own trachea. Spitting blood, Danator still did his best to continue exerting lethal pressure on his foe's throat, but the jungle warrior also redoubled his efforts and cut several muscles on his foe's strangling arm, rendering it useless. Freed from the deadly grip, Felifax raised his blade again, this time slashing it across Danator's throat with supreme effort, nearly severing his head completely.

The Tiger Men left his slain adversary and rushed to Felanthus' cage to combine his own strength with that of his sibling in ripping open the lock-damaged cage door. As both pushed with their combined effort, the door slowly began giving way. Unfortunately, the conflagration had attracted the attention of both Tornada and Nolter, who appeared several feet away from them.

"I have no idea who you are, or how you could have slain my New Adam, interloper," Tornada spat with fuming ire, "but you will pay dearly for your intrusive compromising of my lab and ruination of our work."

To make good of his threat, Tornada hit a hidden switch under a table that not even Nolter was privy to which instantly opened the locks on the other three cages. The two scientists then quickly moved out the front door and bolted it shut. They then rushed towards a private vehicle on the other side of the grounds that Tornada made sure was there in case such a hasty retreat was warranted.

"Push, brother!" Felifax shouted as he and his sibling each gave one great simultaneous heave of the cage door. It was finally wrenched open, and the two Tiger Men stood side by side at last.

Gouroull began pounding his battering ram fists against the bolted front door, determined to smash it open and pursue Tornada and Nolter. His attempt was disrupted when a Deep One, crazed from its weeks of captivity, leapt upon him and tore its talons into his chalky flesh. Rivulets of black ichor seeped from the wounds, but Gouroull fought back with equally savage fury. He slammed his back against the nearby wall, and the crushing force dislodged the Deep One. Undaunted, the aqueous creature leapt at him again, but this time the spawn of Frankenstein met the attack with his own prodigious might and the two titans began pounding at each other furiously.

On the opposite side of the room, the other equally crazed Deep One rushed at Felifax. Felanthus pushed his brother aside with a mighty shove and lunged to meet the humanoid's attack head on. Both creatures ripped into each other's flesh with their respective teeth and claws. As Felifax was about to leap into the fray and aid his brother, he was interrupted when the re-agented dead man ran at him howling and foaming at the mouth like the homicidal maniac he now was. The Tiger Man braced for his attack, but was pushed back into the wall by the force of the assault. Felifax blocked the reanimated man's flurry of blows with his own mighty forearms, and then slammed him against the opposite wall, struggling to hold him back.

His acute senses then managed to just barely detect the other reanimated man, who sauntered behind him in preparation for biting into the back of his shoulder. Reacting in the blink of an eye, Felifax whirled around the reanimated man in his grip so that the zombie bit into the flesh of his shoulder instead. The maniacal reanimate bellowed in agony as a chunk of his muscle was torn out by the zombie's teeth. Shifting his rage from Felifax to the zombie, the reanimated maniac rushed into the gaunt walking cadaver, and the two began rolling upon the floor in a mutual death grip. The reanimated man angrily ripped one of the zombie's partially decayed arms off, while the latter moved its head and hungrily bit three toes off of the reanimate's restraining foot. The two animated dead men would soon render each other incapable of further mobility.

Meanwhile, as the marauding Deep One sunk its talons into Felanthus's back, the felinoid retaliated by sinking his own nails into the creature's right gill slits under its clavicle bone and tore the furrowed tissue from its neck. The humanoid leapt back screaming as purplish blood spurted from its gaping wound. Felifax rushed forward and sliced open its belly with his dagger, and the beleaguered creature looked down as its own bowels spattered onto the floor. Felanthus then jumped on the humanoid, fully tearing open its gut wound and ending its life.

On the other side of the room, Gouroull displayed his much-feared power as his walloping fists inflicted great damage upon the other Deep One. The creature continued slashing at him, however, rendering multiple tears in his flesh. The man-monster decided to end this once and for all. Pushing the Deep One against the wall, the Monster quickly reached for an amputation hacksaw sitting atop a table near him with his other arm. Grabbing the serrated metal implement, he smashed its sharp edges into the humanoid's neck. He exerted pressure on the hacksaw against the still struggling creature's throat until it finally ceased all movement, and a full gallon of its purplish blood seeped down its torso.

Gouroull then returned to pounding upon the heavily bolted door until it could stand against his might no longer and flew off its hinges. The man-monster emerged from the facility and scanned the vicinity for any sign of Tornada and Nolter. He finally noticed them standing yards away in front of their escape vehicle. A moment later, Felifax and Felanthus rushed out of the entrance to stand a few feet behind Gouroull.

"Professor, those three survived the attacks from the others!" Nolter bawled.

"I'm not blind, Monsieur!" Tornada spat back. "But our work mustn't end up in unauthorized hands, nor must we make it easy for those three to pursue us!"

Pulling a small rectangular device from his woolen coat pocket, Tornada clicked a switch on it. This activated a large number of explosive devices placed strategically throughout the home, including directly beneath its foundation. Felifax instantly realized what the Professor's gesture indicated.

"Brother, leap down on your belly, cover your ears, and lay flat!" he shouted, and he and Felanthus did just that.

A split second later, the devices were triggered and the laboratory/home exploded with a thunderous blast. Due to lying flat as they did, the Tiger Men avoided both the full brunt of the blast wave and any flying debris. Gouroull didn't escape the blast wave, however, and he was thrown clear off of his feet,

202

landing hard on the ground two yards distant. The explosive devices beneath the laboratory caused the bedrock beneath to collapse inwards until it formed a chasm over 500 feet deep, thus removing any last evidence of the structure. Felifax and his brother lay to the ground for several more seconds to fully recover from the sound of the blast.

While that occurred, Tornada and Nolter—who were just far enough from the blast wave to avoid being unduly affected by it—leapt into the vehicle. The Professor activated the ignition and pounded his foot on the accelerator, and the souped-up automobile sped away towards the closest road at nearly 100 mph.

The two Tiger Men struggled to their feet and watched the vehicle fade into the distance.

"Those vile men may have escaped," he said to his sibling, "but at least I found you at last."

He then warmly embraced his monstrous but purring sibling. Distracted in this manner, neither saw Gouroull rise up on his feet, black ichor dripping out of his mouth, ears, and nostrils. The great injuries he received from being caught directly in the blast wave were already rapidly healing. The man-monster ran over to Felifax and grabbed him by the throat, effortlessly lifting him into the air and hurling him several yards away. He then turned to the angered Felanthus.

"You..." he said with difficulty, pointing to the cat-man. "You are a freak... like me. Not like that one. He is human, and our enemy. You come with me, and together we will... render the human world asunder."

Felanthus roared and crouched in an attack position.

Gouroull took on an incredulous expression. "Why attack me? You are... just like me."

"No..." Felanthus gurgled out with even greater difficulty, his first ever spoken words. "Not... like you!"

The cat-man then sprung on the Monster, determined to tear him to shreds for hurting his brother. Angered and insulted, Gouroull pounded back, knocking Felanthus to the ground. Before the Monster could resume his attack, however, Felifax leapt upon his back and drove his dagger into the side of the brute's throat.

"Cease your attack on my brother, Monster!"

Gouroull howled in pain and moved about trying to dislodge his foe. Felifax continued his assault with a slashing cut across the Monster's throat. Though dark ichor poured in large streams from every inflicted wound, still the man-monster refused to fall. Reaching back with his massive arm, Gouroull grabbed Felifax by his arm and slammed him to the ground, cracking two of his ribs. As he lay there stunned, Frankenstein's berserk creation raised his enormous fist in preparation for splattering the jungle adventurer's head like a melon.

But the recovered Felanthus then leaped forward and raked a gash right across the Monster's left eye, nearly ripping the yellow orb from its deep socket.

Roaring in agonized rage, Gouroull swung back. His fist struck Felanthus with great force and knocked him back towards the gaping chasm.

But before he could fall down the deep crevice, the cat-man grabbed the Monster's arm, braced his feet against the edge of the chasm, and pulled with all of his extensive strength.

"You... go with me..." Felanthus gurgled as he heaved on his opponent's sinewy limb.

Gouroull lost his footing near the edge of the chasm due to the force of Felanthus' pull. Even though he struggled to regain a foothold, it proved futile as he was successfully wrenched over the edge along with the cat-man. Both feel deep down into the darkness of the abyss, followed by an oddly peaceful silence.

Having witnessed this, Felifax screamed in turmoil. The brother he had just found after so long sacrificed himself for the life of a sibling he had just met. Though considered a freak in the eyes of the human race, the last act of Felanthus proved him to be far nobler than the vast majority of the race that scorned him. Rama Tamerlane wept as he sat looking down into the depths of the chasm.

*In the previous episode of this two-parter, John Peel, a regular contributor to* Tales of the Shadowmen *and Doctor Who writer extraordinaire, introduced us to a direct sequel to Jules Verne's classic novel,* Journey to the Center of the Earth, *starring not only the cast of the original, Axel Lidenbrock and his uncle Professor Otto Lidenbrock, but also two more familiar faces, Harpooner Ned Land from* Twenty Thousand Leagues under the Sea, *and German agent Captain Von Horst from Edgar Rice Burroughs'* Tarzan at the Earth's Core. *We left the characters just as they were about to enter the fabulous underground realm of Pellucidar... Now read on!*

## John Peel: *Return to the Center of the Earth*
### (part two)

*Pellucidar, 1872*

### X. First Steps in a New World

Pellucidar! Though the name was unknown to us at that first moment in which we stepped into it, we would soon learn at least a few of its secrets. But our first thoughts were still to put greater distance between ourselves and Captain von Horst and his men. At least out here in this immense fresh world we had a greater chance of losing our pursuers.

And so we set off, Hans in the lead, myself and my uncle together and the good Ned Land bringing up the rear and constantly checking behind us. My uncle was like a schoolboy at Christmas, almost giddy with excitement. He wished to stop constantly to examine specimens of plants and shrubs as we passed them, but this we could not allow. We hurried him past them, and he would cry out a farewell to them, including their Latin names. His disappointment at losing one specimen was abated as soon as he saw the next. I promised him that we would halt as soon as we dared, and he could explore to his heart's content. In the meantime, however, we had to hurry.

I really cannot express just how strange and provocative this world we had stumbled upon was. It was extremely unnerving at first to see the land rising upward all around oneself, instead of staying flat and natural as it does on the surface of our globe. It was as if we were scurrying along the bottom of some immense basin that stretched for thousands of miles, until lost into the distance or the light from that strange central sun. It created a strong feeling of oppression, as if one could expect the walls of this world to suddenly start like an avalanche towards one. It was days before I lost that terrible sensation.

And then there was that sun—though it appeared to cast about the same quantity of light upon us as did Sol upon the surface of the world, it was clearly much smaller than the true Sun, and much, much closer to us. How was it powered? Of what strange form of matter did it consist? I threw these questions at my uncle as we traveled, partly out of curiosity and partly to keep his mind occupied so that he wouldn't stand still and look at another floral distraction.

"Those are good questions, my boy," the Professor replied. "And ones I fear will prove to be very difficult to address, since we scarcely yet know what forces power our external sun. Do the same processes at work in Sol work here inside the Earth? I should doubt it, myself. Any force capable of flinging light and heat across millions of miles of airless space would be far too intense to power a smaller sphere within the heart of a planet and shine through merely hundreds of miles of atmosphere."

"Indeed, uncle," I agreed. "But how, then, could this peculiar arrangement have come about? Science has surely agreed that the Earth is a compact spheroid. We have a rough weight for it—six by 10 to the power 24 kilograms. That allows us to estimate the density of the planet, and allows for nothing like this huge hollow we now find ourselves within."

"Then science is wrong, my boy. It has been wrong in the past and no doubt will be wrong in the future. But science progresses by discarding the false and seizing the new truths we discover. I would say that we can account for the missing mass that should be filling this hollow space by theorizing that the central sun that we see before us is vastly denser than packed earth or even heavier metals."

"Perhaps so," I conceded. "But how is it that we have come to be walking on the *inside* of this hollow Earth, when we began our journey the right-side up on the surface?"

My uncle laughed. "Nothing is more obvious, my boy," he replied cheerfully. "It is by the same process that enables a person in the Antipodes to stand right-side up on the bottom of the world—the change is accomplished gradually, so slight that it isn't even noticeable as one travels. As we descended, we must also have been turning 180 degrees without being aware of it."

This was all a bit much for me; I have not the scientific mind possessed by the wise Professor Lidenbrock. I must have looked a trifle confused and glum, for my uncle laughed again and gestured at the path we were taking.

"Then here's another little conundrum for you, my dear Axel—why do you have no shadow?"

I glanced down and saw that he was not technically quite accurate—I *did* have a shadow, but one cast directly downward, so it was extremely small and tight to my feet. The answer to that was quite obvious, even to me. "Because the sun is directly overhead," I replied.

"And yet we have been traveling for about two hours now, and when we started the sun was *also* directly overhead."

That news made me stop, shade my eyes and stare upward. My uncle, as always, was quite correct: the sun *was* directly overhead, and the sun had also been directly overhead a few hours previously. That puzzled me for a moment, and then I laughed. "Of course! This secondary sun is *always* directly overhead because it lies at the exact center of the Earth! The planet revolves about it."

"Good, my boy, good. Now—deduce from that. What does this fact tell us?"

I considered for a moment and then realized what he was getting at. "If this orb is always overhead, then it can never set."

"Admirable, my dear Axel, admirable. And what follows from that?"

"There can be no night here," I said, slowly. "This is a land of perpetual day, like the polar regions in the summer."

"Far more so," the Professor said gravely. "There, at least, the sun will eventually start to rise and set again. Here in this world it can never do so. Conditions here can never change. This world has known only a single day, and will continue to know only that single day until the source that powers it should die out, and then a single, endless night will descend upon this world. Time as we know it cannot exist here."

"But that cannot be!" I exclaimed. "We can measure the passage of time—we estimated we've been walking two hours already, for example."

"I did not estimate it—I measured it with my watch," my uncle contradicted me. "And our chronometers are the only means we have to measure the passage of time here. There is no morning, noon or evening here, so time is constant. It is always *now*. And another thing follows from this, my boy—there can be no seasons, either."

I grasped the reason for that quickly enough. "Because the seasons are caused by the inclination of the Earth's axis toward the sun," I said. "In the winter, the hemisphere is slightly farther away, and in the summer slightly closer. But here, at the center of the Earth, every region is equidistant from the central sun and can never get closer or farther away."

"Quite so, quite so," the Professor agreed happily.

I gestured about us. We were travelling through a fairly dense forest. "Then how do things grow here?" I asked him. With neither spring, summer, autumn or winter, how do the plants know when to flower, the trees to shed their leaves..."

"Ah, but *do* they, my boy?" he asked excitedly. "Oh, I can see that this is going to be a world that will repay exploring most handsomely! A man might spend a lifetime here just attempting to unravel its mysteries!" He rubbed his hands together in anticipation.

Ned Land must have been listening in to at least a portion of our discussion because he let out a heavy snort. "Maybe for you as a gentleman of science," he said. "But I had rather planned on spending the rest of my lifetime back on the surface of this world, not living like a mole in the heart of it. Can you find us a way out of here again, Professor?"

"Oh yes, I'm certain of that," my uncle said. "As our own descent has proven, there are connecting passages between our own world and this. We know of the one behind us, but there are undoubtedly more of them. And that would explain a few mysteries, I might add."

"Such as?" the sailor prompted.

"Such as the plesiosaurs that inhabit the Central Sea. There are too few for a viable breeding population there, and they could not have survived there for the millions of years since they died out on the surface world. This land in which we now find ourselves must be their breeding grounds. I fancy that in the seas here such creatures and much most thrive and reproduce. The same would go for the terrestrial animals we have encountered. Sooner or later we shall stumble across herds of such creatures, I'll wager." He looked at the sailor with twinkling eyes. "As for passages back to our world—we then, they must exist because they help to explain some of the mysteries of science. There are tales around the world of strange creatures—one or two at most—that are sighted and that cannot possibly exist. However, if such creatures as live here were to stumble onto a passageway that leads outside of the crust of our world, why, then, that would be perfectly reasonable!"

At that moment Hans halted and gave a sharp motion that indicated we should be silent. We immediately did so, and I wondered what our sharp-eared and –eyed guide had noticed that we had not. We were walking through thick forestland at this point. As we stood there, we could hear bird cries and songs, and then, faintly, rustling sounds. A smile crept onto the face of our guide, and he indicated that we should stop, so we did so.

A moment later a group of deer slowly emerged onto the faint track we had been following, some fifteen feet ahead of us. They appeared as startled to see us as we were to see them—all, that is, save Hans, who had somehow heard their approach. He had his rifle up and fired before the panic-stricken family could dart back into the hidden depths of the forest.

All save one, who had crumpled and fallen, shot expertly through the heart.

"Well done, my friend, well done!" Ned Land enthused. "An end to eating the jerky at last! Fresh meat for our feast tonight."

"Not *tonight*," my uncle corrected the harpooner, "for in this strange world night will never fall, save at the end of its days, as in some Nordic myth, and then it will be endless night."

"Let's not quibble," Ned Land laughed. "Whenever it may be, thanks to our good friend here, we eat well!"

Hans had stepped forward, his knife drawn ready to start the process of preparing the slain deer. Ned Land was lowering the pack he was carrying to go to his aid when there came a fresh player to the stage.

There was a low growl from the trees, and then a blur of motion. As if from nowhere, a large, powerful form now stood on the pathway, its amber eyes turned balefully in our direction. It was a huge cat, standing a good five feet at the shoulder. It was striped like a tiger, and its powerful body rippled with muscles. As it growled again, my attention was drawn to the two scimitar-like teeth that protruded from its upper jaw. This was some saber-toothed cat, the likes of which no man had seen since the end of the last Ice Age. Though it was clearly a powerful hunter, it was obvious that it was also an opportunistic thief should the chance arise.

It wanted the deer Hans had killed. For my part, I was quite willing that it should have its desire. Even armed with modern rifles, I was by no means certain we would be able to take down such a monstrous creature as this. Much as I would enjoy fresh meat, I wasn't sure that it was worth fighting for. Hans, however, didn't even flinch. Armed only with his knife, he crouched over his kill, refusing to back down. The tiger growled another warning, but Hans merely raised the knife slightly.

Ned Land seemed to barely pause for thought, either. He had, strapped to his pack, one of the harpoons he had brought along on the expedition in the hopes of spearing some gigantic sea monster. What faced us now was no aquatic animal, but as far as the sailor was corned, one monster was as good as another. He drew the harpoon and let his pack fall.

Somehow the tiger realized who was the greater threat. It turned its attention from Hans to Ned Land. The sailor faced this creature of the land with as much aplomb as he must have faced the giants of our terrestrial seas. He stood, feet apart and braced, the harpoon steady in his hand. The tiger must have been desperate for food, for it seemed to sense it was in danger. But it, too, did not lack courage, and it refused to back down. Instead, it crouched and sprang.

Ned Land did not—as I had expected him to—throw the harpoon. Instead, he merely moved slightly aside and then thrust his weapon with all of his might into the great cat, burying the hard iron point deeply between the tiger's shoulders. The huge paws caught him a glancing blow, thrusting him aside as the tiger landed on the pathway. It stood there, mouth agape and roaring its defiance. Somehow I managed to gather my wits and raised my rifle for a killing shot, but it proved unnecessary. Ned Land knew his job well, and the roar of the tiger was its last effort. Its great heart must have burst, for there was a sudden outpouring of blood from its mouth, and it collapsed, lifeless, to the ground.

Hans hurried to the sailor and helped him back to his feet. The Icelander's normally impassive face was split by a broad grin, and he clapped our nautical friend heartily on the back, almost sending Ned Land sprawling again. Then our guide looked down at the massive dead beast and shook his head in wonder. He had, of course, never seen a monster such as this in his life before. Nor had any of us, and I would have been heartily glad for some reassurance that we never would again.

The sailor reclaimed his harpoon and started to clean it. Then he stopped, staring over my shoulder. "We are not alone," he said, quietly.

I looked around, and saw what he meant. Silently, a small group of men had slipped from the shade of the trees. There were six in all, tall, muscular and also on the hunt for food, it would seem. Each man carried a long spear tipped with a stone point. They were all very much alike—dressed only in loin-clothes, with rough sandals. Each had a belt that held a stone knife. Their skin was a reddish hue, darker even than the natives of North America, and they had long, dark hair and eyes almost as dark.

Were these primitives also planning on attacking us to steal our deer? We held ourselves at the ready, but made no hostile move. "Let us wait and see what these men have in mind," my uncle said softly, and it seemed a good suggestion to us all. Would they be friendly—or should we be attacked?

### XI: Back To The Stone Age

After both sides had stared at one another for quite a full minute, my uncle stepped forward slightly. "Can we assist you gentlemen in some way?" he enquired.

Ned Land snorted. "I'd hardly call them *gentlemen*," he grunted.

"Now, Mr. Land, there's no need to be rude," my uncle said. He looked expectantly at the six warriors. They looked at one another, and then one nudged a second with the butt of his spear. The "elected" individual glared at his companion, but stepped forward and spoke earnestly for several sentences, not a word of which did we understand. He then waited and looked at us.

"Perhaps we should try another language?" the Professor mused.

"Begging your pardon," the sailor said, "but I've heard many a tongue spoken on my various voyages, and not a one of them sounded like *that*. And they don't look like scholars to me who might understand Latin or Greek or some other dead tongue."

"I fear you are correct, Mr. Land," my uncle agreed with a sigh. "But what are we to do?"

"Well, uncle," I said, "they've made no move to attack us, which means that while they may not exactly be friendly, neither are they actively hostile. Why not make an overture of friendship by offering to share our food with them?"

My uncle beamed. "A capital idea, my boy! There are times when I do believe you're actually learning to use that mind of yours." He turned to Ned Land. "You have probably had more experience with less civilized people than any of us. Perhaps you would care to conduct the negotiations?"

"Right you are," the sailor agreed amiably. He looked to the savages and made a point of finishing cleaning his harpoon first, to make the point that we were far from helpless. Then he gestured at the dead deer and the slain tiger. Then he spread his arms toward the six men and then gestured to the rest of us. His meaning was abundantly clear, that he was inviting them to share with us.

The warriors conferred briefly in their strange tongue, and then the one who had been elected leader made a point of laying down his pear and his knife before stepping forward. He held out his hand and when Ned Land did the same, the warrior clasped his arm and grinned widely.

We were friends, it seemed.

I need not tell you how much that relieved us all. These stone-age savages had never seen a gun before, and probably thought that our weapons were merely clubs. The metal-tipped harpoon, too, was something utterly new to them, but at least that they could recognize as a weapon, and Ned Land as a skilled warrior. They were much taken with our burly sailor, and kept looking from him to the slain tiger in admiration. Later, when we were able to converse with them after learning their language, we discovered that very few people had ever managed to kill what they called a *tarag*. Ned Land was held, therefore, in great respect. Back at their village, the women pried loose the two great teeth and handed them to the sailor as a trophy. He was more than happy to receive them, and wore them on a thin cord about his neck from that moment on.

At that moment, however, the warriors simply helped us pack up the two kills, gutting them where they lay and leaving the entrails for the scavengers. They also made two carrying poles and strapped the kills to them. Four of the warriors were elected to carry these, while the remaining two walked with us alongside them as we traveled to their village. My uncle seized the chance to converse with their spokesman as best he could, learning words for things as we walked along.

Our new companion managed to tell us that his name was Halar, of the Sarak people. He made an effort at grasping our names, though he couldn't quite get his tongue around "Axel", which came out more like "Askel", but it was close enough for me to understand him. Despite their savage appearance, the men turned out to be remarkably open and friendly.

"Don't make the mistake, my boy, of thinking of them as ignorant idiots," my uncle warned me. "They may be less technologically advanced than we are, and their grasp of science may be rudimentary to non-existent, but there's nothing wrong with their brains. This is their world, and they are clearly very well suited to it."

Their world, it turned out, was Pellucidar, the first time we had heard this name.

We soon reached their village—I say *soon*, but it was, of course, impossible to tell how long it took us. My uncle's watch had stopped, which was strange, as he always kept it wound. Then Ned Land discovered that *his* watch had also stopped, something it had never done in all his days of voyaging our surface oceans. As a result, we had absolutely no way to measure time, for the sun, of course, was constantly overhead, no matter how many hours or days might have passed. We could only estimate our journey, then, by the fact that we were not tired when we reached the village, and therefore judged that our trip was not a long one.

We were the center of attention from the moment the women noticed us. Our clothing was considered strange and somewhat amusing, and many of them pinched at the cloth and commented amongst themselves about it. For their own part, the women wore almost as little as the men—short skirt-like things and halters for their chests—leaving large areas of their skin uncovered. Whilst this would never have passed muster in polite society, our sailor, at least, approved of it. And, truth be told, the women were as beautiful as the men we met were handsome. Still, they all made me realize just how much I missed my dear Gretchen. And the tribal children made me miss my own daughter.

The children were lively and happy, investigating everything. The younger children wore no clothes, and the older ones dressed as the adults. Everyone seemed to be in good health, something we noted with interest. My uncle, in fact, had started our visit with trepidation.

"I've no doubt these people are as friendly as they would seem," he informed me. "But it is not treachery I fear but disease."

"Disease?" I asked him, surprised.

"Yes, my boy. Recall the lessons of history. When the Europeans first voyaged to the Americas, they met peoples who had never known European diseases, and who had germs of their own that *we* had never before encountered. As a result, neither side had immunity to the sicknesses that plagued the other. Whole peoples were wiped out as a result. And he we are, in a world that may possess diseases more deadly than the Bubonic Plague—to which the natives may be utter immune. Or the slightest sneeze from one of us might give these friendly fellows a cold from which they may never recover."

"But these look to be the healthiest people I have ever encountered," I objected.

"Which does not mean they are not the carriers of some fatal malady," my uncle warned. "We must take great care to observe one another—yes, and the natives!—for any signs of illness or infection, and if it does occur, we shall have to enforce strict quarantine measures. We can take no chances, my boy. If even one of us gets ill, we dare not even think of returning to our world. We could become plague bearers such as the world has never known!"

I confess, he scared me greatly with these terrible thoughts. To be exiled here, never to see my Gretchen and child again! That terrified me more than the thought of dying of some unknown illness.

As it turned out, of course, my uncle's fears were groundless—the inhabitants of Pellucidar have great immunity to any kind of disease. In fact, in all of the time we were among them, I never even heard a single child sneeze. But it was several weeks—I *think* it was weeks—before we felt sure we would be safe.

But back to the events of that first day. Ned Land was the hero of the hour. I have mentioned that he was given the great teeth of the tiger, and that he wore them proudly. This made him very popular with the laughing ladies, who value strength and skill in hunting more than anything else. My uncle was sure the sailor received several offers of marriage, which he thankfully did not understand or accept. The women then skinned and cooked the deer and tiger. I was rather surprised at the latter, since I have always understood that carnivores for some reason make poor eating. But the members of the Sarak tribe wasted nothing, and the tiger was cooked and devoured by them with every evidence of great enjoyment. I for my part stuck with the venison, which was a trifle burnt but absolutely delicious after so long on our rations.

The tribespeople did not practice agriculture—my uncle hypothesized that they were still at too primitive a level of culture for that—but the women and children had gathered some roots and plants from the forest, which they made into a kind of stew to go with the meat, and so we ate very well. After a hearty meal, almost everyone elected to sleep. There were a few guards posted, for there are a number of animals in Pellucidar that will happily attack and devour people, as well as other dangers of which we were quite unaware at the time.

Another consequence of the perpetual, unwavering daylight in this world is that there is very little variation in weather. It was constantly like a warm summer day, hence the lack of clothing by the Sarak people. Truth be told, I was a trifle uncomfortable in my own clothing, but nothing would induce me to shed any of the layers. Both Ned Land and Hans, however, went shirtless after a short while, though neither went quite so far as to resort to loin cloths. This warmth also meant that bed sheets were unnecessary, as, indeed, were houses as such. The people had only slight shelters to shade them from the sun while they slept.

In truth, they slept much less than we do in our world, though neither I nor my uncle could account for that. Our best guess was that perpetual sunlight may have affected the human need for sleep somehow, but there was no way for us to test that hypothesis, so it remained little more than a conjecture. But we discovered that our own need for sleep much reduced while we were in Pellucidar, though now we are home and safe in our own beds, we have reverted to our earlier need for several hours a night.

I found their lack of housing most peculiar, but my uncle—as always—had a ready explanation for it. "These are a primitive people," he reminded me. "They have few possessions, all of which they can easily transport with them. Because of the weather, they have no real need for shelter, so why should they build houses?"

"But what about… privacy?" I asked.

He laughed, good-naturedly. "They understand privacy differently than you or I," he said. "They do not know greed, either—for no one has more or better than anyone else. Envy? Pfah! Theft, too, is likely unknown."

"You think them faultless, then?"

"My dear boy, they are still human beings, and, as such, I am certain must be prey to sins—just not the ones we fall prey to. Jealousy and anger probably exist here as much as in our world."

This was true enough—the people here had their faults, but various crimes that exist all too frequently in our world could not thrive here. What was there to steal when your neighbor had only the same things you had, and when the identity of the thief would be transparent almost immediately? The only thing one person might have that another wanted was food, but that was held in common anyway. The men hunted and everything that was brought back was shared with the tribe. The women and children gathered roots, fruits and edible plants which, again, were shared.

People being people, no matter where they lived or what sort of culture they possessed, they still managed to have human emotions and thus human conflicts. Men angered one another, and these arguments sometimes ended in fights. They were rare, however, for all able-bodied men were needed to hunt to feed the tribe, so the chief of the tribe was empowered to settle conflicts when they arose, and his word was law.

I sighed. "You make this place sound almost like Paradise reborn," I said to my uncle.

He glanced at me and shook his head. "My boy, one thing I have learned in life is that where there may appear to be a paradise, then there is also a serpent in the garden."

In actual fact, there were two serpents in this garden—one of which we had brought with us...

## XII: The First Serpent

As I have already mentioned, our good friend and companion Ned Land proved to be most popular with the unmarried females of the Sarak. His skill as a harpooner made him a reliable provider as a hunter. We had been accepted into the tribe quite easily, and as a result we now had duties to perform. My uncle was excused from hunting on account of his age, but Ned Land, Hans and I accompanied the other men on their expeditions, under the leadership of Halar, who had always been accepted before as the greatest hunter. But Halar had never killed a *tarag*, so he soon found his status challenged by the regard everyone felt for Ned Land.

Any other man might have been jealous, but this was not in Halar's easygoing nature. Instead, he appeared to be glad to have such a skilled hunter to add to his parties. The sailor, of course, had no desire to usurp Halar's position as chief of the hunters, and readily accepted the other man's orders and friendship, so this was not a problem.

There was, however, another problem, and one not so simple to sort out. Among the unmarried females was Alaya, daughter of the chief, Tomak. Alaya was acknowledged as the most beautiful woman of the tribe, and rightly so in my opinion. I thought her almost the equal in looks to my darling Gretchen, though her temperament could hardly match that of my dear wife. She was tall and lithe, extremely pleasant to look at, and, as I have mentioned, the chief's daughter. This made her the most eligible catch in the tribe, and don't think that she was not aware of this fact! As much as anyone in the tribe of Sarak, Alaya was spoiled. The men all vied for her favors, and the women all sought to be her special friend to gain status. And Alaya—Alaya played everyone off against everyone else.

It had apparently been understood that she and Halar would be mated—but that was before our arrival, and the ascent of Ned Land to most successful hunter. For such was indeed the case. The men of Sarak all had their stone weapons, which were surprisingly effective in their skilled hands, but Ned Land had his invaluable metal-tipped harpoon, a far better weapon.

We all had our rifles, too, but we refrained from using them as much as possible. Our ammunition was severely limited and we conserved it against a true need. Besides, the tribe had no concept of what a rifle could do, never having seen a firearm before, so they didn't even recognize them as weapons. As a result, when we went hunting Hans and I used spears and knives of stone that the tribe made and presented to us, while the sailor used his harpoon. One of us would take along a rifle, in case of emergencies, but it chanced that we never really had occasion to use one.

Alaya had seen the shift in status of Halar, and even though Ned Land didn't press his situation, it was evidently very obvious to the women of the tribe, and to none more so than Alaya. She found excuses to be close to the sailor, to hand him some delicacy at the feasts, or to fetch him water when he was thirsty. He, for his part, enjoyed the attentions of the most beautiful of the women of the tribe, and enjoyed spending time and attention on her. I could not wonder if he was not falling in love with the savage maiden, and mentioned this to my uncle.

"I had not noticed," the Professor said, thoughtfully. "But this might complicate matters for us."

"How so?" I asked. "Surely his emotions must remain his business?"

"Yes, yes," my uncle said impatiently. "But how will this affect our little group? I do not imagine that you are in favor of our staying here for the rest of our lives?"

I thought—as I did so often!—of my dear Gretchen and our girl, and shook my head vehemently. "No indeed!"

"Good. Nor do I, or Hans, - who is eager to get back to the girl he was wooing. I had thought to remain here merely a short while to build up our strength, to learn what we can, and to sharpen our language skills. Tomak assures me that there is only one common tongue throughout all of Pellucidar, which I find quite peculiar but helpful. I am building up a map of this area of this subterranean world and hope we can set off soon to explore it. Given that Captain von Horst is undoubtedly close to the place where we entered this world, I do not think it wise to attempt to return to the surface through that passageway. I am hopeful that we may be able to discover an alternate route, and propose that we set off again on our journey quite shortly."

"You think some alternate route exists?" I asked him, eagerly. I had not considered the possibility myself, and had assumed that we would have to retrace our steps to return to the surface.

"I believe there must be others," he answered. "It would be most logical. But finding one may take some doing. It is clear these primitive peoples have no inkling that there is another world, let alone that it is reachable from here. If we are to escape, then we must discover a route by ourselves. Allow me to think on that, and let us assume one will be found." He looked a trifle worried. "Now— will Ned Land accompany us or not, do you think? I must confess that I have grown used to his company and find him exceedingly helpful as a member of our expedition. I would not gladly leave him behind—but if that is the way his heart may carry him, neither would I attempt to compel him to go with us." He clapped me on the shoulder. "My boy, you are quite close to him—perhaps you would be good enough to sound him out and ascertain his intentions?"

I promised my uncle that I would do so—but events precluded me from carrying out that intent, events provoked by Alaya herself.

As I have said, she was rather spoiled and tended to take for granted that what she desired would be immediately given her. It appeared that she currently desired Ned Land, and had laid her plans to take possession of him. But her plans were not progressing as swiftly as she had hoped, for the sailor was proving difficult for her to pin down. She was not the only unattached girl flirting with Ned Land, though she was undoubtedly the prettiest. However, all of the girls seemed to me to be extremely attractive—perhaps their scant attire had something to do with that!—and certainly it seemed as if that might be the case with our harpooner.

Annoyed by her lack of success, Alaya elected to attempt to allay her annoyance in that time honored female way—taking a bath. In our world a lady might simply order her maid to prepare her water for her and then take a leisurely soak to her heart's content, but in this primitive society there were no baths, no heating and no maids. Instead, the accepted method of bathing was to simply undress and plunge into the closest river—away from prying male eyes, of course. This is what Alaya elected to do, taking along a handful of her close friends, probably with the intent of complaining about men in general and Ned Land in particular.

I should at this point explain that we had heard for some time a curious expression amongst the members of the tribe, and one that made little sense to any of us. A mother might warn an unruly infant to behave or "the Mahars will get you." We took it to be the generalized kind of warning that parents always give to keep their children in check and thought nothing more of it. However, the phrase was also used in some of the few laws that these people had. On the whole, their legal system was quite simple and splendid: don't do anything to anyone else you wouldn't wish done to yourself. And in most cases, the punishment for breaking this law was simply that the offense would be repeated upon the offender. As my uncle had noted, there was very little law-breaking for the very reasons he had given.

There were, however, a few injunctions that were more specific. One of these was that women should never travel more than a quarter mile from the village unaccompanied by a warrior—"else the Mahars will get you." Again, we thought little of this, given the dangerous nature of Pellucidar in general. We had already encountered one *tarag*, and were told that these ferocious sabertooths had no fear of man. And there were other animals almost as dangerous, such as the *jalok*. We had not encountered any of those, but they were described to us as something like a large, ferocious wolf that frequently hunted in packs. So the admonition against going unaccompanied by an armed man made perfect sense—to everyone but the spoiled Alaya, who was having nothing to do with any man if she could not get the one she desired.

It seemed that her favorite spot to bathe was almost a mile from the village, where the river twisted and made a pleasant pool, and she decided to go there with her friends. And, of course, she informed no one in the village of her plans, partly so that nobody could try and dissuade her and partly because she was annoyed and didn't wish to talk to anyone other than her silly friends.

Meanwhile, we were in the village having a time of leisure. Our last hunting trip had been a success, and we had brought down a *thag*—a kind of oversized elk—with enough meat on its bones to last everyone for almost a week. If it were possible to measure a week in this land! The men were using their free time to repair their spears and knives, or to make new ones. I was watching one of the skilled craftsmen preparing a new blade the way it had been done during our own Stone Age, fascinated by the swift and assured way he used a stone to flake a flint core. In his own way, this man was just as much a craftsman as any watchmaker or instrument maker in our world. As I have said, the men of Pellucidar are not stupider than the men of our world—they simply have less access to information than we have. When it came to living the lives they did, I doubt if any modern men could do as well, let alone better. The stone axe or knife or spear maker was a skilled craftsman, working with precision and care.

It was while I was watching him work that one of the lazing hunters gave a cry and pointed to the path to the river. One of the village girls was heading up it, but she was barely able to keep her feet. Two of them men dropped what they were doing and hurried to her aid. One of them caught her as she fell, and carried her back to the village, where the older women shooed the men aside and took charge of the unfortunate girl. Out of curiosity, I had wandered across and could see she was covered in lacerations, mostly superficial, but that a large bruise was forming on one shoulder, and her arm was held at an angle that looked extremely uncomfortable.

"Sagoths," she gasped, opening her eyes and wincing from the pain. "Sagoths attacked us by the river."

We had heard nothing in the village, which was puzzling if the attack had occurred so close, because the river was only a hundred yards or so away. One of the older women understood what had happened, however, and elicited the fact that Alaya had taken the girls a mile from the village, against the laws and all sense. Alaya and four girls had been captured, and this girl had barely managed to escape to run for help.

"What does this mean?" my uncle asked Halar. "What has happened to them?"

"The Mahars have taken the girls," the hunter replied, grimly.

"The Mahars?" I asked, confused. "But she mentioned some people named sag..."

"Sagoths," Halar explained. "They are not people—at least, not people like us. They are brutish and twisted, and they serve as the strong arms for the Mahars. Alaya and the others will be taken to their city."

This was all new to us, but my uncle managed to drag some information from the tribespeople. They feared speaking of the Mahars out of a superstitious belief that if they were spoken of, somehow the Mahars could know of it. This was why the villagers had spoken so little about these creatures. They were, we were told, utterly inhuman and evil, and lived in great and terrible cities all over Pellucidar. There was one not too far away from the village—they had no real measuring system, so "not too far" might mean a handful of miles or else a journey of a week. They did agree that the girls would be taken to the city, however, and that a rescue party must be mounted to try and intercept them. Once the women were in the city, escape would be impossible.

The rescue party would have to move swiftly, and it would be unwise to make it too large. "It is possible that this was done to lure the hunters away in order that the Sagoths might raid the unprotected village," Halar explained. "So we have to leave enough men with weapons here to defend our women and children in that event."

It was decided, then, that a party of six of us should suffice. Halar and Ned Land would lead. Hans and I would go along, as well as two more men from the village. We hastily grabbed our weapons and some dried meat—since we did not intend to stop to hunt for our meals—and said our farewells.

"Take care, my boy," my uncle said, warmly, clasping my hand. "Come back safely—and, hopefully, with the missing women."

"Don't worry able me, uncle," I told him. "I have Ned Land and Hans with me, as well as Halar. I shall be perfectly fine." I hefted my rifle. "No matter what kind of creatures these Sagoths might be, a bullet should stop them in their tracks."

And so we set off, hurrying down the path to the river. Halar was grim, clearly very concerned for his friends, and especially Alaya. Even Ned Land seemed subdued; clearly the savage girl meant a lot to him. We reached the kidnap point quite swiftly, and it was not hard to see evidence of the affair. Plants had been crushed on the bank of the river and there were small patches of blood. Halar bent to examine the disturbed ground and then looked up at us.

"They were taken in this direction," he said, pointing. "There are at least a dozen Sagoths in the raiding party. Let us hurry, for they cannot be too far ahead of us."

Silently, we followed him. A skilled hunter, he could see traces of the passage of the kidnappers invisible to my city-bred sight. We moved quickly up to where the trees began to grow farther apart, and there was grasslands favored by the thags. Here he stopped and scowled.

"Ah, we are too late after all," he said. "They have taken to *lidi* here." Even my untrained eyes could see that the ground was much disturbed and that there were prints of some large creature.

"What are *lidi*?" Ned Land asked.

"Huge lizards," Halar answered. "They are used as transport. They can walk for long periods of time, and it is not likely that we shall be able to catch up with them." He shook his head. "They will be able to return with our women to the Mahar city before we can reach with them. Our rescue attempts are doomed."

*XIII: The Rulers of Pellucidar*

This pessimistic outburst did not sit well with Ned Land—nor, truth be told, with me. I was in full agreement with the sailor when he gestured at the clear prints and said: "Even a blind man could follow that trail! Even Axel here!"

"Hey!" I exclaimed, annoyed at the insult.

Ned Land clapped me on the shoulder. "No offense, lad, but your tracking skills are somewhat lacking. Even you must agree to that." There was a certain amount of truth in what he said, no matter how much it stung. But in my defense I will say that he would make a terrible geologist. He turned back to Halar. "There is the trail—why should we not follow it? Do you not want the women back? Do you not want Alaya back?"

"Of course!" the hunter exclaimed angrily. "I have known them all my entire life. I do not wish to go back to their families and tell them we have lost them to the Mahars. But what other choice do I have? The sagoths will reach their city before us, and once they do, we cannot rescue the women. There is, then, no point in even trying to follow them."

"Why can't we rescue the women from the Mahars?" the sailor demanded.

"If you knew the Mahars, you would not need to ask that," Halar answered.

"But we *don't* know the Mahars," I said. "We've never seen them, and this is the first time any of you have even talked about them—and even now you are not being clear on the subject. Tell us about these Mahars and why they are so invincible."

The savage looked frustrated. "We do not talk about them," he said. "It is said that if you mention their names, they can hear it and listen to what you say."

"In that case," Ned Land growled, "they must already be listening in, because we've mentioned them an awful lot. So nothing you tell us now could draw their attention more, could it?"

Halar considered the point, and then nodded. "If they can listen, they are listening already," he agreed. His companions didn't like the sound of that, and they moved away from us as Halar finally deigned to explain matters to us. "The Mahars consider themselves the masters of Pellucidar, and with good reason. They have strange powers, many of which I do not understand."

"Which probably don't exist," Ned Land muttered under his breath.

"No!" the hunter exclaimed. "These powers exist. They are able to fly, for one thing, and to speak without using their voices. They are immensely old and wise, but very, very inhuman. In appearance they are like the *thipdars*."

For the first time I started to get worried. We had seen *thipdars*—the native word for creatures we would call pterodactyls—and they were large and powerful hunters. It would explain how Mahars could fly, if they were related to these creatures. I exchanged a worried look with Ned Land.

"They live together in great cities throughout all Pellucidar," Halar continued. "The one closest to us, where these lidi are heading, is a hundred times the size of our village, and hundreds of Mahar live there. The Sagoths are their servants, but they take humans as slaves whenever they can. At least as slaves. The Mahar eat flesh, and it is said that they find humans quite tasty."

"Thundering seas!" Ned Land exclaimed. "Alaya and the other girls are destined for the dinner plate, and you won't lift a finger to save them? What kind of a man are you?"

"A practical one," Halar replied. "What is the point of going to the Mahar city only to be taken in our turn? It would help no one in that event."

"Then I am an impractical man!" the sailor vowed. "My friends and I have powers of our own that these Mahar have never encountered." He shook his rifle. As I have said, we had never used them in the presence of our savage friends in order to conserve our small supply of bullets. But here I was in full agreement with my companion that this was a cause in which some ammunition must be spent. Halar, of course, thought our rifles were simply wooden sticks—probably some sort of good-luck charms—and had no idea of the damage we could cause with them. "Whether or not you go with us, Halar, I am going along." He looked at me expectantly.

"I cannot abandon these women," I said, simply. "How could I ever face my sweet Gretchen again if I should have to tell her that I abandoned four of her fair sex to be slaughtered and devoured by reptiles?"

"Brave lad!" Ned Land said. He looked to Hans. Here there could have been a problem in communications because Hans only spoke Danish. He had the intellect to learn other languages, but it simply did not interest him. He was able to communicate with my uncle, and that was sufficient for him. To my surprise, then, he indicated that he would go along with us. He had evidently understood some at least of the conversation, though I could never be sure how much.

"Well, then," the sailor said, turning back to Halar, "the three of us are going along. If you are not, you'd better return to the village and let them know there what has happened."

Halar was clearly caught in a dilemma here. He was afraid to go on, convinced our quest was useless and our fates sealed. But he was clearly loathe to go back and abandon the woman he had hoped to marry and her companions. He squirmed, wrestling with this problem for several minutes before finally composing himself. "I shall accompany you to your deaths," he decided. "But my tribe can spare no others." He therefore ordered the other two hunters to return to the village and to let everyone there know what we were doing. "Tell them to hold a great funeral feast for all of us," he instructed.

"But not just yet," Ned Land snapped. "Give us the option to live first."

"Then when should they hold our funerary feast?" Halar asked.

Ned Land grinned broadly. "At the next full moon!"

I glared at him. "You know very well Pellucidar has no moon."

"Aye, lad, that I do," he agreed cheerfully. "So if they wait for it, it should give us quite sufficient time to rescue the women!"

I had to admire his optimism, as well as Halar's courage. We set off together, following the tracks of the *lidi*, despite the fact that he was marching off to his death. He could not have the confidence that we had in the power of our guns, but he accompanied us anyway. As it turned out, he was soon to be enlightened, though not through any event of our choosing.

The jungles of Pellucidar are thick and plentiful, probably owing to the warm climate that exists throughout this interior world. As there are no seasons, they are a profusion of color and growths. Ferns dating back to the Jurassic era rub fronds with flowering plants of far more recent periods. Likewise the fauna is just as mixed. I have mentioned the ferocious *tarags*, wiped out after the last Ice Age on the surface of our world, but their companions the cave bears also existed here, along with the Irish elk. From earlier epochs were the eohippus, the dog-sized ancestors of modern horses. Going further back in time were land creatures such as the *lidi*—which I was to discover looked very like reconstructions of the brontosaurus—and even small bird-like creatures that looked more like lizards with rudimentary feathers. In the seas and lakes there were the plesiosaurs I have mentioned, and in the skies were the great *thipdars*, pterosaurs of our world.

Along with these, of course, were some creatures that as far as science knows never existed upon the skin of our planet. The most obvious example, of course, would be the Mahars—intelligent and malevolent reptiles—along with their brutish servants the Sagoths—half-ape and half-human. Pellucidar was indeed a most strange environment. And, far too often, a very deadly one.

The *thipdars* are the hunters of the Pellucidarian airs. They take eagles on the wing and even sizeable beasts like small antelope from the ground. When they are hungry—which is much of the time, as flying takes much energy—they will even attack and devour people. Some time into our journey, we became the objects of one such creature's attack.

It was Halar who spotted this, as we were still sufficiently new to Pellucidar not to think automatically of scanning the skies for trouble. We grew up in a world, after all, where the skies are perfectly cheerful and safe. Halar gave a cry, and pointed upward. We followed his gaze and saw one of the winged predators swooping down. We were caught in the open, crossing a river clearing, and there was no safety for us to rush to. We were forced, therefore, to stand and defend ourselves. Ned Land, Hans and I all raised our rifles, while Halar hefted his near-useless spear. I held my fire, knowing that my companions were better shots than I, and far more likely to hit the creature. I would wait until the last possible moment to use up any of my precious bullets.

It turned out to be unnecessary, as I had suspected. Hans, our best shot, fired first, when the great winged beast was little more than thirty feet from us. It was a brilliant shot, straight through one of the *thipdar*'s large eyes and into its brain. The beast was dead before it hit the ground before us. We were forced to dive aside as the immense creature tumbled to a bleeding halt.

Ned Land and I clapped Hans on the back, and our guide smile back modestly at us. Halar was completely shocked.

"How did you do that?" he cried in wonder. "Your wooden sticks threw thunder at the *thipdar*, and it died!" He shook his head, astounded. "For the first time, I begin to think that your magic may indeed match that of the Mahars." Now he had seen what a rifle could do—even though he could not understand *how* it worked—his mood improved immensely. He finally had confidence in us and our sound-throwing sticks. We did not inform him that we had only a small supply of ammunition. Now that he was optimistic again, we did not wish to destroy his hopes.

Ned Land drew his knife and eyed the dead *thipdar*. "It was going to eat us," he observed, "so it seems only fair that we should return the favor." He considered for a moment and then asked Halar: "Are *thipdars* good eating?"

"I do not know," the hunter answered. "No one I have ever heard of has ever killed one before."

The sailor laughed. "Then let us find out!" he exclaimed.

*Thipdars*, I might add, are excellent eating. They taste more like steak than chicken. We cut and cooked up a supply of the beast's meat, leaving the rest of the carcass for the roaming *jaloks* to find and scavenge.

We moved on. As I have said, it is almost impossible to estimate time in Pellucidar, with its endless day. We walked, following the ever-present *lidi* tracks, we ate and from time to time we slept. Sometimes we were attacked by the local animals, sometimes we attacked them for food. Time passed.

We entered another of the grassy plains that sometimes stretched for several miles at a time. But this time we knew immediately that there was something wrong. We could hear the snarls of *jaloks* ahead of us before we left the shelter of the last trees. They were clearly fighting over food, which meant something had killed another creature ahead of us. It might have been them, it might have been some other beats, for *jaloks* are not above chasing off lesser animals and stealing their prey—or of simply scavenging what some greater killer had left behind. Normally we should simply have skirted a site like this, but it was clearly from directly ahead of us on the path we were following. We conferred on the matter for a brief moment, and decided we should be ready with our rifles in case of need, but that we should take a look at what was happening ahead.

We were quite unprepared for what we saw when we stepped from the trees. The *jaloks* were there, of course, and clearly scavenging what had been killed by one of the monsters that lived hereabouts.

It was a dead *lidi*, the first I had seen. Knowing that it was a brontosaurus was one thing, but seeing the immense beast laid out on its side, huge portions of its muscular body torn out, was quite another. It was a small mountain of flesh. Impressive as it was in death, I could only imagine how majestic it must have appeared alive. Some great carnivore—perhaps a tyrannosaurus or one of its relatives—had slaughtered the beast and eaten its fill, leaving the carcass for the hyena-like *jaloks* to feast upon.

"Look!" Halar exclaimed, pointing at the corpse. I could see what he meant—there were the remains of some immense howdah beside the dead creature. And, as we looked closer, we could see, scattered about it, the corpses of several sagoths.

This was the *lidi* we had been following. It and its passengers had been slaughtered.

We were too late.

### XIV: City of the Mahars

I stared at the scene of the massacre, stunned and depressed. After everything we had gone through, the savage land of Pellucidar had claimed more victims. Alaya and her friends were dead.

Then something penetrated through my shock and hopelessness. Halar was scouting about, and did not seem to be as depressed as I would have expected for a man who had lost his love. He was giving the feasting *jaloks* a wide berth—they were intent on their grizzly feasting, but spared us a glance and a heart-felt growl of warning from time to time—but he was clearly looking for something in the long grass.

"Poor Halar," I said to Ned Land. "He refuses to give up, even with the evidence before us that we have failed. He must truly have loved Alaya."

"I'm not so sure his brains are addled," the sailor said. "He seems sure of his purpose." He shook his head. "Though I cannot..." He broke off as something suddenly occurred to him. "Friend Axel, look at those corpses."

"I'd rather not," I confessed. I do not have a very weak stomach for such things. "I'd prefer not seeing Alaya and the others with their insides on their outsides."

"Nor will you," he said. "They are all without exception only Sagoths."

"What?" I turned to gaze of the scene of the massacre and saw that he was correct. Beside the dead *lidi*, the only victims in sight were the brutish forms of the ape-men. "Perhaps the *jaloks* ate the tenderer females first?" I suggested.

"They're not that tidy eaters," he replied. "There would be bits of the women left behind in that case, and I can see none."

At that moment, Halar gave a cry and gestured for us to join him. The *jaloks* growled at us again, but as we were moving further from their feast, they then ignored us. We hurried to join our friend the hunter, where he was pointing excitedly at the ground—and fresh *lidi* tracks.

"The second *lidi* escaped this fight," he explained. "Alaya and the others must have been on this one."

I was confused. "There was a second *lidi*?"

Halar laughed and clapped my arm. "Axel, my friend, you are a good companion, but probably the worst hunter I have ever known. Did you not know we were following a pair of *lidi*?"

I had to confess that I did not. My misapprehension was aided by the fact that the word "*lidi*" means both a single creature and multiple beasts. One *lidi*, two *lidi*, a herd of *lidi*... I felt such a fool, and my face must have shown it, for Ned Land laughed and slapped my back.

"Don't worry about your lack of tracking skills, lad," he said. "I didn't see the second set of tracks, either." He turned to Halar. "So we still have our trail?"

"Better than that, my friend," the hunter replied. "Look—there are signs of blood along the way. The second *lidi* escaped the attack, but it must have been wounded. It is walking slower now, and is undoubtedly carrying extra passengers. We now have a chance of catching up with it before it reaches the city of the Mahars."

That was good news indeed, and we hurried to follow the tracks, feeling of lighter heart now. Added to this good news was the fact that the bodies of the Sagoths left behind us meant that we also faced fewer foes than before. We moved faster than before, hope giving us extra strength. The *lidi* we were following was less steady upon its massive feet, and the trail of blood showed that it was probably getting weaker. Everything gave us encouragement.

And so we went. We stopped to eat at one point, but we refused to rest, sure our goal would be in sight beyond the next ridge, or through the next copse of trees. The blood trail that we followed had not coagulated, so clearly the *lidi* was not far ahead of us.

And finally we were correct—we came to the crest of a hill and there, at its base below us, lumbered the *lidi*. We had caught up with it—but not it time! It was approaching what was clearly the city of the Mahars.

And *city* is certainly the word for it. This was no village composed of wooden shelters such as those the tribe of the Sarak dwelt in. This was a sizeable community of stone-built houses, and towers. As Halar had informed us, it was clear that this was home to hundreds of creatures, not simply a few dozen. The stone had been hewn and lifted into place, creating structures that showed design skills. Though still far below the standards of a European city, this was the sign of the highest culture we had yet seen within the Earth. It was clear that these Mahars were as far above the Sarak culturally as those humans were above the *jaloks*.

There was one peculiarity that stood out about these buildings—the windows in the towers were huge, far larger than needed to simply allow in light. Then I saw a couple of flying creatures, larger than men but smaller than *thipdars*. They circled one of the towers and then came in to land on the ledge of the window. They waddled inside, and vanished from view.

They had obviously been two of the Mahars, since Halar had said they could fly, and the "windows" were actually their doorways into their buildings.

As we stared down at the city, the *lidi* we had been following arrived at a large pen area beside the closest buildings. There were several other *lidi* stabled there, and I could make out a mixture of humans and Sagoths in attendance upon the beasts. I heard Halar give a growl of anger and pain and saw that the brutal guards were forcing the four women they had captured down from the *lidi*. Cuffing their prisoners about the head, the Sagoths led them into the closest of the buildings. The remainder of the Sagoths and their human slaves set about removing the howdah from the *lidi* and then to examine and tend its wounds.

"Just too late," Ned Land growled. "It will be difficult to find the women in that maze of buildings."

"We cannot give up now," I objected. "Not when we are so close."

"I wasn't proposing retreat, my friend," the sailor said. "Merely bewailing our luck. But we don't know where the women are being taken, not do we have a plan yet to rescue them."

Halar gestured at the *lidi* pens. "The workers there will know," he said simply. "We shall ask them."

"They work for the Mahars," I pointed out. "They may betray us to the Sagoths."

"No man would work willingly for the Mahars," Halar stated. "I am sure they will aid us if we ask it of them."

I have to confess that I was nowhere near certain of this—and neither was Ned Land, judging from the skeptical glance he gave me. But then he sighed. "We have no other real choice," he agreed. "But I think we should single out just one of the slaves—the less people who see us there, the better I shall like it."

We conferred and finally agreed to a plan. We should sneak down under cover of the rocks and trees until we should be able to slip unseen into the compound. One of the slaves had been left to feed the newly-arrived *lidi*, and we should approach him while he was alone and speak to him. Because he was human, we hoped he would help us, but if he tried to raise an alarm, we were ready. Only three of us should appear at first, and Ned Land would make his way behind the man. If he gave any indication of intending to betray us, the sailor would jump him and subdue him.

We gave Ned Land a few moments to be on his way before Halar, Hans and I moved cautiously toward the *lidi* pens. Once we were close, we revealed ourselves to the startled slave.

The man jumped, and looked around quickly. "Are you insane?" he demanded. "The Sagoths are nearby. If they see you, you will be captured and enslaved as I am—or worse."

This did not sound like the speech of a man who intended to betray us to his masters, so I stepped forward. "We are here to rescue the women the Sagoths just brought in," I explained. "They are our friends, and we will not abandon them to their fate."

"More fools you, then," the slave growled.

"Do you know where they have been taken?" I asked him.

"To the Mahars, of course," he replied. "The Masters must decide the fate of all captives."

"Do you know how to get there?" I enquired. "Can you direct us?"

"I do know," he admitted. "But I cannot direct you—the way is winding and complex. Being strangers here, you would get lost—and then the Sagoths would capture you."

Ned Land stepped up close behind him, startling the man. "It sounds to me like you have many excuses for taking no action," he growled.

The slave looked from one of us to the next and then sighed. "You are right. I have been here a long time, and have accepted my slavery, not wishing worse." He looked up, and there was a new spark in his eyes. "But—enough! I will be a slave no longer. It may be that this is the time of my death, but even death is preferable to remaining a slave."

"That's the spirit!" Ned Land encouraged him. "You have become a man again, whatever befalls you."

"Come, then," the newly minted man replied. "I will take you to where you may see into the Great Hall of the Mahars. And if I die—I die in the company of men, and not of animals."

"What is your name, friend?" Halar asked him. "And of what tribe?"

"I am Siom, and I was once of the Dathar tribe."

"I have heard of the Dathar," Halar commented. "It is said that they raise great warriors. I am glad that you are with us, and am certain now that we will rescue our women." This little speech gave our new friend fresh pride and courage. Halar added to that by passing him a spare stone knife.

Our new friend led us quickly into the city. In moments, I had lost all sense of direction, but Siom seemed to know precisely where he was going. We had our weapons hidden from sight, but had no need to skulk in the shadows. The idea that any humans would invade the city of the Mahars was completely unthinkable, so any Sagoths who saw us assumed we were on some errand for the Masters, and completely ignored us. Their arrogance was working in our favor!

The Sagoths were huge brutes, more gorilla than men, though they had some rudimentary intelligence and could speak the common language of Pellucidar. There is nothing like them in our world, of course, but we sometimes found this to be true in this lost world. There were many relics of bygone eras still alive and thriving here, but there were also chimera, creatures the surface world has never seen—or, if once seen, they are long dead and science has discovered no trace of them so far.

Chief amongst these are the Mahars themselves. We caught our first glimpse of the Masters as we passed one of the houses. Inside were three of these creatures, all of them sleeping. They stood taller than a man, and in general form looked like smaller relatives of the great *thipdars*. But their heads were larger, to accommodate greater minds, and the claws on their wings possessed long and slender fingers that enabled them to manipulate objects as well as any man.

I do not know the origin of these creatures, but when I discussed the matter later with my uncle he agreed with me that these were somehow evolved from the *thipdars* over the long eons they had been isolated in Pellucidar, as men had once been shambling brutes like the apes. This was the only sense we could make of the matter, and we must let it rest unless we somehow discover further evidence.

Siom led us finally to the Great Hall. Herein were gathered hundreds of the Mahars, each on ledges in tiers, looking down to a stage in the center of the immense hall. We slipped in at a side entrance and were in time to catch the proceedings, though Siom cautioned us against taking any actions here. Not only were there hundreds of the Masters, but there were numerous Sagoths also. We were vastly out-numbered, and any attempts to free our women would surely lead to our own capture.

And our women were there—I could see Alaya, who stood tall and proud, despite the scratches and bruises that showed she had put up strong resistance to her capture. The other three women tried to emulate her, but they did not possess her haughty manner or her strength of spirit, and they looked cowed.

One of the eeriest things about the proceeding that followed was that none of the Mahars uttered a word. It seemed that they did not possess vocal chords, and cut utter no audible sounds. Instead, Siom explained, they somehow communicated with each other directly, mind to mind, though some strange sense that they alone possessed. I wondered how they then could communicate their wishes, but soon discovered the answer to that.

One Sagoth, older and greyer than the rest, came forward. He was cloaked in an air of authority, and it was he who spoke for the Masters. It seemed that one in a thousand Sagoths possessed the sort of mind that could receive messages from the Mahars and understand them. As a result, this speaker was a valued member of the race, and most useful to his Masters.

"Gilaks," he said, solemnly. *Gilak* is the Mahar word for humans, but it means "beast", for the Mahar do not consider people to be intelligent, merely animals. They split all creation into Mahar and non-Mahar. I cannot say I do not understand this, for do we humans not do the same thing ourselves? It is because they consider humans on the same level as animals that they feel no guilt in enslaving them or eating them as they wish; no more than we should about devouring or domesticating a cow.

"Gilaks," the Sagoth repeated. "It is decided that no more slaves are needed at this time. You will therefore be taken to the Pits." It made a gesture and the Sagoth captors seized the women and dragged them from the hall. Other matters were to be taken up, it seemed, but they were of no interest to us.

"What are these Pits?" Ned Land demanded of Siom. "And where are they?"

The ex-slave shuddered. "The Pits lie below this building," he explained. "There Mahars who search for knowledge experiment upon captives. They wish to know all that there is to know about our world, so they study everything. Your women will be given over as subjects for study."

"They sound like scientists," I said. "They mean to examine the women?"

"Yes," Siom replied. "They will be taken apart to study their blood, their muscles, their hearts..."

*Dissected!* I fell horror rising within me. Given the level of culture I could see about me, I doubted that this would be done at all humanely. "We can't allow that to happen," I exclaimed.

"The paths to the Pits lie this way," Siom said, urgently. "If we move swiftly, we may be able to intercept them before they reach the depths." He looked at us earnestly. "Once they reach the Pits, we shall stand no chance of rescuing them—it is too well guarded."

"Then let's hurry, man!" Ned Land snapped.

We hurried indeed. Siom knew his way and he led us into the tunnels under the buildings. These were not well lit, but we had sufficient light to see what we needed—ahead of us were the three Sagoths carrying out their Masters' orders to take Alaya and the others to their fate.

228

Thankfully, Alaya was struggling, and she caught sight of us as we approached. Clever girl, she started screaming and kicking at her captors more than before, so that the three Sagoths' attentions were entirely on her. When we attacked them from behind, they suspected nothing until the last second, by which time it was too late, and then went down, clubbed unconscious.

Alaya laughed, and threw her arms about the sailor's neck. "Nedland!" she cried—she had never comprehended our strange custom of possessing two names, and always made his name a single word. "I knew you would rescue us!"

"You're not rescued yet, lass," he growled, disentangling himself from her clutches. "All of you, stay with us. Siom, lead us out of here!"

"With pleasure, my friend," the ex-slave said gladly. We headed back toward the surface, more than happy to leave those dark, unwholesome tunnels behind us. We were starting to feel optimistic about our chances when there came howls and cries from behind us.

Our victims had been discovered, and a hue and cry was raised!

We were still in the city of the Mahars, which was being roused to action against us.

### XV: Pursuit!

"Hurry, man," Ned Land urged. "They must know where we are heading."

Siom nodded, and increased his pace. We followed, readying our weapons for the inevitable fight. Thankfully, so far the pursuit was behind us, so we were not cut off. We emerged at the surface again, and started to rush through the streets toward the safety of the waiting forest. However, our speed of flight roused the suspicions of the slaves and Sagoths in the city streets, even before they heard the sounds of alarm from behind us.

"We must make for the *lidi* pens," Siom called out, between gasps for breath. "It is our only chance!"

Trust ourselves to those mighty but slow-lumbering beasts? It didn't make sense to me, but what other choice did we have but to follow our new friend's lead? Accordingly, we sped along in his wake. Our path was not unhindered, but we did have surprise and desperation on our side. Halar's spear and Ned Land's harpoon soon tasted blood, and I used my rifle as a club, wishing to spare the bullets as much as possible. Even the women were no strangers to combat—they were, after all, savages, and unused to sitting idly by while their men fought. They snatched up weapons from the fallen Sagoths and laid about themselves, giving far more blows than they received.

But, in the end, there were only nine of us against a city full of foes, and there could only be one conclusion to this chase unless we could produce some miracle. Something did change then, but not in our favor.

The Mahars had been alerted to our rescue attempt by this point, and several of them leaped from their buildings and into the air in pursuit of us. As in ancient Rome, there were more slaves in the city than Masters, and the one thing that the Masters could not tolerate was a successful slave uprising. Our little escapade had to be cut short before it might inspire others to emulate us and fight for their own freedom. It was vital, then, that the Mahars crush us, and be seen to crush us.

Four of them were in the air when we spotted them, and they were swooping down toward us. It was clear that the time to conserve our ammunition had passed. "Stand and fire, my friends!" Ned Land called out, and Hans and I paused to obey. The sailor and the duck hunter were both superb shots, and even I managed to be more than passable. Our three shots plucked three of the Mahars instantly from the air. Hans fired a second time, this time with his revolver, and we gave a cheer as all four of the Mahars plunged to the ground. Two were dead instantly, both shot through their eyes. The other two died crashing into the walls of buildings as they fell.

Our actions produced a momentary lull in the chase. The Sagoths had no idea what we had done—all they knew was that we had made noises, and four of the Masters had mysteriously died. This event gave them pause, and I have no doubt they accredited us with supernatural powers. But, magic or not, they had been ordered to stop us, and they feared the wrath of the Mahars more than they feared our ability to throw invisible death. With a great roar, they charged after us again.

We fled onward, reloading as we ran.

The slaves took no part in the chase—they simply melted to one side out of our path. I do not think this was so much because they supported our actions as that they had been trained to fear, and would only act upon receiving orders. They were no longer true men or women, but beaten animals. We had truly been lucky to have stumbled across Siom, who had not had his will completely beaten from him yet. And it was he who saved us.

He had not paused while we had shot the Mahars but rushed ahead of us, reaching the pens of the *lidi*. Here he wrenched blazing torches from the stable walls and threw them to us.

"Fire the feed stalls!" he called out. "The *lidi* are terrified of fire and will panic." He laughed. "I have long been planning to escape this way myself, but lacked the courage to act alone." He immediately torched the foodstuffs closest to him. The rest of us, even the women, rushed about the pens, setting fires as swiftly as we could.

The Sagoths caught up with us then, and we were forced to use more of our few remaining bullets on them. By the time that the fires were blazing full strength, we were completely devoid of ammunition, but more than a dozen Sagoths lay dead. Now we were forced to rely on our stone spears and Ned Land's mighty iron-tipped harpoon.

But we had bought the fire the time it needed to take a firm root. Gushes of flame leapt all about us as we retreated toward the safety of the forest. And now the *lidi*—as Siom had predicted—began to scream and panic. They crashed from their stalls, and hurtled themselves in all directions, seeking to escape the flames. As a result, more Sagoths died beneath this huge feet, and several buildings collapsed, fanning and spreading the flames.

More Mahars had now arrived, along with the Sagoth speaker, but they were no longer interested in capturing and punishing runaway slaves—their entire city was being threatened by fire and the stampeding beasts. They were forced to order the Sagoths to fight the flames and to turn to recapturing or killing the crazed *lidi*. As a result, we were able to slip away unmolested at last, and into the jungle. As we hurried off, we could see the smoke from the blazing buildings behind us, and hear the cries and screams of the dying, as well as the bellowing of the *lidi*.

Siom was laughing and dancing with joy. "We have taught the Mahars a great lesson this day!" he crowed. "We men will not be enslaved forever!" I could not blame him for his enthusiasm, and, indeed, joined in his rejoicing.

"Save your breath," Ned Land advised. "As soon as they have extinguished the blaze and dealt with the *lidi*, they will be after us. We'd better be far, far away by that point!"

He was correct, of course, and so we hurried onward.

Finally, though, Hans indicated that we should rest, and we were all more than happy to concur with this. We were thoroughly exhausted from our adventures, and sank to the ground happy. After a short rest, though, Alaya sprang to her feet and threw her arms again around Ned Land's neck.

"You came for me, Nedland!" she cried, one eye cast in Halar's direction to see how the hunter was taking this. "I knew you would!"

"We *all* risked our lives for you and the other women," the sailor growled. "And it would not have been necessary if you had only been sensible and listened to the wise laws of your own people. Your selfish actions endangered not only the lives of your friends but those of your rescuers also."

Alaya didn't like the sound of that. "What are you saying?" she cried. "I am the daughter of a chief! I will do what I wish to do!"

"And that's the problem," Ned Land growled. Abruptly, he grabbed her and spun her round, pulling her face-down onto his lap. He then proceeded to give her a thorough spanking.

I did not know what to do. It disturbed me to see a young woman treated like a child, but if anyone had asked for trouble more than Alaya, I could not think who it might be. Halar was more troubled, for I could see that he loved the girl. Yet he did not wish to go against the will of the sailor in this matter, so he simply stood there, conflicted, waiting. The other women looked on, giggling and laughing to see Alaya spanked. They would probably have volunteered to help out if they were asked, as it was their lives she had so carelessly endangered. Hans, stoic as always, simply kept watch behind us for any signs of pursuit.

As for Alaya, she struggled and twisted and screamed, but it was impossible for her to break free of Ned Land's grip, and she was forced to endure the whaling that he applied. I do not know how much actual pain he inflicted—though I did not see her sit down or lie on her back for the rest of the journey home—but she certainly suffered indignities that she had never in her life known before. I suspect a good deal of her screaming was due to outrage, but eventually the sailor stopped and released her. Rubbing her tender portions, Alaya glared hatred at him.

"Nobody has ever treated me like that before!" she screamed.

"And that, I think, is the problem," Ned Land said, composed. "If your parents had applied a little correction like that to you when you were younger, perhaps you would not have grown up so spoiled."

"I hate you!" she yelled at him. "I hate you, and I shall be avenged!" Then she spun and glared at Halar. "And you! I hate you also, and will punish you for this!"

"But what did I do?" the hunter asked, helplessly.

"Nothing! That's what you did—nothing! When you could have stopped him at any time."

"To be honest," Halar said slowly, "I thought he had every right to do as he did. You endangered us all by your actions and needed punishing for your selfishness."

"You!" she spat at him. "On you I will have the greatest revenge of them all!" Then she spun on her heels and walked away. It would have been more effective if she wasn't limping for the pain of the spanking.

"Well," Ned Land said, brushing off his hands, "I think that's enough rest—on we go, my boys!"

And so we continued on our escape. There were no signs of pursuit, though Halar said that, sooner or later, it would come. I asked him if the Sagoths were likely to attack his village in retaliation.

"No," he replied. "The Sagoths are vicious, but they are cowardly at heart. They would not attack an armed village. But they will lurk close by for a while, hoping to take anyone foolish enough to venture out alone." He shrugged. "We shall simply have to take greater care for a while. Eventually the Sagoths will tire of waiting, or the Mahars will have something else for them to do."

That was something of a relief, for I had been worried that the Mahars would be so angered they would order an attack on the Sarak. Thankfully, it seemed that their reptilian minds didn't turn in the direction of vengeance.

Alaya, on the other hand, could think of little else. I suspect she was hurt more in her pride than in her flesh—though I did notice she didn't sit down or lie on her back the whole trip home—but whichever hurt the most, her tongue barely stopped. She threatened Ned Land with all kinds of terrible vengeance when she returned to her father. And when she tired of abusing the sailor, she started in on poor Halar instead, vowing all sorts of repayment for his inaction.

After a while I simply stopped listening to her litany of dire punishments. Ned Land paid her no mind, of course, but Halar looked very sad and downcast whenever she yelled at him.

Aside from the verbal abuse, the journey back was quite uneventful. I had along my compass, but it turned out not to be needed; the inhabitants of Pellucidar possess some strange ability to know exactly where they are in their world at any moment, and where their home lies. Halar set the pace and direction and we simply followed along. The trip was interesting enough, and I caught sight of many animals and plants I should dearly have loved to examine, but it was clearly better to press on, back to the safety of numbers at the Sarak village. I took notes, but could do little more.

Siom proved to be a good addition to our party. He was a skilled hunter, and joined with Halar and Hans in providing for our needs on the journey. His mood had much improved since he had escaped his captivity and he became an amiable companion. One of the rescued women seemed to find him quite appealing, so I took it upon myself to ask him his plans.

"My people, the Dathar, live a long journey from here," he said, exchanging a smile with the girl. "They have long since celebrated my death—I see no need for me to return from the dead. Halar has said that I would be welcome with his people…"

"And there is a certain appeal in that," I finished for him, with a laugh. "I understand the draw of a good woman." I sighed, thinking once again of my sweet Gretchen. "Siom, do your people know of any route that leads away from Pellucidar?"

He looked at me, puzzled. "Where is there but Pellucidar?" he asked. "He gestured, taking in the scope of the world we could see. "It is clearly all that exists."

So we were out of luck once again—nobody, it seemed, even dreamed of another world beyond Pellucidar. If there was an alternate route for us to escape from this inner Earth, it seemed that none of the locals would be of use in discovering it.

Finally, we reached the river bend close by the Sarak village from where Alaya and the others had been taken. Our pace quickened with the end of our journey now so close. I confess, I was eager to see my uncle again—yes, and the members of that savage tribe. I almost thought of their village as "home" myself. Alaya, of course, was ecstatic—she was within minutes of being able to get her father to punish her two would-be victims. Ned Land seemed unaffected by her repeated threats, but poor Halar—lost in his wretched love for her—looked downcast and beaten.

We hurried into the village and then slowed and finally halted. There was nobody in sight.

True, there was no way when anyone could possibly know when we were to return. There were probably men out hunting and women out gathering. But there was never a time when the entire village was left completely empty like this. Worried, we looked about, and called out for my uncle, for Tomak and for others, but there was no reply.

Ned Land was lost for an explanation. "The pots are ready for a meal," he said, pointing to one of the well-stoked fire pits. "Everything looks normal—and yet there are no people. What can have happened?"

I had to confess that it was a complete mystery to me. It looked as though everyone had been here just a short while ago, but there was no one here now. It was puzzling and very disturbing.

And then I saw movement, out of the corner of my eye. As I started to turn, a voice called out: "Gentlemen! It pleases my heart to see you again."

It was von Horst. He and one of his men held their rifles leveled, aimed directly at us.

### XVI: The Second Serpent

"Von Horst," Ned Land breathed. "So, this is your doing?"

The officer inclined his head slightly, and gestured with his rifle. "You will carefully lay down all of your weapons," he instructed. "And instruct your savage companions to do the same." He was speaking German, of course, which none of the locals understood. I learned later that he had not bothered to even attempt to learn the Pellucidarian tongue. It was typical of his arrogance.

As we had no other choice, we obeyed his instructions. Our friends had seen the effects rifles could produce, of course, and understood the threat von Horst posed.

"Where is my uncle?" I asked him. "And the rest of the tribe?"

"They are in the jungle with the rest of my men," von Horst replied. "They will return when I instruct it. I didn't wish for you to cause trouble, and had them removed when my scout reported you were returning."

"So, what do you plan now?" Ned Land asked him.

"To complete my mission," the soldier said. "This is a fascinating land, and one that Herr Bismarck will no doubt wish to occupy. There are many resources here that Germany can use, and very little to stand in the way of our occupying it."

I could just imagine what Pellucidar would be like with a modern army marching through it. It was a savage land, but one also of great beauty. It did not belong to Germany or any other nation that might seek to expand its frontiers; it deserved to stay as it was, wild and free. I said as much to von Horst and he laughed.

"My dear Axel, you are so naïve! We may not have discovered our soldiers as yet, but I have seen some of the great beasts that live here. Imagine some of these dinosaurs turned loose on a battlefield! They would strike terror into the hearts of our foes. The armies of Germany would be invincible! And there is little here to prevent us from taking whatever we wish—merely a few half-naked savages armed with primitive stone weapons."

Sadly, what he said was perfectly true. We had brought a serpent with us into the strange paradise that was Pellucidar.

He pulled a whistle from his pocket and sounded a sharp blast upon it. A short while later, the people of the tribe began to filter back into the village from the trees. Amongst them was my uncle, looking older and more tired than I recalled. I hurried to his side to help him, and his face lit up at the sight of me.

"Axel, my dear boy—you are safe, and returned to me!"

"Yes, uncle," I agreed. "Safe—which is more than I can say of you, I'm afraid."

The Professor glared at their escort, two German soldiers with their modern weapons. "Yes, my boy. These ruffians descended upon us a short while ago, and have taken control of the village. They have killed three of the locals, including—I am sorry to say—Tomak. I was forced to tell them what had befallen you and your companions, and they have been waiting for your return ever since."

"And not to celebrate it, I'll be bound."

"Indeed not," he agreed. "That evil man has vile plans to exploit this land and its inhabitants. We are all that stand in his way—for the moment."

The villagers came together in the center of the village and slumped to the ground. They were frightened and their resistance had been shattered by the power of the Germans' guns. Von Horst indicated that Halar and the other natives should join them, and all but Alaya did so. She refused to leave our side and von Horst simply shrugged. "Let her stay—what can it matter?"

To my astonishment, Alaya answered him in perfectly acceptable German. "These men have insulted and injured me—I wish to see what happens to them."

"You can speak German?" I asked her, amazed.

She gazed at me in contempt. "You think only you are clever enough to listen and understand another tongue?" she asked me coldly. "I have been studying you as you studied us." And she had never let slip any of this before! My respect for her intelligence and my fears for her cunning rose both at the same time.

"Well," Ned Land said to our captor calmly, "are we to hear what you plan?"

Von Horst shrugged. "It is really very simple," he replied. "It is what I have been intending all along. Now that we are at the center of the Earth, we have no further use for you. Indeed, it has become clear that you do not stand with the glorious progress of Germany, and would interfere in any way you could with my aims. Therefore I intend to have you shot at dawn."

The sailor laughed heartily at this threat. "Well, you'll have a long wait, then," he gasped. "From what I understand from Professor Lidenbrock, there will never be another dawn here, for there won't ever be an end to this day."

"You are mistaken," the officer snapped. "Dawn will occur whenever I order it. The sun may not set or rise here, but the hours will follow good German order. I deem it now afternoon and once I have slept, it will be dawn, and you will be executed. Unless you would prefer to die now?" he offered.

"I'll take dawn," Ned Land decided.

"Good."

Alaya scowled. "You will kill him?" she asked.

"Indeed I shall," von Horst agreed. "Does this bother you?"

"Yes," she answered. "It will be a quick death, and I would prefer him to die slowly. He has insulted and offended me." She looked at the officer. "Give that one to me—and him," she added, pointing to Halar. "I will kill them for you, but it will not be quick."

Von Horst laughed. "Woman, I admire you. I am tempted to do as you request. It might be amusing to watch. But I have ordered these men shot, and shot they will be. My orders are to be followed implicitly. I am sorry if this upsets your pretty self, but you will simply have to live with it."

Alaya looked disappointed at this news. Then she pointed to Halar. "You ordered nothing to be done to him—let me have him, at least, and a knife."

That made the officer laugh again. "You are quite the bloodthirsty one, aren't you?" He stroked her face. "I'll tell you what—you come with me, and if you please me, I will grant you what you wish."

Alaya smiled happily. "And can I watch you have Nedland shot?" she asked, eagerly. "It will be too swift, but I should very much like to see him die."

"Persuade me," he said, suggestively. He turned to his men and then gestured to our small party. "Tie them up and keep them apart from the natives. Watch them closely. If any of them get away, you will be punished in their place." He put an arm around the willing Alaya and led her off.

The remaining Germans did as they were instructed, binding myself, my uncle, Ned Land and Hans. The sailor merely said to the man binding him: "Weren't there more of you when we left?"

"This cursed land has taken them," the man replied. "And soon it will take you, too." He and his companion moved off, and they took turns in watching us.

"Well, we're in a pretty kettle of fish now," my uncle said. "There may only be three of them left, but they are more than enough to help von Horst carry out his vicious plan. They have all of the guns and all of the ammunition. These poor locals have no chance against them."

"Perhaps one of us can get free?" I suggested.

"I'm afraid I've been tied rather expertly," Ned Land said. "But even if one of us could somehow break his bonds—then what? We can't wait for nightfall and escape under cover of darkness, for that may not happen for another million years." He inclined his head toward the soldiers. "If we try anything, one of those two will cheerfully shoot us."

"Then there is no hope for us?" I asked him, dismally.

"There is always hope," the sailor answered. "But, to be honest, I cannot at the moment see what it might be."

"And we have a greater problem," my uncle added.

"Greater than being killed?" Ned Land asked.

"You must learn to look beyond yourself," my uncle chided him. "Men of science understand that human lives are ephemeral, but the search for truth is eternal."

"If you'll excuse me, Professor," the sailor answered, "I'm not a man of science, I'm a man of harpoons, and at the moment I'd rather search for escape than truth."

"Pish-tosh," my uncle said, dismissively. "Did you not hear what von Horst said? He intends to return here with an army of occupation, and to enslave the population and exploit its animal life. That we cannot allow."

"That we cannot stop," the sailor argued. "We're to be his first victims, remember?"

"Then we must apply our intellects to the subject of escape," my uncle announced. "And, once that has been achieved, we must then decide how to stop his foolish plans. Mixing two environments that Nature has separated for millennia can only lead to disaster for both."

I must confess, I fell into a gloom. My bonds were too well tied for me to slip them, and it seemed to me that the soldiers had the upper hand. The thought that I should never see my sweet Gretchen or our child again occupied my thoughts far more than my impending death. I resolved that if we managed to get out of our dire straits somehow, I would press my uncle for an immediate return to our own world on the outside of our globe.

I do not know how long I was held a worse captive of my thoughts than I was of my bonds, but after a while, I felt Hans kicking me on my leg. At first I simply ignored him, wallowing in my loss, but he persisted, and I looked up to rebuke him. As I did so, I saw him nod in the direction of the guards and make a shushing noise.

Immediately, I saw what had caught his sharp eyes: beyond the two soldiers there was furtive movement. It took me a few seconds to realize that what I was seeing were three of the women of the village creeping up behind our guards. Then, with a sudden rush, they jumped the startled soldiers, who had been watching us and not the village. Each of the women carried clubs and they employed these in swift and deadly action. As soon as the guards were dispatched, the three women hurried across to free us with their stone knifes.

To my intense surprise, two of them were women we had freed from the Mahars. Their leader was none other than Alaya.

Even Ned Land was startled by this turn of events, especially when he was the first person Alaya cut free of his bonds. "What's this?" he exclaimed. "I thought you had defected to von Horst's side because you were so mad at us."

"I'm *still* mad at you, Nedland," she snapped. "But I am first and foremost of the Sarak tribe. I could not allow these wicked men to harm any of us—not even you or Halar. And they slew my father."

One of the other women had cut me free. "But I don't understand," I said. "You went off with the soldier."

Pah!" She spat on the ground. "He was a fool. He wished to lie with me, and thought I was a savage and a fool and would readily agree." She gave a rather wicked grin and held up her stone knife. I could see that there was blood on it. "I killed him. It was what he deserved."

"I'd be inclined to rather agree with you, my dear," my uncle said, shaking off his own severed bonds. "And those two guards?"

"Dead also," she said with pride. "They will never threaten us again."

"Which leaves just one man," Ned Land said, grimly. "I trust, Alaya, you'll leave this one for me?"

"You are a man," she replied. "I assume you wish to appear to be useful. You may have him. He is down by the river, watching over the rest of my people." She looked every inch the savage princess. "Now my father is dead, they *are* my people."

"Indeed they are, my dear," the Professor agreed. "And you have undoubtedly saved all of their lives by your courageous actions."

Ned Land slipped off, to finish off the last of the soldiers. Hans and I went to the two fallen men and confirmed that they were indeed dead. He and I stripped them of their weapons, but left them where they had fallen. We now had rifles and ammunition again, which made me feel a lot better. I returned to my uncle, offering him a revolver, which he took.

"Let us go and see to von Horst," he said.

"Come," Alaya said. She was getting quite used to giving orders. She led us to the modest dwelling where the soldier had taken her, and then stopped in shock. "He is gone!" she exclaimed.

It was true—von Horst was nowhere to be seen.

### XVI: A Return From the Center of the Earth

I could see a pool of blood where the soldier must have been stabbed by Alaya, but evidently the blow had not been a fatal one. As soon as she had left to free us, von Horst must have seized his opportunity to escape.

There was no time to waste—as long as he was at liberty, we were still in grave danger. I pointed to the blood and said to Hans: "We must follow and stop him." Our guide nodded his comprehension. To my uncle I said: "Tell Ned Land when he returns what has happened and what we are doing." Then Hans and I set off at a trot on the trail of von Horst.

As I have said, I am not a great tracker, but even I could see the trail of blood left behind by the wounded man. He had headed for the river, probably to try and join his last surviving soldier and in the hopes that the two of them could somehow together turn the tables again. But his wound appeared to be severe, and he obviously wasn't traveling very swiftly.

The river came into sight, and we saw that the blood trail abruptly led off parallel to it. The reason for this was quite obvious—he had reached the river after Ned Land, and had seen the sailor freeing the tribe. Alone and wounded, he couldn't take on Ned Land, so he had fled.

We followed on, and after a short while we heard a cry from behind us. Ned Land and Halar joined us, the sailor armed with the dead German guard's rifle and revolver. We were now quite the war party, but the trail of blood was getting more difficult to see. The wound must be closing up, obviously. But we now had Hans, Ned Land and Halar, and von Horst's path was as clear as day to them.

We heard the sounds of crashing far ahead of us and paused a moment. Was some savage Pellucidarian beast hunting? Well, no matter—we had rifles and bullets again, and nothing this land could breed would stand up against those! We went on. In a matter of moments we reached the edge of the trees and promptly halted.

Something was indeed hunting—Sagoths! They had fallen upon von Horst, and in his weakened state he could not resist them. They were dragging him to where their *lidi* was waiting, clearly with the intent of taking him back with them to the Mahar city.

I raised my rifle, ready to shoot. To my surprise, Ned Land gripped the barrel and pushed it aside.

"What are you doing?" I asked him. "We must rescue him!"

"Why?" the sailor asked, simply. "This will solve all of our problems. If we attempt to rescue him then one or more of us might be injured or killed—and he is not worth that price. Besides, what would happen if we *did* rescue him? We should have to take him back to the village where Alaya would undoubtedly have him killed for murdering her father. Should we risk our lives for that?"

"But… to leave him with the Mahar!" I protested.

"As I said, a perfect solution. To them we are all *gilaks*, animals. I doubt they can tell that von Horst isn't one of us, so his capture and execution would probably satisfy them that they have paid us back for firing their city. They will be less inclined to harass the Sarak after this."

"They will send him to the pits." But my protests were growing weaker.

"I can think of no one who deserves such a fate more." Ned Land clapped a hand on my shoulder. "Your sentiments show you have a good heart, Axel, so allow me to offer you a ray of hope in this situation. The blood trail we have followed shows that von Horst was badly injured. It is quite likely that he will not survive the journey back to the Mahar city, and that the Masters will be left to dispense their idea of justice on a corpse. If it will make you feel better, believe this."

"He is right," Halar said. "Alaya can be quite… vengeful, as you know. The German would not be allowed to live in any event."

It had all become rather moot anyway, for the Sagoths and their captive had reached *the* lidi and were setting off on their return trip. It would now mean another lengthy pursuit if we were to attempt a rescue, and I could see that none of us had the heart for that—including me. "Very well," I agreed. "Let us return."

As can be imagined, there was much rejoicing when we returned. Alaya heard our story and let slip a curse.

"I wished to slay him myself," she growled. "I do not know how I failed the first time, but I should not have failed a second. Ah, well," she added, looking happier, "maybe he *will* survive the trip and the Mahars will kill him."

"In the meantime, my boy," my uncle said, "*we* can now plan our trip home."

"Home…" I repeated, happily. Gretchen!

"Yes indeed," he said. "The soldiers are all dead, and we have their weapons, so we can retrace our steps with ease just as soon as everyone is ready to go." As he said this, he looked pointedly at Ned Land.

The harpooner looked back and then laughed. "You think I'd want to stay here?" He shook his head. "Professor, I cannot wait to look upon a good, clear sky and an honest ocean again."

My uncle blinked in surprise and looked at Alaya. "I had thought…" he said, weakly.

Ned Land laughed again. "We sailors like to have a girl in every port and a home in none. Besides, Alaya is now the head of this tribe, and she will need a good, steady hunter beside her to help her."

"I need nobody," the savage said, coldly. Then her face softened. "But it may be that my heart will change and I will forgive Halar. *If* he tries hard…" I could see that she was enjoying the thought of tormenting our poor friend. But I suspected that with her as a prize at the end of it, Halar might endure.

And so we laid our plans to return to the surface of the Earth. The tribe insisted on a great feast to say goodbye to us, and we packed a good deal of food for our return journey. We had discovered the place where the soldiers had hidden their own supplies before they raided the village, and so we had our equipment and more than enough ammunition to last us on our return trek through Pellucidar.

Alaya, in her usual thoughtful mood stared at our guns with some lust in her heart. But then she sighed and said: "Those rifles of yours might be of help to us, but it is perhaps best that you take them. Sooner or later their supplies would run out and we could not replace them. I would not want my hunters to get too reliant on something they could not keep."

My uncle smiled. "I think you will make quite a wise ruler, Alaya."

"*If* you can control your temper," I could not resist adding.

She laughed. "If I could not control it, Axel, you would be leaving our village unable to sit down for the remainder of your journey."

We said goodbye to our friends with mixed feelings—but, in my case, mostly a longing to return to my wife and child. We were able to retrace our path with ease. The journey was—well, as this was Pellucidar it was hardly uneventful. But we won through, back to the passage that led back onward and downward—though, eventually, upward—to Iceland again.

As we took our last look at Pellucidar, my uncle called us all together. "This is a savage and often frightful land," he said. "But it has its own beauty and its own nobility." He held up his rifle. "Yet a few hundred well-armed men might be able to conquer this place and kill or enslave the inhabitants. They could turn it into another European colony, a slave-state run for the benefit of the rich and powerful of our world. My boy, my friends—I do not think that we should allow this to happen."

Ned Land nodded. "You think we should keep quiet about what we have found?"

"I do indeed. And I am sure that no one would doubt the word of Professor Lidenbrock and his nephew if we say that all we found were rocks and tunnels, and that there is nothing here of any value."

"And how are we to explain that von Horst and his men are no longer with us?" I asked him. "They will certainly be missed."

"Those brave souls were lost in a cave-in," my uncle said, with a slight smile. "We shall say they died heroically, saving our lives. That should satisfy everyone."

"Even Herr Bismarck?" I asked. "Surely he knew of von Horst's plans?"

"Even Herr Bismarck," my uncle assured me. "We do not know that he was aware of those plans. If he was not, then it is no problem. If he did—well, he could hardly admit to it, could he? Being a pragmatic politician, I am sure he will make the best of a bad situation. And even if he *did* plan to exploit the inhabitants of the underworld—he could do nothing without our help. And I think this time we shall all decided that we have had quite sufficient of our subterranean explorations."

I laughed. "I know that I, for one, have!"

And so we returned. To our surprise, our ship was still waiting for us. The Captain heard our story and sighed, but accepted it. We were quite astonished to discover that we had been missing only some six months. It had seemed to be so much longer—but, as I say, time plays strange tricks in Pellucidar. We said our farewells to Hans—who went off to see whether he still had a fiancée or not—and then to Ned Land, who was intent on finding berth on the next whaler he could board. He left us with a firm promise to visit the house in Koenigstrasse.

And about that—what can I say? I need not tell you of the great pleasure it was to see my dear Gretchen and our growing daughter again. I told her the true story of our adventures, of course—I cannot lie to my wife!—and then I set myself to write this account and to seal it for my daughter to read when she is old enough to understand and appreciate it. I shall leave it to her, then, whether to publish it or to pass it on to some child of her own.

There are just two further points to add. First, about a month after our return, my uncle received a note from Iceland. He beamed as he read it, and then showed it to me. It was written in careful, cramped Danish, which I could not read, of course. My uncle explained: "It is from Hans; it seems that his Habby was indeed a most sensible girl and waited for him. They are now married."

This was excellent news indeed.

The second point concerns the Gun Club of Baltimore. It was the story that they were attempting to reach the center of the Earth that impelled this entire adventure, but we had at no time seen them. The reason for that became clear—they had not, in fact, even set foot in Iceland. They had indeed gone to the Arctic Circle[5], but for entirely other reasons. What had therefore started our entire adventure off, then, was nothing more than unfounded gossip!

---

[5] If you wish to know why, you can find the story in "The Purchase of the North Pole" by Jules Verne.

*Like Brian Gallagher with the Vampire Captain, Martin Gately with Rouletabille, and Travis Hiltz with Doctor Omega, Pete Rawlik has been using* Tales of the Shadowmen *to craft a series of stand-alone stories that feature the same, ongoing protagonist, in his case H.P. Lovecraft's Robert Peaslee. The latest of these chilly little gems is yet another exploration on the theme of what truly lies beyond Death, and the fate of those who would peer behind the everlasting curtain...*

## Pete Rawlik: *The Ylourgne Accord*

*France, 1919*

It was July of 1919 and I was no longer in Paris. I wish I could say that I had finally given up on the city, or that it had given up on me, or that the local authorities had demanded that I be reassigned. None of that happened. The truth was that, regardless of what I had seen, of the maddening things I had witnessed at Locus Solus [6] and the Paris Opera House, I had remained mostly unaffected. My nervous condition seemed to be controllable, mostly through liberal administration of spirits. If my work suffered, my superiors said nothing. I did my job, insured the security of the delegates, and made sure that nothing unseemly happened to any of them. I assumed that, on the day the treaty was signed, my services would no longer be needed, they would pat me on the back, and I would soon be headed back to the States like so many of my fellow agents.

But the Army had other plans.

There was a conference, a meeting of scientific minds, to discuss how some of the recent advancements in medicine were going to be dealt with in the future. Like any such conference, there were concerns, and while the French were in charge of overall security, each delegation, including those from the defeated Central Powers, were bringing their own protection. Our delegate, a man I had never met, had requested me personally. Despite how it was expressed, as a request, I really had no choice in the matter; I knew, as any good soldier did, that it was an order, no matter that it was framed in pleasantries.

The meeting was to be held in the south-central part of France, in the province of Averoigne, an area dominated by a dark virgin forest that few have penetrated. The territory is sparsely populated, with the only city being Vyones, the foundations of which had been first laid during the Dark Ages. Vyones would have been a scenic destination, but I was not to be so fortunate. The conference was to be held in the ruins of the ancient fortress Ylourgne, amidst crumbling

---

[6] See "Revenge of the Reanimator" in *Tales of the Shadowmen* No. 10.

walls and fallen masonry. The place had a weird reputation and the locals shunned it. There had been a catastrophe once, a "horror" about which I could only find the vaguest of references. The woods were said to have been haunted by werewolves and worse. There was a reference to a "Beast of Averoigne" which, right or wrong, I took to be another werewolf not unlike the tale of the Brotherhood of the Wolf which had plagued Gévaudan. The ancient, dark forest had done its best to reclaim the ruins of Ylourgne, but there were areas where nothing would grow, and only dead barren soil remained.

The French had found a use for such a place, and had already begun laying the foundations and earthwork for what would become the L'Ossuaire d'Ylourgne, a memorial cemetery for those who had fallen during the Great War, regardless of nationality. The work was being done primarily by a firm out of Paris, but with so many partners and sub-contractors, it seemed like a veritable army of architects, masons and carpenters had descended on that ancient site. It was an international call, a rallying cry for those who cared about such things, and it seemed a charitable and popular thing to which to donate. Even my client, the enigmatic Meldrum Strange, had contributed to the building fund.

Meldrum Strange was an affable man; to call him rich would have been an understatement; he dealt in information by profession, but was also an industrialist. He was Carnegie, Vanderbilt and Morgan all rolled into one, with triple the ego to boot, but without the haughty superiority complex. On the drive through the countryside, he actually talked with me; he had a deep melodious voice and seemed genuinely interested in what I had to say. As we conversed, we discovered that we knew people in common. Strange had even studied briefly at Miskatonic University, where he had earned his undergraduate degree, before moving on to study business abroad. He had a soft spot for Miskatonic U and was proud that his son Hugo was studying medicine there. As affable as he was, Strange seemed tinged with regret. There was work to be done, important work; he was engaged in some great undertaking that, he implied, would be a boon to all men, but the President had asked him to attend this conference personally, and when the President asked you to do something, Strange suggested, it wasn't really a request.

"There are duties, responsibilities a man must accept," Strange said, "regardless of his wants, no matter what they cost him professionally, or personally."

When he said that, I took it to heart, for it reminded me of my own sentiments, and I knew that this was a man worth knowing.

The conference village, including a great reception hall, had been built in the last few months by the assembled legions of workmen who were now busy rebuilding the fortress, transforming it into a great memorial chapel. One day, these outbuildings would serve as the offices and homes of the resident caretakers, but until then, they would serve our purposes. The great hall had incorporated stones from the ruin itself and, in the archway above the entrance, was carved a phrase which, I supposed, was meant to inspire unity amongst the fallen, the mourners and even perhaps the delegates. It was written in medieval French but was easily translated as:

*THEY THAT COME HERE AS MANY SHALL GO FORTH AS ONE*

It was beneath this inspiring motto that dozens of delegates, professional diplomats, men of science, and even men of business gathered. Dr. Astrov had come from Russia, General Mazovia from the Polish Republic, Dr. Lorde and General Duval represented France, the Austrians had sent von Schelling and Dr. Miklos Sangre, while the British a man named Richard Steadman. The Germans had suffered during the war, many of their best and brightest had been lost or fled; the man they sent to represent their interests was known to everyone else as a cruel and vicious man, a criminal who would have been arrested had he not been traveling under diplomatic papers, Dr. Cornelius Kramm, whom the more sensational of journalists called "The Sculptor of Human Flesh."

When Strange saw Kramm, he warned me to be wary of the man, but also to keep a close eye on him. "He's a dangerous man, ambitious, manipulative. He ran his own crime syndicate in New York and Paris, The Red Hand. It took an entire team of adventurers to bring him and his brother down. He had been presumed dead."

"In my experience," I declared, "dangerous men have a habit of not staying dead."

He looked at me incredulously, as if I had said the most important thing ever. "Do you know what this conference is about, Lt. Peaslee?"

I shook my head, "I don't have clearance for that."

He thumped me on the back as if we had been boyhood friends. "You have what clearance I say you have, and right now, I need you to understand why we are here, what has happened, and what we hope to do about it."

It took me hours to read the files that Strange gave me, and even then I didn't want to believe what they revealed, but I knew it to be true, I knew what could be done to the dead. It was possible to give the deceased a semblance of life, to give them motion and some sense of self. They could be given purpose, tasks, even played with. I know this because I had seen it done, not once but twice. Of the men described in the files, I was familiar with one name, that of Doctor Herbert West, who had been involved with the events at Locus Solus. The files had a picture of West, a mousy man with a shock of blond hair. They had pictures of his colleagues, as well including the nondescript Daniel Cain and the stoic Canadian Major Sir Doctor Eric Moreland Clapham-Lee who had died tragically and then been victimized further by West himself. I stared at that photo of Clapham-Lee, his piercing eyes and strong nose seemed so familiar. I had seen this man before, but where I could not recall.

The next day, the purpose of the conference was made plain to me when General von Schelling opened up with a plea to the other delegates for a sense of human decency. "This science of reanimation, this thing that was released on the battlefields of Europe, we must put a stop to it. I do not deny that we ourselves are guilty of exploring the procedure. Our agents have obtained Herr Franken-stein's notebooks; we have carried out our own experiments." His voice became proud and frightened at the same time. "I tell you, this path leads not only to abominations, but endangers the very balance of world power. If this technology were to fall into the hands of the Persians, Chinese, Japanese, or even one of our own rebellious colonies, it could be the end of European dominion of the globe, and could potentially cast us back into a new Dark Age."

This little speech set the delegates ablaze and the room exploded into a ca-cophony of accusations and excuses. The delegates quickly fell into old political alliances, and familiar lines were drawn. The chairman, General Duval, mo-tioned for security to take action and several guards moved from their stations their hands going for their guns.

I tapped Strange on the shoulder and suggested we withdraw. Instead, he stood up, slammed his fist onto the table and bellowed out at the others. "Are you fools? Have the last few years of war taught you nothing? Millions lie dead and you still bicker. Your precious alliances and treaties have led you to war and the brink of destruction. Your nations lay wasted and your landscapes ruined and still you cling to old ideologies and familiar patterns. If we are to survive, as men, as nations, as a species, you must find a new way of thinking, for all our sakes."

The crowd was stunned into silence, and the room grew still. Duval raised a finger and his agents paused. Something electric was passing through the crowd, something contagious. I could see it in their eyes, and in the way they stood. They were ready, ready for change, they just needed a leader, someone to show them the way, a way forward. Was that man Strange? Looking at him as he stood there, the bulk of him, his great grey beard and powerful eyes, he was like some Old Testament prophet. He was Moses ready to lead his chosen peo-ple to the Promised Land.

Then the lights went out.

It took an hour for someone to find the fault. By that time, the delegates had left the hall and wandered out into the gardens. Strange and I had taken ref-uge in the shade of an old oak. Together we watched as Kramm and Sangre talked furtively. They kept looking over their shoulders like they were afraid of being watched, which of course they were. We ourselves did not go unnoticed and were soon joined by General Duval and Richard Steadman.

"A rousing speech, Mr. Strange," commented Steadman. He wore a tall, black hat, rectangular glasses and an ascot to accent his suit. His hair was neat and blended into a thick dark beard. His voice was accented but not one I recog-nized, he was obviously a member of the Commonwealth but beyond that I knew nothing about his origins. "Tell me do you think it will make a difference? Do you really think you can change human nature?"

Meldrum Strange took a drag off his pipe. "Explain yourself, if you would?"

"Our history, our legends, our myths they all suggest that any time we develop a new technology, a new idea, a new invention, we tend to succumb to its most deleterious of effects or uses. Eve, Prometheus, Pandora. Innovations tend to have disastrous beginnings, and men never seem to learn, or change."

"I take your point, sir, which is why I intend to at least try. Would you have us do nothing, and let history run its course? Should we leave well enough alone?"

Steadman made an odd noise that seemed to express his displeasure, "Would that Frankenstein, West, Cain, Hartwell and Tsiang had left well enough alone."

Strange nodded, "You forget Clapham-Lee, Mr. Steadman; surely he was as much to blame as all the others?"

The British delegate turned and walked away. "I assure you Mr. Strange," he called back, "Clapham-Lee has not been forgotten, least of all by me. But I do not blame him for any of this. He is as much a victim as anyone else."

Duval gave a strange little salute and said "Be seeing you," before trotting off after Steadman.

That night, while Strange slept I reviewed the files once more and familiarized myself with more of the men that were documented within. I had of course known about Victor Frankenstein, who had meddled with the dead in the 1790s, but I was not familiar with the exploits of his descendent Henry, nor those of the mysterious Dr. Pretorius. Nor did I know about those other "children" of Frankenstein. As for the name Tsiang, it was in reference to an unfortunate event that had occurred on the Franco-Austrian front. Tsiang had been a priest of Siva who, in his attempts to please the French, had created undead soldiers, nearly invincible things that only stopped moving when the enemy forces reduced them to ash.

No matter how many files I read, I kept coming back to Doctor West and his colleagues. West had used the war as a source of subjects for his experiments in perfecting his own method of reanimating the dead. Like West, Cain and Clapham-Lee were graduates of Miskatonic University. There was another man, a doctor named Hartwell; he had done something to soldiers as well, but the details were vague. Looking at their photographs, these men didn't look mad, or even dangerous. Yet they were just that, not only to others, but to themselves. Major Doctor Sir Eric Moreland Clapham-Lee had by all accounts died when his plane was shot down, but West had claimed the body from the morgue, a body which had never been returned to Toronto for proper burial.

This information was classified. The British knew; West, Cain and Clapham-Lee had served in their forces, but the other allies didn't, and neither did the Central Powers. They knew that the dead had been brought back, but they didn't know by whom or how. Strange and I intended to keep it that way and if possible put the genie back in the bottle.

The other factor we had to contend with was the civilian angle. West and his followers had not confined their work to wartime. They had experimented at home, amongst unsuspecting townsfolk, and they had not been as discreet as they thought. Despite the risks, military intelligence had decided to keep the activities of these men a secret from local authorities, and even other Federal agencies. It was, as Meldrum Strange suggested, the only way to keep the knowledge from spreading across the world and disrupting the natural order of things.

The next day came early. One of the security men woke me before dawn; there was a man outside the gate that was asking to see me. I suggested that I meet him at one of the smaller rooms off the hall, but the officer shook his head. The stranger refused to come any further down the road. If I was to see him, I would have to go to the gate. As reluctant as I was to leave the comfort of my bed, I dressed and allowed the officer to drive me out to the edge of the property, where the dark forest swallowed the road.

The man waiting for me there had all the trappings of an Indian mystic, the sash and his turban; the great, bushy tawny beard that covered his face all suggested this, but his skin and his green eyes betrayed his Western origins, as did his voice; his French was tinged with an accent that suggested he was from Brittany.

"I am Sâr Dubnotal, the Great Psychagogue. I come bearing a warning."

I lit a cigarette and invited him to come with me to the village but he refused. "This place is a necropolis, a city of the dead; I am too sensitive to journey any closer."

"You are mistaken," I told him. "The construction has just begun; there are no dead yet interred here."

Dubnotal shook his head. "You are mistaken, sir; the dead have held sway here for centuries. The construction of the ossuary is merely a formality. You sleep in a grave for thousands."

I was frustrated with his mystic mumblings and vague inferences. "Your warning, sir, what is it?"

His tone betrayed that he was equally annoyed with me. "I know what you and the others do here; the voices of the dead have told me. The say you are a good man, that you might do the right thing, and let the dead rest. There are others who do not share your sentiment. They would seek the power for themselves."

"Kramm and Sangre?"

"I cannot say. The dead do not utter the names of the living; it is unseemly. I beg you: do what you must to prevent the spread of this madness. If you do not, our world, and the next, will suffer."

"Why didn't you find me in Paris, and tell me this there? It would have saved you the trip."

"Indeed," said Sâr Dubnotal, "but then it would not have been nearly as dramatic, and you would not have taken me seriously." With that, he bowed, turned, and began to walk away.

I called after him, "Where is your car and driver?"

As he marched, he looked back. "I need no car, Mr. Peaslee. I walked here from Paris. I shall walk back."

"That's more than two hundred miles!"

"One can always use more time to think, Mr. Peaslee. To reflect on what one has said, and what one has heard. You should try it some time."

I took a drag from my cigarette and watched as he disappeared beyond the first curve in the road.

Strange was waiting for me when I returned. "Anything I should know?"

"According to a very odd mystic, the dead think I am a good man. They are counting on me to do the right thing, and let them stay dead."

Strange harrumphed but whether it was at me for being a good man or the dead for having an opinion, I didn't know, "Anything else?"

I nodded, "I think Ylourgne has secrets that we haven't been told. I think there is a reason the French have decided to build the memorial here. I also suspect that Kramm and Sangre might not be our only concerns."

"Of whom do you have suspicions, and why?"

"When Steadman spoke of Clapham-Lee, he used the present tense. The man was supposed to have been killed, twice at that, but I suspect that he is still alive, or at least no longer dead. I think he might even be here in Ylourgne."

Meldrum stewed for a moment and then gave me instructions. "I'll be in committee all day; we're supposed to be drafting an accord making the use of the reanimated as soldiers a war crime. Most of the delegates should be there. Do what you can to learn more about our opponents, both those we know about and those we don't." With that, my massive employer left me assured that I would carry out his orders to the best of my ability. It seemed that the dead were not the only ones who had faith in me.

It has been my experience that if you want to go through someone's things, it is best to make sure that your target is otherwise occupied. In this case, I made sure that Kramm's security was busy going through my room, leaving me free to go through his apartments. I spent twenty minutes opening draws and skimming files. In the end, I learned that Kramm knew less than Strange and I. He had files on the Frankensteins—they were slightly more robust than ours—but his files on West and Cain were weak, and, as for the others, those files were little more than single pages. Kramm may have been the enemy, he may have had an agenda, but from what I could gather, he wasn't the player that the strange mystic had warned me about. The only thing of any interest that Kramm possessed was a photostatic copy of an ancient book written in German. While my reading of that language is satisfactory, this volume had been printed using a black letter type I was unfamiliar with, and thus I could not immediately ascertain its contents. I took the book, believing that neither Kramm nor his security would report it missing out of embarrassment.

Once I was secure in the quarters I was sharing with Strange, and had assessed the covert search that Kramm's man had done, I settled in to study the book I had taken from Kramm. It was entitled *Von Unaussprechlichen Kulten* and attributed to Friedrich Wilhelm Von Junzt. After only a few pages, I discerned that its contents consisted of accounts of the rites, practices and beliefs of secretive cults and unsavory orders scattered throughout the world. Von Junzt had apparently traveled the globe collecting what knowledge he could on these pagan religions, and, in some cases, even participating in certain ceremonies amongst those believers which still remained extant. It was a compendium of horrors detailing the most fiendish sorceries and necromancies. So terrible were the things written and hinted at that I dare not mention them here, save for the one section of that grimoir which was most pertinent to my own tale, for there was in that hideous book an entire section on Ylourgne.

Indeed, there were two entries for the ruined castle, which apparently had been built by a line of marauding barons who had been exterminated by the Comte des Bois d'Averoigne. The first chapter related the tale of Gaspard du Nord a would-be wizard who did battle with a monstrous creation of his former master, the Necromancer Nathaire. In the spring of 1281, Nathaire and his ten disciples fearing a church-led purge against sorcery, had fled Vyones for the ruins of Ylourgne. Not long after, there came to cemetery of Vyones and all the other boneyards of Averoigne a plague in which the newly-buried dead, chiefly those stalwart men who had died in misadventure, would simply not stay buried. Not even the pious Cistercian monks were immune to the fiendish call. The source of this necromancy was, of course, Nathaire and his followers, who used the reanimated bodies to construct a titanic golem of flesh and bone with Nathaire's face and his voice, that strode across the countryside attacking peasants and nobles alike. Only through Gaspard's limited knowledge of necromancy was the creature stopped and laid to rest in a shallow grave by the River Isoile, not far from Vyones.

The second section dealt with a legend that grew up in the area almost two centuries later. In 1476, shepherds reported that an area along the Isoile had been disturbed and great holes had been rent in the earth. Investigators sent out by the Comte confirmed that the riverbank had been disturbed, and that something large, perhaps many things, had been removed. A trail of damp clay led from the riverbank through the woods to the road. The road itself was disturbed, for whatever had traveled down its path had not been carried by horses or cart.

Whatever had been moved down the road had been dragged to the ruins of Ylourgne where even the Comte's men dared not follow.

There then grew up around the ruins tales of lights and noises emanating from the crumbling stones, and, in the months that followed, rumors of witchcraft, more specifically of a coven that drew their power from the evil that had been done at Ylourgne. Some say it was Nathaire and his disciples who had returned as a cohort of *liches* who haunted Ylourgne. Others suggested that this was the work of *L'Universelle Aragne*, the deposed King Louis XI, who was still resorting to necromancy in his war against the Duke of Burgundy. Whatever the truth, by the time Von Junzt visited the area, he found little evidence of occult activity. There were lights and sounds, but the sources could not be discerned, and Von Junzt left after a week, disappointed and as perplexed as he had been when he arrived. Though he was insistent that someone had inscribed in the ruins a quote in medieval French from Nathaire, perhaps as an epitaph:

*THEY THAT COME HERE AS MANY SHALL GO FORTH AS ONE*

It was the same saying that decorated the great hall, but in this context, it was no longer a message of peace, but rather of the dark and twisted necromancy that had allowed Nathaire to transform hundreds of the dead into a single titanic, golem of flesh: the "Colossus of Ylourgne." The thought that the memorial cemetery was being built in such a place, and that the conference, a conference focused on the science of reanimation, seemed too much of a coincidence. I made for the door, fully intent on taking my suspicions to Strange, but I barely made it through. Someone was waiting for me on the other side, someone who had something large and heavy. I was knocked unconscious by a man I never even saw.

When I finally regained my senses, I was handcuffed to a chair. The room was dark, except for a single bare bulb swaying back and forth from a dangling cord. It was such a cliché that, even in my semi-conscious state, I was forced to chuckle. As I did, there was movement in the dark, several forms shuffled about beyond the range of my sight.

"Is that you, Kramm?" I managed to mumble, "or is it Sangre? Perhaps both of you? Not that it matters. Show yourselves, or do you prefer to skulk in the dark like rats?"

A match was struck and a flame sputtered to life illuminating a man whose face I knew, a face with a beard accented by a fancy cravat: the British envoy Steadman! He took a drag from his cigarette and smoke filled the air. It seemed to billow up around his head like a fog.

"We are sorry, Lt. Peaslee. We hadn't meant to be so heavy-handed, but you had obviously put some things together and put our time table in jeopardy. We needed to remove you from the playing field before you got yourself hurt, or before you could spook the enemy and put them on guard before we could flush them out into the open."

"Them being Kramm and Sangre?"

A second figure stepped out from the darkness; it was, as I suspected, Doctor Kramm.

"The Austrians aren't capable of such deviousness; with the loss of the war, they have been placed in a most difficult position. They no longer have any desire to possess the reanimation technology, nor do they wish to see any other nation possess it. It is a terrible power, Lt. Peaslee, one that the Austrians fear could reshape the globe, and wrest it from European control. It is a childish fear, but one that cannot be ignored. But where are my manners? I must echo my ally's apology for your poor treatment."

I stared at these two men and, despite the questions running through my head, I voiced only one: "Can someone please take these handcuffs off me?"

As Kramm undid my chains, Steadman opened the curtain and let in the fiery light that roared outside. The conference village was on fire, and a long line of cars was slowly making its way out of the gates, carrying the delegates to safety.

"Am I to understand that you blew up the conference?"

It was Steadman that supplied the answer to my question, and many others that I was thinking.

"We warned everybody anonymously first. I realize that it may be somewhat anticlimactic, even rushed, but I saw no reason to drag things out. Whatever the greater plan was for this place, whomever was behind it, this brings it to an end. It has accomplished at least one task."

"Which was?"

Kramm smiled. "The players have been revealed. They have made themselves known. This in itself has changed the game. The field has been leveled."

The heat was getting to me. "What of the memorial, the conference, the accords?"

Kramm's smile turned into a chuckle. "The French can build their memorial cemetery someplace else. This place will be left as a ruin. As for the conference, and the so-called Ylourgne Accord, the lesser nations have already signed it. Though for various technical reasons, France, Great Britain and the United States have refused to endorse it."

"Strange won't stand for this."

"Meldrum Strange has been bought and paid for with what he holds most dear, information." Steadman spewed as if the idea was bitter in his mouth. "He is not the idealist you thought, Peaslee; he is a realist. The conference is finished, despite the fact that the Ylourgne Accord has been signed, it is for all intents, pardon the word, dead—or, at best, useless."

My head was swimming.

"Reanimation *is* the future, Peaslee," exclaimed Steadman. He took off his coat. "There will be no restrictions, and the nations of Earth will be free to pursue whatever studies in reanimation they desire." He took off his cravat and then proceeded to remove the rest of his disguise. "General Duval, Strange, Sangre and the others like them can do what they want. And they will. And one day, the Undead shall outnumber the living and they shall rule the world."

Then Steadman took off the last of his disguise.

I ran, fleeing the awful thing that Steadman had revealed. I fled toward the cars fleeing the conference. Meldrum Strange found me and took me back to Paris. I was discharged a week later. My discharge was honorable, but my nerves were destroyed; it took years of therapy before I could sleep easily. Though I will admit that, even now, I carry certain scars from those events.

After all these years, what Richard Steadman did still haunts me; it was a little thing really, almost nothing compared to the other things I had seen, but perhaps it was all that needed to happen to push me over the edge. Perhaps it was the fact that Strange had struck a black, unholy bargain with the man, or that Kramm stood there laughing. Regardless, when I close my eyes, I still can see that face, Steadman's face, as he took off the false beard and revealed his true face, a face that I had seen amongst Strange's files—the face of Major Sir Eric Moreland Clapham-Lee, the decapitated man that Herbert West had resurrected in Flanders.

He was there, standing before me, his disembodied head in his hands, and he was laughing; he and Doctor Kramm were laughing.

And I knew that I had witnessed a new and terrible terror, and I was too weak to do anything to stop it.

*Mephista is a female embodiment of evil created for a series of horror films starring the beautiful actress, Edwige Hossegor. But she acquires an unholy life, independently of Edwige, and embarks on an evil spree. She is usually defeated by the private detective Teddy Verano. Mephista and Verano are characters created by the prolific French writer Maurice Limat (1914-2002), also the author of a popular space opera series starring Chevalier Coqdor. Three Mephista novels are scheduled to be translated and released by Black Coat Press in a single volume in 2015...*

## Frank Schildiner: *Saint and Sinners*

*Paris, Marchecoul, 1970*

The freaks were dancing about in several circles, their actions frenzied as they drank the blood of sacrificed goats and acted as if they were reenacting the rites of ancient Bacchus.

I thought it was a sorry sight, young and old behaving like fools. An elderly couple stood above the crowd, watching and waiting as their followers misbehaved. They were the leaders of the cult, but in my opinion, they looked more like a wealthy suburban couple than the high priest and priestess of a Satanic cult. The man was large, fleshy, and resembled a retired academic, or a wealthy art gallery owner. His wife was tiny, shrunken with her gray hair pulled back in a loose bun. She was like one of the nosy neighbors everyone fears, always full of advice, opinions, and many, many invitations to card and coffee parties.

All of this silliness was being performed before the ruins of the castle of Marchecoul which had once belonged to the Devil-worshipper, Gilles de Rais. Gilles, a.k.a. "Blue-Beard," had fought besides Joan of Arc against the English; he was a powerful nobleman who had chosen to devote his life to murdering children and trying to raise the Devil. Why? I had no idea. I had a hard enough time figuring out the motives of modern criminals, let alone the ones who fought in the Hundred Years' War.

"Well, well, well, this has just gotten quite interesting," Mephista crooned, staring at the scene without the need for binoculars.

She was easy to look at, a raven-haired beauty with dark eyes and a figure that caused traffic accidents whenever she walked down the street. Despite that, I found her as attractive as the said traffic accident, for I knew what lay beneath her polished surface.

"How so?" I asked, not lowering my binoculars. They were an essential item for a private investigator, as useful as a camera and more important that the .32 snub nose revolver in my belt.

"Have you noticed the old man leading this farce? His name is Steven Marcato. He and his wife are Satanists who reside in Manhattan," Mephista stated, sounding very happy with her information.

"And this is relevant, how?" I asked, bored by the spectacle.

These cultists were trying too hard to be wicked, pretending to be evil for a lark more than any true belief. They were all in too deep to back out when the scene became boring and would kill to keep their secret.

"Did you know that Marcato is the nephew of Morcata—the reason we are here in this delightful locale?" Mephista explained, giggling slightly at the end.

I rolled my eyes, but saw her point. I was in this horrific location for that exact reason. The fact that my partner in this job was a succubus possessing the body of film actress Edwige Hossegor was beside the point.

It had all begun in my office back in Paris...

Mephista was sitting on my desk, her perfect legs crossed, as she swung her foot with obvious boredom. She'd arrived that morning without explanation and made a nuisance of herself as I tried to finish my report on a particularly ugly divorce. I had just handed off the pictures to a messenger and was counting the small envelope that would cover rent and food for this month, when the woman walked in and everything changed.

She was of medium height with mousy brown hair, watery blue eyes and sallow, yellow skin. Her shoulders were hunched and their position didn't seem inherited, but rather the slumped look of one beaten down by life. This woman was not what I expected from a client; usually, they're far more furtive when coming to see a PI like myself. Also, I just couldn't picture someone so beaten down by life to want any help; that type usually just shouldered their burden, so to speak.

She introduced herself merely as Miss Micheala. When she spoke, and I could do nothing else but listen. Her voice was light, musical and sounded so pleasant on the ears I found myself leaning forward to hear more of what she had to say.

"My nephew from America has been taken by Satanists, Monsieur Verano," she said. "I know you're going to doubt me, but they are real worshipers of the dark powers."

"Why would they kidnap your nephew?" Mephista asked, surprisingly leaning away from our new client.

Usually she tried to vamp them, but something was causing her to recoil. An odd one, Mephista... We were something partners, other times enemies. Her whims were dangerous and more than a few men and women had died because of her charms. Today, we would work together—next week, who knew?

"They wish to use him to bring back an ancient master of dark magic. His name was Morcata and he died many years ago in England." Miss Michaela explained, "while battling..."

"...The Duc de Richleau," I interrupted. "Yes, my father told me of that battle. He helped the Duc and his friends deal with the remainder of the cult."

Miss Michaela smiled, her brown-stained teeth still shining despite their lack of whiteness.

"Yes, I am glad you understand. To bring such a man back, they require a great rite as well as a body. My young nephew is naturally gifted in the mystic arts, poor little Simon. They seek to drive him out and return that monster back to the world in his body."

"That will require a location steeped in blood," Mephista stated, hopping off the desk and backing up to the water cooler near my right arm. "The closest is beneath the Paris Opera House..."

"No," I said, shaking my head. "The Phantom is back and controls that area again. Also, all the places where the guillotine was used during the Terror is his grounds again. He won't let any such horrors in, unless he controls them."

"I think I know the place," Michaela said, handing me a thick envelope. "I have included extra for travel expenses."

"Have you spotted the boy?" I asked, still scanning the worshippers as they danced. None fit the description of a young man, not even close.

"No," Mephista replied, sounding aggrieved, "I am becoming bored by all this capering. Let us go down and kill them all."

I shook my head, "I'm not being paid that much. We just need to disrupt the rites and release the boy. That's what the client wants."

The rites came to a sudden halt as Morcato raised his hands and chanted something that sounded like, "Eco, eco," or something like that. Satanists don't realize how silly they sound when they try to be serious.

It was then that the scent of brimstone hit my nose; I fought back the urge to sneeze and gag. Mephista stood up straighter; this was a smell she reveled in, the scent of her birth. The fact that I knew such information demonstrated why my life was nothing close to the way I envisioned it as a child. I'd planned on following my father into the private investigation field and spend my life dealing with divorce cases and the occasional theft, murder or mad scientist. An interesting life, but one I understood since I was raised in that world. But instead, my job now seemed to involve Satanists, succubi and the like; divorce cases were relaxing in comparison...

"One comes, one of my kind," Mephista practically sang as she bounced up and down on her heels. "It will begin soon!"

The she-demon was correct as I spotted two men leading a young man, a teen from the look of it, over to the stone altar which was still covered in goat gore. The boy was tall, blond and seemed completely willing to follow the cultists; there was no struggle to bring him to the place of sacrifice.

This didn't fit Michaela's description of a kidnapping victim, but I was past caring. Disrupting this group's rites was necessary for now, I did believe that they planned on bringing back that evil mastermind, Morcata.

I turned to tell my plan to Mephista, but she was already gone, running across the grass with the light skip of a happy child. But I knew all too well her only thought was the theft of lives, of draining victims and leaving mere husks behind. I ran after her, my thin frame feeling slow and cumbersome in comparison to Mephista's airy form.

As I was neared the site, Morcato raised a large golden chalice above his head and said something that was echoed by the group. Smoke began to appear around the altar and the Satanists began to shriek, a horrific sound that filled the air. The smell of brimstone and burning flesh caused me to gag as I reached for my gun with fumbling fingers.

A figure appeared in the smoke, the naked body of a muscular youth coalescing first to all eyes. Then the head formed, but not a human one, rather that of a goat. The creature made no sound, but its red eyes seemed to scan all present, causing many to drop to their knees and howl with despair.

"Mine!" Mephista screamed and leapt upon the demon as a cat would dive upon a mouse.

The goat-headed demon opened its mouth to scream or curse, but was unable to do so as the succubus clamped her mouth on the goat lips and bore the demon to the ground.

Pushing through the crowd, I spotted the boy, Simon, drinking deeply from the chalice of goat's blood. I stopped, aimed and fired my gun, shattering the vessel and causing the blood to spray upon him, Morcato and his wife.

The latter two shrieked and fled, while Simon fell to his knees, grasping his head, covered in blood.

In mere moments, the clearing was empty, except for Simon and me. I had no interest in following Morcato and his followers; that wasn't my job. Instead, I just stepped up to the boy and lifted him to his feet.

"Your aunt, Miss Michaela, hired me to rescue you," I explained, handing the young man a handkerchief.

Simon looked at me with confusion.

"I don't have an aunt. I'm an orphan. But it matters not, you did me great service. I joined briefly with Morcata and to learn his knowledge, but not his foolishness. The trappings they used were a joke, a sad jest and mere showmanship and puppetry. I do not require such stupidity. I shall be an immortal. I shall be the king of witches and I will repay your kindness."

With that, Simon turned and walked away, ignoring that he was covered from head to toe in goat's blood. Mephista appeared at my side a moment later, watching Simon's form grow smaller.

"He will be powerful, but accomplish little. Too full of himself and unlucky to ever become a true problem for the world. Perhaps that is why we were sent," she stated, watching him vanish in the distance.

"Perhaps," I agreed, still confused as to who hired us.

I didn't ask what Mephista did to the demon, I didn't want to know.


It was a month later that I had my answer. I was walking back to my office, having spent the whole night chasing Mephista through the Père Lachaise Cemetery to stop her from gaining an amulet that would make her nearly impossible to destroy. I was exhausted and planned on sleeping in until a client appeared at noon with my pay, and then spend a week or so doing as little as possible.

Tossing the Talisman of Huitzilopochtli in the air and catching it, I was surprised to see my office door open. Then I remembered that the cleaning woman came in before office hours, so I knocked and stepped inside. She was emptying the waste basket into a small cart as she straightened and didn't turn around.

"So sorry, I'll be out of your way, sir. Just finishing up," the cleaning woman mumbled, turning my and keeping her head low.

It was "Miss Michaela," but dressed in the blue uniform of a cleaning woman.

I wanted to speak, but I spotted she was wearing a necklace containing a Catholic medal. I knew immediately which saint, but stepped closer to see... It was indeed St. Michael, the archangel who fought the Devil for the Lord.

Closing the door as she left, I shook my head and lay down on my couch. My life was far too strange; I hoped my next client was something simple like a messy divorce.

*Sam Shook is new to* Tales of the Shadowmen, *a project which has always prized itself on giving a break to talented first-time writers. Earlier, we crossed paths with BBC TV detective Jim Bergerac; in this story, it is yet another BBC TV detective, the unflappable, swashbuckling Adam Adamant, from the short-lived 1966-67 series created by Donald Cotton & Richard Harris, who heads to France to cross swords (literally!) with none other than Arsène Lupin...*

## Sam Shook: *A Professional Matter*

*Baker Street, 1902*

*To this day, I am not entirely sure whether it was Devanne's mysterious book, or the challenge issued by another son of England, as to why my friend, Sherlock Holmes went to France on that fateful night...*
Observation of Doctor John Hamish Watson

"Well now," Holmes mumbled as he held his pipe in his mouth, "tell me, Mr. Adamant, what is this 'matter of great importance' you mentioned?"

The man sitting opposite the Great Detective took a sip of tea, and began:

"You have more than likely heard of my exploits before, and know that I fight crime for Queen and country. In 1898, a certain Inspector Ganimard of the Sûreté requested I come immediately to France to catch the master burglar Arsène Lupin, who they believed stole a great sum of money from the management at the Palais Garnier. 'Well,' I said 'it sounds like you are need of a man of my talents.' I grabbed my trusty sword stick and departed immediately. *After all, I thought, how difficult can catching a simple thief be?*"

*Paris, 1898*

"Hello inspector, have you any good news on the case?"

Ganimard sighed, "I'm afraid not, Monsieur; all we know is that Arsène Lupin had to be the one who performed the deed."

"Have you at least found any evidence?" I inquired.

Ganimard laid three calling cards on the table, all baring the same name: *Arsène Lupin.*

"Strange," I murmured, "why would he implicate himself?"

Ganimard kept his steel gaze upon me, "He didn't." He reached into his waistcoat pocket and tossed four more on the table. "Lupin never leaves any evidence he does not want left, and he seldom leaves anything to chance."

This was going to be more difficult than I first thought.

"We found a bag full of these behind the Opera house," he continued.

I was rather bewildered at this news. "All right, then," said I, "what else do you know?"

"We know that MM. Eugène Bertrand and Pedro Gailhard, the Managing Directors of the Paris Opera, were having a dispute over the profits made during the last season, and so they went to check the safe in their office. Now, they had locked their office from the inside only thirty minutes ago, and because of its location, no one could possibly get in or out unseen. Well, can you explain how the Devil someone managed to ransack the safe and escape unnoticed in broad daylight?"

Astonished by this, I had to ask, "Was there anything out of the ordinary in the Opera that day?"

"They only said that they had the feeling that someone was following them."

There was no good explanation to my knowledge. "Well, time to go to the Opera, then."

I learned nothing more than I knew already, save that an inebriated stage hand claimed he had caught a glimpse of a phantom carrying a sandbag. I spoke with the Directors and they showed me their office. There was no way for Lupin to get in through any windows undetected, so he had to have already been in the room, or somehow followed them in. The problem was, even if he had managed that feat, there were no places to hide. I even checked the room for trapdoors or hidden passages, but there were none. I decided, however, that I did not need to figure out how he did it. All I had to do was capture him.

After exiting the Palais Garnier, as I contemplated visiting my friend Oscar Wilde, who was knowledgeable of gossip and rogues, by mere chance I happened to overhear a man say:

"A letter from Arsène Lupin, can you believe it?"

I heard a second man reply, "What did it say?"

I hid around the corner to hear the rest of their conversation.

The first man spoke up, "It warned my uncle that, at the public showing of his collection, Lupin would rob him of his famous green paste Idol of Princess Hermonthis!"

The second replied, "Detestable business. Will he hire any gendarmes?"

"No," answered the other, "I don't think he wants to bother the guests. Besides, if what they say about Lupin is true, it will make no difference."

I jumped on my chance. "Excuse me, gentlemen, I would be glad to offer *my* services." They looked at me inquisitively. "I understand you are trying to catch a thief."

The Collector's house was on the edge of the city. He lived practically in solitude, yet there were many guests. The evening came and went. I'll spare you the details, Mr. Holmes, and just say that the night was uneventful. I was surprised to be wrong, and almost went about my business, when I happened to catch a glimpse of a figure leaving the mansion, and swiftly walking into the darkness alone.

I gave pursuit, but kept my distance at first, just to be sure I was chasing the right man. Then I saw a small green object in his hand! At that moment, I knew it had to be Lupin. I kept following, but he looked back, panicked, and ran like the devil. Without waiting a moment, I went after him. He rounded a corner, but when I went around there, he was gone.

As I passed by a beggar wrapped in a raggedy blanket, I noticed a small shop ahead. The door was wide open, and I started to become suspicious. This was too easy. I entered and began my search; though the shop was small, there were enough places for someone to hide. I started feeling like I had just walked into a trap when, without warning, I heard the door lock. I ran to the large window and, as I looked through the glass, I saw the beggar cast aside his wrappings to reveal a handsome young man in an evening suit. The man whom I had been following had passed the idol to the real Lupin, who then sauntered off.

Time was of the essence, so I positioned my cane in front of me, using it as a ram as I smashed through the window and landed in the street. The accomplice attempted to grab me, but a good anointing sent him reeling into unconsciousness. I took off in Lupin's direction. He darted into a restaurant, so I sprinted through the door, almost knocking over a waiter, but keeping my eyes on the thief. I saw him take a salt shaker from a table and empty it into his coat pocket. Enigmatic fellow, is he not?

Through the kitchen, out the door, and back into the street we went. I could almost reach out and grab him as we ran through yet another alley. With one last push, I jumped and tackled him to the ground.

"Arsène Lupin," I grunted, "we meet at last."

Lupin, however, was a skilled combatant, and the next thing I knew, he elbowed me in the face, and shoved me onto my feet, causing me to stumble. With one fluid motion he rolled over and stood up. It would take more than that to best me, so I merely laughed and drew my sword.

"Surrender, or defend yourself."

Lupin tucked his cane under his arm, pulled out a cigar, clipped it, and then began to light a match.

"Who do you think you are, Englishman?" he said.

I sliced the cigar in two. "My name is Adamant, sir; perhaps you've heard of me?" That got his attention. "Now I say again, defend yourself!" I saluted.

Looking at my weapon, then to me, he said, *Mieux qu'on dise 'il court-là qu'il gît ici...*"

He ran toward the back of the ally, and frantically looked from left to right. I charged him. I was foolish enough to believe he was cornered. At the last moment, he jumped out of the way, and I lodged my sword between two bricks. I looked over my shoulder and was surprised to see his wiry figure kicking open a

261

wooden door in the side of the passage wall. I reached out to grab his cape, but he darted in too quickly. I dislodged my weapon and once again began to track him.

As my eyes adjusted to the darkness, I could tell I had emerged in the green room of a small theater. I treaded carefully, wary of my opponent's trickery. He was not downstairs, so I walked up the stairs which led backstage. Still there was no one in sight, so I walked upstage. Through the darkness I was able to make something out in the middle of the stage. It was a note, with the message *Look up* scrawled on it. I did just that, when, suddenly, I felt something tighten around my leg and I was snatched up into the air.

After a few disorienting moments, I was greeted to the sight of my enemy working his way across the catwalk. Judging by the noose-like knot around my ankle, he had rigged a snare trap for me. But I was not going to let him escape, so I started swinging to and fro until I was over the catwalk. With a well-timed cut, I severed the rope. Though it wasn't the most graceful landing, I was free.

I rose up and was after him once more. When I reached him, he took up his cane and struck at me. We fought all across the catwalk, my swordplay against his. Yet, neither could get an advantage.

"I see you're well versed," I said as he jumped from the catwalk to a small adjacent platform suspended by ropes.

I followed; Lupin leapt to the neighboring platform. He kept running, but I blocked him off, swinging on a rope to get in front of him. I cut one of the cables holding him up, throwing him off balance, and I followed up with a thrust, injuring his hand and disarming him.

"But I'm afraid you're off your rhythm." I put my sword to his throat, "I grow weary of this, Lupin, let's be done with it."

I motioned with my other hand for him to give up the stolen item. He produced the idol, but the infernal thief tossed it in the air!

Distracted, I didn't see him as he reached into his coat, grabbed some salt, and threw it in my face.

When I could see again, Lupin was gone, and thus I left the theater. It was getting late so I walked under a street lamp and reached into my pocket to check the time. All I felt some thick paper where my watch should be, and as I pulled it out, I saw it was a calling card:

*Merci beaucoup – Arsène Lupin*

Upon seeing this, I crushed it in my fist.


The next day, I returned to Ganimard to give my report. The Inspector looked at the card Lupin gave me.

"So close," he mumbled. "*C'est la vie.* I am afraid Lupin will have to wait for now; something damnable happened last night." Ganimard slid forward a photograph that was so horrid in nature... I wish not to think about it.

"By Saint George! I have investigated murders before but... this is pure savagery." I looked back up at Ganimard. "Who could have done this?"

"That is why I still need you, Monsieur Adamant. France is home to numerous criminal masterminds and any of them could be responsible."

"Rest assured inspector, I will avenge these men."

By the time I had arrived, the bodies had been taken away, but the stains were still there. I saw an old man whom I took to be a policeman a few feet ahead, looking over the area with great interest.

"Good morning, Monsieur," I called.

Without taking his eyes off the scene, he replied, "*Bonjour, Monsieur.*"

I approached the older man and looked him over; he had dirty grey hair and dark rings under his tired-looking eyes.

"Inspector Ganimard did not mention that you would be here. Adam Adamant at your service. Who are you exactly, sir?" I questioned, offering my hand.

The man looked at me, and then looked down at my outstretched hand, only to ignore it, and returned with, "Inspector Ledoux."

I put my hand down. "Do you know who they were?" I asked, pointing my cane toward the ground where the bodies once lay.

Ledoux responded, "As far as we can tell, members of the Diogenes Club, here on orders from Monsieur Mycroft Holmes. From what we found, they had no valuables stolen."

"Lupin, that blackguard! I knew he was crafty, to steal from the Opera as he did, but I didn't think him capable of this!"

Ledoux shook his head, "Murder is not part of Lupin's *répertoire*, and I believe the man who did this was the same man who robbed the Opera."

"Who are the suspects?" I inquired.

"The Sûreté has no idea," muttered the Inspector.

"Do you have any clues?" I asked.

Ledoux replied, "I don't just have clues. I know who did it. Follow me."

Sherlock Holmes looked on at Adam Adamant with a sort of morbid, though stoic, curiosity, at this point.

"I suppose, Mr. Holmes, you already have the mystery solved, don't you?" he half-way jested.

The good doctor's typewriter had ceased its rhythmic clicking as Watson looked inquisitively at the client.

The facial expression of Holmes remained unchanged.

"What did Ledoux do next?" he asked.

We followed footprints, made of what I now believe to have been dry blood, to a nearby hotel. We were about to enter when the door suddenly swung open. Ledoux pulled me away, hushed me, and listened. He then beckoned me to follow him.

After some time, we found ourselves at the Collector's house that Lupin had robbed earlier. We stood several meters or so away, hiding around the corner of an abandoned building. Standing on the front porch of the house, holding a grimoire, was the Collector. From somewhere, we heard a voice say, "Charles le Sorcier, eh? You're sure this is the correct book?"

The Collector nodded.

"Now, for the idol of Princess Hermonthis and the deal is done. I get what I want, and you get to live," the voice said.

The poor old man began to quake and said that it had been stolen the night before.

The voice again spoke up, "I gave you a lot of time to hand over the idol, and still you don't deliver. I'll give you one last chance: get it to me by midnight, or I swear neither Heaven nor Hell will protect you from me!"

Then, I hope to God that I can describe what happened next--something truly unbelievable. The grimoire was ripped from the old man's hands as if by some unseen force, and began to float away. It was now horrifically apparent where the voice was coming from...

"That... *thing* is the murderer?! Is he a specter, or else what form of trickery is this?" I asked quite distressed.

"He's supposedly an English scientist who's gone astray and is now in league with some cultists."

"Cultists... Do you mean to say that he's working for sorcerers?" I inquired; I always have been wary of black magic.

"Not exactly," replied Ledoux, "They seem to believe in an ancient religion filled with eldritch monsters, many unpronounceable names, and they worship something they call Nyarlathotep..."

That did not make me feel any better. I was just about to ask him how he knew all this when, almost as if he read my mind, he said, "I found a letter from them to that invisible fellow. All I know is that they are from America, but I don't know what they need the book and the idol for. I can't imagine anything good coming of it."

I was trying to find some way to piece this all together. We went to a café for a few hours to attempt to make some sense of it.

"Is there anything extraordinary about Princess Hermonthis, or her idol?" I questioned.

Ledoux removed his hat and ran his hand through his grey hair.

"That old collector was known to say that he was given it by the Princess herself when she took him to a realm where all the pharaohs lived eternally."

"And who is Charles le Sorcier?"

"He was an alchemist and magician; the son of one Michel Mauvais."

"Now, how is this connected to this cult you mentioned?"

Ledoux looked into his coffee cup, as if he could divine the answer from it. Then he finally spoke up:

"I know the book contains a summoning spell; I'm sure they'd find some use for it. Other than that, I don't know. Does the name 'Nyarlathotep' mean anything to you?"

The name did, in fact, hold some meaning for me. After a moment of reminiscence, I recalled how once, for reasons to complex to explain at the moment, I had made contact with Miskatonic University. The curator there had mentioned this "Nyarlathotep" and how some believed that, through sacrifice, he would grant knowledge of abominable secrets. I conveyed this to Inspector Ledoux.

He shook his head, "This only raises more questions. If I were to wager a guess, I would say that they want access to the pharaohs' realm for some reason, but for what, I don't know."

There was one last part of this mystery that I had yet to understand.

"Why do you think those men here under Mycroft Holmes's orders were killed?" I asked.

Ledoux looked distant, as if he was witnessing something I could not see, and I could detect sadness in his voice. It was the sort of melancholy that one can only gain from old age and experience.

"I don't know why madmen work as they do. Maybe they do it out of greed, or even revenge. Sometimes, I'm not sure if there is any motivation at all. Sometimes, I think that they do what they want because evil is all they can do."

There was, for some time, a pensive silence. Finally, I inquired, "Was there anything of interest found on the bodies."

Ledoux then handed me a pocket Bible. I examined it, and discovered that on the bookmark were several series of numbers. When I pointed this out, the inspector looked at them for a few minutes. Suddenly, his face lit up, "It's a code! Let's see what it says."

I found that each series of numbers corresponded with a book, chapter, verse, and word. It makes sense that England's worst kept secret would use books to convey secret messages, considering it's officially only a reading club.

When finished, the message read: *Behold they knock and the Pharaoh openeth the door and bringeth iniquities upon the Earth.*

My face paled. It now struck me as to what they desired. The curator at Miskatonic University had also told me that one of the most infamous followers of Nyarlathotep had been Pharaoh Nephren-Ka, a man so evil that Egypt did its best to expunge all record of his existence. They wanted to summon him from the realm of the dead pharaohs, and the idol was their catalyst.

I told this to Ledoux, who, in turn, informed me that, according to the Collector, the immortal pharaohs were nigh invincible. Imagine what a man as wicked as Nephren-Ka would do once he was returned to our world! The cultists' plan, normally, would have sounded like folly to me, but I knew if your brother cared enough to send those men to investigate, Mr. Holmes, then the threat was far from idle.

We then paid and left, formulating a scheme to best the cultists and their invisible partner.

We returned to the Collector's house. Knowing we could neither get him anywhere safe, nor enlist the police within the time we had, we told the old man to hide in the attic, and we would defend him.

We waited anxiously to enact our ambush, bracing ourselves for what was to come. Late in the night, from the top story window, we saw eight men approaching the house. Taking the lead was the invisible fellow, dressed in a grey long coat, a hat, with bandages and dark glasses on his face. Behind him was a man armed with a saber; trailing behind him were thuggish-looking men brandishing axes and Bowie knives.

"All right, old man, come out of there!" the Invisible Man called, pounding his fist on the door. "Blast it all! Wake up and get out here or we'll break in, kill you, and I'll take the idol myself!"

A minute passed before the Invisible Man said, "Very well then, give me that axe!"

The house's windows were thick and we could hear one cracking as he struck them. We hurried into position, and it was not long until, with a thundering smash, the window was shattered, and they entered.

"Well, now, I wasn't expecting company," I said tauntingly as they gave me a look of surprise. "But don't worry," I continued, "I am quite prepared!"

As I drew my weapon, Ledoux popped out from behind the curtains and smashed a chair over the Invisible Man's head.

"They got Griffin!" one of them yelled.

*That's one*, I thought.

Saluting, I said, "Whenever you're ready, gentlemen."

One of the men with an axe came at me screaming, "Ia Nyarlathotep!"

I kicked a stool toward his legs, tripping him up, and I followed up with a good kick to the temple. As the one with a knife tried to gut me, I lunged, piercing his heart. *That's three.*

I locked blades with two other knife-wielders, and, looking over my shoulder, I saw Ledoux knock two others out at once by slamming their heads together and ramming them into a wall. *That's five.*

I pushed the two in front of me back, and quickly dodged the swordsman as he attacked me with his saber. As the fight wore on, I began to feel overwhelmed, and I looked around for my companion.

"Ledoux!" I called out, but no response was made. "Ledoux, confound it man! Where are you?!"

I looked around while avoiding or parrying strikes from my foes, but I could not find the Inspector.

The next thing I knew I was disarmed. The saber-wielder thug slashed at me wildly, and, from the corner of my eye, I could see both of the knifemen rushing me.

I braced myself as they charged, and, at the last moment, I ducked, causing the swordsman to slay both knife-wielders!

As he looked on with shock, I quickly kicked the weapon from his hand, and delivered two jabs to the face and a right hook to his jaw. While he stumbled around, I picked up the shaft of my cane and struck him on the back of the head.

I walked into the next room, and there I found the Inspector.

"Ledoux," I said a trifle flustered, "where were you...?"

I stopped myself, for I was shocked when I looked at the desk in the room. On it stood a green paste idol.

"More importantly, how did the idol get back here?" I asked.

Just as Ledoux opened his mouth to speak, we heard a noise in the main room. We rushed in to investigate, and, to our horror, saw Griffin's clothes and bandages discarded on the floor.

We made a mad dash for the door, but Ledoux suddenly went flying into the wall and something punched me in the stomach before striking me to the ground. The sound of an unpleasant laugh filled the room. I struggled to lift myself up.

"Griffin," I grunted, recalling the name the cultist had said, "why... do you cast your lot... with them?"

"Last I heard you were dead," Ledoux groaned.

The disembodied voice replied, "No, dear Inspector, only wounded. Surely you don't believe everything you read? As for you, Mr. Adamant, do you understand that they offer me something more valuable than any money I could take?"

I knew I couldn't get him to reveal his whole plan, but if I could keep him talking, I could figure out his location. "And, what would that be?" I asked.

"Power!" he bellowed, "power to make the world crawl at my feet, power to rule an empire!"

*God save us, he's completely mad.* I now was on my hands and knees. "And I suppose... you think yourself an emperor?"

"Invisible Man the First, resuming his reign of terror," he gloated, kicking me in the torso. "And, like Mycroft Holmes's men, you shall become its victim!"

I rose as quickly as could, and began turning left to right, still not knowing where exactly he was. Without warning, a cold, rough hand grabbed me by the throat.

"But don't think of it as murder..." As he gripped even tighter, everything began to go dark. "...Think of it as judicial killing."

Before I sank into oblivion, Ledoux jumped onto Griffin's back and began to choke him.

I lay prone for a moment, watching as Griffin fell to the floor, in order to injure the Inspector on the broken glass. I heard Ledoux cry out in pain. I wobbled to my feet, and stumbled toward where I had left my sword, only for Griffin to take one of the knives and throw it at me, pinning my coat sleeve and cape to the wall.

Ledoux had released his grip by this point. Griffin was picking he Inspector up by his lapel, and was about to stab him with a large piece of splintered glass, when the Frenchman reached to the shelf behind him, grabbed a wine bottle, and smashed it on the Invisible Man's head. The bottle was not thick, so it did not render him unconscious, but he was riddled with cuts. Wine dripped off of him, and some blood trickled down his face. I could finally see him!

I slipped out of my coat and cape, retrieved my sword, and lunged at Griffin. I was still a bit dazed, so I only managed graze his side. He grunted, dropped Ledoux, and grabbed one of the axes on the floor. The Inspector was still lying on the ground, recovering from his wounds.

"Yield, Griffin, for whether by my blade or by the rope, I guarantee you will die!"

I evaded a swing from his axe, but he tripped me. He charged; however, I flipped him over me, and he tumbled headlong into the fireplace. I rolled onto my feet. He came out, covered in ash. I dealt him a powerful uppercut. He stumbled back, and I asked again, "What will it be?"

He spat in my face, and then tried to ram me. I leapt out of the way, saying, "Bad form!" and, with that, I gave him cut across the back. He spun around, swinging the axe, and disarmed me. He butted me in the face with it, knocking me down. He lifted up the axe to finish me off, but at the last moment, Ledoux used what strength he had left to toss me my sword.

I stabbed at the Invisible Man, deeply piercing his shoulder. With a yell, he dropped his weapon. His arm useless, he swore and cursed as he clumsily ran away. *That's eight.*

The next day, after spending the night at the infirmary, I returned to Ganimard's office to make my report.

"Congratulations, Monsieur Adamant, we are indebted to you for solving this case. Now all that's left to do is to catch this Griffin character."

*The Devil you will*, I thought, but kept to myself.

I chuckled and replied, "Thank you, Inspector, but I can't take all the credit. The man you sent acted valorously last night."

Ganimard raised an eyebrow. "I never sent any man," he said.

I looked on with confusion, but before I could object, Ganimard said, "Also, someone left this parcel for you."

I opened it up, and inside were my watch and an envelope that read, *From Inspector Ledoux to M. Adamant*. Inside was a note. I walked outside and down the street before Ganimard could say anything, and opened the envelope.

*Dear Mr. Adamant,*

*Ledoux is dead. He died back in 1879 while he was hunting the Phantom of the Opera. I wished to return this, as a way to say thank you, and because I see you value justice. I have been pursuing the Invisible Man ever since he attempted to rob the Opera and pickpocketed that letter from him after one of those mercenaries gave it to him. I stole the idol in order to catch Griffin and protect the Collector. Lupin is seldom a wanton thief. I also assure you that Griffin did not leave the Palais Garnier with a single franc. I hope he has use for a collection of calling cards.*

*Sincerely,*

*A. L.*


I chuckled and wondered out loud, "I wonder what happened to the stolen money?"

A mailman walked by and, with Gallic panache, lifted his hat and whispered, "I can't tell you all my secrets, now can I?"


Holmes now was leaning far forward, smoking his pipe vigorously.

"Did you arrest him?" he asked.

Adamant hesitated for a moment.

"I gave him a head start," he replied, meekly.

Holmes cocked his head, "You let him get away?"

"I did. You must understand, it was a conundrum, for he undoubtedly stole, but he was a man of honor, Holmes, and it was justified. Not only that, but he saved my life."

Holmes laid his pipe on the table. "Do you regret your decision?"

"No," muttered Adamant before turning to look out the window, "not entirely…"

"So you want me to go after France's best burglar? That sounds, quite elementary."

"Did my story fall on deaf ears, Great Detective? I've told you how crafty Lupin is, and one good deed does not properly redeem him. He is still a problem…"

"A problem you let escape. That fact cannot be forgotten. If I were in your situation, I would have stopped him with ease."

Adamant sighed. Little did he know that the words that were forming on his tongue would be an ember in a greater flame that would light a decade-long rivalry.

"It's difficult, Holmes, it's a professional matter."

*Arsène Lupin returns in this story that takes place on the eve of 813, his greatest adventure, soon to be released in a new translation by Black Coat Press. In David Vineyard's tale, the cunning Lupin, posing as Sûreté Commissioner Lenormand, is facing two other thieves who may be just as good as he is. How will he outwit them (if he does!) in this ballet of deception and legerdemain?*

## David Vineyard: *The Legacy of Arsène Lupin*

*Paris, 1911*

Even a thief has a sense of honor. More so a thief such as my friend Arsène Lupin. However Machiavellian his mind, however ruthless his purpose, his honor was as prickly as that of a Spanish grandee, and some things were not to be tolerated.

"A travesty, my friend," he spat.

We were at our favorite sidewalk café, enjoying a warm spring day in Paris and a glass of Pernod. Arsène Lupin was gone as far as the greater public was concerned, and my present companion was Prince Sernine, a respected and well-liked figure in the city, known for his taste and style. That he was also M. Lenormand, recently promoted to the Head of the Sûreté Nationale and France's greatest sleuth since Vidocq, and that all, in turn, were in fact Raoul d'Andresy, the Duc de Charmerace, and more names and faces than I cared to imagine, all leading to the single identity of Arsène Lupin, seemed a fine joke in those days, before the darker ones to come.

But, for the moment, Prince Sernine was indulging in a rare moment of righteous anger.

"A travesty, I say! That a man like that should possess the sword of France's greatest hero is an assault upon every Frenchman's honor. The sword of the noble d'Artagnan in such hands! You realize that such a insult to France herself cannot be allowed to stand?"

The man "like that" to which my friend referred was none other than the Comte de Guy, a noble of questionable title who had purchased his nobility with a fortune rumored to have been acquired by means as questionably as his title. The one thing certain was that he had shadowy connections among the underworld, ties to governments other than his own, and a beautiful daughter, if such she was. Rumors flew around such men, not all of them about money, and the most recent was hardly a rumor at all, since it had been the subject of articles in virtually every newspaper in France.

"Vulgar man that he is, that de Guy couldn't wait to go to the press to announce his purchase. See: *Le Comte de Guy is pleased to announce the acquisi-*

*tion of the sword of d'Artagnan, Marshal of France, hero of legend and fact, the brave Gascon, the king's Musketeer...* You saw the headlines, my friend. Common, vulgar, an insult not to be borne!

"Lenormand has heard rumors of how the Comte has come by that sword. There's been talk of dealings with the Chinese fence, Hanoi Shan—his path has crossed Lupin's before—rumors of a murderous thug named Gurn, an elderly woman whose throat was slit in her bed—by the hand of this same Gurn, no doubt; half-whispered rumors of Cagliostro, Saint-Germain, and the Englishman Barrington, who had defrauded the great Cagliostro of a fortune and the sword; talk that the sword had once been in the trust of one Prince Rodolphe; that it was stolen by Colonel Bozzo-Corona or by that young rogue Rocambole; that British cracksman took a shot at it; and there was a suggestion the Devil Doctor in Limehouse, had shown an interest; Josephine Balsamo's name came up... There were even rumors of Lupin's involvement, though it would be an insult if there had not been."

The Prince paused, and I could not say what it was that I saw flicker across his keen eyes for an instant.

"Rumors are a great aide to the policeman, but also a great obfuscation," he continued. "They swirl like mists around the detective's head, and only the sharpest eye can spy the telling detail, perceive that which others miss. The Englishman to the contrary, it is as much an art as a science. The law of the perfect moment, as great as the letter of the law, applies in such situations. The work of a great detective, like that of a great thief, is a matter not of chance, but of opportunity seized.

"In truth, it was young Rouletabille, the journalist, who brought it to the attention of Lenormand, and almost as soon as the words had left his mouth, I knew Lupin had to act, whatever threat it posed to my ultimate plans. How fortuitous then that, on that very afternoon, Comte de Guy had been in my offices!

"You have seen the pictures in the popular press; he looks more like an English cleric than a nobleman: strong aquiline features, large white hands, thick brown hair beginning to show some gray, and—one must admit—a good tailor and some taste in clothes, whether it is his own or not. Lenormand could not quite place the accent, but he was not of French origin. At best, the Channel isles or Martinique. Just that morning, he called at the Quai des Orfèvres seeking an audience with M. Lenormand himself, bearing letters of introduction from the public prosecutor, a respected judge, and the Secretary of the President himself. One can hardly blame Lenormand for ushering him into his office with some haste.

" "M. Lenormand," de Guy began, "we are assured that you are the man we seek—France's greatest detective and most honored policeman. The prosecutor and the Minister of Justice both sang your praises and assured me that you are indeed the man I need.'

271

"Lenormand did his best to show humility: 'And how so, Monsieur le Comte?'

" 'As you may know, my daughter possesses several valuable and irreplaceable jewels. She wishes to show these off in the proper setting, therefore this weekend we are giving a masked ball. Only the *crème de la crème* will be there, nobility of several countries, ministers of state, ambassadors, industrialists... It is vital, therefore, that we provide the best security for them and for my wife's jewels and our own modest collection. It would be a national scandal if something should happen; our reputation ruined, your own force embarrassed, the honor of France...'

"Lenormand was well aware that said *modest* collection included a folio from Shakespeare, paintings by Leonardo, Caravaggio, Degas, Goya and Manet, Louis Quinze furnishings, a number of rare jewels... and the sword of d'Artagnan, less valuable in *francs,* perhaps, but in terms of honor, priceless. Lenormand could hardly refuse him, and Lupin had been eyeing those treasures for some time, as you might imagine.

"Lenormand agreed to meet the Comte on the following day at his château outside Paris, in order to review his security precautions, and better assign the men who would guard the event. Versailles itself would have envied the precautions that were to be taken. And with good reason, for the treasures of Versailles pales compared to some of those held by de Guy—and the ambition of Lupin knows no limit. Even old Lecoq himself might have found himself challenged by this problem!

"Lenormand arrived at the château promptly at ten in the morning. Any time earlier might have risked finding a man such as the Comte abed; any later might have been considered an insult or dismissive of the weighty responsibility.

"If you have not seen the Château de Guy, it stands as a monument to another age. It was built in the time of Louis XIII, and added onto as needed over the years as a bow to modernity—plumbing, furnaces, gas, electricity... Still, it retains the charm of the gilded era from which it is. Even that vulgar Comte could not change that.

"Something must be said of the grounds as well, for they play a role, however small, in the drama that followed. One arrives at the château through a gilded gate, opened by a dour brute whose uniform reveals the bulge of a revolver, and whose accent contains a hint of Corsica. There follows perhaps three quarters of a mile of well-kept road, canopied by ancient elms of impressive age. From this tunnel of green, one emerges into a large drive, still mindful of the days when coaches drawn by fine horses were manned by footmen. To the west lay the stables and a small track; beyond that, a grove of walnut trees.

"One is met at the bottom of a fine staircase by the de Guys' butler; again, something of a brute, obviously armed, with a more pronounced Corsican accent. He escorts the visitor past the massive gilded oak doors. Everything about Chateau de Guy is gilded. There's enough gold paint and gold leaf to build another of M. Eiffel's towers! One is led into a vast entranceway, dominated by a great crystal chandelier that once graced Versailles itself, a gift to some distant de Guy by a grateful Louis XIV, or so the Comte claims. A wide staircase, worthy of the Paris Opera, lies beneath that. A wide landing leads up to different parts of the house, while, at ground level, a set of large double-doors open onto the main ballroom, and to the library opposite, where M. Lenormand was escorted to wait.

"Even so, Lenormand took the time to admire the Comte's library. The folio Shakespeare was under glass; high walls that reached three floors were packed with rare volumes from Iraneus to Voltaire, Rousseau to Proust. It wasn't hard to imagine one of them sitting behind the master's hand-tooled desk or in the deep throne-like chairs. Weaponry of other ages adorned the room and the walls. Crossed pikes hung above the library doors; a suit of 14th century armor stood in a corner; a pair of hand tooled dueling pistols and an ordinary musket from the 17th century were crossed on the walls with swords of the period and musketeers' tunics. A large globe, dating back to the 15th century, stood just to one side of the desk; on the desk itself lay a bejeweled sword, stunningly preserved, shining in the morning sunlight streaming in from the windows behind the desk.

"It was the sword of d'Artagnan.

"In that instant, M. Lenormand faded away; Prince Sernine and all the others became but phantoms, shades that barely lingered in the mind. In that moment, there was only Lupin and the sword. Had anyone been present in that moment, all the disguises in the world could not have concealed him.

" "Commissaire Lenormand," said de Guy, entering through the wide doors, "you will forgive our tardiness, we trust? The preparations for this ball have been quite exhausting, and we fear we overslept, though, in truth, we spent a restless night with concerns about the security. That rogue Arsène Lupin haunted our sleep.'

" 'You need not bother yourself about Lupin," replied Lenormand. "That rogue is long since gone. The cracksman Bunn is in Perth, by all reports, and that Englishman Raffles who has plagued Scotland Yard has not been heard of since the Boer War. That still leaves us with much to be concerned about, Monsieur le Comte, but none of that genius, no Lupin to haunt your dreams.'

" 'What a weight that lifts from our shoulders!' de Guy touched a small button on the globe, and it opened up to reveal a well-stocked bar. 'We did not imagine of course that Lupin would best you, M. Lenormand, but the vulgar press and their accounts of his exploits paint him as a formidable force.'

" "In his day, Monsieur le Comte, but no more. If he lives, I should say he is not half the man he was. Now, if I might, before we discuss details, I should appreciate a chance to explore the estate on my own. I promise not to become lost, and I may have more concrete suggestions for your security afterwards.'

"The Comte was about to speak when the library doors opened, and a most beautiful young woman appeared, just arisen from her bed, no doubt, and wearing a deeply cut gossamer black lace robe that swept the floor like a train and revealed a justly praised bosom as pale as the breast of a dove. Her hair was dark as a raven's, her eyes a startling blue, and, just perceptible beneath the robe and gown, lay a fine body possessed of a dancer's form. She was no more than eighteen if that, Lenormand knew from the press, but her appearance endowed her with a natural command of any room she entered.

" 'Father, forgive me, I was not aware you had a guest. What must he think of me?'

"When she spoke, some of the illusion of grace was lost, for the accent was more pronounced than her father's, if equally puzzling.

" 'Comtesse Emmeline de Guy, may I introduce the famous M. Lenormand, of the Paris Sûreté. Commissaire, this is my daughter.'

"Lenormand took the offered hand and brushed it lightly with his lips. It would not do for a policeman to show too many graces. A history of civil service in Saigon and police work in Paris hardly lent one to noble gestures.

" 'Comtesse, I am honored.'

"The honor was not all in her presence or her beauty, for resting on that luxurious bosom was an emerald the size of a small hen's egg, encrusted with diamonds in a star shape, fastened around her neck by a diamond chain. Tot was the jewel known as the Green Star of Kaipoor. Lenormand had to confess he had not expected to see that great stone here.

" 'You see our dilemma, M. Lenormand. Our darling insists on wearing her baubles, and we are at a loss to deny her. You may imagine the source of such dreams as we have suffered of late.'

"Still, after a few moments of polite, if inane, conversation, Lenormand was able to extract himself and begin those investigations he felt so necessary before making his suggestions regarding the security for the gala to come. Nor would a lay of the land be a bad thing for Lupin.

"Perhaps three quarters of an hour had passed as he studied the various entrance ways and exits from the château; then he moved to the grounds, examining the stables, the gardens, and finally the grove of oaks that hid a small private lake.

"He was in the grove, admiring the picturesque lake, when a walnut struck the top of his hat. Or, to be precise, a walnut shell.

"He turned, expecting to see a squirrel dashing for cover, but instead, lounging in the crutch of the tree, he spied a boy. A boy now whistling a haunting little refrain.

"Though he wore long pants, the boy could not have been older than fifteen. He was fit-looking, had dark hair, regular, handsome features, and startling blue eyes of a candid nature that were quite effective. Most of all, when he smiled he seemed almost beatific.

" 'As the actress said to the bishop in the vestry, *You seem to have me at a disadvantage, sir.*'

The boy spoke excellent French, but Lenormand was a collector of accents and caught the faintest trait of the Englishman, though other than a gentleman's voice, he could not say from where in England the boy was—and he could normally spot such an accent within a few miles of its origin.

" 'And what disadvantage is that, young man?'

"The boy swung his long legs so he was sitting on the limb rather than lying on it.

" 'Why, I'm trespassing, of course. At least, I hope I'm trespassing. It would be rather tedious to have wasted a day's adventure if one weren't.'

" 'You don't look like a poacher,' Lenormand said. 'I don't suppose you are here for the walnuts?'

" 'No,' the young man said, 'not the walnuts.' So saying he cracked and ate another nut.

" 'Then might I ask what...?'

" 'I'm a thief of course,' the boy said, 'though I prefer the term buccaneer. I should have thought it obvious to a policeman such as yourself.'

"Lenormand didn't ask how the boy knew he was a policeman. His picture was frequently in the papers, and there had certainly rumors that he would soon calling on the Comte de Guy.

" 'And what is it you intend to steal?'

" 'My original intent was to relieve the Comtesse of that atrocious big emerald she wears, but having learned that de Guy has purchased the sword of d'Artagnan... That really is an insult that cannot pass, sir. For a pretender like de Guy to own *that* sword, the noble d'Artagnan's, it's rather like displaying the crown jewels in a pawn shop window, don't you think?'

"Lenormand repressed the urge to agree with the audacious young rogue.

" 'I've seen the emerald and the sword. They are very well guarded. You'll certainly be caught if you try; you might even get hurt.'

" 'Good,' the boy said. 'It was beginning to look a bit boring to be frank. Of course, I would liberate them from de Guy in any case. It's high time something was done about him. No offense meant, Monsieur, I understand that law and justice are at best distant cousins, and your position is restrained, whereas my own...'

" 'You seem unconcerned that I might arrest you here and now.'

" 'That wouldn't be very sporting, would it? Anyway, how long could you hold me on trespassing if you did? Not exactly a capital offense, and there is no guarantee that you have a cell that could hold me if you did capture me... and you'll note, you haven't yet, captured me, that is.'

" 'I don't suppose you have a name?'

"The boy paused.

" 'Hmm. Not an entirely unreasonable request. Of course, no need for it to be my *own* name. That's playing *too* fair. Something close though... Sam, no, Sebastian, oh, clearly no, Stinky... no, it doesn't really work in French, does it?... I have it! Stephen, as in St. Stephen, and a last name, something appropriate, but not too ornate... Temple... No, Tombs... No, no... I have it! Tarleton... Stephen Tarleton. I'm quite good at this, aren't I? Of course, I'll get better with time, don't you think?'

"With that the boy stood on the limb.

" 'As the bishop said to the actress in turn, *We all yield to temptation in the end*, and I've quite tempted you enough, I think. I'll be seeing you again, of course, but you might not see me, so a reluctant *au revoir,* Monsieur.'

"And with that, he lifted himself into the foliage, and with hardly a whisper or rustle of leaves, he was gone. Lupin could not have done it better.

"Lenormand returned to the château more than a bit bemused by the youth. Normally, he would have taken the young rogue's braggadocio for just that, adolescent prattle with no purpose other than thumbing its nose at authority and prickling it's backside with a needle. But there remained an aura about the youth, this false Stephen Tarleton, something in those blue eyes, the smile, the way he moved... No, he was convinced the youth was serious and bound to be a spanner in any precautions taken by Lenormand or any plans made by Lupin.

"The Comte was waiting in the library when Lenormand returned. For some time they discussed Lenormand's suggestions for increased security, and the Comte took careful note of each. And yet, he seemed almost too concerned with the position of each gendarme, with the exact movements of Lenormand's men. His grasp of tactics was almost Napoleonic, and Lenormand could not help but note that, for all his guise as a shallow and rather vain aristocrat, his mind was sharp and his intelligence acute.

" 'I have a few precautions of my own,'' de Guy said when they had exhausted Lenormand's plans. 'I'd like to show them to you, if I may?'

"So saying, he drew Lenormand's attention to the musketeer's tunic, musket and sword hanging on the library wall.

" 'It seemed an ideal place to secure the valuables I have acquired,' he said pushing the tunic aside to reveal a wall safe manufactured by the Dale company in New York, one of the most reliable firms in the business, and one that might offer challenge even to Lupin, though that American they call the Gray Seal had remarkable luck with them. If *he* could crack them, Lupin surely could.

"As de Guy opened the safe, Lenormand politely turned away, but the keen ears of Lupin listened as each tumbler clicked into place, a skill not a dozen men on the planet had mastered, much less perfected in Lupin's manner.

"Opening the wall safe, de Guy revealed the contents: numerous red velvet lined trays containing the sparking jewels of his collection.

" 'Lloyd's agent was quite appalled,' de Guy said. 'He seemed to think the collection should be locked away in a bank, but I cannot bear to part with them, and my dear daughter would be devastated.'

"de Guy carefully closed the safe again, replacing the tunic and the musketeer's sword that guarded it.

"After excusing himself and while returning to Paris, Lenormand's mind was awash with thoughts. Save for the boy, this was all too predictable, too easy. He did not sleep well that night, thinking of it, and the next day, his shadow spread over all of Paris, seeking any knowledge or rumor about the Comte or the boy, but finding nothing about the latter and only vague, half-formed rumors about de Guy. Either nothing was known, or his sources feared de Guy more than they did him.

"Even as he made plans for de Guy's approaching ball, his mind was unsettled because nothing quite made sense. The pieces refused to fall into place. Nor was Lupin more certain of his far simpler plans for the ball. The boy lingered at the edges of his conscious mind, almost spectral in his elusiveness.

"Prince Sernine had been invited to the gala, but had reluctantly declined, citing personal duties. It was far more important that Lenormand made an appearance, which he did in the costume of yet another eat swordsman, Cyrano de Bergerac.

"De Guy had chosen Louis XVI as his costume, and his daughter, Marie Antoinette. Her alabaster costume and powdered wig offset the great emerald at her throat and the many jewels bedecking her fingers, as well as bracelets and earrings glittering as if so many living things on her arms. Whether the irony regarding the Queen's necklace had occurred to her or her father was uncertain, but it occurred to Lenormand. That necklace had been stolen as well, by Cagliostro, and then in England by George Barrington, the Picaroon, king of the London underworld. And by he, himself, as a boy, from the Dreux-Soubize.

"Though not a superstitious man, it seemed a poor omen to Lenormand.

"As de Guy's guest list suggested, the guest list was made up of the elite of French society; here, the scion of a great banking family; there, a high-ranking minister; enough high judges for a dozen trials; the thin-blooded remainders of ancient aristocratic lines, and the *nouveau riche* in their vulgar glory; in each case, their wives proudly displayed their own spectacular jewels. Yet, among that crowd, among the servants, Lenormand spotted many a face from the underworld: Paris' infamous *Vampires* and the Union Corse from Marseilles. That English cracksman, Cleek, in London would rest well tonight, for his deadly enemies were all present at this gala event. A slight stirring at the back of his neck reminded him of the Comte's threatening Corsican servants, whose appearance was somewhat lessened by powdered wigs and livery.

"But, above all, he thought of the boy. The foulest criminals in France, the cream of the police, and half of the most influential men in France, and yet, his eye kept wandering, looking at the face of each waiter, each young man, even a few tall young women, expecting to meet those remarkable blue eyes and that beatific smile.

"The boy surely was only an unfortunate coincidence, a schoolboy on holiday, or had wandered away from his school, dreaming of piratical adventures and avenging d'Artagnan, *la belle France's* favorite son. Still, several times, Lenormand made his way to the library to assure himself that the safe had remained undisturbed. Foolish, of course, for how could a fourteen year-old boy crack one of the finest safe's in the world?

"And yet...

"As the hour drew toward midnight, Lenormand grew more apprehensive. As in fairy tales, the witching hour was likely to be the crowning moment of tonight's affair, no matter what else happened, and all his instincts told him that he was right. De Guy pretended to swig champagne, yet Lenormand could have sworn he never drank a single drop; his own men grew restless, and the rogues seemed to be gathering their nerve for a signal, a single moment.

"It was only a few minutes before the clock would chime the midnight hour when the Comtesse approached him, the emerald at her throat. dazzling in the lights from the great chandelier.

" 'A dance ,Commissioner? I should feel, oh so safe, in your arms.'

"Grace demanded that he agreed to her request, and indeed, being near the great stone at the moment of decision seemed a wise precaution. He took her hand and led her onto the floor as a Strauss waltz began. Somewhat to her surprise, the gruff policeman proved an excellent, even gifted, dance partner.

"But always, his eyes strayed to the emerald as the Comtesse chattered and laughed while he pretended to listen.

"The clock began to chime. From a distance, he also heard the bells tolling at a nearby church.

"One...

"Most of the people on the dance floor kept swirling about with no awareness of the moment's inherent drama.

"Two...

"Had the Comtesse's laugh become a trifle forced?

"Three...

"The Comte had disappeared. A tight knot formed in Lenormand's belly.

"Four...

"Still no sign of that boy...

"And so until the last few tolls, ten, eleven, twelve...

"Suddenly, the ballroom was plunged into darkness.

"There was a great confusion; a woman's screamed, men swore as they stumbled into one another. A police whistle blew loudly...

"It was a British bobby's police whistle, for Lenormand had issued none to his men this night.

278

"The Comtesse gasped. Lenormand swore, and, at that moment, the lights came on again.

"The ballroom was a mass of confusion. The Comtesse stood before him, quite pale, quite bereft of the Green Star of Kaipoor.

"At that moment, Lenormand identified himself and, acting on his orders, his men fell upon every criminal at the affair.

"Everyone was searched, no stone was left unturned, no bauble unexamined, but the Green Star of Kaipoor was nowhere to be found.

"When Lenormand made his way alone to the library, he found the safe empty, and the jeweled sword of d'Artagnan missing.

"Nor could he account for the Comte—or his daughter, who had disappeared as surely as the young thief.

"The sword of d'Artagnan was no longer in vulgar hands and the fabulous jewels of Comte de Guy had vanished.

"And neither have been seen to this day," Lupin concluded.

"But," I stammered, "the sword was presented at the National Gallery only days ago... I assumed Lupin..."

"No, the boy got to the sword and the emerald and made off cleanly with them, right through the police lines; he cleaned out the safe as well. Lupin could not have done it better. It's a pity really."

"That he got away?"

"No, that he got away with nothing."

"I don't follow?"

"Because you hear, Maurice, but you don't listen. You will recall that Lenormand remarked on the casual security de Guy displayed in regard to the jewels and the sword. For a man haunted by the specter of Arsène Lupin, he seemed far too casual about both the security of the jewels and their theft. And with good reason, for the stones in the safe and the emerald worn by the Comtesse were less than they appeared. There was something that smelled far from sweet. Something the boy had neatly foiled, saving Lenormand some embarrassment.

"Has it not occurred to you, knowing the jewels were false, that the Comte could hardly have planned to display them as he said? No, the jewels were bait for his guests, who would no doubt wear their own finery. The whole business was an elaborate set-up for an audacious robbery during which the Comtesse would be relieved of the Star of Kaipoor, just as the other ladies were of their own jewel. No one, police included, knew that the false Comte had set all this in motion in order to rob his guests and appear to be a victim himself.

"Lenormand had heard rumors from his forays in the underworld of numerous criminals gathering for a big job, and it seemed natural the ball was their target. He was convinced they were allied with the Comte, but how to prove it? Police were posted all over the estate with descriptions of half the rogues in Europe, most of whom were attending the party. The Comte had been solicitous about knowing the placement of each policeman, but Lenormand had not been entirely forthcoming about the number of men he would assign to the case.

"But the boy, le jeune Monsieur Tarleton, as he claimed to be, struck too soon. The commotion he caused foiled the Comte's perfectly timed plan, and when Lenormand doffed the tragic face of Cyrano, the police discreetly fell on the larcenous among the guest. All the Comte could do was feign concern over the loss of a bit of paste and crystal, and relatively worthless stones."

"I suspect your young rogue would be shocked to hear the role he played," I began

"Ah, but you underestimate our young friend. Why do you think he announced to Lenormand in the first place that he would be at the ball to steal the jewels? He knew by his own methods, or at least suspected le Comte's complicity. He wanted Lenormand and the police to have a strong presence to foil le Comte, but having no idea what those plans were he struck too soon.

"As Lenormand's forces looked fruitlessly for the boy and closed on the Comte's cohorts, Lenormand returned to the library. The open safe yielded little but a note left behind by the boy which he pocketed without looking at. Being in need of a drink, he opened the globe to reveal the bar inside, and drawing out a bottle of Napoleon, he noticed the globe weighed more than it should if it were hollow, even with the bar. It was a matter of seconds to find the release and the bar raised to reveal a concealed section. The Comte was so certain of it that he didn't even have a safe. The jewels—the real jewels—lay there for the taking. No Green Star of Kaipoor, of course, but a sufficient amount of real stones to have lent credence to the Comte's stories of fabulous wealth.

"No doubt de Guy will be somewhat less sanguine when he discovers that, too, is empty."

"But the sword? The boy..."

"The boy stole a sword certainly, and presented it with some honor to the National Gallery, but it was no more authentic than the jewels or the Green Star of Kaipoor."

"Then de Guy didn't have the real sword of d'Artagnan or the real Green Star?"

"As for the emerald, no, Lenormand was quite certain of that, because, you see, many years ago Lupin had acquired it, and since, it has rested among his treasures. The boy stole a replica, itself of some worth, the stones are genuine, but nowhere near the quality of the original. Lenormand realized it the instant the Comtesse entered the room wearing it that morning."

"But the real sword..."

"Yes, De Guy did have it, and he was clever about it. A touch of the American writer Edgar Poe there, but then, he was really too clever—and not the only one to have read Poe. You've noticed he had made no claim with regard to the sword hanging in the gallery. The sword on display was all gilt and deception. What would a soldier do with such an ornate toy? No, the real sword of d'Artagnan, nicked and tarnished, hung on the wall with the musket and the musketeer tunic, guarding the safe, still vigilant after all this time. That was a soldier's weapon. Not that bejeweled toy."

"You have it then?"

"I do, and I shall hold onto it for a time rather than return it to that rascal de Guy. The boy was quite right. It was intolerable for a man like him to possess such a noble hero's sword. I hope, if he realizes it, that the boy thinks me worthy of it."

"Then the boy got nothing."

"I wouldn't say nothing. Is not a lesson from Lupin himself of some value? And there were a few real jewels among the false stones. I should think he will make a tidy profit, though I don't really believe he cares for the money half so much as the adventure and the justice of the thing. The world will hear more from this clever young fellow. He might even rival Lupin one day. I imagine he is quite satisfied with having embarrassed the Comte, however. For him, the 'loot' is, I suspect, only a way to keep score."

"What of the Comte?" I asked.

"Rumor has it that he and his daughter departed this morning for Le Havre and points south, and since Lenormand has nothing on him as yet, it is just as well. Most of his staff are under arrest, many belonging to the Union Corse. Having made inquiries, it turns out the château was merely leased and much of the furniture and decorations rented. All an elaborate facade to aid in an audacious crime on a grand scale. Some credit there as well, Lupin himself could not have done better, save for the execution. The Comte cannot be faulted for not having anticipated a fourteen year-old Robin Hood anymore than Lenormand or Lupin."

"You mentioned a note from the boy, your young Robin Hood, what did it say?"

Lupin paused and withdrew his wallet from which he drew a scrap of paper and unfolded it, placing it on the table.

"Our friend's calling card," he said.

It was a crude drawing of a stick figure with a jaunty halo, and beneath that the initials S.T.

"The young devil," I swore.

"Oh, I don't know," Lupin said folding the card and returning it to his wallet. "I like to think it is a tribute to Lupin's legacy, and, in any case, who among us is to say who is a devil and who a saint?"

*We end this year's collection of Shadowmen stories with a short, political vignette by Jared Welch, who contemplates the respective ideologies of the French Revolution and the Black Coats, and the fork in the road that France faced in the 1790s with a choice between chaos and empire...*

## Jared Welch: *The Revolutionary and the Brigand*

*Corsica, 1789*

June 12th, 1789

My name is Albert Lecoq. I was born in Normandy, now I work for the *Cercle Social*, and Nicolas Bonneville has sent me to Corsica to assist Philippe Buonarroti in his attempts to garner Corsican support for the Revolution.

I arrived on the Island a few days ago, and I was soon introduced to Pasquale Paoli.

"Corsicans are divided into three camps, right now," he explained. "Those who are Royalists, those who sympathize with the Revolution, and Nationalists who seek only independence for our island."

"Monsieur Bonneville believes in the sovereign right to independence of every nation," I assured him. "And further believes that nothing done in the cause of Revolution is valid if it violates any of the inalienable *Rights of Man*."

"And do all the Jacobins see things that same way?"

"Bonneville and Brissot's faction is the one that holds the most influence today."

Here, Buonarroti interjected: "As an Italian myself, I can assure you I care deeply about the plight of my Corsican kin..."

Something in his voice made me doubt his sincerity, but I chose to ignore that for now.

"Corsica is a very deeply and traditionally Catholic country, going back to ancient times," Paoli continued, with concern in his voice. "The Jacobins all seem to be Atheists or non-denominational Deists."

"Monsieur Bonneville believes very strongly in the right to Freedom of Religion," I explained.

Suddenly, we were interrupted by the sounds of gunshots coming from outside in the distance. After some time passed, a man came in to update Monsieur Paoli on what had just happened.

"It was another gang of *Veste Nere*, Monsieur. Some of my men tried to pursue them, but they got away."

"They're getting bolder it seems," replied Paoli.

"*Veste Nere*?" Buonarroti inquired.

"A brotherhood of brigands, like the Camorra in Southern Italy, or the Beati Paolo of Sicily," Paoli explained. "Their leader is known only as 'The All-Father.' He rules over them from the old Convent of the *Brothers of La Merci*, near Sartene. I was allied with him once, long ago, in the days of Rinaldo Rinaldini and Nicolas Patropoli. But any devotion to the good of Corsica he may have once felt has long since been replaced by Greed."

After exchanging some whispered communications with his men, Paoli spoke to us again: "I'm afraid I cannot make any promises at this time."

He then bade us farewell.


Back at the main office of the *Giornale Patriottico di Corsica*. Buonarroti and I passed some time drinking.

"This hasn't gone as well as I'd hoped," I said in disappointment.

"I have a new plan," Buonarroti replied.

"What is that?"

"These brigands, the *Veste Nere*, we'll convince them to side with the Revolution."

"Are you serious?" I asked. "Criminals who are only interested in money?"

"Trust me, I can talk their leader into it. Tomorrow, we set out for Sartene!"


June 15th, 1789

We arrived at Sartene; Buonarroti had skillfully arranged a meeting with The All-Father. That rural bandit looked surprisingly spry for a man whom we were told was 67 years-old. His hair had turned white, but his face was not yet very wrinkled.

"So, you wish to enlist my assistance in your cause?" he asked us with an amused smile on his face.

"My name," Buonarroti began, "is Fillippo Giuseppe Maria Ludovico Buonarroti. In Florence, a few years ago, I was inducted into the order of the Illuminati, where I was given the name of Camillus. But I've decided I do not agree with the views of my fellow Illuminati, such as Nicolas Bonneville, Jacques-Pierre Brissot, Condorcet, and Francois Babeuf, nor those of Lebrenn and Gerolstein. They feel that the power of Government must be restrained and lessened in order to achieve Utopia. Myself, I have come to admire Maximilien Robespierre. Like him, I believe Man must be forced to be Free, and that the State must be given the power to enforce Liberty and Equality. The people should be taxed in order to pay for a powerful Government that can manage all their problems. Those who refuse to abandon their faith in the Rotting Wretch of Nazareth should be exterminated."

My eyes widened in shock at this speech. I, too, had been inducted into the Illuminati, where I'd taken the name Thrax. Bonneville and Condorcet believed in Equality of opportunity, but forced, absolute Equality was inherently incompatible with Liberty and Freedom.

I looked at The All-Father and he just smiled mischievously.

"It sounds like a bit of a contradiction in terms there," he remarked.

"Perhaps," said Buonarroti, "but once we've looted all the churches of France, we'll have much gold, silver, and valuable treasures with which to reimburse you for your service."

The All-Father appeared to be contemplating everything he said.

"Your legend," Buonarroti continued, "is still infamous in Italy. I have seen *The Brigand's Painting* and heard its tale. Join us and you can add untold riches to your vaunted treasure."

"And what do you intend to do about those who believe in smaller government?" inquired the All-Father.

"Robespierre is clever; he intends to take out all his rivals for power by pitting them against each other."

"So?" I felt inclined to ask. "Robespierre still believes in Monarchy; he just wants himself to be King?"

"It is true that Robespierre's ego may very well be too big for his own good," Buonarroti conceded. "He might think himself to be a god."

"There are only two things that live forever," the All-Father interjected. "God who is Good, and I, who am Evil."

This statement intrigued me. Was he claiming to be the Devil Himself?

"Very well," the All-Father declared. "My *Veste Nere* shall assist your Revolution. Both here, in Corsica, and on the continent, for we already have a significant presence in Marseille."

A victorious smile appeared on Buonarroti's face. I merely looked around and contemplated what I'd just learned. I feared that the seeds of our great Revolution's self-destruction had just been sowed before it had even begun.

The All-Father simply rubbed his hands together and said: "I think this may well be my last affair."

# Credits

## Gilgamesh Revisited

| Starring: | Created by: |
|---|---|
| Gilgamesh (The Man of Bronze) | inspired by Lester Dent and Guy d'Armen |
| Ut-Napishtim (Natas) | inspired by Sax Rohmer and Guy d'Armen |
| Enkidu (The Lord of the Lions) | inspired by Augusto Pedrazza, Franco & Fausto Oneta |
| Shamhat (The Priestess of Atlantis) | inspired by Pierre Benoît |
| Humbaba | inspired by Merian C. Cooper & Edgar Wallace |

**Matthew BAUGH** lives and works in Albuquerque, NM. He is the pastor of a small church and an editor for Permuted Press. He is also an author and a regular contributor to *Tales of the Shadowmen*. His first novel, *The Vampire Count of Monte-Cristo*, a mash-up of the classic story of adventure and revenge with vampires, ghosts and Faustian bargains, is now available. Matthew is also the co-author, with *TOTS* contributor Win Scott Eckert, of *A Girl and Her Cat*, which continues the adventures of classic TV heroes, Honey West and T.H.E. Cat. He is currently editing Volume 2 of *The Lone Ranger Chronicles*.

## The Darkness in the Woods

| Starring: | Created by: |
|---|---|
| Joseph Balsamo | Alexandre Dumas |
| Captain Clegg/Christopher Syn | Russell Thorndike |
| Nathan Slaughter | Robert Montgomery Bird |
| The *Jibbenainosay* | Robert Montgomery Bird |
| Atala | F-R. de Chateaubriand |
| **Co-Starring:** | |
| Childress | Nic Pizzolatto |
| **Also Starring:** | |
| Charles-Phillipe Aubry | |
| **And:** | |
| *The King in Yellow* | Robert W. Chambers |

**Nathan CABANISS** is based out of Atlanta, GA, where he lives a life consisting primarily of danger, intrigue and Netflix. His stories have appeared in *Voluted Tales* and *Cranial Leakage: Tales from the Grinning Skull*, and he can be found online at his website, *Girls, Guns & Cigarettes*, where Nicholas Roeg films and the finest in Italian exploitation trash are held in equally high regard. He is the creator of *Beyond Order & Chaos*, an online, interactive superhero novel still forthcoming. He is a regular contributor to *Tales of the Shadowmen*.

## Don't Judge a Book by Its Title

| Starring: | Created by: |
|---|---|
| Ash Williams | Sam Raimi |
| Countess Irina | Jesus Franco |
| The Giant | Jesus Franco |
| Baal | Renée Dunan |
| Sâr Dubnotal | *Anonymous* |
| **Co-Starring:** | |
| The Ghostbusters | Dan Aykroyd & Harold Ramis |
| Vampirella | Forrest J. Ackerman |
| Paul Bearer | Vince McMahon |
| The Undertaker | Vince McMahon |
| Morticia | Charles Addams |
| Abdul Ahazred | H.P. Lovecraft |
| Buffy | Joss Whedon |
| **And:** | |
| *The Necronomicon* | H.P. Lovecraft |

**Matthew DENNION** lives in South Jersey with his beautiful wife and daughters. He currently works as a teacher of students with autism at a Special Services School. Matt has been a huge fan of Edgar Rice Burroughs ever since he first picked up *A Princess of Mars*; he is also a big follower of Sherlock Holmes, Doc Savage, Spider-man, Batman and James Bond. In addition to being a regular contributor to *Tales of the Shadowmen*, he also writes stories involving giant monsters for *G-fan* magazine.

## The Trial of Van Helsing

| Starring: | Created by: |
|---|---|
| Boris Liatoukine | Marie Nizet |
| Baron Vordenberg | based on Sheridan Le Fanu |
| Professor Van Helsing | Bram Stoker |

| | |
|---|---|
| Polly Bird | Paul Féval |
| Mircalla Karnstein | Sheridan Le Fanu |
| Laura | Sheridan Le Fanu |
| Countess Marcian Grigoryi | Paul Féval |
| **Co-Starring:** | |
| Count Dracula | Bram Stoker |
| Doctor Hesselius | Sheridan Le Fanu |
| Otto Goetzi | Paul Féval |
| Orlok | Henrik Galeen |
| | & F.W. Murnau |
| Lucy Westenra | Bram Stoker |
| "Brides" of Dracula | Bram Stoker |
| **Also Starring:** | |
| Rasputin | |
| **And:** | |
| Selene, the Sepulchre | Paul Féval |
| Brescia Air Show (1909) | reported by Franz Kafka |

**Brian GALLAGHER** has a BA in Politics and Society and lives in London. He works in the media and for many years has written on the politics, economics and many other aspects of Croatia and has been quoted in Croatian and international media. In relation to that he has written extensively on Croatian-related cases at the International Criminal Tribunal for the Former Yugoslavia. He has always been interested in science fiction, classic horror, comics and is proud to be a lifelong *Doctor Who* fan. He is a regular contributor to *Tales of the Shadowmen*.

## *Rouletabille vs. The New World Order*

| **Starring:** | **Created by:** |
|---|---|
| Joseph Rouletabille | Gaston Leroux |
| Hugo Danner | Philip Wylie |
| Anthony "Buck" Rogers | Philip Francis Nowlan |
| Ward Baldwin | David McDaniel |
| Cyrus West/Cyrus Smith | Jules Verne and John Willard |
| **Co-Starring:** | |
| Herbert Brown | Jules Verne |
| Sherlock Holmes | Arthur Conan Doyle |
| Scarecrow of Romney Marsh | Russell Thorndike |
| Captain Crouan | Philip Wylie |
| Kapitan Mors | *Anonymous* |
| Abdnego Danner | Philip Wylie |
| Dr. Grierson | Martin GatelyMartin Gately |

Ian Hassett
**Also Starring:**
Adam Worth
Ned Ludd
**And:**
The Maracot Deep
Locksley Hall
UNCLE/THRUSH

Sir Arthur Conan Doyle
Alfred, Lord Tennyson
Sam Rolfe

**Martin GATELY** is most recently the author of S*amdroo and the Grassman* in *The Worlds of Philip Jose Farmer 4 - Voyages to Strange Days* and of the comics novella *Sherwood Jungle* in the *Phantom: Generations* series. He is a regular contributor to the UK's journal of strange phenomena *Fortean Times*, for which he also created the *Cryptid Kid Investigates* comic strip. His writing career began back in the 1980s when he wrote for D C Thomson's legendary *Starblazer* comic-book. He lives in a decaying mansion in Nottingham that has a view of a former insane asylum. He is a regular contributor to *Tales of the Shadowmen*.

## *Once More, the Nyctalope*

| | |
|---|---|
| Jacques Roll (The Invisible Man) | Jean de La Hire |
| Leo Saint-Clair (The Nyctalope) | Jean de La Hire |
| Briar Rose (Belle) | Randy Lofficier |
| Aristide Clairembart | Henri Vernes |
| Tryphon Tournesol | Hergé |
| Jérôme Fandor | Pierre Souvestre |
| | & Marcel Allain |
| Dutil-Parrot | Jean de La Hire |
| René Belloq | George Lucas |
| | & Philip Kaufman |
| Brunehilde | based on Richard Wagner |
| Siegfried | based on Richard Wagner |
| Votan | based on Richard Wagner |
| **Co-Starring:** | |
| Sylvie Saint-Clair | Jean de La Hire |
| Simone Desroches (Belphegor) | Arthur Bernède |
| Auguste Cahizac | Emmanuel Gorlier |
| Mathias Lumen | Jean de La Hire |
| Leonid Zattan | Jean de La Hire |
| Glo von Warteck (Lucifer) | Jean de La Hire |
| Gnô Mitang | Jean de La Hire |
| **Also Starring:** | |
| Karl Haushofer | |

Paul Langevin
Marcel Priollet
Léon Blum

**Emmanuel GORLIER** lives in Puteaux, near Paris, with his wife and three children. He has been a fan of science fiction since the first grade and a devvoted player of *Dungeons & Dragons* for 30 years. That is probably why he became a tax accountant. He has contributed to *Enter the Nyctalope* and *Tales of the Shadowmen*, and is the author of *Nyctalope! L'Univers Extravagant de Jean de La Hire*, a Nyctalope companion book published in France. He is a regular contributor to *Tales of the Shadowmen*.

## *Meeting with the Mir Beg*

| Starring: | Created by: |
|---|---|
| Joseph Rouletabille | Gaston Leroux |
| Blaylock | Micah Harris, Loston Wallace |
| Emeric Belasco | Richard Matheson |
| The Mir Beg | based on Robert E. Howard |
| **Also Starring:** | |
| Houdini | |

**Micah S. HARRIS** is the author (with artist Michael Gaydos) of the graphic novel *Heaven's War*, a historical fantasy pitting authors Charles Williams, C.S. Lewis and J.R.R. Tolkien against occultist Aleister Crowley. His most recent publications are *Lorna, Relic Wrangler*, with illustrator Loston Wallace, the collection *Slouching Toward Camulodunum and Other Stories*, and the electronic release of *The Frequency of Fear*. He is a regular contributor to *Tales of the Shadowmen*.

**Loston WALLACE** is a freelance artist who lives with his wife in North Carolina. His large body of work includes merchandising art for children's book tie-ins with major movies and the animated versions of Batman and Krypto. He has drawn *Flash Gordon* for Kings Syndicate and the *Rocketeer* and the *Spirit* for IDW. With Micah Harris, he created *Lorna, Relic Wrangler* for Image comics. This is his first appearance in *Tales of the Shadowmen*.

## *All Roads Lead to Mars*

| Starring: | Created by: |
|---|---|
| Doctor Omega | Arnould Galopin |
| Fred | Arnould Galopin |
| Denis Borel | Arnould Galopin |

| | |
|---|---|
| Jason Spell/Time Brigade | Claude Legrand |
| | & Edmond Ripoll |
| John ***/Lectroids | Earl Mac Rauch |
| Captain Spencer | Clive Barker |
| Setissi/Ice Warriors | Brian Hayles |
| | and Arnould Galopin |
| John Carter | Edgar Rice Burroughs |
| Thea | based on Thea Von Harbou |
| Sorns/Seroni | C.S. Lewis |
| Bent Oyarsa/Eldils | C.S. Lewis |
| Tiziraou | Arnould Galopin |
| Oompa-Loompas | Roald Dahl |
| **And:** | |
| Pyramid of Mars | Robert Holmes |
| Barsoom (Mars)/Helium | Edgar Rice Burroughs |
| Mars Rover | N.A.S.A. |
| Malacandra.Mars | C.S. Lewis |
| Thulcandra/Earth | C.S. Lewis |
| Chroni-synclastic infundibulum | Kurt Vonnegut |

**Travis HILTZ** started making up stories at a young age. Years later, he began writing them down. In high school, he discovered that some writers actually got paid and decided to give it a try. He has since gathered a modest collection of rejection letters and had a one-act play produced. Travis lives in the wilds of New Hampshire with his very loving and tolerant wife, two above average children and a staggering amount of comic books and *Doctor Who* novels. He is a regular contributor to *Tales of the Shadowmen*.

## Dream's End

| **Starring:** | **Created by:** |
|---|---|
| The Time Traveler | H.G. Wells |
| Manse Everard | Poul Anderson |
| Barbarella | Jean-Claude Forest |
| Lord Dianthus | Jean-Claude Forest |
| Nado | Jean-Claude Forest |
| Duran Duran | Jean-Claude Forest |
| Sinahu | Mika Walhari |
| Dard Kelm | Poul Anderson |
| **Co-Starring:** | |
| Weena | H.G. Wells |
| The Eloi | H.G. Wells |

| | |
|---|---|
| The Danellians | Poul Anderson |
| Professor Ping | Jean-Claude Forest |
| **Also Starring:** | |
| Mahu | |
| General Ramose | |
| Paatenemheb | |
| Queen Nefertiti | |
| Merye | |
| Thutmose | |
| Akhenaten | |
| Smenkhkare | |
| Tutankhamen | |

**Paul HUGLI** has a degree in Zoology, and has written for everything from *Cracked* magazine to general interest pamphlets, and for most of the first, second *and* third tier adult magazines. He is the author of three published "adult fantasy" novels, and the acclaimed *Traci Lords Companion*. He has also been employed as a science/math instructor, and as a "Floor Manager" at a local "Gentleman's Club." In addition, he once owned/managed Destiny Bookstore, which dealt in SciFi, comics and adult "fantasy" magazines, for 30 years. He now has three novels in the works. He is a regular contributor to *Tales of the Shadowmen*.

## *Shadows Reborn*

| **Starring:** | **Created by:** |
|---|---|
| *L'Ombre* | Walter Gibson |
| (aka Alaric Kentoff; | Philip José Farmer |
| Frédéric-Jean Orth) | and Alain Page |
| Thelda Blanche Bouchard | Walter B. Gibson |
| (aka Angelique Blanchet) | |
| Runa Valda Kritchnoff | based on Maurice Leblanc |
| | and Walter B. Gibson |
| Mimile Justin | Louis Feuillade |
| | Arthur Bernède |
| | Edward Bock |
| | Leslie Edgley |
| | and Raymond L. Schrock |
| Pierre Lecoq | Paul Féval |
| | Walter B. Gibson |
| | and J. Donald Wilson |
| Sanger Rainsford | Richard Connell |
| (aka Lamont Cranston) | and Walter B. Gibson |

| | |
|---|---|
| Margot Phoebe Lane Dale | Clark Alexander |
| | and Edith Meisner |
| Alice Duprès | Edward Brock |
| | Maurice Tombragel |
| | and Cornell Woolrich |
| John Sinclair | Wilfred H. Petitt |
| | William Castle |
| | and Alan Radar |
| "Ragging" Rassendyll | Philip José Farmer |
| Major (later Police Commis- | Walter B. Gibson |
| sioner) Weston | |
| The Rampaging Beast (aka King | Merian C. Cooper |
| Kong) | & Edgar Wallace |
| Doc (Savage) | Lester Dent |
| Ed Somers | Eric Taylor |
| Marko Vukcic | Rex Stout |
| Nero Wolfe | Rex Stout |
| Don Parker | Edward Bock |
| | Leslie Edgley |
| | and Raymond L. Schrock |
| Dr. Ira Burbank Franklin | Eric Taylor |
| | and J. Donald Wilson |
| Luther Burbank | Walter B. Gibson |
| Nurse Carroll | Aubrey Wisberg |
| Kenton Lane | Philip José Farmer |
| M.K. Simmons | George Bricker |
| Colonel Bozzo-Corona | Paul Féval |
| Captain Driscoll | Merian C. Cooper |
| | & Edgar Wallace |
| Donald Gale | Eric Taylor |
| Joe Conroy | Wilfred H. Petitt |
| | & William Castle |
| Pat (Savage) | Lester Dent |
| Dr. Crawford | Aubrey Wisberg |
| Robert Bianchini Drake | Robert Bloch |
| | Louis Feuillade |
| | & Arthur Bernède |

**Co-Starring:**

| | |
|---|---|
| Humbert Kenneth Allard | Karl Edward Wagner |
| The Black Coats | Paul Féval |
| The Seven Silent Companions | Walter B. Gibson |
| Roger Crowthers | Walter B. Gibson |
| Marie Margot LaSalle Dale (aka | Frank L. Packard |

Tocsin)  
James Dale (aka The Gray Seal) — Frank L. Packard  
The Revenant — Rick Lai  
Noel J. Hendricks — Aubrey Wisberg  
The Secret Raiders — Louis Feuillade & Arthur Bernède  
Judex — Louis Feuillade & Arthur Bernède  
Mrs. Harrison — Wilfred H. Petitt & William Castle  
Lecoq de la Perière — Paul Féval  
Marguerite Sadoulas — Paul Féval  
D.A. Bryan — Dashiell Hammett  
Lee Gentry — Ben Hecht and Charles MacArthur  
Lefty & Toni Vigran — Eric Taylor and J. Donald Wilson  
Bernard Sutton — Max Pemberton  
Juan Gonzalles — Robert E. Howard  
Jethro Clayton — Walter B. Gibson  
Arsène Lupin — Maurice Leblanc  
N'a-qu'un-Chasse — Louis Feuillade & Arthur Bernède  
William Lane — Edgar Wallace  
Marielle Gibson — Rick Lai  
Benjamin Gibson — Horatio Alger  
Angélique LaSalle Gibson — Rick Lai  
Andrée Duprès LaSalle — based on Lara Parker  
Angélique Bouchard — Dan Curtis & Art Wallace  
Emile Bouchard — Walter E. Grauman  
Sonia Kritchnoff — Maurice Leblanc  
Countess Cagliostro — Maurice Leblanc  
Rip Van Winkle — Washington Irving  
Rhea Gutman — Dashiell Hammett  
Desdemona — Rick Lai  
Madame Palmyre — Renée Duran  
Jerry Mason — Edward Bock Leslie Edgley and Raymond L. Schrock  

**Also Starring:**  
Tsar Paul I  
Tsar Alexander II  
Margo Channing

Mayor Jimmy Walker

**And:**

| | |
|---|---|
| Ramsey Arms | George Bricker |
| The *Crow's Nest* | Eric Taylor |
| | and J. Donald Wilson |
| Szinca girasols | Walter B. Gibson |
| Blue Diamond | Maurice Leblanc |
| Black Pearl | Maurice Leblanc |
| Standard Savings Bank | Cornell Woolrich |
| *Daily Register* | George Bricker |
| Aldebaran Hotel | Walter B. Gibson |
| Blackspear Holdings | Jean-Marc Lofficier |
| Club Royale | George Bricker |

**Rick LAI** is an authority on pulp fiction and the Wold Newton Universe concepts of Philip José Farmer. His speculative articles have been collected in *Rick Lai's Secret Histories: Daring Adventurers, Rick Lai's Secret Histories: Criminal Masterminds, Chronology of Shadows: A Timeline of The Shadow's Exploits* and *The Revised Complete Chronology of Bronze*. Rick's fiction has been collected in *Shadows of the Opera, Shadows of the Opera: Retribution in Blood* and *Sisters of the Shadows: The Cagliostro Curse* (the last two titles are available from Black Coat Press). He has also translated Arthur Bernède's *Judex* and *The Return of Judex* into English for Black Coat Press. Rick resides in Bethpage, New York, with his wife and children. He is a regular contributor to *Tales of the Shadowmen*.

## A Fistful of Judexes

| **Starring:** | **Created by:** |
|---|---|
| Michel Kerjean | based on Arthur Bernède |
| | & Louis Feuillade |
| Mattie Storin | Michael Dobbs |
| Jim Bergerac | Robert Banks Stewart |
| Diamante Lil | Robert Banks Stewart |
| Teddy Verano | Maurice Limat |
| Peggy Masters | Robert Banks Stewart |
| David | Nigel Malcolm |
| Barney Crozier | Robert Banks Stewart |
| Charlie Hungerford | Robert Banks Stewart |
| Judex | Arthur Bernède |
| | & Louis Feuillade |
| BlackSpear Holdings | Jean-Marc Lofficier |
| | based on Paul Féval |

**Nigel MALCOLM** lives in Kent, England. He works as a teacher of English as a Foreign Language. He is a long-term *Doctor Who*, *Star Trek* and *Prisoner* fan—long before all the new-fangled versions came along. He is still working on that elusive steampunk novel and various short stories. He is a regular contributor to *Tales of the Shadowmen*.

## The Noble Freak

| Starring: | Created by: |
|---|---|
| Rama Tamerlane (Felifax) | Paul Féval, *fils* |
| Professor Tornada | André Couvreur |
| Lance Nolter | Edward Mann |
| | and Robert D. Weinbach |
| Adam Danator | André Couvreur |
| Felanthus | Christofer Nigro |
| | based on Paul Féval, *fils* |
| Deep Ones | H.P. Lovecraft |
| Grououll (Monster of | Jean-Claide Carrière |
| Frankenstein) | based on Mary Shelley |
| Renanimate | H.P. Lovecraft |
| Zombie | George Romero |
| The Moss | Theodore Sturgeon |
| **Co-Starring:** | |
| Djina Tamerlane | Paul Féval, *fils* |
| Grace Parker Tamerlane | Paul Féval, *fils* |
| Sir Ralph Napper | Paul Féval, *fils* |
| Sir Edmond Sexton | Paul Féval, *fils* |
| The Frankensteins | Mary Shelley |
| Dr. Herbert West | H.P. Lovecraft |
| Dr. Stuart Hartwell | H.P. Lovecraft / Peter Rawlik |
| Dagon | H.P. Lovecraft |
| Roger Kirk | Theodore Sturgeon |
| **Also Starring:** | |
| Stéphane Leduc | |

**Christofer NIGRO** is a writer of both fiction and non-fiction with a strong interest in pulps, comic books and fantastic cinema, and a regular contributor to *Tales of the Shadowmen*. He may be known to some by his extensive writings in cyberspace, including his websites *The Godzilla Saga* and *The Warrenverse*, as he is an authority on the subject of *dai kaiju eiga* (the sub-genre of cinema specializing in giant monsters), and the characters featured in the fondly remembered comic magazines published by Warren. He has recently revived and expanded Chuck Loridans' classic site MONSTAAH, and has since been published in the anthologies *Aliens Among Us* and *Carnage: After the Fall*. He is presently at work on a novel, and works as a website administrator and freelance editor.

## *Return to the Center of the Earth*

| **Starring:** | **Created by:** |
|---|---|
| Axel Lidenbrock | Jules Verne |
| Professor Otto Lidenbrock | Jules Verne |
| Captain Von Horst | based on Edgar Rice Burroughs |
| Ned Land | Jules Verne |
| Mahars, Sagoths, lidi, thipdars, jaloks | Edgar Rice Burroughs |
| Alaya, Halar, etc. | John Peel based on Edgar rice Burroughs |
| **Co-Starring:** | |
| The Gun Club | Jules Verne |

**John PEEL** was born in Nottingham, England, and started writing stories at age 10. John moved to the U.S. in 1981 to marry his pen-pal. He, his wife ("Mrs. Peel") and their 13 dogs now live on Long Island, New York. John has written just over 100 books to date, mostly for young adults. He is the only author to have written novels based on both *Doctor Who* and *Star Trek*. His most popular work is *Diadem*, a fantasy series; he has written ten volumes to date. He is a regular contributor to *Tales of the Shadowmen*.

## *The Ylourgne Accord*

| **Starring:** | **Created by:** |
|---|---|
| Robert Peaslee | H.P. Lovecraft |
| Meldrum Strange | Talbot Mundy |
| Doctor Astrov | Anton Chekhov |
| General Mazovia | Victor Halperin |
| General Duval | Victor Halperin |
| General Von Schelling | Victor Halperin |
| Doctor Lorde | Cyril-Berger |
| Doctor Miklos Sangre | Jean Yarbrough |
| Richard Steadman | Peter Cannon |
| Dr. Cornelius Kramm | Gustave Le Rouge |
| Sâr Dubnotal | Anonymous |
| Eric Moreland Clapham-Lee | H.P. Lovecraft |

**Co-Starring:**

| | |
|---|---|
| Hugo Strange | Bill Finger & Bob Kane |
| Herbert West | H.P. Lovecraft |
| Daniel Cain | H.P. Lovecraft |
| Stuart Hartwell | H.P. Lovecraft |
| Victor Frankenstein | Mary Shelley |
| Henry Frankenstein | William Hurlbut |
| | & John Balderston |
| Dr. Pretorius | William Hurlbut |
| | & John Balderston |
| Tsiang | Victor Halperin |
| Gaspard du Nord | Clark Ashton Smith |
| Nathaire | Clark Ashton Smith |
| The Colossus of Ylourgne | Clark Ashton Smith |
| The Beast of Averoigne | Clark Ashton Smith |
| **And:** | |
| Miskatonic University | H.P.Lovecraft |
| Locus Solus | Raymond Roussel |
| Averoigne | Clark Ashton Smith |
| Vyones | Clark Ashton Smith |
| Ylourgne | Clark Ashton Smith |
| Brotherhood of the Wolf | Christophe Gans |
| | & Stéphane Cabel |
| The Red Hand | Gustave Le Rouge |
| Friedrich von Junzt's *Von Unaussprechlichen Kulten* | Robert E. Howard |

**Pete RAWLIK** holds a B.S. in Marine Biology and manages monitoring projects in the Florida Everglades. He has been a fan of the Lovecraftian fiction since his father sat him on his knee and read him Lovecraft's *The Rats in the Walls*. His fiction has appeared in *Talebones*, *IBID* and *Crypt of Cthulhu*. His literary criticism has appeared in *The New York Review of Science Fiction* and in *The Neil Gaiman Reader*. He is a regular contributor to *Tales of the Shadowmen*.

## *Saints and Sinners*

| **Starring:** | **Created by:** |
|---|---|
| Teddy Verano | Maurice Limat |
| Mephista (Edwige Hossegor) | Maurice Limat |
| Steven Marcato | Ira Levin |
| Mrs. Marcato | Ira Levin |
| Simon Sinestrari | Robert Phippeny |
| | & Joe Solomon |

**Co-Starring:**

| | |
|---|---|
| Morcata | Dennis Wheatley |
| Duc de Richleau | Dennis Wheatley |
| Teddy Verano Sr. | Maurice Limat |

**Also Starring:**
Gilles de Rais

**Frank SCHILDINER** has been a pulp fan since a friend gave him a gift of Phillip Jose Farmer's *Tarzan Alive*. Since that time he has published articles on *Hellboy*, the Frankenstein films, *Dark Shadows* and the television show's links to the H.P. Lovecraft universe. He has had stories published in *Secret Agent X, Ravenwood, Stepson of Mystery, The Black Bat Mystery, The New Adventures of Thunder Jim, The New Adventures of Richard Knight* and *The Justice Files*. He is a Senior Probation Officer in New Jersey and a martial arts instructor at Amorosi's Mixed Martial Arts. Frank resides in New Jersey with his wife Gail who is his top supporter. He is a regular contributor to *Tales of the Shadowmen*.

## A Professional Matter

| **Starring:** | **Created by:** |
|---|---|
| Sherlock Holmes | Arthur Conan Doyle |
| John H. Watson | Arthur Conan Doyle |
| Adam Adamant | Donald Cotton |
| | & Richard Harris |
| Ganimard | Maurice Leblanc |
| The Collector | Théophile Gautier |
| Arsène Lupin | Maurice Leblanc |
| Ledoux | Gaston Leroux |
| Griffin (Invisible Man) | H.G. Wells |
| **Co-Starring:** | |
| Mycroft Holmes | Arthur Conan Doyle |
| Nyarlathotep | H.P. Lovecraft |
| Charles le Sorcier | H.P. Lovecraft |
| Michel Mauvais | H.P. Lovecraft |
| Nephren-Ka | H,P. Lovecraft |
| Phantom of the Opera | Gaston Leroux |
| **Also Starring:** | |
| Eugène Bertrand | |
| Pedro Gailhard | |
| **And:** | |
| Idol of Princess Hermonthis | Théophile Gautier |
| The Diogenes Club | Arthur Conan Doyle |
| Miskatonic University | H.P. Lovecraft |

**Sam SHOOK** is a 19-year-old university student majoring in history, and he would not be caught dead without a nice outfit and a hat. An actor, fencer, singer, and panpipe player, he has always been a bit different from the rest of his friends in Oklahoma. While most of them like things such as hunting or cars, he has always enjoyed reading and writing. He has been creating stories from a young age for the entertainment of himself and others. Through those simple tales he honed his skills, and he decided to make a career out of it. *A Professional Matter* is his first published story.

## The Legacy of Arsène Lupin

| Starring: | Created by: |
|---|---|
| Arsène Lupin / Lenormand / Prince Sernine | Maurice Leblanc |
| Comte de Guy (Carl Peterson) | H. C. (Sapper) McNeile |
| Comtesse de Guy (Irma Peterson) | H. C. (Sapper) McNeile |
| S.T. (The Saint) | Leslie Charteris |
| **Co-Starring:** | |
| Sherlock Holmes | Arthur Conan Doyle |
| Hanoi Shan | H. Ashton-Wolfe |
| Gurn (Fantômas) | P. Souvestre & M. Allain |
| Cagliostro | Alexandre Dumas |
| Comte de St.-Germain | Chelsea Quinn Yarbro |
| George Barrington | Ernest Dudley |
| Prince Rodolphe | Eugène Sue |
| Colonel Bozzo-Corona | Paul Féval |
| Rocambole | P.-A. Ponson du Terrail |
| Devil Doctor (Fu Manchu) | Sax Rohmer |
| Joséphine Balsamo | Maurice Leblanc |
| Rouletabille | Gaston Leroux |
| Lecoq | Emile Gaboriau |
| Smiler Bunn | E.W. Hornung |
| A.J. Raffles | E.W. Hornung |
| Jimmie Dale (Gray Seal) | Frank Packard |
| Dreux-Soubize | Maurice Leblanc |
| The Vampires | Louis Feuillade |
| Hamilton Cleek | Thomas & Mary Hanshew |
| **Also Starring:** | |
| Maurice Leblanc | |
| D'Artagnan | |
| Edgar Allan Poe | |

**David L. VINEYARD** is a fifth generation Texan (named for his gunfighter/Texas Ranger great grand-father) currently living in Oklahoma City, OK, where the tornadoes come sweeping down the plains. He has useless degrees in history, politics, and economics, and is the author of several tales about Buenos Aires private eye Johnny Sleep, two novels, several short stories, some journalism, and various non-fiction. He is currently working on several ideas while battling with a three month old kitten for household dominance and the keyboard of his PC. He is a regular contributor to *Tales of the Shadowmen*.

## The Revolutionary and the Brigand

| Starring: | Created by: |
|---|---|
| Albert Lecoq | Philip José Farmer |
| | based on Paul Féval |
| | & Emile Gaboriau |
| The All-Father | Paul Féval |
| **Co-Starring:** | |
| Nicolas Patropoli | Paul Féval |
| Beati Paolo | Luigi Natoli |
| Rinaldo Rinaldini | Christian Vulpius |
| Lebrenn | Eugène Sue |
| Gerolstein | Eugène Sue |
| **Also Starring:** | |
| Filippo Buonarroti | |
| Nicolas Bonneville | |
| Jacques-Pierre Brissot | |
| Condorcet | |
| François Babeuf | |
| Maximilien Robespierre | |

**Jared WELCH** lives in Racine, WI. He is a long-time fan of Batman, J.R.R. Tolkien, C.S. Lewis, Nintendo, Buffy, Pretty Little Liars and the Star Wars Prequels, and has now become a very big fan of Paul Feval. He is currently working on a few plays, novels and essays about Bible Interpretation. This is his second contribution to *Tales of the Shadowmen*.

WATCH OUT FOR

# TALES OF THE
# SHADOWMEN

*VOLUME 12: CARTE BLANCHE*
**TO BE RELEASED DECEMBER 2015**

Rick Lai, Jean-Marc Lofficier, David McDonnell, Brad Mengel, Sharan New-man, Neil Penswick, Pete Rawlik, Frank Schildiner, Stuart Shiffman, Bradley H. Sinor, Brian Stableford, Michel Stéphan, David L. Vineyard.

### Doctor Omega and the Shadowmen (2011)
Matthew Baugh, Thom Brannan, G.L. Gick, Travis Hiltz, Olivier Legrand, Serge Lehman, Jean-Marc & Randy Lofficier, Samuel T. Payne, John Peel, Neil Penswick, Dennis E. Power, Chris Roberson, Stuart Shiffman.

### The Nyctalope Steps In (2011)
Matthew Dennion, Emmanuel Gorlier, Julien Heylbroeck, Paul Hugli, Jean de La Hire, Roman Leary, Randy Lofficier, Stuart Shiffman, David L. Vineyard.

### Volume 8: Agents Provocateurs (2011)
Matthew Baugh, Nicholas Boving, Matthew Dennion, Win Scott Eckert, Martin Gately, Micah Harris, Travis Hiltz, Paul Hugli, Rick Lai, Joseph Lamere, Olivi-er Legrand, Jean-Marc & Randy Lofficier, DavidMcDonald, Chris Nigro, John Peel, Dennis E. Power, Pete Rawlik, Joshua Reynolds, Frank Schildiner, Michel Stéphan, Michel Vannereux.

### The Many Faces of Arsène Lupin (2012)
Matthew Baugh, Anthony Boucher, Francis de Croisset, Matthew Dennion, Viv-iane Etrivert, Matthew Ilseman, Maurice Leblanc, Alain le Bussy, Jean-Marc & Randy Lofficier, Xavier Mauméjean, André Mouëzy-Eon, Thomas Narcejac, Jess Nevins, Bradley H. Sinor, Jean-Louis Trudel, David L. Vineyard

### Night of the Nyctalope (2012)
Matthew Dennion, Martin Gately, Emmanuel Gorlier, Julien Heylbroeck, Travis Hiltz, Jean de La Hire, Roman Leary, Jean-Marc Lofficier, David McDonald, Chris Nigro, Philippe Ward.

### Volume 9: La Vie en Noir (2012)
Matthew Baugh, Nicholas Boving, Robert Darvel, Matthew Dennion, Win Scott Eckert, Martin Gately, Travis Hiltz, Paul Hugli, Rick Lai, Jean-Marc Lofficier, Nigel Malcolm, DavidMcDonald, Christofer Nigro, John Peel, Neil Penswick, Pete Rawlik, Josh Reynolds, Frank Schildiner, Bradley H. Sinor, Michel Stéphan.

### The Shadow of Judex (2013)
Matthew Baugh, Nicholas Boving, Thom Brannan,Matthew Dennion, Emmanu-el Gorlier, Travis HiltzRomain d'Huissier, Vincent Jounieaux, Rick Lai, Jean-Marc & Randy Lofficier, David McDonald, Christofer Nigro, Dennis E. Power, Chris Roberson, Robert L. Robinson, Jr.

**Volume 10: Esprit de Corps (2013)**
Matthew Baugh, Nicholas Boving, Nathan Cabaniss, Anthony R. Cardno, Matthew Dennion, Brian Gallagher, John Gallagher, Martin Gately, Emmanuel Gorlier, Micah Haris, Travis Hiltz, Paul Hugli, Rick Lai, Olivier Legrand, J.-M. & Randy Lofficier, Patrick Lorin, David McDonald, Nigel Malcolm, Xavier Mauméjean, Michael Moorcock, Christofer Nigro, John Peel, Pete Rawlik, Josh Reynolds, Frank Schildiner, Brian Stableford, Michel Stéphan, David L. Vineyard and Jared Welch

**Harry Dickson vs. The Spider (2014)**
Nicholas Boving, Bill Cunningham, Matthew Dennion, Martin Gately, Travis Hiltz, Paul Hugli, Nigel Malcolm, Neil Penswick, Jean-Paul Raymond and Michel Stéphan

CPSIA information can be obtained at www.ICGtesting.com
Printed in the USA
BVOW09s0008031214

377328BV00001B/148/P